DAVID

THE WARRIOR KING

DAVID J. FERREIRA

Bridge-Logos

Alachua, Florida 32615

Bridge-Logos
Alachua, FL 32615 USA

David—The Warrior King
by David J. Ferreira

Copyright ©2009 by David J. Ferreira

Printed in the United States of America.

Library of Congress Catalog Card Number: 2009924755
International Standard Book Number 978-0-88270-929-1

DEDICATION

To Monique—my sweet sister,
whose life has been a light on my path—
with all my prayers, blessings, and love.

ACKNOWLEDGMENTS

Firstly, allow me to give praise to God for His unfailing love, blessings, and inspiration.

I would especially like to give tremendous recognition to my agent and editor, Frances Bond. It was she who first recognized the talent from my meager attempt at a first novel (or perhaps it was purely compassion!), and has since worked conscientiously with me on this book, editing draft after draft, answering question after question, guiding the progressing work down the road to literary perfection, until it was finally ready for submission.

Then, of course, to my brother Louis—I am indeed indebted for your patience and support in reading the book a hundred times over, as each draft came from the printer. Though you often groaned at the prospect of reading it yet again, you did; and each time with familial dedication. Also, thanks to my mom and dad for your support—especially my mother. Thank you for all your prayers.

Of course, every author has one person in his or her life who has instilled the love of fiction and for me that one person would be Mrs. Smith. Thanks for the hours spent reading *Macbeth* with such passion, and giving us more than just English education, but also a life of teaching. Your love of poetry and fiction has certainly rubbed off on me—in a good way.

Pastor van Eeden, thanks so much for your words of guidance in one of the biggest choices of my adult life.

I extend my gratitude to Professor van Heerden for his time reading the manuscript to ensure that it is as historically and archeologically accurate as a work of fiction would permit.

And lastly, to Mary Ruth Murray—thanks for sanding down the final draft for printing perfection, and for your kind and encouraging words that have made the dream of publishing my writing all the sweeter.

For those whom I neglected, it is with the support of all my friends and family that this book has come to publication.

FOREWORD

The Old Testament scholar, Walter Brueggemann, has pointed out that "David is one of those extraordinary historical figures who has a literary future. That is, his memory and presence keep generating more and more stories." David Ferreira's book, *David*, is precisely such a new story.

The truth about David that is offered in the Bible is not a simple, unambiguous piece. It moves in a variety of directions and can hardly be reduced to a single formulation. We should not be surprised by this, given the various pieces of literature about David that come from different hands in different contexts for different purposes. Each of them touches a dimension of this "larger-than-life" person. In addition, the person David seems to be inscrutable, very down-to-earth, and harboring tensions and ambiguities.

Now that is what makes a good story, which explains why many modern Bible readers find the David narratives absorbing literature. Furthermore, such narratives feed our imaginations in various ways. A wonderful example is how this book, *David*, came into existence. The biblical narratives about David inspired the author to enter the world of the ancient Near East, to create context, and to imagine possible details of events that are portrayed only in outline in the Bible. Scholarly analyses of the biblical narratives about David have also revealed that these texts are characterized by subtlety, ambiguities, surprises, inscrutability, development and polyvalence—all of which are essential ingredients of a rich and thick plot. These ingredients have also found their way into David.

Biblical scholars have identified at least four modes of truth concerning David in the Hebrew Bible. Each concerns a particular literature, reflecting a particular social context and a social hope, each making a particular theological claim. Brueggemann, for example, has identified four presentations of the person David in the Old Testament:

- The trustful truth of the tribe (1 Samuel 16:1–2 Samuel 5:5)
- The painful truth of the man (2 Samuel 8-20 and 1 Kings 1-2)
- The sure truth of the state (2 Sam 5:6–8:18)
- The hopeful truth of the assembly (Psalms 89 and 132; Lamentations 3:21-27; Isaiah 55:3; 1 Chronicles 10-29)

The book you are reading has been inspired by the trustful truth of the tribe in particular, which covers only the narrative about David's rise.

If this fictional story about David entertains some truth of David, which truth does it offer? There is evidence that the historical reality of David has been taken seriously. The reader is also confronted with the truth by which David lived. But this book also discloses a reality which clusters around the person of David, a truth made possible because we linger over the memory of David and the possibilities that are associated with it.

I trust your reading experience of this delightful book will be as fulfilling and exciting as my journey with the manuscript.

Prof. S. W. van Heerden
Dept. of Old Testament and Ancient Near Eastern Studies
University of South Africa

PREFACE

I wrote this novel with the intention of creating from the Bible a physical universe for the characters in the world of David ben Jesse. It has been an interesting journey that has taken me through the much finer details of the biblical texts. It was a great few months that made me fall in love with the ancient Israelites.

I chose David, not because of the namesake, but rather because of the universality of the character. Not only is he one of the best-known characters in the Bible, he also experienced immense trials and difficulties before he received God's multitude of blessings. He had to be equipped with the right knowledge, strengths, humility, and skills to become one of the greatest kings in history. The story tells of an ordinary man from a rural farm in Bethlehem, who achieved more than most monarchs in our 6000 years of recorded history. It speaks of the truth that our destiny lies not outside of us, but is rooted in our selves by God. It then gives us the capability to attain the greatness that we can only imagine, and then actually create through passionate dreams, prayer, and hard work.

To touch on the fictional side of the book—some of the characters that were born from my writer's psyche, in order to enhance the reality of this world, were the soldiers and captains Ludim, Ziph, Tilon, Jarim, Eliel, Saran, and Ozra the strategist. Also Jonathan's cook Nepheg and servant Akkub,

Saul's assassin Zidka, and the women Keturah, Princess Achsa and Ladiah, the royal concubine and prostitute, were characters I envisioned. I tried to use only biblical names for my fictional characters, and I have to admit, I chose names for the characters by sound. If they sounded like they could match the characters I had locked in my mind, then those were the names I chose. When it came to David's army and Mighty Men, I used the names that are given in the Bible, and created personalities, dialogues, and descriptions around those names.

Early on, the characters were so real in my imagination that they led in the unfolding of the book, and I like to think the Holy Spirit guided me.

To my knowledge, there is no information about Jonathan's wife in the Bible. Princess Achsa, as said, is completely fictional, as were the scenes of husband and wife together, and all their dialogue. I wrote in the problems of infertility for the royal couple, because it is recorded in the Bible that Jonathan did not have many children, so I thought this would be a realistic scenario as to what could be the reason.

In the book, Queen Ahinoam of Israel is also largely fictional. We know that she existed from the Bible and other ancient texts, but nothing is known about her apart from some of her lineage. I wanted to create a strong woman who was so beautiful, in both mind and spirit that she could cope with the temperament and disposition of King Saul and the emerging nation of the Hebrews.

Most of the scenes with the Philistine King Achish are completely fictional, as very little is known about him or his reign. As mentioned above, Ladiah is a product of my creativity and she came quite unexpectedly, but I found her to be a wonderfully interesting character who enriched the scenes in Philistia.

David's successive wars add much of the fiction to the novel, largely because of the Bible's succinctness—many wars are written about in mere sentences. I had to do considerable research on ancient warfare, the weapons and armor of the ancient Israelites, as well as their tactics, army formations, and military ranking. I tried to recreate the battles in which Saul hoped to send David to his death, but instead made him more powerful and successful. These wars flowed from the rich data I gained from reading numerous academic materials, and they built bridges for me between the major events that brought David from being an unknown soldier to a beloved son of the nation, and ultimately, king.

The work contains many facts, but also fictional characters, events, and places. I spent over six months researching for the novel, and read over ten archaeological books on Ancient Israel, numerous translated Jewish texts, fifteen different Bible commentaries and Bible translations of the Books of 1 and 2 Samuel, and also many university journals and theses on King David and the lives and times in 1000 BC. To my surprise, there was much I did not know about the Davidic texts, and I found the enlightenment quite thrilling.

Some of the problems that I encountered were those surrounding Saul. Because of his depression, he became very irrational and obsessive about David. I had to create a plausible explanation for his actions within the reality of the character and also that of the reader. Saul's personality is so complex that a large part of the book is dedicated to explaining his words and deeds. Nevertheless, it was worth the research, because he is an amazing character who grounds the book and forces much growth in all the characters around him.

I must say that as much of a pleasure it was to recreate a biblical history, it was also intense, because I had to scrupulously keep with the written facts, and thus did not have the freedom of many other historical fiction authors. There was a constant fear that I might write something that was not in harmony with the Bible or that would mislead a reader into believing something that was not scriptural.

However, I haven't had enough. In subsequent books on David, I would like to follow his kingship, how he brought the twelve tribes together as one nation, and built a kingdom that was feared by all the Middle East, from Phoenicia to Egypt, and beyond.

As a final note, I would like to mention, as we historical fiction authors so often do, that any errors are solely mine, although I endeavored to work in a realistic structure within the bounds of fiction.

Characters

Main

David – Son of Jesse, second king of Israel.

Saul – Son of Kish, first king of Israel.

Secondary

Abner – Saul's general and influential cousin.

Achish – Philistine king.

Ahinoam – Saul's wife.

Eliab – David's eldest brother.

Jonathan – Saul's son, eldest prince of Israel.

Ladiah – A courtesan and later Achish's wife.

Michal – Saul's daughter and David's wife.

Tertiary

Abiathar – Priest to David who survived Saul's slaughter at Nob, and the son of Ahimelech.

Abigail from Carmel – David's second wife, and the widow of Nabal.

Abinadab – David's second eldest brother.

Abishai – Zeruiah's second son.

Achsa – Jonathan's wife.

Ahimelech – priest who gave David bread and Goliath's sword, and was murdered for his actions.

Ahinoam from Jezreel – first a servant to Abigail; later David's third wife.

Amasa – David's nephew, his sister Abigail's only son.

Asahel – Zeruiah's youngest son

Bathsheba – Beautiful daughter of Eliel who was infatuated with David, but was rejected by him.

Doeg – Saul's henchman.

Ehud – Saul's captain over a thousand.

Ish-bosheth – Saul's youngest son.

Joab – Zeruiah's oldest son.

Merab – Saul's eldest daughter.

Ozra – Strategist.

Pelet – David's soldier

Rizpah – Saul's concubine.

Samuel – Prophet who anoints David king.

Shammah – Daivd's third eldest brother.

Zidka – Saul's informant, Philistine mercenary spy.

BACKGROUND CHARACTERS

Abigail – David's sister, her son is Amasa.

Abinadab ben Saul – Saul's son.

Adriel – Merab's husband and Saul's son-in-law.

Ahijah – Saul's priest.

Akkub – Jonathan's personal servant.

Eliel – Younger soldier on guard when Saul stabs Tilon for mocking him

Hushai – One of David's guards in the wildernesses.

Jaasiel – Abner's son.

Jarim – New recruit who spots Goliath along with Ziph.

Keturah – Woman who warns David and Eliab of Saul's plans in the city of Keilah.

Ludim – Captain in Saul's army.

Malchi-shua – Saul's son.

Mephibosheth – Jonathan's only son.

Nepheg – Cook in the army.

Nethaneel – David's fourth eldest brother.

Ozem – David's sixth brother.

Raddai – David's fifth brother.

Saran – Philistine officer at the garrison David burned.

Sérèn – Five princes of Philistine (Gath, Gaza, Ekron, Ashkelon, and Ashod).

Tilon – Older soldier, who mocks Saul in his tent.

Zeruiah – David's sister; mother of Joab, Abishai, and Asahel.

Ziph – War veteran who spots Goliath with Jarim.

PART ONE

CHAPTER ONE

Dark clouds rolled across the sky as light rain began to drizzle over the lush green and rocky Vale of Terebinth. The Israelites had assembled their forces and had already set up camp in organized areas when the military council gathered. Abner's velvet cape flared out behind him as he strode through the rows of small tents, which were spattered with black mud from the Judean hills. At the center of the encampment stood the royal tent, surrounded by guards and bustling servants tending to the king of Israel. The tent was large, made from woven goat hair and layered with animal hide to withstand the elements. Two guards at the entrance, armed with spears and shields, saluted and opened the two flaps as the general approached. Without a word, Abner entered.

The interior was stately; the ceiling draped with silk and the floor layered with thick carpeting. Abner's presence seized the council's attention as he stepped inside. The general greeted the men with a nod and summoned a young servant with a flick of his hand. He moved to the king and kneeled. The general was a burly man with wrinkled sunburned skin and gray chest hair curling over his soft leather tunic, but the fire of life gleamed in his hard eyes.

"My king, I am at your service."

"Please, my dear Abner, tend to yourself. This council needs you," Saul said. Abner took a towel from the young servant and dried his face and beard. Throwing the damp cloth on the floor, he rose and joined the council of six men sitting on folding stools.

"The Philistines will not proceed. They wait for us, my king," Abner said in a deep voice as he looked squarely into Saul's piercing blue eyes. A large leather map lay spread out over a low, dark wood table, arranged with small blue and red clay figures representing the forces at war. Three men stood opposite Abner—Captain Ehud, Captain Ludim, and the strategist Ozra, all focusing their attention on the general. Abner moved alongside the table as he thought about their options.

Saul remained silent, running his hand through his thin beard.

Who will it be? Saul thought. *Abner? It could be him.* He regarded the general. His eyes shifted to his captains. *Perhaps one of them,* Saul considered. He had asked himself these same questions a thousand times, but he could never be certain. He feared that he would only know the snake in his midst when it was too late, and he would die a horrible death from its poison.

The king felt listless suddenly.

One of my sons? Saul thought, narrowing his eyes, his lips trembling. *Jonathan?*

"We should also remain," Abner said confidently after a moment's silence.

"Insanity," the strategist cried out, jumping to his feet. The council was shocked that a man without rank would speak to the great Abner in such a tone.

"Our provisions are vanishing with each passing day and the soldiers are getting fat from doing nothing. And it is costing Israel a fortune in gold to *wait*." Abner turned to face the thin man, trying to hide his anger behind a plastered smile.

"It is one thing to learn about war from scrolls, but trust me, it is an entirely different thing to learn it from experience, Ozra."

The strategist snorted.

"It is clear that the Philistines want us to move out onto open ground so their chariots can cut through our forces."

"I have already thought of that, good general," Ozra said. The strategist removed his hands from the heavy folds of his robe, and indicated a spot on the map. He then rearranged the red and blue clay statues, and with this gained Abner's full attention.

"Right there we will construct wooden spikes, protruding from the ground," he said. Swiftly he moved the red ceramic chariot and the infantry soldier simultaneously to where he had pointed. "They will be well camouflaged by the dusty winds of autumn, and at the speed that the chariots race, the charioteers will not be able to see them. All their vehicles will be destroyed." Ozra placed the red statue on its side, his eyes brimming with excitement.

"Naturally, their infantry will follow to clear out the last of our foot soldiers, only now there are no more chariots." Quickly he took hold of the blue archer, and slid it a short distance toward the red Philistine infantry. Abner's face relaxed as the strategist continued. A young scribe sat on the left hand side of the king, writing on large piece of thin papyrus parchment rolled out on a small table.

"The archers take out the infantry and our foot soldiers will deal the final blow. Victory," Ozra said.

"How can you assume that the Philistines will send out their mêlée troops directly after their chariots?"

"They will not expect us to be able to destroy their precious chariots," the strategist replied. "They are too arrogant."

"No. There are too many uncertainties. I will not risk it," Abner said vehemently, his temper rising the more Ozra argued.

Shaking his head, the general asked himself why he was debating. He was second only to the king and princes of Israel. The strategist did not have any rank and had only been included in the council to give advice.

Ignoring the small man, he turned and faced Saul. "King Saul, it's imperative that the army doesn't advance. Our fortifications are well under way. If the Philistines dare come closer, our archers will destroy their troops."

The king came out of his musing.

Ehud rose to his feet, "I agree with General Abner, my king. Their chariots are their only advantage and they cannot use them in a battle if we hold our position. Our infantry will destroy their men and we will have victory." Ehud waited for Abner to agree.

"Unlike some people, Captain Ehud thinks before he speaks," Abner said, annoyed, and the council laughed.

Ozra lowered his head in frustration as he tried to control his temper. He knew that if he were to lash out, he would certainly lose his position. He sighed in despair.

"With a king like ours, how can we not win?" Captain Ludim spoke above the whispers.

Saul sat back in his chair, still not saying a word. His eyes scanned his council as he thought about what little he had heard.

"I think it best if we hold our position. Our best option is to wait for them to make the first move. And besides, if God blesses us with enough rain, their chariots won't be able to ride through the mud," Saul said calmly.

"My king, I will pray for rain," said the priest Ahijah, sitting at Saul's right hand side.

"It is decided then," Abner said.

Suddenly Saul's eyes became blank, and his breathing heavy. Now looking into Saul's face, the general did not look into those piercing eyes he knew so well, but instead saw something in his cousin's eyes that he had not seen for a long time. It unsettled him.

"My king, what vexes you?" Abner inquired, concerned as he moved closer to the throne.

"The council is dismissed," Saul said abruptly, holding the bridge of his nose between his thumb and finger. The men looked with amazement at Saul, frowning with uncertainty.

"But my king, we have so much more to discuss," Ehud said after a brief moment of silence.

"I said *leave*," Saul snapped, smashing his clenched fist down on the armrest of his chair. The servants and scribe bowed and hurried outside. Each council member quickly kneeled before Saul and left in silence.

Ozra irritably marched past Abner and was the last to exit, murmuring to himself as he left, "Dear and glorious Abner, one day they'll know. I'll show them, all of them." He hated them for their mockery.

Abner was the only one not to leave. Saul did not say a word, and only stared bleakly ahead of him.

"Yes, the little worm irritated me also," Abner, said with a straight face. Saul smiled at his cousin's weak attempt at a joke.

"You know Abner, this is the first time today that I have smiled," Saul said shaking his head. The king's face turned somber once again as he sighed, feeling the weight of the world pressing him down.

"My sons?" Saul asked, weak with dejection.

"They should be two days' ride from camp, sire. They will be happy to see you, especially Jonathan."

"And I them," Saul nodded in acknowledgment. "You're the only one I can speak to, cousin. I have advisors and priests that I talk to, but although they listen, they do not hear."

"I hear, my king," the general replied and knelt. Saul ran his hands through his perfumed hair.

"Something is not right, Abner. I know it. I can feel it. For the first time in my life, I wake in the mornings tired, if I've slept at all. I feel ..." Saul caught his words, clenching his jaw as he shut his eyes. He could not say it. *"I hate what I've become."*

Saul's face went blank. Abner could not stand to see his beloved cousin like this. In the past months, Saul had become a different person. "I shall not sit upon the throne for much longer, my dear Abner."

"How can my lord say such a thing? I will personally smite the man that tries to take the crown from you," Abner said passionately, angered by the king's words. How could he be so weak? What had become of his cousin, the ruler of Israel?

"I am all alone. He left me, Abner," Saul confessed. Looking troubled, he continued, "How could he leave? I have sinned against Jehovah."

"Are you talking about the prophet again? Samuel is old and living in Ramah. Why does he torment you so? In all your days, will you not forget him?" Abner asked almost in a whisper, shaking his head.

"I will always think of him, Abner," the king said.

"What happened? What did he say to you?" Abner asked, gripping the king's hand affectionately.

Saul did not answer him. *They can never know,* he thought. He feared the rejection he would see in their eyes, and a pang of grief made his lips tighten into a thin line. He could hear Samuel's words in his mind as clearly as if it had happened yesterday, and he drew in a sharp breath. Saul closed his eyes as if in pain and looked away. "I p-pray you, leave me to my thoughts."

Abner rose and moved quietly to the tent flaps. He looked at Saul once more, and then left the tent.

He has taken everything, Saul thought miserably. *I have nothing left to live for. He has rent the flesh from my bones. I will never know true happiness again.*

"But who is to replace me?" he whispered with an uncontrollable surge of anger.

Heavy gates of hardwood and bronze swung open as the carriage approached, escorted by a royal retinue of twelve guards, ten attendants, and several packing asses.

Abner, gray with age, was sitting at a small writing desk with a long papyrus scroll stretched open before him. With his left hand, he was writing to his wife at Gibeah.

A partial shadow cast across the floor drew his attention to the tent entrance. A young boy hastily entered and fell to the ground before the general. He was panting and barely able to speak.

"Blessed be our great general," the young herald gasped, and took a deep breath before he continued.

"The princes have arrived at the gates."

"Ah, blessed news," Abner said. Placing the reed pen in the inkwell, he rose and patted the child on the shoulders. He had instructed the herald to wait at the gates and inform him immediately when the royal carriage arrived.

"You did well, lad." Smiling, the herald bowed and quickly exited. Abner leaned over the papyrus scroll and blowing quickly, dried the thick black ink. Carefully he rolled it up and put it away. He belted his sheathed kidon to his side and, resting his hand on his bronze sickle sword, left the warmth of his tent.

Abner entered Jonathan's tent to find the young prince lying on his bed, exhausted from his journey. Servants worked about the large tent as they brought in Jonathan's personal belongings. Jonathan had closed his eyes only for a minute, desiring a long sleep, but knowing that there was too much to do. When he opened his eyes, he found the general standing at his bedside, looking at him amiably. Jonathan was a slender man, his body toned from training with the spear and kidon. From a young age, the prince had been fascinated with the bow and arrow, and was now one of the most skilled archers in all of Israel. Saul had taken personal interest in his son's mêlée training, and forced Jonathan to practice with his instructor daily.

"Morning, my prince," Abner said. Jonathan smiled and then closed his eyes again.

"Not a moment's peace," he muttered.

"Happy to see you also, prince," the old man snorted.

"Abner, if I had to see your ugly face in the middle of the night, I would certainly die of fright. Thankfully, the sun is shining brightly."

"Yes, I know it doesn't take much to scare a simple woman like you."

Jonathan gasped and jumped up from his bed, "I'll show you what this *woman* can do."

Abner stepped back and lifted his fists in front of his face. Skilfully moving his feet, the general spoke with a forced frown, "It has been a long time since I taught you a lesson—or two."

"Come here, you fat old Benjamite." Grinning, Jonathan embraced the general warmly with a slap on the back. "It is truly good to see you again, uncle."

"And you also, my boy. There are so many things that I want to talk to you about."

"I am sure that there are, uncle, but I pray you, let me at least bathe and have a good meal," Jonathan said.

"I will order the cook to prepare something for our breakfast. Freshen yourself, and I'll arrange for us to be served in my quarters." Abner moved to the door, turned, and said, "Should I have the servant bring some lavender for your bath, or perhaps some myrrh ointment, m'lady?" Smirking, he left without waiting for a reply.

The day had grown hot by the time the two men had finished their meal of pomegranates, dates, nuts, goat cheese, and some fig cakes with honey, and were sitting back and enjoying a goblet of wine. Abner belched as he loosened his belt.

"How is my wife?" Abner asked softly.

"She misses you a great deal. She cried when I left. I have a letter for you," Jonathan said with a sympathetic smile. He understood the emotions he saw in the general. He missed his own wife already. It was always those first few weeks that were the hardest. He thought of her then, her whisper on his skin, the smell of rosemary in her hair, and the love he adored seeing in her eyes. The weeks he had been with Achsa were worth more than gold to him. They both sat in silent thought.

"And Achsa, and your mother and sisters?" Abner said finally, bringing Jonathan from his musing.

"They're well, and they send all their love. Where are my brothers?" Jonathan asked when he suddenly remembered them.

"I left them with your father. Will they stay long this time?" Abner asked gulping his wine, hoping for something he knew would not happen.

"No, I don't believe they will. They only came with me at my mother's request, and they will be gone again tomorrow. I know them." Jonathan said distantly, clenching his fists. "They always do this, and they're hurting my father more than they realize. I wish they wouldn't come."

Abner looked into his cup in mute empathy.

"Since my lord left, your father has become estranged from his council. He doesn't sleep at night, and he has again become violent at times," he said, sitting up straight. A servant handed him a clay drinking bowl with some coriander oil for his indigestion. He drank from the vessel, pressing his fingers into his uncomfortable gut. Abner belched softly into his fist.

"Yes, I realized when I went to greet him," Jonathan replied. "I didn't see my father this morning, but someone else. His eyes have become dull and his hair is nearly fully gray."

"The only thing that seems to help is his armor-bearer's music. He plays the kinnor and sings to him. The young man that's so good with the sling, what's his name?" Abner murmured as he thought, taking another sip from his cup.

"David. His name is David ben Jesse. He has been serving my father for nearly three years, and still you don't know his name," Jonathan said, teasing him. "And yes, he's especially skilled with that leather slingshot of his. He amazes me sometimes." Abner did not reply.

"I just realized I haven't seen David yet. Where is he? And why hasn't he been playing to my father?" Jonathan continued.

"He was sent home for the winter," Abner said. "I think your father still mourns for the prophet. Samuel's words struck him deeper than we thought."

"Abner, it's been close to four years since he left. How can he still long for that prophet? There are other prophets. If only we knew what Samuel had said to him."

"He doesn't speak about it. And God knows I've tried to get it out of him," the general said with a sigh. "Something will have to happen soon. We'll have to think of a way to lighten his spirits."

"My dear Abner, I think you are making too much of this. My father is stressed and tired. What he needs is a good rest. The coming winter break will do him good," Jonathan said with a slight frown.

Abner glared at the young prince, making him feel slightly uncomfortable. "Well then, only time will tell, won't it, my dear Jonathan?" Feeling offended, Abner downed the contents of his goblet and rose from his seat of cushions on the floor.

The swaying pale green grass scratched at David's legs as he stood taking in the crisp morning air. He loved the early hours of dawn, and as he did every day, he walked through the endless hills of Bethlehem and sang a prayer. He was almost never without his kinnor, and he played the crude harp with skill, perfected through the years. It had been his music that had brought him to Saul's court more than three years before.

He thought of the royal family every day, wondering what they were doing and if the king were well, if Saul needed his music to calm his troubled mind. He smiled as he thought of Jonathan, and was still amazed that he and the prince had such camaraderie, despite the age difference. He knew that Jonathan saw him as the son he and Achsa could not have. The prince and his wife had been trying to have a child throughout their marriage, but with all the tonics the physicians gave her to drink, and the balms and ointments they put on her belly, she remained barren. David wondered if she would ever be pregnant.

His legs were cold and wet from the dew, and he climbed on a large boulder. Before him, the highlands bristled with black sheep grazing on the shimmering grasslands.

David was a handsome young man with wild red hair and green eyes, which showed through patches of dark filth that smeared his skin after weeks of herding his father's sheep. He watched the sunrise, remembering the battles he had fought beside the king, carrying his shield for him, protecting him. He had never killed a man; though he had seen men die by Saul's hand many times. He had watched his three eldest brothers, Eliab, Abinadab, and Shammah ride out to the battle in the Elah Valley, and he hoped Saul would send for him.

Nethaneel, Raddai, and Ozem were still too young to be called out to war. Both his sisters were married and had strong healthy sons nearly his age. David was the youngest of eight siblings. If he had not played for Saul at his court, and if his father had not permitted it, he would never have become the king's armor-bearer so young.

He hated the sudden cold winds that would blow over the highlands in winter. It prevented him from practicing his aim with the sling and even though he tried to ignore the cold, he would tightly wrap himself in a soft leather blanket, and sit miserably with only his thoughts to entertain him as the piercing gusts bit at his exposed skin.

He recalled how the prophet Samuel had anointed him, and he often thought how it would all play out. He was torn between emotions. He loved the time spent with the royal family, but also feared how it all would end. It was something that had to happen.

There's nothing I can do, David thought simply.

"God's will be done," he told himself, shrugging delicately.

When it was light enough, David slid from the boulder and searched the waving grass for small stones he could shoot with his sling. After filling his shepherd's bag with the white rocks, he scratched a circle on the boulder as a target. Easily he loosened the long braided flax straps dangling from his belt, pressed a rock into the small leather pouch, and spun the weapon, clenching his teeth as he launched it with a grunt. David chuckled proudly when the soft limestone smashed into white powder in the middle of the circle.

He didn't notice the dark clouds sweeping across the steel blue sky, and only after his bag was empty, did he notice the change in weather. The sky echoed with thunder.

The herd seemed nervous and he assumed it was the lightning that scared them. He searched the fields with his eyes, though he knew that the swaying grasses would make it impossible to spot a stalking predator.

Suddenly, a lion raced from its cover. The hunter chased a young ram and even before David could load his sling, the predator pounced. The sturdy sheep kicked violently as claws cut into his flesh. It spun around and tried to defend itself, but the lion locked its jaw around the ram's neck, suffocating it.

A stone struck the beast between the eyes, and blood spurted from the wound as the animal roared in pain and dropped its prey. David came to the dazed hunter, lurching in circles. He grabbed the beast by its mane and struck it with his rod, cracking the lion's skull with a heavy blow. The animal dropped into the grass. David removed a small blade from his belt, and cut its throat. With terrible sounds the creature jerked in spasms as it died.

David waited for the predator to stop moving. After some time, he trotted home to call servants to help him, knowing the skin would soon spoil if he waited too long. The hide would make fine leather.

Chapter Two

Two soldiers, armed with spears and daggers, leisurely worked their way along the camp fortifications as morning broke over the Judean hills. The night torches, greased with animal fat, were still burning and the camp would soon wake, signaling the end of the night watch. Winter had come early this year and the first rains had fallen weeks ago.

"Why are we not marching out to meet the heathen in battle? I tire of this," Jarim said, pushing his hands underneath his arms to keep warm. He was a young inexperienced soldier, only recently called to the army after he had come of age.

"I have complete faith in our king. I am sure there is a good reason why he waits," Zuph, an old and battle-hardened man said as he blew warmth onto his freezing hands.

"Not from what I've been hearing lately," Jarim replied in an undertone.

"After Samuel left King Saul, the king doesn't think about anything else. He mourns for the prophet from the moment he wakes till the second he closes his eyes to sleep." The young soldier looked his comrade in the eyes and whispered, "They say he cries at night."

"Unbelievable. After everything Saul has done for our glorious Israel, this is how his people, my brothers, repay him. How can you even believe such lies?"

"Everybody is saying it; how can I not accept what I hear as the truth?"

"If I hear another word of this, I will personally report you to General Abner. Do you understand me?" Zuph said, his eyes hard and cold, poking a finger against the young patrolman's shoulder. The color drained from Jarim's face, as he dropped his head. They marched on in silence.

After awhile, the young soldier spoke hesitantly, looking at the dark mud, "Were you there when it happened?"

"Yes," Zuph said taciturnly, his vigilant eyes constantly scanning the expanse outside the camp for any movement.

Jarim lifted his head and gazed out into the bare hills, "Is it true? Did Samuel reproach King Saul?"

"You know it is true; everyone knows it. Why do you even ask?"

"I just wanted to hear it from somebody who had actually been there." After a moment he asked, "Did he proclaim that God would anoint another as king over Israel?"

"Oh, goat dung!" Zuph rasped as his anger flared up.

Suddenly, a slight movement in the distant darkness caught his eye.

"Quiet!" he whispered sharply and readied his spear for the throw. The old man searched the dawn until finally his trained eyes focused on the outline of a man. It was a Philistine.

"It's an ambush. Sound the alarm!" he shouted back into the camp. Within seconds, several trumpets sounded throughout the encampment.

"Warn the general. Now," he barked. Frightened, the young soldier stumbled back, and then sprinted into camp. "Ambush! Arm yourselves!" he shouted as he ran.

Zuph drew his dagger and readied himself for an attack, his eyes still scanning for more enemies. *Is it a night attack,* he thought, *or is it a spy from their camp? No, it couldn't be,* he decided; he would not have spotted a professional so easily, even with his trained eyes. What was happening?

A massive Philistine and his shield-bearer stood roughly three hundred meters from the Israeli camp. Fully armored, he howled into the morning, "Israel!"

The air was bitter. Tensions were high as morning broke over the ranks of Philistine warriors lining the horizon, their hosts spread across the crescent mountain range. The red sunrise spewed streaks of clouds across the sky as the sun rose between the two forces, Israel to the north and the Philistine military to the south.

Saul walked hastily through the working army, receiving "Hail, King Saul" wherever he went, barely acknowledging the men, his mind in disarray. Clouds of white dust billowed behind him as he marched.

When Saul finally reached the front line of his army, he stood frozen as he gazed out over the rocky Elah, not believing what he was seeing. In the distance loomed a dominating figure, with a backdrop of skilled warriors against the horizon. In front of him his armor-bearer, hardly half the size of the giant, hid behind the Philistine's shield. Even from afar, the man was enormous. In width, the Philistine champion was nearly twice that of Saul, with his shoulders heavily set. His legs were like tree trunks. With arms the circumference of pillars, he possessed hands that could easily wrap around a man's head. Apart from his freakish and grotesque physique, he was even more strikingly armored.

King Saul stood out like a colorful jewel, his regal attire making his royalty instantly evident.

Displaying bulging pectorals, the champion's chest heaved as he filled his lungs with air. "I am Goliath of Gath, a champion of the Philistine legions."

His coat of mail, weighing a hundred and seventy pounds, played a foreboding high-pitched jingle, like two deadly blades colliding. His brass-swathed body gleamed, from the solid helmet sheltering his gargantuan head to the tightly woven coat of mail hanging to his lower thighs.

"Why are you coming to draw up in battle array?" he cried, his voice cutting through the distance.

"Am I not a Philistine?" he shouted lifting the spear with a shaft like a weaver's beam into the air. He swung the spear parallel to the ground, pointing it at the Israelite masses.

"And you, servants of Saul?" His war-painted arm muscled as the hard bronze tip, weighing roughly twenty pounds, drew to the ground. Goliath brought the spear up straight and held it for a minute as he looked across the Israelite forces and then lifted it again. The spear rested level with his shoulders as words exploded from his throat.

"Choose you a man and let him come down to me. If he is able to fight and kill me, then we will be your servants." He grinned.

"If I prevail against him and smite him, then you shall be our servants, and serve *us*."

Saul was dismayed as he heard the Gath shout.

"I defy the armies of Israel this day. Give me a man that we might fight together." Goliath wanted nothing more than to battle against the best warrior of his enemy. He thought of the glory and riches that would be the reward for his feats. He did not even consider the fact that any man, much less an Israelite, might defeat him.

Saul sighed as he heard the defiant Philistine.

"Let it be known that I will give any man who slays that Gath, riches beyond his wildest dreams. His father's house will be free in Israel," Saul announced. "I will even give my daughter to that man."

Whispers spread through the formation as the men thought they would be princes of Israel. Suddenly the men paled as they heard Goliath's violent screams, and fear quickly took hold of them again.

Saul waited calmly, scanning the faces of his fighters. After awhile, he realized that no man had enough courage to face the Gath. The monarch moved back into the lines of his men, pausing only briefly at his general's side.

"Array the forces against the might of the Philistines. We shall fight these uncircumcised heathen," Saul instructed Abner.

"It is done, my king." With a firm fist, Abner saluted Saul as the king returned to the calm of his tent. He would be surrounded by opulence and comfort but it would bring no relief, for his mind was in chaos. The coming night would be a long one for both the king and his camp.

The sun threatened the distant horizon, its rule over the land finished as night descended. That entire day the Israelite battalions had endured demeaning insults and taunts from the colossus. His threats grew more intense with every passing hour until finally, when it was clear to him that no one would take up his challenge, he returned to his encampment of pitched white tents, shaded blue by the approaching darkness. Single fires spread throughout the camp, illuminating the wafting haze of smoke escaping into the night, while savage howls and screams filled the air.

A cold morning breeze wafted across the Elah Valley, stirring the thick, green leaves of the turpentine trees spread across the two miles of open ground. Snowflakes fluttered onto the muddy battlefield.

Eliab took a deep breath as he and his two brothers stood side by side, looking at the forces of the Philistines. The air was rich with the scent of the trees.

"God save us today," his lips barely moved, his eyes fixed on the terror that threatened across the distance. Abinadab heard his elder brother whispering to himself and looked at him curiously. Was this fear he was sensing? No, not his eldest brother. Now fear of his own crept across his broad face. He kept his eyes locked on the face of his brother, seeking comfort and courage. Nervously, Abinadab put his hand on the leather hilt of his kidon. It was comforting to know that the weapon was at his side. He twisted his fist nervously around the end of the sickle-sword, his eyes on the horde of Philistines that waited across the valley, their armor glistening, sending flashes of light across the Elah. The Israelite offensives anticipated the attack, their fear exaggerated by the whispers of a few soldiers that traveled easily through the quiet air, as they moved from one man to the next.

"They outnumber us at least five to one. We will not see the sun set on this day," one coward muttered to the warrior at his side. Abinadab's head turned upon hearing those terrifying words, shaking the thick black curls protruding from a yellowish helmet, as the color left his cheeks. Shammah, Abinadab's younger brother, could not help but catch the sudden movement.

"What worries you, brother?" Shammah's brow arched as he looked at Abinadab. He coiled his arm around his bronze-tipped spear and rested it against his chest.

"How can you even ask such a question? Did you not hear?" he snapped.

"That man has the heart of a pig. Truly, he is exaggerating," Shammah replied surprised at his brother's doubt. He took a deep breath as he rested his hand on his brother's shoulder. The sudden coldness of the chain mail spread through his hand. Abinadab jumped with fright at his brother's touch.

"Be a man. What would father think if he saw you now?" Shammah said sharply. Abinadab lowered his eyes to the dark mud and waited for his courage to return. He looked at his brother and forced a smile. With a sigh, he released his grip on his sheathed blade, straightening his body as his tense muscles relaxed. Abinadab saw the ridiculous grin from his younger, yet taller, brother. They both managed to chuckle over the craven behavior. Abruptly, Eliab prodded his elbow into Abinadab's side.

"Look, the Gath returns." Eliab's eyes were locked on the Philistine army. Abinadab stood on his toes, stretching his well-muscled body to look over the tarnished helmets of his fellow fighters.

The giant stepped from the enemy lines and marched forward.

The wind was rising, causing the tent flaps to snap gently against the two soldiers on guard. Their spears hung at their sides as they stood in front of the opening. Saul was sitting in his tent contemplating what Goliath had said. Tapping his thumb on the armrest of his throne, he stared at the leather map as he worked through tactics and strategies. Jonathan entered the tent, his eyes showing his anxiety.

"The Gath is at it again," he said.

"This cannot continue. It ends now." Saul replied gritting his teeth.

"What will you do, father?"

"No man has the courage to fight him in single combat, so we'll have to battle. Our fate is in God's hands," the king said as he stood up from his throne. "Today is the thirty-ninth day. Disease is breeding in the mud and the unexpected cold is disastrous for morale."

An icy draft blew into the tent as Abner stepped inside, his lips blue. He kissed Saul's hand.

"I assume my liege has heard," the general said. Saul nodded.

"What are your orders, my king? The armies are ready for battle, sire."

"Let's attack these dogs with everything we have."

The valley came alive as scores of Philistine and Israelite foot soldiers charged at one another from both ends of the Elah.

As fast as his rippling muscles could accelerate his lumbering bulk, Goliath led his brethren into battle. The Gath's deep-set eyes locked onto a target. His triceps tightened as he reached between his shoulder blades and freed a bronze javelin hanging at his back. Swiftly aiming, he skilfully launched the weapon with a sharp grunt. The thin metal staff whistled through the air, arching widely before it spiraled downward into a soldier's abdomen, his protective coat of mail useless. Blood splattered against the inside of the chain mail as the fiery red tip penetrated his flesh. The Israelite wrapped his fingers around the shaft, his face contorting with pain, as he tripped, still at full stride and dropped into the mud. He died instantly. Goliath did not see his victim go down as he kept his eyes on the ascending Israelite forces.

"You are all cowards. I challenge thee, fight me one on one!" he screamed over the chaotic din. He brandished his spear, performing for both the Israel and Philistine armies. The first unfortunate warrior approached the giant unwaveringly, baring his teeth as his muscles flexed while he charged. Goliath brought his arm down in full swing, striking the man against his side. His body convulsed in spasms as it was tossed through the air, his fall broken by his fellow soldiers.

The veins curled across his forearms as Goliath flexed his muscles and gave a series of growls. Fear struck some of the Israelites as they turned from the monster, fleeing back to the safety of their camp. The soldiers who maintained their courage, now danced vigilantly around him, not sure how to strike, their feet sliding through the slush as they cautiously stayed outside of striking range. Afraid, they jumped backward as the infuriated Gath paced forward.

A thunderous scream exploded from a stout and well-armored Israelite. His voice roared out, inspiring courage and rage in his comrades. In response, the entire Israelite battlement emitted cries of war into the dawning day.

☗

The youngest son of Jesse jogged lazily to the battle camp of Israel, moving to the casual pace of an ungainly ass. In the near distance, the sight of the garrison was a welcome relief. He had been riding on the ass from Bethlehem since before dawn, occasionally walking to save the beast of burden. After nearly twenty minutes, the young man and a family servant finally walked past the first wagon, entering the camp with renewed energy. The donkey bellowed as David brought the beast to an easy halt.

Suddenly his ears filled with the war cries of the fighting soldiers. David's eyes were filled with excitement, he could not believe his luck; he was going to witness the battle. He charged deeper into the camp, his red hair streaming behind him. The servant only smiled at his enthusiastic master as he led the beasts to the trough, still pulling a small wagon.

David hurried through the encampment until he reached his brothers standing in formation, their attention shifting between the Philistine hordes and Captain Ehud, waiting for him to sound the war horn.

The morning before, Abner had sent out the militias in three waves, losing roughly two eleph, composed of sixty-five men, in the meleè combat.

"Eliab, Abinadab," David cried. Eliab's eyes grew wide as he saw his brother running toward them.

"What are you doing here?" Abinadab asked. "We are about to march out. This is no place for heated youths."

"He's a fierce warrior," Shammah snorted mockingly.

Eliab glanced at his brother, but said nothing.

David acted as if not bothered by his brothers' hostility. "Happy to see you also," he replied sarcastically. With that, Goliath again approached the Israelites.

"Arrgh, look at him—he's massive!" David gaped at the colossus, and decided that he had to get a better view. His remembered how his father used to tell him of the giants that lived in Philistia, but he never could believe the lurid tales of his ancestors. He laughed with excitement as he quickly moved to the front, hearing the Gath scream.

"Why hasn't somebody gone to cut out that heathen's tongue?" David asked a soldier standing beside him, appalled.

"Would you fight that?"

David did not answer.

"What shall be done to the man that kills this Philistine?" he inquired.

"It is said that to the one who does this, the king will award great riches," the soldier said bitterly.

"Why did you come here?" Eliab suddenly grabbed David by his upper arm from behind and pulled him back. "And with whom did you leave those few sheep in the wilderness? I know your pride," he whispered accusingly. "You've come here only to see the battle, haven't you?"

"What have I done?" David said, upset. Eliab only glared at him. "Is there no answer?" He grunted as he pulled his arm free.

Turning to another soldier, he asked again. "What reward for killing the Gath?"

"The king will give that man his daughter, and make his house free in Israel. Riches will be his."

David looked at Goliath as he thought.

"I will kill him."

Saul had summoned David to him when he heard that his armor-bearer would fight Goliath. David was stalwart in his youth, his eyes gleaming with confidence. He had the physique of an ardent fighter.

David smiled as he knelt before Saul, taking the king's hand into his own and pressing it against his forehead. "It is good to see you again, my king."

"What are you doing here, my boy? Did I not send you home to your family?" Saul asked smiling down at the son of Jesse whom he had come to love greatly over the past years.

He's a fine young man, Saul thought, beaming at David, *well mannered in court, and educated.* The king realized how he had missed David while he was away.

"My father sent me to the captain of a thousand men, to bring him corn and loaves of bread for kif halak. But I have not yet met with him, sire," David said, and rose to his feet.

Saul regarded his faithful shield-bearer. "Now, what's this I hear about you going out against that mighty Philistine?" he asked. *David is small compared to the giant,* Saul thought, *and he isn't even the official age of twenty-one to be a soldier.*

"Let no man's courage fail because of that Philistine. Your servant shall go and fight with him," David said, and bowed his head.

"David, you are not able to battle with him. You're an adolescent, and he, a man of war from his youth."

"My king, I have kept my father's sheep for many years and there came a lion and took a lamb out of the flock. And I went after him, smote him, and saved the creature out of its jaws. And when the beast attacked me, I caught it by the beard and slew it. Your servant has killed both the lion and the bear. This uncircumcised Philistine will be no different, because he has defied the armies of the Living God."

The war council listened to the young man. David ran his hand through his wild hair and swept his gaze across the mighty men. "The Lord has delivered me out of the paw of the lion and the bear; He will save me out of the hand of the Philistine."

Saul nodded satisfied, his eyes bright with pride. "Then go, and the Lord be with you."

"Truly, my lord is a great king," David said.

Saul rose from his seat. His rich halug tunic fell to his ankles, and he carefully removed his coat of mail. The council gasped at this, but did not comment.

Saul gave David his armor and put a helmet of brass on his head. David girded his sword and essayed to leave, but the protective suit was too large, and he moved around the tent first, trying the metal corselet.

"I cannot go with these because I have not tested them," David said.

CHAPTER THREE

oth encampments waited in anticipation for an accomplished warrior to march out against the Philistine champion. This battle called for a man of immense stature and well-sculpted body, a man skilled in the art of combat and good with the kidon and spear, a man hardened by the slaughter of war.

The hosts cried out in amazement as the son of Jesse dressed in a plain halug and carrying a staff appeared. Some wailed in dismay, while others shouted with rage. Feeling betrayed by their reaction, David froze as he looked at his countrymen. His heart pounded.

"I shouldn't have let him go out there. If anything should happen to him...." Saul murmured, his face tight with worry.

Jonathan placed his hand on his father's shoulder, and forced a smile. "Remember what David told us? That God had delivered him out of the paws of the lion and the bear. Yahweh will give him victory today, I'm sure of it."

"Yes, now he goes with God," Abner replied, detached.

The Philistines laughed and taunted. Goliath faced his people and lifted his arms in display.

"What's he going to do—beat me to death?" he said to his shield-bearer with a snigger.

"Am I a dog that you come to me with a staff?" he shouted, as his face straightened. "I curse you in the name of Chemosh." The Gath snorted mockingly.

"Come, little man, I will give your flesh to the birds and to the beasts of the field," he sneered, flailing his sword through the air. The Philistines hailed their champion, beating their spears against their shields.

David stopped. "Give me strength, God," he prayed, his lips barely moving. "You are the creator of all things, the Might of Israel."

Steadily, he started moving.

"You come to me with a sword, a spear, and shield, but I come to you in the name of the Lord of Hosts, the God of the armies of Israel, whom you have defied," David shouted. "This day the Lord will deliver you into my hands, and I will strike you and cut off your head. Today, I will give the carcasses of the hosts of the Philistines to the carnivores of the air and to the beasts of the Earth. All the world shall know that there is a God in Israel." He felt the cold air bite at his uncovered skin as he paused for a moment, his lips shaking. He wanted to rub his hands together for heat, but resisted the urge.

"And all in this assembly shall know that the Lord doesn't save with the sword and spear, for the battle is the Lord's and He will give you into our hands," David cried passionately, raising his fists in the air. Israel shouted and cheered wildly.

"Abner," Saul asked, intrigued by the spectacle, "inquire whether David, who we know is of the tribe of Judah, is from the clan of the Perez or from the clan of the Zerah?"

"As your soul lives, oh king, I cannot tell," Abner said.

Goliath planted his spear and sheathed his sword. "I will rip this runt's head from his shoulders with my bare hands."

Screaming, he broke into a sprint. The opposing hordes quieted as the Gath stormed on, his screams muffled by sudden gusty winds. Calmly, David stopped, undid his sling from his belt and loaded one of the five smooth stones he had collected from the brook. Swirling the leather weapon faster and faster, he took aim and fired.

In a flash of blackness, the rock struck the colossus squarely in the face. His head snapped back as his skull cracked. Torrents of blood gushed from his forehead as Goliath wheezed and stumbled. With the stone lodged in his brain, he plunged into the mud, dead.

David ran across the valley as the entire Israelite army exploded into shouts of victory.

Panting, he unsheathed Goliath's golden kidon and took hold of his beard. David hesitated for a moment and then hacked at Goliath's neck, grimacing in disgust. Blood spattered across his face and hands, as the blade easily cut through the flesh. With a few strokes, it severed the spine and David lifted the head into the air. He shuddered as he held the massive head up for all to see.

The Israelite shofar, the horn of war, blew triumphantly and the Israelites swept across the Elah Valley. The Philistines retreated, abandoning their camp as they scattered toward their cities. Israel routed them all the way to Ekron, slaughtering hundreds of the enemy as they fled.

♔

The blood had dried on David's skin by the time he walked into the encampment, carrying the Philistine's head.

"An amazing display of valor," said Abner, eyeing the young man. "You must be proud of such a victory."

"I give God the honor, not my own soul, for I am but His servant," David said firmly. Abner's eyes shifted to the mass of bloody flesh and black hair, dangling from David's fist.

"Well answered, man. Who did you say your father is?"

"I didn't."

Abner's eyes narrowed. "You dare disrespect me, you who hasn't even a full beard?"

"It wasn't my intention, and I apologize, sir." The general did not know what to make of the young man staring at him. Was he being impertinent, or was he just strong-minded? He decided it was the latter. He liked that quality in a man. David reminded him of his son who was nearly the same age.

"The king wishes to speak to you. Follow me."

Saul and Jonathan had gathered with council to discuss the aftermath of the battle. As usual, the royal scribe sat in the corner and recorded every word.

"I assure you, father, now that we control the mouth of the Judean ridge, the Philistines will return," Jonathan said. "We can now adequately defend the highlands, and launch incursions into Philistia. They're vulnerable."

"And we effectively have the Vale of Terebinth and the trade route that leads through it," Saul added, pointing to the map where a thinly painted line indicated the road leading to the northeast. "We just have to keep it."

"We'll have to upgrade the garrison," Jonathan said. "Construct heavier fortifications, build more watchtowers, and even add some outworks. It could take many weeks," he murmured.

"I want it done in a week. I'll speak with Abner about it. We'll do whatever is necessary," Saul said.

The general entered the royal tent and announced the young man. All eyes fell on the large head of the Philistine as David came in, his body still stained by blood and mud.

"Finally! I was wondering when my general would bring you to me," the king said. The strong smell assailed Saul's nose as David kneeled before him.

"You have done Israel a great honor this day," Saul said, placing his hand on David's head. "May God bless you and your house."

"Whose son are you, David?" he asked as he motioned him to stand up.

"I am the son of your servant Jesse, the Bethlehemite, my king."

"He is the descendant of Boaz and Ruth. There is a lot more to David than meets the eye," Jonathan announced proudly. "You have a very wealthy ancestor, brave David. As this council well knows, David writes psalms, sings, and plays the kinnor with passion. And now he kills Philistines on the side." The men chuckled.

"Ah, yes. Now I remember," Saul said, smiling.

Abner watched David, analyzing his posture and movement. He took pride in knowing what people were thinking and feeling by reading their body language and behavior. He had never before felt it necessary to do so with the young armor-bearer, but his daring exploit changed everything.

"I have ordered that a feast be held in your name, David ben Jesse. Tomorrow night we shall celebrate your victory. It is well deserved," Saul said, looking into David's lively green eyes.

"Keep Goliath's armor and sword. And as for that, I will have my servants treat it. It's up to you to decide what you want to do with it afterwards." Immediately a young servant approached with a woven basket, covered the head with a cloth, and carried it away.

"Ask of me anything, anything at all," said the king.

"If my king doesn't object, may I take leave to wash and prepare for tonight?" David asked and bowed again.

"You had better, you look as if you've just cut off a man's head," Saul said, laughing at his own joke. David kneeled and kissed Saul's hand.

"My servant will take you to the quartermaster for lodging and then have people tend to you. Inform him that I personally sent you, and that he must see to it that you get the best."

"I'm looking forward to speaking with you later on," Jonathan said as David bowed before him.

As David left, Saul called out after him, "David, tomorrow morning I want you back in the training camp, fighting with the best of my warriors."

"He has a good heart, father," Jonathan said after David and the royal servant had left.

"Yes. He is a strong young man, and God is with him," Saul replied playing with a heavy ring on his finger, thinking.

Jonathan thought for a moment. "Father, perhaps you should give him more than just a feast in his name and some gold coins."

"What do you have in mind?"

"Well, as you know, father, he is well educated and has a brilliant mind. You have seen how he is with the men, and after today, they'll respect him. And certainly as your soul lives, he has proven his loyalty to the crown."

"What are you suggesting, my son?"

"Announce him officer over a cohort of three eleph," Jonathan said candidly.

The soldiers had looted the Philistine encampment and divided the goods between themselves. David had been offered first choice, but did not want anything. Everything was taken, the wood—already burning in several fires—the dry foods, the livestock, and even the tents. Nothing remained but the broken bodies littering the Elah.

A strong hand touched David on the shoulder. He was startled and turning, saw Eliab.

"Brother, are you always in the habit of sneaking up on people?" he asked, pulling the thick fur skin tighter around his body. David had slipped away from the celebrations, wanting to be alone, and was sitting on a hill just outside of camp.

"It's a fine evening," Eliab said, the cold stinging his skin. "We're not all that different, you and I. Sometimes at night,

I also go someplace to be alone, just to think and clear my head."

"We are brothers, aren't we?" David said distantly.

"What troubles you?" Eliab asked, as he sat down beside him. David did not answer but looked across the open dale, its beauty enriched by the moonlight washing over the endless rolling hills of the Judean ridge.

"Only hours ago, hundreds of Philistines lined the horizon, and now...."

"You had a brilliant victory today, brother," Eliab said.

"God gave him into my hands. I only hacked off his head."

"That's what's wrong. Now I see," Eliab spoke quietly and leaned in closer. "It was your first time, wasn't it?"

David nodded. "I have been in battle with King Saul and have seen men cut down by his own blade many times before, but it's something entirely different seeing someone else kill than to actually do it yourself.

"Yes, you smote a man, but he challenged us. He cursed Israel. You heard. You should be proud. God gave you a glorious victory," he said, putting his arm around David. "You, my brother, saved Israel from the heathen."

"I can still feel the flesh ripping under the blade, and hear his neck skin tear." David said curling his upper lip in disgust.

"I felt the same way after killing the first time," Eliab confessed, looking away. "I still see his eyes and the way he looked at me when I cut open his stomach. It haunts me in my dreams. Nevertheless, I know that Israel is the light in a dark world; we fight for a better life. Never forget this." David searched his brother's face. For the first time since Samuel, the last judge of Israel, had secretly anointed him king, he saw his brother looking back at him.

"Little brother, it's when you start enjoying the slaughter that you should be troubled." He was silent for a moment, and then suddenly spoke, his voice different.

"We all wanted to be anointed, every one of us. And I was very envious when the priest chose you," Eliab said. "I wish you could've known what I felt that day—the disappointment, the rejection, the guilt of knowing that I should have been happy for you. I couldn't understand why you and not me."

David remembered that his brother had a thin scar across his cheek, though now his beard covered it. The physician had shaved the hair on his face and he felt ashamed for weeks.

"And I can only imagine the battling emotions you must suffer, little brother. You're still young," he said.

"Will it get easier?" David asked, looking ahead of him.

"I fear not, David," Eliab said chuckling. "It will only get worse."

David looked up at the stars, and sighed. "Sometimes I also wonder why God chose me. I don't have your strength, Shammah's wisdom, or even Ozem's obedience," he admitted.

"God knows exactly what He's doing," Eliab said softly. "I am sorry for the way I've treated you these past months."

"It didn't upset me because I knew you were all only jealous," David said with a childish grin.

"You brazen little worm. Just because you killed a Philistine, and have red fluff growing on your face, doesn't mean that I can't still give you a good wallop," he snapped and grabbed at the hair gleaming in the light. David winced at the sharp pain and punched his eldest brother on the shoulder. With a quick hand, Eliab slapped David at the back of his head, sending him reeling forward. David rubbed his head violently as he glowered at Eliab and leaned forward as if going to wrestle him.

"Don't make me whip you," Eliab barked, pointing his finger at his younger brother.

"That hurt," David growled.

Eliab burst into laughter. "You should see your face. It's nearly as red as your hair." Reluctantly, David gave a weak smile.

"Come on, we must be getting back. We've been gone far too long, and if father learned that we had left the feast, he would give us both a thrashing," Eliab said as he rose to his feet. "The king holds a banquet in your honor and you disappear for most of the night. An insult, you must admit."

David and Eliab were immediately swept up in the merriment of the celebrations as they walked into the camp. The men danced and sang as they played on kinnors and tambourines. Grabbing a goblet of ale, Eliab drank deeply and then handed it to David. "Taste this, it's magnificent." Accustomed to drinking wine, David looked at the foamy drink warily. He had never tasted the soldier's drink before. Laughing, Eliab lifted the goblet to his mouth and forced his brother to take a gulp of the dark liquid. Frowning, David choked as ale streamed down the sides of his face.

"It's horrible," he spluttered as Eliab slapped him on the back.

"We men of war don't drink that watered-down grape juice," Eliab said. Wiping his mouth, David had another go at it.

"Ha! Now you're truly a man," Eliab said grinning widely. He cheered as he took another goblet from the table and downed half of it.

"We had better get to the king's feast before somebody notices that you are gone, even if I prefer to remain here," he said putting down the jug.

The atmosphere in the royal tent was lively as members of Saul's family, commanders, officers, and high-ranking soldiers celebrated. Musicians played sweetly on flutes and skilfully plucked at the strings of kinnors. Several servants walked around the room with wooden trays, serving goblets of diluted wine.

David and Eliab entered and quickly moved into the crowd, looking for their brothers. Abinadab and Shammah were conversing with Captain Ehud.

"The man of the evening," the captain cried, lifting his cup. Suddenly an older man, with a neatly trimmed beard, introduced himself abruptly and began talking to David. Eliab joined his brothers and smiled as the man dragged David off.

"So I pray you, tell me how you did it?" the man asked as he took a goblet of wine from the tray and offered it to David.

"Did what?" David asked, politely rejecting the cup.

"You know, defeat the Gath. You can tell me. You're secret is safe with me," the man whispered.

The music stopped and the men hushed.

"Where is the lad—no *man*—whose acts of bravery will be told throughout history?" Saul said, searching the group of men. Relieved, David turned from the man without a word and made his way through the crowd.

David moved to Saul and bowed deeply before the king. Kissing his hand, he rose and stood at Saul's shoulder, facing the guests.

"Your victory has inspired me, David ben Jesse. Your bravery is among the best I have ever seen," Saul said and the men applauded. Saul waited for silence.

"I am sad to say that the good Jesse ben Obed has now officially lost a son, but happy to say that I have gained an officer," he continued.

David stared at Saul. All eyes were now on him.

"David has been a trusted armor-bearer, he is well educated on the facts of war and tactics, and he has a strong mind, a faithful spirit, and a loyal heart. He is among the bravest of men I know. That is why I have decided to promote him in rank to officer over two hundred men … if he is up for the challenge?" This was a major honor. Soldiers would serve years in the army before they would gain rank as a commander over a unit of ten to fifty men. Usually the general would promote the soldier. David would now have up to two officers over a hundred who would report to him, and in turn would have to answer to his captain over a thousand fighters.

"How can I accept such an honor, my king?" David asked shaking his head. "I am but your servant. Why would you favor me so, my liege?"

"The army needs more men like you, my boy." The men applauded.

"As long as I am king, bravery and a strong arm will always be rewarded," Saul said and signaled with a hand. The music began again and the men cheered when a line of servants entered carrying platters of food, from beef roasted in bay leaves and lamb prepared in sweet-basil and served in a honeyed mint sauce, to cooked vegetables and spiced cakes. The men all sat down on silken cushions, and waited for the king to help himself first. Tantalizing smells pervaded the tent.

Saul chose selectively from the many platters, and dished out only the best. Jonathan, Abner, and David then did the same.

David was standing on top of the highest hill and had just finished his morning prayers to the Almighty God of Israel. His breath turned into gray wisps of cold air as he looked out over the broad horizon, the sun coloring the endless undulating hills with gleaming white and yellow. The thin hair on his bare arms stood up from the cold as a gentle wind caressed his skin. He closed his eyes and filled his lungs as he lifted his arms. On that hill, he was free.

Suddenly David heard the grass rustle behind him. He instinctively eyed his weapons lying a few steps away, and reached for them.

"It's rather a quest to find you so early in the morning. If it weren't for the watchmen who saw you walk up here, I would never have found you," a deep voice said behind him. David immediately recognized it and was relieved to turn and see Jonathan and several respected men, as well as his personal servant, approach him. "Everybody is still asleep after last night's festivities and you're watching the sunrise."

"I was never a man for much sleep, my prince," David chuckled and bowed his head as the prince walked closer. The small crowd remained at a distance as Jonathan towered over him, almost as tall as his father, the king.

"You don't have to bow every single time you greet me, David. We are friends, are we not?"

"How can a simple soldier be a friend to the prince of his country?" David asked honestly.

Jonathan placed his hand on David's shoulder, "How long have you been serving my father and me?"

"Two years and eleven months, my liege."

"And how many times have I confided in you and sought your advice?"

"I do not keep count, my prince." He grinned.

"You are more than just a soldier. You've defended my father's honor and life in battle, and me as well, David. I see you as a friend."

The prince waited for a moment, then continued, "Please call me Jonathan and not by my title. You are an officer and from now on I will love you as I do my own soul, and trust you beyond all reason." He waved for the men to gather around them to witness his berith with the son of Jesse.

Jonathan loosened his leather girdle. The prince then removed the rich, heavy robe that hung over his shoulders and draped David with it, as was the custom.

David stood frozen and silent, and then as Jonathan waited, he exchanged his own robe with the prince. This was a tremendous commitment between two men, and David did not have time to reflect on the weight of the matter. It was life binding and he would be cursed if he dared break the vows.

Jonathan took his belt, with his dagger and arrows, and fastened it around David's waist. Then he sheathed his sword on the leather belt. The kidon had a striking iron blade with an ivory hilt, fashioned with furrows to fit the grip of the fingers, and a large onyx stone encrusted in the pommel. There were very few iron weapons in Israel and the prince had just given him one.

The Philistines still held the monopoly on iron making, and with no ironsmiths in the land, the Israelites had to survive with bronze and the Philistine blades they acquired as spoils of war. David admired the artistry with a light stroke of his fingers. The gleaming hilt was smooth, and it almost felt as if it could yield against a firm grasp. He still preferred a wooden handle, he decided. It had a better grip, and his hands did not sweat against the surface as much.

"David, I pledge all of my strength, support, and protection. When a man attacks you, he attacks me," Jonathan said and placed the bow into his hands. "Now take my bow and my sword to seal this covenant, my brother." David took it hesitantly.

"Do you have nothing to say?" Jonathan asked.

"My prince, Jonathan, I lay my life at your feet and swear total allegiance to my lord, and Israel," David said and firmly embraced him.

"Now let us proceed with the cutting of the covenant."

An animal was sawed in half and the two sides were laid down beside Jonathan and David, who stood in between the bloody halves, symbolizing that they were dying to themselves. They walked a continuous figure eight through the sacrificed beast, together beginning a new walk with their covenant partner, unto death. The number eight spoke of more than perfection, of new beginnings, and a never-ending bond.

"I say, 'May God split me in two if I break this covenant,'" David intoned, and Jonathan spoke in similar fashion. The prince took David's blade and cut his palm. He watched as David did the same. They raised their right hands and mingled their blood, symbolizing to all that they were now one. As they gripped their hands and their lifeblood mixed, solemnly, they exchanged names. David accepted Jonathan's last name, and Jonathan accepted David's. The two brothers rubbed their hands together, scarring their skin as a permanent testament to the covenant—a mark that bore witness to the berith.

"All my property and all my possessions are now yours, David, son of Jesse," Jonathan said as he beamed at his new brother in covenant.

"And I give you all that I have, my property and my possessions," David said, as the Hebrew ritual dictated. David now had the right to speak and buy in the prince's name, as could Jonathan in David's name. The gravity of the bond struck David for a moment, and he stood in silence, shaken.

"Now, my brother, let us seal this berith and eat together, you and I," Jonathan said, and he looked across at the men. The ritual had taken far longer than an hour. "I will feed you my bread and I will drink from your cup. The blood of the grapes and all will know that you are now in me, and I in you." The prince sent his servant back to the encampment to arrange with the cook to prepare a breakfast, and then turned toward the camp, stained red by the blood of the ceremony.

The men were spirited in their congratulations.

"Shall we go taste what old Nepheg has prepared for us, Officer David?"

"I still have to get used to that title," David laughed, and joined the prince. The men walked leisurely to the camp.

In the course of two days, David had gained immense political power and influence, and inevitably, fame. He was now the king's beloved officer and the blood brother of the eldest prince.

CHAPTER FOUR

ronze clanged as the blades of two kidons pressed onto each other. David's arms shuddered under the pressure as Jonathan forced the blade down, sweat streaking his brow. He held his opponent's gaze, his biceps burning.

The prince spun around, keeping a small shield close to his side, and stepped away. David grinned at what he thought was a retreat. He rushed toward Jonathan and thrust his sword. The prince blocked and spun one final time, hitting David's blade from his hand, sending the kidon sliding across the floor. In a following move, he brought his sword around skillfully, but David was quick with his shield and the sharp blade thudded against it.

David stepped backwards as the prince hacked at his shield. Jonathan's blows were too swift and precise for him to sidestep. He knew that he was vulnerable; he had lost his kidon, and Jonathan was bearing down on him hard. The pressure increased.

His rage surged and he roared as he charged forward blindly, pushing the prince across the sparring tent. He shoved him aside with a grunt and quickly darted for his blade. As he snatched up his weapon, he felt the cold metal of Jonathan's curved blade against his neck. He grunted in frustration, and his body relaxed.

"You made two major mistakes," Jonathan said, winded as he lifted his blade.

David opened his mouth to speak, but Jonathan silenced him with a sweaty palm. "No David, I don't want to hear it. Just listen for once."

"Your first mistake, you lost your kidon. Quite the blunder. Secondly, you lost your temper. Next time don't get angry, and above all don't lose your sword. It's very important that you keep a cool head in battle, or else you won't have one at all." Jonathan said panting. "I have to admit, you did put up a good fight. You're getting better." Two servants handed them cotton towels and stepped away.

Over two months had passed since David had gained his rank, commanding his elephs personally, supervising their training, keeping them fit, and learning their strengths and weaknesses. He had formally requested before the royal court that his brothers Eliab, who was already commander-over-ten, and Abinadab and Shammah, who were light infantry, serving under Eliab, be added to his cohort. With Jonathan, Captain Ehud, and the priest Ahijah speaking for him, and Abner and a few other officers against him, the council had been at some odds over the appeal. When Saul voted for David, it was recorded on scroll. Abinadab and Shammah were now his commanders-over-fifty and Eliab had a hundred men under him.

"I almost had you for a moment, though," David said chuckling with a rasping breath, closing his eyes as he wiped the sweat from his face and neck. He wondered if he would have been able to match the prince's strength for much longer if Jonathan had not broken from the fierce lock of blades when he had.

"Your head would be rolling in the mud. But I'll make a ben-hayil out of you yet," Jonathan said as he dried his chest and underarms. "You have gotten a strong arm and fast movements over these past months. Use that to your advantage.

You have an admirable sense of fighting, David. You still just need to refine your skill. But with your brilliant mind, you'll strike me successfully soon enough." It had been over a year since they had given up wooden swords and had been training with the more dangerous bronze.

"You are too kind," David said moving to a low wooden table standing against the tent canvas.

"No, not at all, David. If I have my way, you'll be a captain soon," Jonathan said, and studied David for a reaction. Although Jonathan had mentioned it before, David felt like exploding with excitement, but he composed himself, and only smiled at the prince.

David loved his sparring sessions with Jonathan, and he grew stronger and more skilled each day. When he arrived at Saul's court, he was a fighter trained by his father, but now he was a warrior. His father had a sharp mind, and the tactics and battle histories David had learned from the retired combatant had impressed the king immensely.

"Let's go through the fight, so that I can show you where you can improve," Jonathan said, smacking his lips.

"You have a good defense, but still need to improve on the offense. Let's be serious for one moment. By the next moon, it'll be spring and my father will want to see that he didn't make a mistake in trusting you to command three eleph. You will have to prove your worth. And I know Abner. He will press that your cohort be the first to foray into Philistia when the snow melts, just so that he can throw it back into my face when you don't return."

David sighed as he suddenly remembered his old concerns. *What if I fail?* he thought again. *I am responsible for the lives of over two hundred men.* Nodding with tight lips, he pushed aside his feelings of anxiety, and decided that he would face up to his fears. They would not rule him.

His eyes narrowed as he welcomed the challenge.

Jonathan liked the confident energy he felt pouring off the young man, but continued. "You will be fighting warriors who want your blood on their swords. You've been in battle with my father, fighting at his side. You've seen what it takes to survive out there. Only the strong stay alive, David."

He put his hand on the back of David's neck and gripped him gently. Leaning in close, he said softly, "The last thing I want to see is you dying out there. I want you to be ready for those uncircumcised heathen. Now focus and let's begin."

Saul woke with a start and sat up straight, his eyes focusing in the dark. A windstorm howled outside, the canvas jerking with the powerful gusts. Suddenly he caught a brisk movement, and he knew that he was not alone.

"Who's there?" he whispered as he desperately searched the darkness. Finding it hard to breathe, he listened for the low groan that had awakened him, but the tent was still.

Feeling uneasy, he dismissed the sound as the wailing wind, and sank back into his pillows, the covers clinging to his heated body. He closed his eyes and listened for the slightest sound.

Then he heard it again. His heart raced as he flung himself up, and reached for his iron kidon. An eerie hiss originated from the farthest corner of the tent as Saul imagined seeing the outline of a heavily built man. The hiss became louder and he saw the subtle movements of the lurking figure.

"I will cut out your heart," he said, waving his blade. Saul wanted to call for the guards, but the words caught in his throat.

Without warning, a large creature jumped at him. Saul's entire body tensed to the point of physical pain. His face twisted in fear. He tried to react, but it was as if his mind had detached from his body.

The monstrous devil came within an inch of his face, its deep-set eyes piercing him. It exhaled its musty breath into the king's face, and he gagged at the foul smell. It moved even closer and Saul whimpered as he looked away, gritting his teeth as he felt heat emanating from it in waves. Weakly, the blade slipped from his fingers.

Saul went pale as the black scales of the creature scratched his skin. It growled and slime oozed from its mouth.

The demon roared with bloody fangs.

Saul jolted up from his bed at the night terror. His lungs swelled violently with a harsh breath and he screamed, his mind in a daze. He was alone in his tent, and he heard the wind crying.

Two guards rushed in to find their king sitting on the edge of his bed looking at them as if death had touched him. His bewildered stare frightened them.

"Why didn't you help me? You heard the beast growl. You cowards!" he cried. The guards looked at each other, uncertain how to reply. Tilon, a burly guard, was the first to speak. "Was there something here, my liege? We did not hear anything. What has caused this?"

"What did I just say? Are you saying that I imagined it? How dare you! It stood there, right in front of me, growling," Saul rambled. "It snarled and hissed. How could you not have heard it? You idiots, where were you when I needed you?"

"What exactly did you see, Lord Saul? Was it a wild dog? We can still hunt it down and smite it, if my lord so wishes."

"It wasn't a dog. Do you think I would look like this if it were a mutt, or any animal for that matter?" Saul rushed his words, doubling over with his conflicting emotions. "It was a sable demon, with blood-splattered claws and deadly fangs and … and … and thorns on its scaly skin."

The guards shared a silent glance, realizing that he must have dreamt again. Tilon nearly smiled, but caught himself.

"Perhaps it was the wind you heard, my liege. I have heard the wind make ..." Eliel broke off as Saul shouted at them.

"Get out—out!" Stiffly, they bowed and turned.

"Next it'll be ghosts wanting to steal his nightgown," Tilon said under his breath, and chuckled as they left the tent.

The men braced themselves as they stepped into the wind, and properly closed the tent flaps behind them.

"Can you believe that? A thorny beast," he snorted. Eliel just smiled, shaking his head as he held his body stiff against the cold.

Suddenly the guard groaned with pain, his back arching as sharp metal pressed through him. Eliel staggered back, stunned by the dying man. Tilon's face contorted and he coughed blood over his clothes, the protruding blade tenting his tunic at the chest. The blade twisted in him, tearing through his body as he gurgled.

"Never mock the king of Israel," a rough whisper came from inside the tent. The impaled body went limp and then fell from the blade as Saul pulled back his kidon.

"Do you also have something to say?" he asked murderously, his words muffled by the gusty winds. Eliel's voice had gone, his body so tense that he could barely shake his head in reply.

"I thought so. Good," Saul said with a sadistic smile, cleaning the blade on his white nightgown, sniffing as if nothing had happened.

"You will not tell anybody what has happened tonight. Nobody must know. My name cannot be blemished. You will say that you argued and when he attacked, you simply defended yourself. Do you understand me?"

Saul went on without pause. "If you dare tell a soul, I will hear of it, and you shall suffer the same fate. Now get somebody to remove that heap of flesh before it stinks up the air. I don't want flies in my tent."

Eliel stood in horror, looking down at the corpse. He did not know what he would do, and cared little. He just wanted to get away from the wild king. Eliel turned and then ran off.

Coldly, Saul wiped his hands on his clothes as he stared after the soldier, and then stepped back inside. He climbed into bed, still covered in blood, feeling exhausted as he sighed with depression. Closing his eyes, the silence of the tent filled him and the distinctive hiss of the beast played in his mind. His body went cold at the memory. He thought he had been rid of the terrible nights.

Saul buried his face in the pillows, and began to sob uncontrollably.

David pushed his kidon away from his body slowly, letting out a rush of air over his lips. His arms burned and the blade began to quiver after holding it steady for a moment. He had awoken before dawn for prayer and training as was his routine and now, his body was aching from practicing. A single droplet of sweat hung from the tip of his nose, trembling before falling as he brought the sword around in a slow sweep, as if performing a dance. The only sign of his consciousness was his eyes blinking away the salt stinging him.

Jonathan stormed into David's tent, snatched a folding stool, and sat down without a word, his lungs burning as he breathed wildly. David froze at the sound, and spun on his heel to face the intruder, gripping the hilt of his iron kidon more tightly. He relaxed slightly when he saw the prince and instinctively listened for sounds of fighting. What was happening? He had been training for hours, and his body was ready for a fight.

"Jonathan, are you well? What's wrong? My prince, what's happening?" he asked again, only louder and David saw Jonathan come from his thoughts.

DAVID

"Achsa is with child!" he said, and the ends of his mouth turned up. He was shaking and still couldn't believe what the herald had told him. There must have been a mistake. They had wanted this for longer than he cared to remember, and over the years, he had miserably made peace with the fact that he would never have a son.

David shouted in excitement, clamping Jonathan's shoulders and shaking him as he laughed joyfully. "You old man! You thought it would never happen." David embraced the prince, slapping him on the back.

"Oh, Lord, blessed be Thy name! Achsa is pregnant!" Jonathan said coming from his daze as reality began setting in. He burst into happy laughter, and jumped up from the chair, though his legs felt like water.

"Achsa is having my child," he said again through his exhilaration.

"Can't you say anything else?" David asked and he could see the amazement in his stare.

"I don't want to," Jonathan said shaking his head, grinning like a small child.

"Have you told your father?" David asked.

"I haven't told anybody, David. Y-you are the first," he said. "Will it be a boy or a girl?" Jonathan asked. He sank onto the small chair. His mind was racing. "Will it be healthy? Will it like me, David? How am I going to raise a child?"

"Yes. Yes. You will be a great father, Jonathan. And does it matter if you have a son or a daughter? We need to celebrate," David said and pulled Jonathan to his feet. "But first we have to tell your father and Abner."

Jonathan gazed into his goblet as he swirled the last of the dark wine at the bottom. In one gulp, he downed the spiced wine, and struggled to focus on his friend. It had been a long night and the muscles of his face were hurting from all the smiling, but he couldn't bring himself to stop. It had been a day filled with festivities, and afterward, a large feast. Saul had ordered cups of wine for all his officers, captains, and generals. Afterward David and Abner had walked with Jonathan to his tent, and they continued their celebrating there. Abner had retired to his bed a long time ago and the moon had passed its zenith.

"You are a good friend, David. If I have a son, I want him to be like you," Jonathan said. "Do you remember saving my life?" David thought for a moment, but could not recall the event. "You were with my father, and he was hacking at Philistine flesh. I fell and you were the one who stopped his sword from taking off my head."

David couldn't remember this, but decided not to say anything. After several cups, he had begun to feel the effects of the wine, and had stopped drinking then.

Jonathan belched and held the empty vessel above his head. "More wine, Akkub."

When the servant picked up the clay container, David discreetly signaled him not to fill his cup. "Don't you think we've had enough for tonight?" The prince smiled, and nodded as he put the goblet on the low table.

"And that wasn't the only time. You have gotten me through difficult times, David," Jonathan continued. "When my father was ill, you played for him and his soul was healed. You helped me get over my own insecurities when Achsa couldn't conceive, and only then could I comfort my wife as a good husband. You always put other's needs before your own and you always know what to say to make me feel better. You're my pillar, even if you don't know it."

David looked away as he clenched his jaw. He did not know how to respond to the prince's praise.

"I love you, David," Jonathan said, and held his head. "I do believe I'm beginning to feel the wine."

David laughed. "Yes. I think I must retire to my own tent and sleep the few hours that are left of the night," David said and rose. "I thank you for your kind words, Jonathan," David said warmly at the door.

Jonathan took David's shoulders firmly and embraced him. "There's no need. Everything I said was true. I will see you tomorrow, my friend." He clapped David on the back.

CHAPTER FIVE

The sun burned David's skin for the first time in months. His men were all bare-chested in and around the fighting ring, roaring and cheering for the two fighters battling it out. It had not snowed for weeks and the strong gusty winds that signal the end of winter had gone. Rumors had spread across Philistia, and he was now the most notorious Israelite in all Palestine. Some hated him for killing their beloved champion, while others admired him for his bravery and skill with the sling.

David studied the fighters, assessing the capabilities of his men, learning who was the strongest, fastest, and bravest of them.

During the first few weeks, his soldiers had derided his youth, but followed his orders nonetheless, some simply acting out of their military obligation. However, one tenacious soldier had challenged his authority in front of the entire cohort. He was forced to have the man whipped, something he despised ordering, but it was the only way. The man had returned in silence with long welts across his back. After that, he did not again dare disobey another order from his ranking officer, but despised him silently.

David's father had taught him never to befriend the men he had to command, but earn respect and not force it. This was something he struggled with, and he had wished many times that his father had been there to tell him what to do. He thanked God that Eliab and Jonathan were there to guide him.

With a few strikes, Pelet had again won the fight in the ring. He was the most skilled with the buckler and among the best in the elephs. His speed was unmatched, even by David.

"Gather in formation," Eliab suddenly bellowed. The soldiers scattered from the battling-pen and within seconds stood perfectly aligned, holding their spears and shields at their sides. Pelet panted and tried to stand erect despite his tiredness. Eliab stood with a straight face, his strong posture inspiring reverence.

David was amazed at how quickly his brother had demanded authority from the men, and had gained it seemingly without effort.

"You are men of war, and I am your officer," David said loudly. The men saluted as one, hitting their fists onto their chests with loud thumps. David knew the names of all his men, and had gotten to know their likes and dislikes, their worries and desires; he even knew a few names of some of their families.

"You have trained hard these past months. And now you have truly become one unit. One that should be reckoned with. I could not have been given braver and stronger men than you. Together, the Philistines will hear our name and tremble," he continued proudly, his voice carrying to the last of them. The men looked at him, their bearded faces showing their veneration.

David paused slightly to give more weight to his words. "We are the warriors that shall bring utter destruction to our enemies. And that is why we shall be known as Gibbôr— *Mighty Men.*" The men began chanting the name repeatedly, the power of their voices sending a chill down David's spine. He fed off their energy.

"Join me now, my brothers. I ask you to commit to our glorious cohort. Swear loyalty to me and fight valiantly for Yahweh and our holy inheritance—Israel. Together we shall have victories and magnificent triumphs."

David searched the faces of his men for a moment and then turned to Eliab and nodded. His brother stepped forward.

"Those who will join us recite this vow after me," Eliab said. "If you are not willing to sweat and suffer for this cohort, leave now. You will not have another chance."

The formation did not break. Nobody left.

After looking over the four hundred war-scarred men for an anxious moment, he said, "Yahweh is almighty. I am an honorable man, serving my country and fighting to protect her towns, the cities of my ancestors, and the lands of my descendants."

The soldiers of Gibbôr were now part of something bigger than an army. They had formed a brotherhood, a cohort of skilled warriors who would die for one another without thought.

"Well done, little brother," Eliab said with a wide smile. "What are your orders? The day is still young."

"Let them march in formation. Press them till nightfall. I want them working together like the mortar and pestle. The one is useless without the other," David said. "And tomorrow, let them fight in pairs tied together. I want twelve men in the pen at a time. Let's see how they handle that. Also double their combat training."

He looked ahead blankly as he said softly, "I will show them what God's anointed can do. All of them."

"They will come, their greed assures me. They want my land so that they can give it to their snot-nosed brats," King Achish of the Philistines muttered irritably as he sat on his throne with his fingers curled around a goblet of dark wine. The battle at the vale of Terebinth was still fresh in his mind, the loss still eating at him. His humiliation and rage were festering. "Where will they attack?"

"I would think that they would raid the garrison at the eastern border of Ekron, my king," a military advisor answered.

Achish's eyes bored into the man, "You *think*? Find out exactly where they plan to strike. And don't waste my time with guesses." He hurled the cup across the stone floor, spilling some of the wine on his pleated tunic. The four women sitting around him winced behind their multi-colored veils at his sudden burst of violence.

"Now look what you made me do. This halug was cut from the finest imported silk. Now it's ruined. I'll buy another finer one from your monthly wages." He wiped the warm fluid from his stomach, feeling the soaked cloth cling to his skin, and with a flick of his fingers, he sprayed the wine on the advisor.

"Y-yes, my lord," the advisor stammered, closing his eyes as the drops splashed in his face.

"Why did I give you all that iron? Did the rat not accept our offer?" Achish asked, knotting his thick eyebrows as he licked his stubby fingers clean.

"He did indeed, oh lenient one. He told me personally that is where they will attack. They will strike by the light of the next full moon."

The Philistine king smiled lewdly at the women as he pulled them closer, wrapping his flabby arms around them. He smiled as he stroked his bare paunch, playing with his frizzed black hair. His skin was covered in black tattoos.

"The iron was a good investment then. I want you to make sure from our informant if that is undoubtedly the garrison, and then double the men. Have all the reinforcements attack from the rear after our foes engage and then hammer at them from the front and the back." Achish pursed his lips. "It shall be chaos for the Israelites," he said, his stomach quivering as he snickered. "We will nail their bodies to our walls."

"What do they call that Israelite whelp?" he thought aloud.

"Do you mean the warrior who slew Goliath, my king? They call him ben Jesse."

"I know what he did. How can I forget?" Achish snapped. "Bring this ben Jesse to me, *breathing.* I would like to meet the Israelite who smote that insolent Gath. He must be quite a man."

CHAPTER SIX

lades of wild grass brushed David's leather armor as he crept dangerously close to the Philistine outpost. He had stripped off his heavy armor, his shield, and spear in case he had to make a quick retreat. He had only a small leaf-shaped dagger placed inside his bronze belt and a hand-axe.

David sat on his haunches, his muscles burning. Looking out over the swaying grass that reached as high as his face, his eyes followed the moving points of light at the Philistine garrison. He studied the movement of the patrol, and within an hour, he had figured out the route and time of each of the thirty sentries.

The soldiers of Gibbôr waited tensely in the fields for their officer to return. David had them remove any metal that could send a flash of light into the enemy camp, alerting the guards of their presence. They wore leather armor and had smeared their blades and spearheads with black mud. They sat in total silence.

Suddenly Eliab heard the call, the bell of a roe deer. It was a welcoming sound. Quickly he got up and waved his sword through the air, and then disappeared back into the grasses. David moved closer to his brother. Breathing heavily, he sat back on his haunches.

"There are thirty of them. We have, at the most, ten minutes before they meet up. We'll have to be very quick," he whispered.

"Only thirty? How many guards?"

"I couldn't see. They were all inside the garrison. There are four at the gates, which will make it difficult. I would guess that the walls are three meters high and they keep the gates open for the patroling men."

Eliab frowned as he wondered for a moment. "With thirty sentries, I would say that we are almost evenly matched. Let's take the gatemen first. Then the sentries and, lastly, we close the gates and burn it all."

Abinadab and Shammah crawled closer and Abinadab spoke in a low voice. "Good to see you back without any holes in you."

"Your concern is touching," David replied with a thin smile, and shifted his weight onto his other foot.

"So what are we dealing with?" Shammah asked.

"We're looking at a hundred and fifty to two hundred men. But we only have to kill thirty-four. It's almost too good to be true. In fact it is," David murmured as he thought.

"A trap, perhaps?" Eliab asked.

"It can't be, I would have noticed something," David said almost to himself. "If it is indeed a trap, how did they know we were coming? And where are all of their men? No, everything looked fine. I have a good feeling," he finally said shaking his head. "Let's just get this over with."

David sighed with relief as Shammah waved the torch at him. All the sentries outside of the fortification were dead and his men now patroled the walls. The Israelites had surrounded the stronghold, and at David's orders engaged in the assault. It was a quick takeover. Eliab, Pelet, and two other soldiers had crept closer to the gates, disposed of the gatekeepers, and hid the bodies in the grassy coverage of the plains. Israelite soldiers disguised as Philistines manned the posts at the gates and as each of the sentinels passed, they were silently assassinated.

Knowing that the worst was over, David emerged from cover, and hurried to the garrison. The rest of the patroling guards would exit the gates in good time, so they had more than enough time to slay them all.

Eliab and Pelet made quick work of the men as they in turn exited from the gates. Everything was going brilliantly. They had now killed nearly all the watchmen and nobody even knew that they were there.

"That should be all of them," David said. "Ready the archers and then come in after us."

He and a group of three men cautiously entered the garrison, and quickly made their way to the center, knowing that was where the officers' quarters would be.

Without any effort, David opened the door to the wooden building, holding his kidon ready. They entered and found the officer sleeping with two prostitutes in his bed.

Eliab moved across the room and with the end of his hilt, hit the officer square in the face, rendering him unconscious. Pelet and Abinadab jerked the naked women out of bed and put strong hands over their mouths, muting their screams with a thick cotton cloth. With ease, Eliab lifted the man over his shoulder and carried him out. Pelet had to draw his dagger to get the prostitute he had in hand to cooperate. She cried vehemently as he led her outside.

Suddenly cries of pain filled the night as David's men ripped open the tents and slaughtered the sleeping Philistines in their beds. Minutes later the military base fell deathly silent, the only sound coming from the breeze sweeping over the grasslands.

The officer felt his head throb as he woke from a sharp pain. David struck him again and then pressed his blade against the officer's neck. The Philistine—Saran—came around slowly, his vision going in and out of focus. His face hurt.

"Philistine *filth*. I'm going to cut off your head," David whispered harshly, grabbing the man by his wild beard. Saran felt cold earth press into his skin and realized that he was lying on the ground, completely naked. His face was mottled with anger and blood began to drip again from his broken nose.

"Why are there so few men in this garrison?" David asked, jerking him by his hair. The officer snorted and spat at him, baring his teeth. David closed his eyes as he fought not to grab the man by the throat. Wiping the spittle from his face, he rapped the man's jaw, bursting his lower lip. Screeching in pain, the Philistine cursed in Semitic.

"No! I pray you don't hurt him," one of the prostitutes cried, and covered her face in horror. What David saw in her eyes made him realize the advantage they had. David glanced at Pelet and knew that he had also seen it.

"Tell me," David demanded.

"Do what you will to me. In all my days, I will not fear a stinking Israelite," Saran hissed. He knew that Goliath's killer would use his lover to break him.

Without waiting for David to give the order, Pelet shoved the prostitute closer, and brought the knife up to her chest. She firmly held the blanket around her, her body trembling as she sobbed. Saran struggled to hide his sudden worry as he looked at the woman. Her eyes begged him, tears flowing down her cheeks, but still he refused. Painfully, he looked away.

"I will cut out her heart," Pelet barked, his hand quivering. He prayed that the Philistine would speak before he had to harm the woman. He didn't know if he could. Her scream broke the tense silence as Pelet pierced her skin with the tip of the blade.

The officer roared and Pelet's hand stopped.

"Leave her alone. I will speak. I will tell you anything," he said, almost crying. David did not show his relief, increasing the pressure on the man's throat instead. The officer choked quietly, his face contorting as the blade cut his skin.

"Many nights ago I received the orders to send half of my men to the garrison at Ekron. One of your own had told my king where you would attack. That's all I know."

David had heard what he wanted.

"Run. And go tell your king what has happened here tonight. Tell him that we will raid other garrisons. Let him try and stop us," he said, removing the blade from his neck. "Now get out of my sight."

Cautiously the officer rose under David's angry glare, and then looked at the women in silence. He waited uneasily for a moment, and when David nodded, he exhaled slowly with a quivering effect. Eliab and Pelet shoved the women to the Philistine without a word.

Frantically they ran off into the night. Gibbôr looked after the fleeing figures until the darkness swallowed them.

"Burn it. Burn everything," David ordered.

Achsa touched the seal on the papyrus parchment gently, rubbing her thumb over the letters of his name.

"Jonathan, my love," she whispered and then carefully untied the string and broke the seal. She unrolled the letter and began reading, smiling at his anecdotes. He was the only one that could make her laugh, even with the constant discomfort of her pregnancy. After finishing, she pressed the letter against her massive belly, believing that her baby could feel the rough paper on her skin.

"This is a letter from your father," she said to the child inside of her. "And he loves us so much." She hadn't seen Jonathan in nearly eight months, and she ached for his touch.

She rolled up the parchment, tying the string around it again, and placed it in a large ceramic container with all the other letters. She hoped he would be with her during the birth. He promised her every time he wrote, and she counted the days as she watched her stomach swell, feeling the child growing inside of her. She refused to admit that she might have false hope and she told herself each day that he would be by her side when the baby came.

Achsa called for the servants and allowed them to undress her. Uncomfortably, she lowered herself onto the bed, and waited as servants pushed pillows behind her back and head. For all the joy her unborn child gave her, it caused her just as much pain. She wondered when her back would give out, moaning because of her huge belly. The servant girl rubbed olive oil onto her gleaming skin and Achsa crooned to her baby as the woman massaged her. She imagined having a son. Closing her eyes, she could see his golden hair and hazel eyes. He would be just like his father, she thought, taking in the distinctive smell, enjoying the feeling of the restorative emollient on her tired body.

⁂

Saran and the women walked wearily across a large fenced piece of land, which they assumed was a farm, hoping to find someone who could give them some clothes and shoes, and something to eat. Their feet were hurting, and the skin on their heels and toes were chafed from the days of walking.

Saran laughed and pointed when he saw a small house in the distance and hurried to it. The women forgot their discomfort as they ran after him. Soon they could have water on their lips.

As they approached, they saw that the stone dwelling was old and decrepit, and he cursed loudly when he thought that no one might be living there. He shouted, but nobody came from the building. Saran began circling the broken structure in search of rainwater that might assuage their thirst.

"Soldiers aren't welcome," a deep voiced sounded from within the house. Saran squinted as he tried to see into the dark doorway, making out the figure of a well-built man. How did he know he was a soldier? Was it his scars?

"We just want some clothes and something to drink," Saran said and covered himself with his cupped hands. His body became stiff when the man came out from the shadows holding a mallet.

"I said soldiers aren't welcome," the man grunted again. "But the whores can stay." When Saran noticed the large man was leering at the women, he knew there was trouble. Unconsciously he sized up the man, and knew he could defend the women, even though he was unarmed. The women quickly moved behind him.

A flash of light, reflected from a moving metal object, caught his eye from inside the house and he stepped back in the realization that there were others.

"Run," he suddenly said to the women, grabbing his lover's wrist and jerking her after him as he ran.

Saran heard the men stumbling through the door of the house and sensed they were on his heels. He didn't look back at how many there were, as he imagined feeling a hammer smash into his back.

The other prostitute tripped over her feet and crashed into the grass with a painful cry. Saran's lover looked back, and tried to free her wrist, but Saran screamed at her, and pulled her away.

They could hear the chilling screams of the woman being ravaged behind them as they ran. He didn't even feel the thorns cut into his feet and he swore he wouldn't stop until he reached Ekron.

Saul could see Jonathan feel the sun's fury as he sat in his tent, sweat running into his beard.

"Achsa tells me her belly is huge. She complains about all the aches and in the same sentence writes how happy she is with the life inside her. Mother and the physician think it'll be a boy," Jonathan said with an affectionate smile and Saul could see his son thinking of her. "I wish I could see her, father. What if I never again see her like this? Thank God, I haven't heard of any trouble with the child. It is healthy, and she writes that he is almost kicking right through her. He's going to be a fighter someday." His son chuckled at the thought.

Saul felt his old self, and when he touched Jonathan's shoulder to comfort him, he felt love that only a son could inspire. He knew what he was fighting for.

Jonathan hesitated for a moment. He seemed guilty, and Saul could not help thinking again that he might be the one who would replace him. The thought made him numb inside. "The physician thinks that the baby might be growing too large for Achsa's small body," he said, and Saul saw him running his fingers through his beard, and wipe the sweat from his hand on his knee length halug.

"Achsa will be fine, Jonathan. Don't concern yourself with things that are out of your control. I need you here with me, my son. You must have a clear head to make decisions. She'll be fine," Saul said.

"I miss her, father," Jonathan admitted softly, almost to himself.

"That I understand. All of us miss our loved ones, but it is the burden of a man. We must all suffer it, my son," he said, strengthening his grip slightly.

Then Saul's eyes focused on something behind Jonathan. From the corner of his eye, he could see the prince turn in his seat to see what he was staring at, but it did not seem as if Jonathan could see it. When his son turned back to look at him, he gasped softly, and Saul understood that his expression must have been dreadful. Saul's body began to shake and it looked as if he were barely breathing.

"Father, what's wrong, are you cold?" Jonathan asked. When Jonathan tried to touch him, he spoke almost as if in a daze.

"He won't hurt you, Jonathan, I promise. He won't hurt you." Jonathan turned his head back in a sweeping glance, but still he could not see anything. Saul could see his son studying him, watching how his eyes followed the presence around the room.

"Who won't, father?" asked Jonathan, his body stiff with fear.

"Don't you see him? Don't be scared, my son, he won't harm you." Saul said. Jonathan jumped up from his seat and looked around the tent again, but could see nothing. They were alone. Jonathan stared at him again and Saul knew that his son was looking at his eyes, trying to determine where it must be. Terrified, he looked at the evil creature standing right beside his eldest son.

"There's nobody here, father. Look at me," Jonathan cried, shaking him violently. Saul looked at his son for a moment, and remembered the guards' reaction when he had seen the demon again. They had laughed at him and thought he was mad. Jonathan would also think it. No, he couldn't tell him, he thought. The thing still glared at him, the void in its eyes seeming endless.

Then Saul woke, moaning from the dream. He was bathed in sweat, and the room was quiet. He sat up and looked at his manservant sitting quietly in the corner. His son wasn't there. They were alone.

It all seemed so real, Saul thought clutching his head. Jonathan, Achsa, and the baby—everything. Suddenly he longed for Jonathan, and he wanted to tell him everything— his rejection of being king, his nightmares, his constant fearful thoughts about who would dethrone him. They all knew of his acute depression, but little else. He had no one who would support him, no one to help him. He was so tired.

Minutes later Jonathan entered the tent, as if he had heard his father calling.

In the early hours of the afternoon, a weary messenger walked into the Israelite camp. Covered in a light coating of dust, he carried only his sheathed kidon and an empty water skin, his mouth parched from the heat.

Abner was reciting his daily report to Jonathan, who was relaxing on a padded chair. He hated standing before the young prince explaining everything he had done the previous day. His words came quickly as he stood straight, reminding himself not to let his irritation show. He would usually meet with Saul, but the king had suffered another dream the night before, and they all could see the toll it was taking on him. The king looked as white as the morning mists and could barely gather the will to speak. He had retreated into himself, and would stare at nothing for hours.

Jonathan looked at the general vaguely, only hearing every other word as he thought about his father and what was happening to him. Jonathan had gotten used to his father's sudden change of moods and knew it best to leave him alone when it happened. He had almost grown accustomed to the random fits of rage and depression. He saw his father's skin grow pale in his mind's eye, and sighed at the disquieting image.

"Abner, did you see my father this morning?" Jonathan asked suddenly, interrupting him.

"No. You told me to deliver my report to you and give your father time to rest," Abner answered through his teeth. Jonathan didn't seem to notice.

"Yes, I remember," Jonathan said distantly, combing his beard with his fingers. "This is the second time I've seen him like this."

"Couldn't he sleep again last night?" Abner asked.

"He was so pale. And he was shaking with the coldness of winter in him. He looked as if ... death were about him," Jonathan said meeting the general's eyes. "I am worried about him, uncle."

Abner's eyes softened as he drew in a slow breath. "Your father has a lot of years still in him. Strong blood flows through our veins, Jonathan." He placed his hand on the prince's shoulder and tightened his grip affectionately. "You and I and your father, we're fighters, boy."

"You don't understand, Abner. When we last spoke, he asked after Ish-bosheth. He told me how guilty he felt because he couldn't stand to have such a weak son," Jonathan said, raising his eyebrows at the general. Abner looked surprised.

The tent flaps opened suddenly and the messenger entered. "We'll speak of this later," Jonathan grunted as he shifted his attention to the young soldier.

"I bring a message from the officer David."

"You may speak," Jonathan said anxiously, sitting up straight.

The thin man rose and swallowed with a dry mouth, "My prince, the first garrison has been destroyed."

Jonathan laughed as he jumped out of his seat, clapping his hands together in excitement.

A smile tugged at the corners of Abner's mouth.

"There were no fatalities and only nineteen injured," he continued. "Officer David burned the garrison, and ..." The man's face tightened as he paused. "... the officer confirms that there is indeed a traitor among us, my prince." Jonathan tensed at the news. It stabbed at his heart that his own blood could betray him. The feeling quickly turned into rage and he took in a forceful breath.

The messenger became flustered under Jonathan's glare.

"Do you know who it is?" Jonathan asked.

"No. Officer David questioned the Philistine officer, but he knew nothing," he said, looking at the ground.

"Is there anything else?"

"Only that Gibbôr is marching for the next garrison."

Jonathan forced a smile. "I thank you for your message. Rest for a while, have some food and drink. I will call on you soon enough."

They watched as he quickly walked out of the tent, both men quiet with their thoughts.

"Then it has to be him. I knew it," Abner said coldly.

Achish gripped the ivory armrests of his regally carved cedar wood throne as the naked officer limped towards him. The obese king knew what had happened, and how the officer he had entrusted with one of his garrisons had failed him. Although the officer was the first, he somehow knew that there would be others. Achish looked coldly at the man.

The muscular soldier of rank could not meet his king's eyes. The sores on his dirty feet were bleeding as he shuffled closer. With a heavy sigh, he knelt before Achish, shaking from exhaustion as he rested his forehead on the titian carpet.

"Forgive me, my king," he said.

"You disappoint me, Saran," Achish sneered and with a pudgy hand wiped away the spittle forming in the corner of his mouth. "How did this happen?"

"They came out of nowhere," Saran said, gripping the long threads of the carpet. "I had eleven sentries on patrol and four gatemen, sire. But the Israelites came like spirits out of the darkness and without a sound slaughtered everybody as we slept.

"Everyone except you," Achish said with a deceptive smile. Suddenly his eyes caught the movement at the wide limestone doorway. His eyes narrowed to small slits as for a moment he wondered at the woman looking in. As she met the king's eyes, she threw herself back behind the wall, hoping that the king had not seen her.

"Who is this sultry one?" he whispered as he ordered the guards to her with a snap of his fingers. Saran's shoulders drooped in despair.

The prostitute tried to hide her fear as she gracefully walked towards him. She had wrapped the white linen blanket tightly around her body. Her shapely form showed through the thin fabric. Achish's mouth twisted as he saw her feet were torn and festering.

"I bring you a message from the Israelite officer," Saran continued in a bitter voice. He knew what would happen to this woman he had come to love at the garrison. Achish did not seem bothered by the officer's tone, the voluptuous figure capturing his attention. She had heated his blood the moment she entered the room, and he was already seeing them together in his mind.

"They said that they will attack other garrisons, and that you should try and stop them," he said and smiled weakly into the carpet. He could not help but feel resentment toward his king. In truth, he despised his every breath, and sneered silently at every command.

The words pulled Achish out of his lustful musing and his expression darkened. "Who is this Israelite dog who dares challenge me?"

"David ben Jesse, the Bethlehemite."

Achish cursed loudly, slamming his fists against the ivory armrests. "Did he say anything else?"

"No, my king," Saran answered bravely, knowing that he would soon know his punishment.

"Give him twenty lashes," Achish ordered the guards, reveling in the woman's expression.

"Thank you, my great king," Saran whispered, grateful for the light punishment, as he began kissing the king's feet.

"And then hang him in the city center," Achish continued coldly, the ends of his fat lips curving up.

Saran jerked his head up. He blinked with disbelief, staring wildly at the king. The prostitute screamed and shrank back quivering as she began to sob. The officer's body convulsed as he clung to Achish's feet, groaning in fear.

Savagely, Saran sank his teeth into the fleshy feet.

Achish growled with pain, and went cold as he saw the man biting inexorably at his flesh. He kicked violently, but the naked man held his feet firmly. Saran took another desperate bite, blood smearing over his face and hands. The king screamed as he struck the officer violently on the back of his head, and then kicked the raging man from him.

Saran fell to the floor, dazed. As he tried to get up and run away, iron tore into his flesh. His eyes glazed and his lips trembled as he felt the coldness of the blade inside him. Achish ripped the kidon out of Saran's back, as he swayed and then collapsed. He did not even feel the other ten stabs ripping his body.

"Bloody animal," Achish snapped and spat, as he stood panting over the sprawled corpse. "Hang him on the palace gates. All shall know that failure does not go unpunished."

The Philistine woman fell at her lover's side, her eyes blank with grief. She dipped her fingers in his blood and looked unbelievingly at it as the realization sank in that her beloved Saran was dead. The sharp pain at her scalp brought her back to the throne room as Achish grabbed her by the hair.

"I can only imagine the things you can do for me," he wheezed and roughly tugged the cluster of black hair in his fist. "You will obey my every whim, until I grow tired of you."

She closed her eyes, and her body tightened at the thought of what would come.

CHAPTER SEVEN

Gibbôr marched in loose formation as the Philistine garrison blazed behind them in the dark night. The sickening smell of burning flesh tainted the air as the flames ate at the corpses.

David did not look back at what he had just done, leading his Mighty Men over the grassy lands. He despised having to attack the enemy in such a cowardly manner. As a leopard at night, they hunted their prey and devoured them.

"Shouldn't we rest the men before we go on?" Eliab asked, sensing his brother's dark mood.

"No. We march farther," he said. He did not want his brother to talk him out of his mood. It suited him, he wanted to feel angry, and he knew that if he met the brawny man's eyes he would long to share what was eating at him. His brother always knew what to say.

Eliab did not reply, but instead waited for David to speak, the silence becoming heavier with each step. He cleared his throat, staring at his youngest brother, but David ignored him.

"All right, out with it," he said.

"I'm just tired, Eliab. I'll be fine after I've slept," he muttered. The moonlight glazed his body, making David look younger than he was. Eliab remembered then how youthful his brother actually was. He narrowed his eyes as he thought of how well David was handling his rank. It couldn't be easy, being so young and having so much responsibility. David had a confidence about him that he could not match. Emotionally, he was very mature; having men in his eleph, war veterans, who were older than he was. David's Mighty Men would follow him anywhere. For a moment, Eliab wondered if he had anything to do with it. He had known several of the men personally before Gibbôr, and he knew that the men feared and respected him, perhaps even so much that they did not dare refuse David's orders. Eliab shook his head lightly at his train of thought.

David felt his brother's gaze on him still, but shook off the urge to talk. Again that itch to tell Eliab everything came to him. He frowned as he resisted.

"Fine, we'll speak again when you have slept," Eliab said with a thin smile.

David glanced at him, surprised that his brother did not press the issue.

"This is not moral, Eliab. This is not how I imagined it would be. We are covered in the blood of our enemies, but I can't be happy over our victory," he said without thinking, and then swore under his breath at his swift surrender.

Eliab chuckled. "What you say is true, little brother, but it is the best way. We haven't lost a soldier yet, have we? Do you think that they would have a problem cutting us open as we slept?"

"It is still not right."

"Would you rather sacrifice the lives of your brothers? War is *never* moral, David. And if you cannot understand this then perhaps you're not meant to be an officer. If you don't want to make the difficult decisions, then I don't think you're meant to lead," Eliab said soberly.

David's face dropped and his body stiffened.

"I think we're done, soldier," David said. Eliab looked at him for a moment and then stepped in behind his brother, taking up his place in the rectangular formation.

However, David knew Eliab was right.

Small beads of sweat flowed down Ozra's face. The heat was unbearable in the tent. He clenched his jaw as he imagined the pain the whip in Abner's hand would give him. He sat uncomfortably on a folding stool with the general pacing threateningly before him. Ozra refused to look at the old man, only gazing bleakly before him. *Did they know his secret? It was impossible.* He forced the idea from his thoughts.

"We know what you did, Ozra," Abner said suddenly, turning a vindictive eye on the strategist. Ozra's body tightened at the general's words. Fear gripped him as he remembered the iron payment in his tent. If they found it, it would mean his death.

"You will do good to just admit it … and save us both the discomfort of this questioning." Abner's words startled the man from his thoughts as he met Abner's eyes. The cruelty Ozra saw there made his throat close up. Abner smiled.

"And what is it you *think* I did?" Ozra said, managing a steady voice. He shifted his eyes from the hard face.

"You're a traitor, Ozra," Abner said. The man did not even twitch at the accusation, and Abner was convinced that it had to be true.

Ozra went cold.

"And you're not?" he said stonily, jerking violently at the iron manacles behind his back. They had him bound like some filthy Amalekite. He was an Israelite, and deserved to be treated as such. The irons irritated his skin. Abner curled his lips in anger, but ignored the strategist's comment and continued more aggressively. "You'd do better to just confess."

His breath smelled of garlic and wine, and the strategist closed his eyes as the heavy smell hit him.

"Had some garlic for lunch? And undoubtedly washed it down with a little too much of Jonathan's fine wine," Ozra said, leaning back from the odor.

Abner struck him with a leather strap across his face. The knotted ends of the tiny whip licked his jaw and blood dripped from the many cuts. Ozra swore, clenching his jaw. He struggled to free his hands from the bruising shackles behind his back, his face burning.

"It is *Prince* Jonathan to you, worm," Abner said softly. The little man spat disgustingly at his feet. A bony fist punched Ozra in the face and he toppled from the small chair. He fell back in such a way that his wrist bone snapped and he screamed. Ozra rolled over and lay face down on the ground in mute agony, his sight blurring. His eye throbbed and blood streaked the side of his face. Abner lifted the thin man as if he were woven from flax, and then slapped him before sitting him down again. His skin was damp with sweat.

"You cannot do this. If Saul should hear that you are torturing me ..." Ozra choked, not looking at Abner. He knew the shrewd general would easily see the fear in his face.

Abner took Ozra's robe in a firm grip and hit him again with the flat of his palm. "It's *King* Saul. For a smart man, you learn very slowly."

"*King* Saul will have your head," Ozra snarled.

Abner chuckled. "I have done nothing wrong. You spoke of both the king and prince of Israel without respect, and I had to correct you. Then you disgraced me with your bodily discharges, and again I had to show you your place," he said and loomed even closer than before. "I told you you'd do well to confess."

Ozra's breathing was ragged. Blood still trickled from his eye, and his broken arm had swollen until it filled the iron band around his wrist with a dark blue engorgement.

"We have proof of your dealings with that dog Achish," Abner said and gripped Ozra's hand and twisted it slowly. "Just tell me what I want to hear, and I'll leave you to hate me in solitude."

Ozra screamed with pain, contorting his face in anger. "I have nothing to say!" he roared through gritted teeth.

Jonathan entered the tent with a gush of cool air.

"Enough, Abner," Jonathan ordered. "I could hear his screams from my tent. How dare you torture him; you *know* our laws." Ozra managed a crooked smile, breathing weakly.

"Free his wrists, now."

Abner sighed as if disturbed by a small child. With the clink of a heavy key, he unbound the man's hands and then stepped away.

"I am sorry for this, Ozra," Jonathan said softly. The strategist let his head drop.

"You hurt me deeply, Ozra, when you betrayed Israel. We have a letter from Officer David stating that you sold information to the Philistines. And we know about the iron." Ozra's body tensed slightly. *They really knew, and weren't guessing in the dark, as he had believed.* He sighed and he knew it was all over.

"There is nothing I can do for you, Ozra, you know this. Our laws are binding. You will be hanged." Jonathan said the words as compassionately as he could. "I thought you would like to confess and die with honor."

A tense silence ruled and then Ozra spoke in a whisper. "May I be alone for awhile to think, Prince Jonathan? Please?" Without a word, the prince left with Abner.

"That was risky, my prince. How did you know Achish paid him in iron?" Abner asked softly when they were outside.

"I found it in his tent. When he heard the soldiers come for him, he did a poor job of hiding it," Jonathan grumbled.

"Idiot," Abner snorted.

Jonathan looked at him angrily. "I told you not to hurt him, Abner. If you ever disobey my orders again, you will be where he is. Do you understand me?" he said, pointing his finger. The general's smile disappeared. *How dare he speak to me like that,* he thought. *He is the crown prince and I'm a general of Israel. I've been with Saul since before his birth.*

"We are in this together, Jonathan. I am not one of your low-ranking soldiers. I am the general of your father's armies. I did what I thought was best at the time," he suddenly said in one breath. "You're attacking the wrong man. We're family, Jonathan. We're bound by blood; remember that." He walked off mumbling to himself.

Jonathan stood in silence, breathing heavily. He could not worry about Abner with everything that was happening with his father. His uncle simply had to understand. Jonathan needed his support during such times.

"Guard the captive and when he is ready to talk, call me immediately," he ordered the four guards, and walked to his tent deep in thought.

Ozra winced as the guard tightened the rope around his neck, the coarse fiber scratching his skin. His chest felt suddenly small, as if there were no space for his lungs to take in air. Oddly, he found his mind empty of any thoughts. This was not how he imagined it. Only hours ago he could not control himself, thinking of everything he had done wrong and wondering if his life could have turned out differently.

"Why did I have to take that cursed iron," he said softly shaking his head. "Why was I so greedy?"

His tongue stuck to the roof of his mouth and he closed his eyes, wishing he could have the taste of a fine wine on his palate. A light breeze turned the sweat on his skin icy as the guard covered his face with a rough cloth that smelled of dust.

He felt the numbed sting of his swollen wrist. *The effects of the tonic are wearing off,* he thought lightly, *not that it mattered anyway. It will all be over soon.* Ozra swallowed nervously.

"You have been charged with crimes against Israel," Abner announced, his voice heavy with disgust. "You have betrayed your king and prince, and you will pay the highest price. Death."

The words sounded in his head, and then his body went numb. The horse he was sitting on shook it's head to chase away flies, almost as if it were sensing his fear.

"Remember, great general. Do not forget," Ozra said loudly, so that all could hear. He wondered what Abner's expression was. He wished he could take off the cloth and just look Abner in the eyes. At least he had angered the general one last time.

"May God have mercy on your soul." A soldier struck the horse on the rear and it whinnied and rushed forward. Ozra slanted backwards, clamping his legs around the animal as he frantically tried to stay on its back, his muscles burning from the effort.

Then the rope pulled him off and he choked violently, kicking the air, swinging from the singing rope.

It was over. For some minutes the body dangled lifelessly at the end of the rope, until finally, Abner ordered it cut down.

Jonathan touched his neat beard as he wondered about what the traitor had shouted, glancing at the general who only looked away nervously.

"Give him a proper burial and make sure you have the priest pray for him," Abner said, and walked back to the garrison. He would never conspire against the king again, he told himself. It was a dangerous business.

Jonathan decided that he would wait until the body was buried and the ceremonies had been completed.

Heat rose from the scorched earth in blurring waves, the humidity only broken by a light breeze sweeping across the hill country.

Achsa's screams resounded over the ancient town of Gibeah, the noise bringing more and more men and women to the high gates of the palace. The watchmen had to shout threats at the crowding Israelites from their stone towers to get them to return to their houses.

Achsa's body was bathed in perspiration as she prepared for the birth of Jonathan's son. Pain gripped her tiny frame again as another contraction built. The cramping was unbearable. Tears, mixed with sweat, flowed from her face as she clamped her eyes shut, and upon the midwife's direction, pushed. A servant pressed a cotton rag to her bottom as Achsa grunted, her skin turning paler with each painful minute.

An elderly midwife sat between Achsa's spread legs, one over each shoulder, and skilfully massaged her large stomach to aid in the delivery.

"Keep her calm and don't stop talking to her. Don't let her lose consciousness," she whispered to the nursemaid, her face hard with concern.

The helping servant quickly moved to the princess' side and sponged her head with cool water.

"It's almost over, everything is going well," Queen Ahinoam lied, letting Achsa squeeze her hand. She didn't let her concern show and smiled down at her.

The baby had not turned in the womb and the midwife now looked down at a wrinkled foot protruding. Delicately she inserted her fingers inside of Achsa, and guided the other foot free. She wiped the droplets of sweat from her brow with her forearm as she waited for another contraction, knowing that there could be several more dangers. There's too much blood, she thought.

Every muscle in Achsa's abdomen contracted again.

"Push," the nursemaid exhorted her. The queen of Israel repeated after the young woman, dragging the word out in a loud cry. Achsa writhed and began to sob softly, her breath becoming dangerously shallow. More red fluid came and the midwife clenched her jaw when she did not see the right hand. Again, her fingers searched until she made out a small fist and finally freed both arms with the aid of another push.

"Hush dear, we are almost there," Ahinoam soothed her.

"The child's too big," the midwife said under her breath, grinding her teeth. It was clear to her that the baby had Jonathan's blood flowing through his veins. The infant was abnormally large, and the princess' body could only handle so much. If she had to remove the head with her hands, she could dent the head, or kill the child, and if she cut the mother she could die from the sickness in the flesh or from blood loss. She waited anxiously as Achsa tried to force the head free from her body.

Her hands quivered as she picked up the small blade, gleaming in her bloody hands. With ease, she cut the taut opening around the infant's head and Achsa screamed.

The baby was finally born and the midwife relaxed, her legs feeling like rubber. With the same blade, she cut the umbilical cord and the nursemaid took the newborn. Moments after, with another lighter contraction came the afterbirth. The blood flowed freely and the midwife tried fervently to staunch the bleeding.

"Well done, Achsa. You did well, my girl," Ahinoam said softly in her ears, wiping away the black hair clinging to her face.

"Jonathan," Achsa whispered in a voice hoarse from screaming.

The baby boy wailed when the nurse burned the umbilical cord then quickly wiped the child clean.

"Do you hear that? He's crying for you, my dear. Finally, you're a mother," Ahinoam said laughing. Achsa did not react and she gripped her hand as firmly as she could. "Look at me. You're a mother, Achsa. Don't leave him. Don't leave us."

The nursemaid wrapped the child tightly in silk, and turned to the midwife with the baby in her arms. The young woman drew in a sudden breath as she saw the pallor of the mother's skin. Achsa rolled her head to look at her baby. She could hear his cries, and managed a weak smile.

"No, Achsa, your son needs you." Ahinoam leaned over the princess, breathing harshly. Her tears dripped into Achsa's hair as the queen wrapped her arms around her. Achsa inhaled in faint uneven gasps, and then fell quiet.

"She's gone. I tried," the midwife said, her throat thick with grief. The queen rocked the lifeless body refusing to let go, crying into Achsa's sweaty hair.

***

Loud wailing broke the still morning when a large body of men and women, clad in black robes, moved through the city. The air was heavy as the sun reached its zenith, and tears stained the bleak sand. Leading the funeral procession were the queen and her daughters followed by four servants carrying the treated body. Achsa's remains had been tightly wrapped in white cotton, with a veil-like cloth around her head. She looked peaceful, as if in a deep sleep.

"Only yesterday I whispered to the child in her womb and now,..." Ahinoam said to her two daughters, choking with tears at the thought. Michal, Saul's youngest daughter and the most attractive, wept into her sleeve. Merab, the eldest, screamed so that everyone could hear, her face twisting grotesquely from crying.

The royal burial cave was nearly a mile outside of the city and only a few could enter. Ahinoam, her daughters, and Achsa's closest relatives stepped into the shaft of the cave face, and climbed the few steps at the end leading through a small oblong entrance. It was dark inside; the shadows of the torches lining the rough walls flickered across the narrow pathway. Ahinoam touched the cold stone, and remembered the coldness of Achsa's body when she and a few servants had wrapped and treated it the night before.

They walked into the entrance hall, which opened up into seven large burial chambers, and waited until the body was brought in last. The noise of the mourners outside had faded.

Merab looked at Achsa's mother sympathetically. The woman hadn't stopped crying all the way to the crypt. She bit her lip as she fought the new tears filling her eyes. Nobody heard the priests' praying, all lost in their grief. The air in the cave was thick and musty.

The queen moved into one of the many rooms followed by four men carrying the body. Four benches lined the dark gray walls of the rock-hewn room and the carriers placed the body on the last available slab.

After what felt like hours, Ahinoam gathered the courage to drag Achsa's mother away from the corpse, and the woman keened in response. She led the woman from the cave, and after a moment, the passage was closed with a heavy stone door. As they walked away, the letters of the deceased's name were being chiseled into the rock.

───

The yellow light from the burning garrison played against David's face as he looked at the flames licking at the blackened wood. In a surge of violent rage, he hurled his kidon into the fire, tasting the burnt air. The sweat dripped from his brow and he wiped it away with the back of his hand. He knew he had to compose himself; his men were all watching him. Breathing wildly, he turned on his heel and raced into the darkness.

Abinadab started to follow, but Eliab placed a firm hand on his chest. "Give him time to think. He needs to be alone."

"It's not safe. He is unarmed and alone in the darkness on enemy lands," Abinadab said, looking at Eliab in surprise. The man had a black expression as he looked out into the shifting shadows, "Give it awhile. If I know David, he'll survive. He needs to do this on his own."

David ran with the wind blowing against him, the wild grass cutting his skin. He longed for Israel, for the days when he used to herd his father's sheep. He was so young then, dreaming of what he was doing now—the brave battles, the glory that comes with great victories. He used to imagine his name chanted by the women of the cities, throwing themselves at him as he returned from the battle. The reality was so different from what he had dreamt. His choices had real consequences, his men were of flesh and blood and when a blade cut them, they bled and died.

David's face flushed from the heat of his sprint until finally he stopped, although his mind still raced. He ignored his itching skin, gasping for air. He saw the lifeless faces of his men, lying in the dust, their blood turning the cold earth into black mud. David clamped his eyes shut and hammered his head with a fist as he tried to figure out what had gone wrong. Had it been his mistake? When all the watchmen had been killed, another soldier came upon his men hiding the bodies. They had tried to run out of sight at David's call, but the Philistine saw what was happening. Was he a sentry? There were sixty sentries; he had counted. David had tried to silence the man's wild screaming, but it took him too long and the alarm sounded. He could hear the bellowing of the horn in his mind and his skin crawled. He wanted to go back and do everything differently. Then he would have seen the sentry in time, and put a stone in his head with his sling before he could alert the garrison. Within moments, a frightful battle raged. Philistine warriors darted from their tents and began cutting them down. By estimating the number of bodies, David's forces had won with nearly half of the men still alive, but most of them bleeding.

David remembered what Eliab had told him. "We are fighting for Israel," David repeated to himself, his whisper almost a breath. He missed his family, his youthful days not plagued by responsibilities, and Bethlehem. He wished his father were there with him. David clenched his jaw when he told himself that his father *wasn't* there; he would have to do this on his own.

He fell to his knees and looked up at the stars piercing through the blackness. He didn't need this. He felt the grainy sand press onto his skin and he could smell the distinctive scent of the grasslands. David's breath had not steadied when he began to pray.

♛

Abinadab marched up and down, crusted in blood and soot. His hands were sweating as he clasped them together tensely.

"I'm going to look for him. It's been too long. What if something has happened? Will you tell father that we let him go alone, and because of that he was cut down by a Philistine blade?" he protested, clenching his fists. Eliab did not look up at him, but passively continued to whittle at a piece of wood with his dagger, "He's fine. He will come back when he is ready."

Abinadab did not reply and as he turned away from Eliab, his worry was replaced by anger. David approached as if nothing had happened, his expression unreadable.

Eliab felt the energy coming from David and when he looked up and met his eyes, something there made his heart quicken. David moved with authority, and Eliab, without thinking, rose to his feet. It seemed that he was not the only one who felt it when the entire cohort stood and saluted the officer, their bloody bodies broken and hurting from the battle. He felt an almost uncontrollable urge to kneel before his brother, but resisted.

Abinadab tensed when he saw all the battered fighters of Gibbôr go down on their knees before David, honoring him in the weak light of dawn. It made the hair on his arms stand up.

Looking at Eliab and Shammah, he bowed on one knee. Then Shammah lowered.

Eliab looked at David with reverence and then after a powerful moment, bowed deeply.

"Look at me Gibbôr—Mighty Men. I have been thinking of the many men we have lost. They shall not be forgotten. They will live on in our thoughts and we shall bring honor to them, with feasts in their names. All Israel will dance because of their bravery. She will sing of their battles. And they will become immortal." The men exploded into cheers, raising their fists into the air.

David continued, the power of his voice silencing them. "We will burn each body and take the ashes to their families along with the spoils of the garrison. We will take nothing for ourselves." He paused to give weight to his words. "Think of them now as we return home."

A smile stole across David's face as he looked around at his men, their hair silvered with cooled cinders. They were the lions of Israel. The men came alive with the news and his commanders began giving orders.

David forced a gaze at Eliab, and placing his hand around Abinadab's arm as he walked by, he pulled him close and spoke quietly. "How many dead?"

"Close to ninety men. And seventy-eight bleeding and bruised," Abinadab answered, sensing the tension between his brothers. "How long will this go on?" he asked suddenly, frowning.

"How long will what go on?" David said, drawing in a deep breath through his teeth.

"You and Eliab. I don't know what he said to you, but you don't want to do this. He is the eldest, and definitely the most stubborn. I know. But he has had your back since the beginning. Don't let this tear Gibbôr apart . . . " he said, resting his hand on David's shoulder.

David's eyes softened and he looked away. "Yes, I know. I'll go speak to him."

It took everything in David to walk up to Eliab. He was sitting on a rock, still whittling an eagle out of a small piece of hardwood with his dagger. The wings and head had already begun taking shape. For the first time, David noticed the silver streaking his brother's beard from his sideburns.

Eliab did not need to look up to know that it was David standing next to him. "Stopped licking your wounds, have you?"

David closed his eyes and forced himself to speak, "What you said hurt me, Eliab. What do you want me to say? That you were right as usual?"

Eliab stopped working with the knife, and stared ahead into the dawn.

"Fine. As usual, you were right. You said aloud what I was thinking, and it hurt more because it came from you," David said and lowered his eyes to the dark soil. "I am just very grateful that you were not hurt in the fight. For as my soul lives, I wouldn't have been able to forgive myself if you had to die still angry at me."

"I was never upset with you, David. I just knew that my words wouldn't have had the same weight if I were to apologize. You were the one who decided not to speak to me, not the other way around," Eliab said, meeting David's eyes. "You had to realize what you were doing. The men need a strong and brave leader who doesn't seem to think about his orders, but silently does so constantly."

He rose and put his arm around his brother's shoulders. David smiled at Eliab, clapping him on the back.

"Now what was that you said about going home?"

CHAPTER EIGHT

Jonathan fell to his knees with raging emotions. His hands trembled as he took earth in his tight fists, fighting against the tears. Slowly he heaved the sand over his head, wailing. His body broke into violent spasms as he sobbed, the hot sand burning his skin.

"You have a healthy baby boy, my prince," the messenger said, his voice shaking. Jonathan did not hear as he wept in sorrow. With determined effort, he took the beautifully embroidered silk robe and tore it, the memories of Achsa filling his mind. He would never see her again, and the thought broke him. He plunged his face into the sand and shoveled it over his head, moaning softly.

The messenger, wrought with compassion, turned to leave the prince to his grief.

"Did she have much pain?" Jonathan asked. He looked up and met the messenger's eyes. The herald hesitated. He knew the truth would devastate Jonathan, and he would not dare lie to the crown.

"I do not know, Prince Jonathan," he finally said, looking away. Jonathan keened.

"Your son has his mother's hair," he said with a thin smile.

"My *son?*" Jonathan asked, and held his breath. The messenger nodded. A weak smile managed to lighten the prince's doleful expression. He lowered his head, and swallowed away the taste of tears and dust in his mouth. "You may leave. I want to be alone." As the man quickly left, he heard Jonathan cry out her name. "Achsa!"

The moon lightened the garrison to a pale shade of blue. Jonathan lay sprawled on the floor wearing a customary head covering of rough cotton. The room spun, and he cursed the liters of wine he had drunk during the night. It was worse when he closed his eyes. All he could think of was Achsa. Her laugh echoed in his mind and his lips shook with raw emotion. When he closed his eyes, he thought he could smell her. Rosemary. She adored the flower. She bathed in it, oiled her skin with it, their room at the palace even led out to a large garden blossoming blue. He thought he was going mad as the smell grew stronger and he opened his eyes when he realized he wasn't dreaming. He sat up, holding his head in an attempt to focus.

Then he saw it. *Is this someone's sick idea of torture?* he thought, and lurched to his feet. He hadn't noticed the ceramic container with the blue clusters standing at the tent entrance. He swayed closer and screamed as he smashed the pot on the floor. Clay shards scattered and the water seeped into the canvas. He snatched the stems, nearly falling over, and broke them in a wild fit, clenching his jaw, groaning with horror.

Slowly Jonathan dropped to his knees, and tears washed over his shining cheeks. He curled himself up on the floor, taking in the smell of the broken leaves as he wept.

The sight of her mother with the infant was something Michal had to get used to. The baby moved restlessly in Ahinoam's arms and Michal laughed into her hand when the child suddenly spewed thick white milk in an arc on her mother's chest. Ahinoam grunted and shot an angry glance at her daughter, as Michal quickly handed a cloth to her mother without being asked. Ahinoam sighed as she dried herself, and Michal felt her stomach turn.

She took the boy from her mother with a sort of fear. As she held him, she began crooning instinctively. She felt strange when she held him, and she could not understand nor control her emotions.

"He's so soft," she said and looked into his clear blue eyes.

She had caught herself several times in the past week, dreaming idly about being pregnant and having a son, and experiencing the father's love and attention. But every time she could not help but feel fear at the thought that a baby couldn't grow inside of her, that she would never be with child.

She remembered the first night when he had cried her awake, and she sat helping her mother through the night.

Privately she desired a baby of her own; it was all she could think about. She stopped her soft singing and touched his rosy cheek gently with her thumb.

"Mother, do you think Jonathan has heard the news by now?" Michal asked, frowning slightly as she thought about how her brother must feel, and how he had reacted to the news. She wondered if he had cried.

"I'm sure he has, love. I wish I were there to hold my son, to comfort him. He must be devastated," Ahinoam said almost to herself, the pain only a mother could feel showing in her eyes.

"He'll be home soon, mama. Then we can hold him and kiss him and support him for as long as he wants to mourn,"

Michal said and when the infant whimpered she rocked him
delicately, smiling down at him.

"He doesn't even have a name. Didn't Achsa mention any
names that she liked or thought of naming her child?" Michal
asked, still beaming at the baby.

"No, my dear. But Jonathan will name him when he
comes," she said. "You'll be a great mother someday, my
girl. Will you take care of him while I bathe?" she whispered,
kissing her daughter on the cheek. Michal smelled the sour
milk on her and nodded, singing to the child in a sweet voice.

At dawn, the first signs of winter could be felt on the
Judean ridge. The hills hid behind the mists and were pale with
shimmering dew. The air cut through David's woolen halug
and leather armor, and his breath turned white in the cold air
as he marched with Gibbôr at his back. They were all tired
and dirty and welcomed the heat of the morning sun to warm
the chill in their bones. They had broken camp in the hours
before sunrise and pressed on, knowing their encampment at
the vale of the Terebinth was within a day's march. They had
been sleeping on the ground for nearly four months, and the
thought of hot food in their bellies and soft beds made them
walk the plains with little effort.

The heat of the afternoon woke Jonathan to the pain of his
sorrow. He felt listless, and did not have the courage to face
another day. Every waking moment he thought of his wife and
the child. He did not know how he would react when he saw
the infant, the son that had taken his wife from him. Could he
hate an innocent child? Would he smile at him with his grief
still burning in him? He wished he had been there, to hold her
hand, and whisper in her ear how much he loved her. He pined
for her. All of this came to him again as he opened his eyes, and
he moaned with anguish.

David drank in the sight of the encampment at the Elah Valley. It had increased since he had last seen it. Massive ten-foot walls now surrounded the garrison with wooden spikes protruding from the earthworks and heavy gates protected the entrance. The guards on the walls spotted the cohort and immediately shouted orders inside the camp. David paused some distance from the garrison and sent a man to the gates. The soldier jogged lazily and, as he approached, slowed to a stiff walk.

"Open the gates. Officer David ben Jesse has returned," he shouted up at the men, feeling suddenly cold again as he stood in the heavy shadow of the garrison.

"Tell me your watch-sentence," the guard said. He hesitated for a moment and then ordered the message brought to the prince.

Jonathan, dressed in a black, ankle length tunic, stared into his cup of wine, his hair curling wildly over his shoulders. How long had it been—weeks, months? He had lost all sense of time since Achsa died.

The sharp daylight that filtered through the tent flaps when the soldier stepped inside, jerked him out of his thoughts, and forced him to squint at the brightness. Jonathan shaded his eyes with his hand as the man lowered himself at his feet.

"There is a soldier at the gate, sire," he said and then rose to his feet. "He says to tell my lord, 'The lions roar at the victory of the sun.' Should we open the gates?"

"David," Jonathan whispered, and a smile broke his somber expression. For the first time in weeks, he felt excitement again. He so desperately wanted David to know everything that had happened since he had left. The soldier blinked as he saw that the tiredness had vanished from Jonathan's face.

"Yes, open the gates. And tell Abner that David has returned," he said as he stood, fixing his tunic.

The gates swung open.

David was welcomed with a cheer from the entire camp as he marched underneath the gates, with his cohort following him in a square formation. He would search out Jonathan first, before he indulged in any other pleasure. He had so much to tell him.

David turned and faced his men. He cleared his throat and a wide smile crept across his face. "Why are you all still standing here? Go. I'll see you around the practice ring at dawn."

The men laughed and as one broke formation, scattering in every direction as they disappeared into the camp.

As he turned to walk to Jonathan's tent, he saw him, and was troubled by the sight. His skin was pale under the sun, and he wondered at the black tunic and cloth wrapped around his head. Was he in mourning? Realizing that he was staring in concern, he forced a smile.

Jonathan embraced him and grinned. "You did well, David. It does me good to see you." David searched his friend's eyes and immediately knew the pain that he tried to hide from the soldiers. Even though Jonathan was allowed forty days of mourning, he did not want to let them see him so weak.

"It's good to be back. You look good," David replied wryly.

Jonathan snorted. "I do, don't I?" He sensed something different in David. The fighting had changed him. His adolescent manner was finally gone. After many months, he was seeing a leader, the one he had known David would become. Confidence emanated from the young officer, his eyes gleamed with intelligence, and his body was powerful with energy.

"Will you tell me about it over a cup of wine?" David asked. Jonathan nodded, and together they walked to his tent. The camp was empty now that the Philistine threat had been crushed, and all the men had returned to their families and farms. Only the three thousand permanent army forces were busy around him, just as he had expected. He had missed it so.

David closed his eyes as the red wine wet his lips. He savored the taste and sniffed its aroma. After taking another sip, he finally opened his eyes, and found that Jonathan had taken on a glazed look.

"Well, are you going to tell what happened?" David said.

Jonathan's lips tightened. "She's dead, David. My wife died giving me a son," he said brokenly.

David gasped in disbelief, shaking his head unconsciously.

"Achsa," he whispered, clenching his jaw. He rose and took the prince in his arms, bunching the black silk in his tight fists.

"I am sorry, my friend. She was a wonderful woman. We will all miss her." David said gently, feeling the loss himself. He was very fond of the woman; she had always been kind and motherly to him when he was away from home. David closed his eyes, as he forced back tears. Jonathan shook in his embrace and cried into his shoulder. He would only cry with David because he had to be a prince and son in front of everyone else, he knew. David clasped the grieving man to him, but said nothing.

"Is the child healthy?" David asked carefully after a long silence. They sat down again and David pretended not to see Jonathan awkwardly wipe away his tears. Jonathan nodded briefly, not wanting to think of the child.

The pain David saw in the prince's eyes was unbearable, and he knew this wound would never heal. In time, he would be able to manage it, but would always carry it with him. He loved the man like a brother, and the prince's agony was his pain as well. He looked away, struggling with his emotions. "Have you been home—to the grave?"

"No. I can't bear it," Jonathan said, his voice breaking. "I can still hear her singing, and smell the rosemary on her skin when we kissed."

David took Jonathan's hands into his own and spoke warmly. "If you like, I will go with you to the grave."

"It is something I must do," Jonathan admitted reluctantly. "You are a good friend, David."

David could not speak. He did not yet fully understand what the man was going through, though he could imagine. He had never lost someone and silently he thanked God.

They shared a silent moment.

"My father will want to see you. He hasn't been well," Jonathan said, feeling the coolness of the limestone against his skin as he sat back in his seat. "He doesn't even speak to me about it anymore."

David took another sip from the wine, the taste lingering after he swallowed. "Has he become more depressed?"

"Not entirely. His eyes have become frantic, wild almost, and he doesn't calm down for hours afterward. He jumps at the slightest noise. I fear for his health."

"Your message had me thinking of him often," David said, as if in thought. "Do you want me to play for him?"

"I think so. Maybe it'll help him unwind," Jonathan said. "But I think we should all return home for a good rest. He hasn't been home for two winters now. My mother and brothers miss him. And I fear he is beginning to pay the price for it. The rains cannot come soon enough."

With a weak smile, Jonathan continued. "My friend, I need you to take my mind off my misery. Tell me of your Philistine successes. Perhaps we should discuss your current rank. After such victories, a warrior and his commanding officers must be promoted. I will convince my father. How does a regiment of sixteen eleph sound, officer?"

Saul's tent smelled stale. David was shocked to see Saul's skin so pallid against the bright colors of his regal garments and wondered when last he had been outside. The king's silver hair was tousled under his crown, and his skin was damp with sweat. David remembered when he had first played for the king and how the man had changed, both in demeanor and in appearance. Saul was growing old.

David longed to find Saul gazing back at him with those powerful eyes that he admired. He had heard that Saul could make the bravest warrior cower with only a stare. He smiled then, as he recalled finding himself tensing nervously under those blue eyes when he had first played at the royal court. Despite his efforts to feign confidence, he had been convinced that the monarch had seen right through him.

Saul's face broke into a web of wrinkles as he smiled when he saw the officer standing there. "David, you're back. I've been wondering when you would return to me. Are all of your limbs still attached?"

"Yes, my king, I'm well," David said with a chuckle. "We were successful in burning all three garrisons."

"I knew you would. You're very resourceful," Saul said distantly, wiping his face on the sleeve of his vesture. Jonathan had told David that by the time he had first been summoned to the court, his father had already become a different man, and with a soft sigh, David wished he had known the real Saul ben Kish.

An uncomfortable silence ruled between the two, until David said, "May I play for you sire?" Saul barely nodded, pressing the bridge of his nose with his thumb and index finger.

David picked up his kinnor, resting the wooden frame on his knee. The sweet sound reverberated from the tight strings as he easily worked the instrument. Saul closed his eyes and the corners of his mouth turned up. As David began singing, Saul emitted quiet sighs, and color came to his face. He felt the energy course through his veins, and with each note, his will strengthened.

"I had almost forgotten how wonderful it sounds, David," he said with his eyes still closed. He began to hum and David played for Saul for almost an hour.

Saul stopped him suddenly. "Walk with me. I want to feel the night air on my skin." The authority in his voice had returned, and his thoughts had become his own again. David's music had calmed him, and every depressing thought had left his mind.

"I've missed our passionate debates, David. And I have been thinking a great deal lately. I long for you to challenge my thoughts. Sometimes I feel like my mind is wasting away out here."

Saul rose from the bed and ran his fingers through his hair. He suddenly realized that he had not eaten in nearly four days. The king began wondering what he would have.

"Are you hungry, David? I'm ravenous," he said smacking his lips.

"I'm always hungry, my king," David said with a broad smile and stood up from the bed. "Have I ever said no to food, especially after being in the wilderness for so long? I am longing for a hot meal and good company with it." Saul clapped him on the back, and David could feel the heat flowing from his body and cringed at the king's touch almost burning his skin.

Saul led his officer outside, and David found himself longing for the discussions they used to have on war tactics, laws, and much more during the course of the evening. He wondered if he should mention Jonathan's plans for his new rank. David's chest swelled with pride when he thought of it again—a captain of a thousand warriors. His old guilt threatened him again, but he would not allow it to plague him. With the king at his side, he told himself that he would never think of it again, and he buried it deep inside himself.

Michal curled her hair around her fingers as she lay on soft cushions in the wide lattice-window of her bedchamber. As she stared out into the small city, the sun washed her skin, making her look golden brown. A red and white silk dress draped her slender body, with a gleaming iron waistband encrusted with jewels tightening the fabric into the folds of her bodice. She dreamed idly about the charismatic man that would soon come home with her father. Biting her lip, she smiled as she remembered his broad face and green-flecked eyes. Her heart fluttered suddenly at the thought of seeing him for the first time in over a year.

Guiltily, Michal thought of her father and brother. She was pleased that they were coming, but she did not really know her father anymore. Most of her life, she had grown up without him, having to share him with all of Israel.

She had become a woman since she had last seen him and would soon be of marriageable age. She questioned how her father could choose a suitable husband for her if he did not know the person she had become. She had only heard rumors of his foul moods and raging fits, and her eyes glistened with tears, as she understood that her father was a stranger to her.

Michal blinked away her tears, frowning as she recalled her mother crying at night every time she read Jonathan's letters. She wished Jonathan would not upset her so with the news of their father.

She bit her lips as she thought of Achsa and the baby. The funeral still plagued their minds. Why did her brother not come home for the birth of his son and to mourn with his family, as a good husband should? Why had he not returned home to hold his son, or visit Achsa's grave? She knew that it had to be difficult for him to deal with her death, but he simply could not cower from it. Now her mother had to care for the child.

"A captain? Son, how can you expect me to do that?" Saul said, leaning forward from his throne. The faces of the council betrayed their interest. Their attentions were centered on the prince.

"Why not, father? David has proven himself to you, to this council—to Israel. In the past, you took any strong and valiant man and made him part of our military," Jonathan said, watching his father.

"He's young, Jonathan," Saul said, frowning.

"And he has a stronger heart and mind than any of your ben-hayil, father. Remember, *he* killed Goliath when your entire army were shaking under their tunics. Why wasn't he too young then?"

"What you speak is true, my prince. But what if he loses his wits on the battlefield?" Ehud said confidently. "A thousand men aren't easy to control; you know this. And he doesn't have the experience that comes with age."

"He definitely has the courage and determination to succeed," Abner added, and this surprised Jonathan.

"As the general says, when Israel needed us, we cowered, all of us. But David fought when we would not," Jonathan said candidly, sweeping his eyes over the bearded men standing around his father's throne. They did not appreciate what he had said, and they frowned, but did not dare express their displeasure. Abner could not help but smile as he read the men's faces.

"Father, when David was your armor-bearer, he was at every council meeting for close to two years. He thinks like a general, he is educated on battle history, and his tactics are noteworthy. He has learned everything from this very council. I have trained him in the art of war. And as we all know, he is exceptionally skilled with the sling and now after my tutoring, with the kidon as well."

The council did not say a word. Jonathan glanced at Captain Ludim and the old man nodded in approval. Jonathan continued, "Father, you took him as a shield-bearer because you knew his loyalty and valor, and only because he was too young then to be a commander. You tested him by giving him two hundred of your core of fierce warriors. Then you tested him further by ordering his cohort to be the first to foray into Philistia. No one can argue; he succeeded brilliantly."

"He did indeed. What is the name of his cohort? Gibbôr, I think." Ludim said, nodding his head delicately. "Gibbôr has slain far more than five hundred Philistines, and lost less than one hundred men, my king. That takes the leadership of a great officer."

Saul looked at the layers of black silk draping Jonathan's body and spoke as affectionately as he could. "I understand your fervor, Jonathan; I'm fond of David as well. But giving him eight hundred more men is.... Son, it's dangerous, if nothing else." He could see the pain in Jonathan's eyes and his heart ached for his eldest son.

"I don't believe it is, father. I have spoken personally to his men. They all respect him. He is loyal, intelligent, and skilled. What more do I have to say to persuade you, father? I have complete faith in him."

The priest spoke next, and everyone listened. "I will have to pray for certainty, but I feel that it carries God's blessing, my king. The Lord is with him."

"I will support him; this council will guide him. He will not fail his rank. I know it, my king. I pray you, father," Jonathan whispered in Saul's ear, and then stepped away from the throne.

"He has indeed changed notably over the months," Saul admitted. "He has become far more mature than his age indicates. I see a strong leader now and not a young inexperienced man anymore." Saul remembered the man's powerful posture. It commanded respect and attention instantly. His eyes were bright with authority. The young man had always been noble, but strangely, he was different. Saul had witnessed David with his fighters and even with the warriors of his respected ben-hayil, his charisma had suddenly become overwhelming, effortlessly inspiring loyalty and bravery.

Saul reflected for a moment, rubbing the broad bridge of his nose. He shook his head as he mulled over the issue.

"Who is for the young David?" Saul finally asked. Five of the six council members voiced their support. Jonathan looked satisfied, but his father was silent.

"Jonathan, at least allow me time to think. I am undecided. I have heard your argument and when I am ready I will announce my decision."

Eliab sat in his tent, enjoying the soft bed and the sensation of warm food in his stomach.

The young boy he had sent for marched into his tent and saluted him. Eliab smiled at the child and motioned him closer. As he sat up from his bed, he grunted at the irritating soreness that still clung to his muscles after the long incursion.

"I want you to do something for me, lad," he said. "I want you to go to Bethlehem." The boy grinned from ear to ear at this and listened attentively, playing with his fingers. He loved such important tasks that would take him into the cities.

"But first I want to know something. Do you know what the officer David ben Jesse has done?" Eliab asked, and the child nodded, his eyes sparkling.

"He killed the monster Goliath," he piped. "And burned many garrisons and killed masses of terrible Philistines."

"That's right. He's a brilliant fighter, isn't he? And he's very loyal to his king and country." Eliab said. "Now, first I want you to go to the good citizen Jesse ben Obed in Bethlehem and tell him about his son. Then I want you to go to Gibeah, to the market there and tell everybody who will listen. Say to them that our glorious Prince Jonathan is speaking of giving Officer David a thousand men to fight under him. Let them know that he and the royal family are coming home. Can I trust you with such a heavy task?" The youngster stiffened again comically, and Eliab ruffled his hair.

"If you do this well, I will give you a quarter-shekel for it." Eliab said and smiled. The boy gaped at him and then whooped, nearly tumbling with excitement.

"I will tell every man in the entire Gibeah, and woman. Yes, I will. And if they don't want to listen, I will scream it to them," he said and rushed out. He raced back in and quickly saluted Eliab and then flew out again. Eliab could hear him shouting as he ran off, and he chuckled.

He thought again about David's pending rank. It was an amazing accomplishment. Now he was convinced that the Spirit of God was with him and he lifted his eyes up and silently said a prayer of gratitude.

CHAPTER NINE

A herald jogged toward the city of Gibeah, his breath rasping from the three mile run. Sweat dripped from his arms and face, and his tongue stuck to his palate, but he had important news. Duty compelled him not to stop.

Gibeah was a small town with tall, reddish, clay-brick houses and well marked roads. He smiled as he saw that the gates were open, and the large, broad wall was a welcome sight for the messenger. The Israelites were coming and going with mules pulling drays laden with trading goods, and women were carrying water jugs. As he approached the city entrance, a guard stepped in his path and held out his spear, motioning him to stop. The militiaman said nothing, forcing the gasping man to speak.

"I am the royal herald. Look, I bear his seal," he said through his heaving breath, holding up the stone bulla. The guard eased as he saw it, and lowered his spear tip to the ground.

"The king is coming!" the herald shouted.

His iron-shod sandals clacked against the stone road as he willed himself to run to the palace. The resting city stirred to life as small crowds of Israelites began to move to the city gates.

At the center of the town stood Saul's fortress palace, a massive stone building with a heavy wooden superstructure and four large watch towers built into surrounding double walls, the outer one almost seven feet thick. The mere sight of it turned the town into a city.

"King Saul has arrived!" the herald shouted up at the palace guards, holding up his hand against the bright sun stinging his eyes. The watchmen hurried inside to alert the household. The herald caught his breath, resting his hands on his knees and then after a moment, ran back. He wanted to be there when his king rode into the city.

Whispering in excitement, the people shoved and struggled to catch sight of their king and the procession of soldiers.

Then a woman began shaking her tambourine, rhythmically tapping it with the palm of her hand. Another woman broke into song and thumped her hand drum and the people spread out along the wide street at the gates, singing and dancing to the hypnotic music.

Saul closed his eyes as he listened to the festivities. Wild cheers sounded through the lively streets as his carriage rolled underneath the massive stone archway, and he waved at his people, touching the hands of the women as they reached out for him. He took a deep breath, enjoying the smells of cassia trees tainted with limestone dust, of rosemary leaves, and piquant herbs growing in the gardens. Finally, he was home.

They hailed him for all of his glory as they capered and cavorted before the oxen pulling his carriage, encircling him in a flurry of movement.

Then a woman saw David before the gates and called out his name. Within moments, the attention shifted from Saul to David riding on a roan stallion. He had dressed for the occasion in fine silk apparel underneath his bronze armor that Jonathan had given him. His red-striped cloak wafted gently behind him, as yellow light shimmered from his swaying chain mail. The people began to extol him. David was stunned by the sudden attention. He had imagined that day many times, and he swept his gaze over his countrymen. A smile stole onto his face.

A chorus began to emerge, "Saul has slain his thousands, and David his ten thousands."

It took Saul a moment to come from his reverie and hear what his people were singing. His fists clenched in anger at the words. The music faded to complete stillness in his mind and he could only hear their treacherous singing. I've freed all of them from the Philistine suppression, he thought darkly. I've built these walls around the city that keep them safe. He looked around at his people, and his breath left him when he saw that nobody was even looking at him.

"I still fight, for *you!*" he roared at them, his voice muted by the celebrations. He jerked his head back and glared at David, who was waving to the masses gleefully.

Saul's eyes widened as he gasped in dread. The color drained from his face, and he clenched his chariot unconsciously, trembling.

"It's him," Saul said in shock, and he lost his voice.

David has been chosen to succeed me on the throne, Saul thought, and anger like he had never known seized him. His face turned purple and his muscles ached as they contracted intensely. *Samuel has chosen David over me,* Saul's mind screamed. He looked stiffly ahead of him, seeing only black in front of his eyes. He couldn't breathe. *It had to be David.*

Jonathan met Saul's eyes for a moment, and his smile vanished. His father's eyes had a glint in them like that of a madman, and it made him shiver. Would his father have another fit? It would shame him, and he feared that his father's reputation would never recover. Jonathan did not shift his gaze from Saul, mentally commanding his father to be calm.

Michal pulled at a tendril of hair anxiously as she waited on the steps of the palace for them. Her mother and sister stood at her side, but she did not notice them. *What would her father look like?* she wondered. *Could he have changed much?* She remembered how handsome he had been; she'd never seen another man like him. She had heard the women say that as her father aged he became better looking; it was one of those unexplainable things. Michal smiled inwardly for a moment, knowing from whom she had inherited her exquisite features.

It has been one year, ten months, and twenty-seven days, she said to herself. She had marked each day and now that she would see him again, she could not understand her emotions. She felt almost afraid. Michal felt her chest close up as the gates of the fortress creaked open and the first soldiers marched into the narrow courtyard. Unconsciously, she craned her neck to see her father in his striking armor, riding in his chariot.

Her father was as cold as she had dreaded he would be. There was no joy in his eyes; they were hard and empty. Her body went numb at the sight of him. She had hoped that he would have at least tried to look pleased to see them.

Saul's face showed the traces of war, and his hair was completely gray with age. She sighed in her disappointment at this, and then shot a glance at her mother. She was beaming with love, and Michal forced a smile.

Staring blankly ahead of him, Saul did not even see his wife and daughters waiting for him on the wide steps of his home. When the oxen bellowed as they were brought to a jolting halt, Saul came from his thoughts and saw his family looking at him. His daughters were dressed in clean white robes, symbolizing their virginity. How he had missed them.

Then he met his wife's eyes. She was crying, but had never looked so graceful. Ahinoam was a short woman, and had gray streaks in her black hair. Saul yearned to hold her and as he stretched out his hands to her, she ran to him. He wanted to enjoy the moment, but he couldn't.

Michal went to Jonathan then, and when she met his eyes, she finally understood. She saw his pain, and began to cry as she took him in a loving embrace. She knew he had been mourning. She could smell the pungent sweat on him and she wished that she could take some of her brother's grief on herself, just to give him a moment's peace. There was no need for words as they stood in silence, holding each other.

David looked at the woman embracing his prince, and his heart throbbed. She was breathtaking. *It couldn't be Michal*, he told himself. When he had last spoken to her, she had still been a small girl. In the two years he had been with Saul, she had become a gem, unparalleled in all of Israel. His eyes followed the curves of her body almost automatically when her brother put his arm around her shoulder. He could see the shape of her body under the white silk. Only the realization of having her see him gaping at her, and the awkwardness of it all, finally made him look away, though her image remained in his mind. He ran his hand through his hair, suppressing the sudden nervousness he felt. *How could the sight of one woman capture his mind so easily?* he wondered. Then he found himself staring at her again.

Michal's eyes fell on David, and her heart raced. He was even more attractive than she remembered. His green-flecked eyes looked deeply into hers, and when he smiled at her with his broad mouth, she shyly lowered her gaze.

The autumn sky was tinted with red as the sun set behind the small city of Gibeah. The coolness of the throne room was invigorating, and Saul could smell lavender in the air. The long travel was exhausting, and he tried to forget the words that his people had sung to David. Even though he longed to get them out of his mind, he could not. His appreciation and love for David had turned swiftly into jealousy and it clung to him like the plague.

"Did you hear what they sang?" Saul grumbled, raking his fingers through his hair. His body was one tense knot.

"How could I not? Since he killed Goliath, they see only him and forget everything you've done for them," Abner said with reserve, reading Saul before he spoke freely.

"They have ascribed to David *ten* thousands …" Saul said with an ugly sneer. "… and to me, but thousands." He traced the engravings on his throne with his finger, and then closed his eyes when he felt his anger rise again. He did not have the strength for it, and breathed deeply to keep calm.

Abner saw Saul's fists tighten, and stepped back in anticipation. He knew Saul's wrath as he had witnessed it many times before.

"And what more can he have but the kingdom?" Saul asked, and relaxed his hands. The king's words shocked Abner. "His vanity is sickening, I cannot stand it. Did you see how he loved the attention? What does he have that I don't? He is a deceitful worm, who smiles at me when he sees me, but in the dark, he conspires for my crown. How could I have been so blind? I'll have to keep my eye on him."

Saul fell silent, possessed by jealousy.

The atmosphere in the room was jovial. Saul sat at a long wooden table and looked at all the people he cared for. The table was spread with delicacies that he loved; from leban—a thick yogurt made from goat's milk—to honeyed dates flavored with aniseed, dried locusts, sweetmeats, cheese, and fig cakes, and enough olive oil for all. It was good to be home.

His daughters looked radiant, with their faces painted and their hair bound. They wore long, sleeveless ketonets with patterns embroidered onto the white silk. Merab, his oldest daughter, had a strong face and a large mouth, and although she was not very attractive, he admired her mind. She would have made a great queen, he thought. Michal was the youngest, and certainly the pearl of all his children.

Saul's eyes fell on his three sons. He had not seen Malchi-shua and Abinadab for many months and he smiled at them. He wondered if they would join the military like their brother. They had always been interested in war, listening avidly as he spoke of his battles and wars. Malchi-shua, to his knowledge, had never missed a fighting lesson or skipped a lecture on tactics. He would make a fine general, he imagined, nodding his head thoughtfully. He would speak to them about it, he decided.

Saul saw Jonathan smiling for the first time since he heard about Achsa, and he was happy to see that Jonathan was enjoying himself. He knew it did him good to be with his family again.

A pang of sorrow stabbed at Saul's heart when he saw Ish-bosheth. His son was quiet and nervous and hardly spoke. Saul saw him as a weakling; he was not like his other brothers. Ish-bosheth did not have any of the virtues of a monarch and did not have the strength of character to rule his lands. He was gangly with light, flowing hair and feminine features that made Saul dislike even the sight of him. His beard was thin on his face and he had a sallow complexion. Saul could not believe that his blood flowed through Ish-bosheth's veins, and he could smile at his son then, because he found comfort in the thought that he would never be king.

Abner clung to his wife, like dried honey to wool, constantly kissing her, and touching her. They spoke softly to each other as if they were new lovers, oblivious of the people and loud chatter around them. He glanced at Abner's son Jaasiel, who was speaking with his eldest daughter.

Saul could not resist the temptation to ogle Ahinoam playfully. His wife blushed as she wet her lips and held his gaze provocatively. When he leaned in closer to feel the touch of her skin, she whispered firmly into his ears, "Not in front of the girls, husband. You'll have to wait until later, my valiant warrior."

"They won't miss us if we slip away," Saul purred, and caressed her lower back lovingly. Ahinoam smiled up at him.

"I missed you," he said softly and kissed her delicately. Ahinoam adored his touch, but when she saw Michal looking at them, she leaned away.

"I have to go see how the servants are managing with the food, husband," she said and then rose from the cushions and left for the kitchen.

David howled with laughter with his companions and Saul was violently jerked out of his fantasizing. He sneered at him, the event hours earlier festering inside of him. He had no proof of his suspicion, but he would expose him, Saul vowed. He noticed how his family looked at David; they loved him. After glaring at the young officer for a moment, Saul saw Merab staring at him affectionately, and he could smile at her. Saul breathed in as he resolved that he would ignore David. He took a yellowish, black locust and pressed the crunchy morsel into his mouth. David would not spoil his first evening with his family.

The nursemaid crooned to the infant as she walked around the small room, rocking the baby in her arms. She beamed at the tiny bundle, and constantly checked to see if the child were too hot or if she had wrapped the swaddling clothes too tightly. Every time she did this, the boy would whimper and wrinkle his brow at the cold touch.

The woman stopped her singing when she saw Jonathan standing there as if he were made of marble. She smiled warmly at him and brought his son to him.

Jonathan did not take the child from her at first, although the nursemaid suggested it a few times. He only stared at the baby and could not show what he was thinking. Finally after what seemed to him like an hour, he spoke, his voice rough.

"He has his mother's nose." Jonathan brought his hand to the newborn's head wanting to touch the mass of clingy black hair, but stopped himself.

"Go on then, he's not fragile. My lord can touch him," the elderly nursemaid said. Gently, he caressed the tiny head, and laughed nervously. He took in the smell of the child as he felt the soft skin of his son.

"He has your fingers, my prince," the woman said, her eyes bright with elation. "Do you want to hold him now?"

Jonathan hesitated, and then the woman placed the infant in his arms without waiting for an answer. Jonathan tried to stop her, but she simply ignored him. His son was so light he feared that he might break him if he dared tighten his grip.

"Relax, and enjoy your son," the nursemaid whispered, patting him on the back. Surprised by the gesture, Jonathan wondered at the strange woman, but made nothing of it as his eyes fell on the pink skin of his baby boy. Silently, the woman left them.

Jonathan smiled faintly and could not believe that he had been afraid that he would hate the child. How could he ever blame something so innocent?

"I shall call you Mephibosheth," he said softly. Jonathan thought about what his mother had told him. She had said that this was Achsa's final gift to him, that he might remember her always. He felt his emotions well up in him, and then he wept for her again.

The child gurgled, and as he held him in his arms, he said his farewells to his late wife and promised her that he would raise their son with the same love that she would have given him.

The morning was a splendid one for Michal as she woke from a dream of David. The shimmering beams of sunlight that filtered through the large window of her room had awakened her, and she smiled as she stretched her arms pleasurably with a soft moan. *What would the day be like with him here?* she asked herself.

Michal sprang out of bed and hurried to her sister's room. She hoped Merab was awake. She just had to tell somebody about how she felt. She could not keep it to herself a moment longer.

Quietly she opened the door to her sister's room and tiptoed inside. She jumped on Merab's bed. Merab gave a short cry of surprise, and snatched off the linen band around her eyes.

"If you ever do that again I will tear out your hair, or something!" she snapped in shock, screwing her eyes up against the stinging morning light. Michal shook with laughter, and Merab smiled hesitantly. "Will my torture never end?"

"Why do you wear that silly thing on your face?" Michal asked, lifting the black piece of cloth from the bed.

"Because every queen has one, from Egypt to Mesopotamia," Merab said tiredly.

"I'd rather not say anything. Did you enjoy last night? What do you think of David? He's even more attractive than before," Michal sighed, folding her legs underneath her.

Merab frowned slightly. "It's too early in the morning for this, Michal," she snuffled, her eyes bleary from sleep.

"By the way you're going on I would think you're happier that David's here than father or Jonathan," Merab said as she rubbed the sleep from her eyes.

"No, I'm glad they're home. Do you think David likes me?" Michal asked, biting her lower lip as she played with a lock of her hair.

"Where did all of this come from, Michal? You never told me that you felt something for him."

"I never wanted to tell anybody because I thought it was a childish love and that it would pass when he left for the war with father. But it hasn't," Michal said contentedly.

"I can see that," Merab interrupted.

"Did you see his eyes? They're greener than the ocean, absolutely breathtaking," Michal continued. Her face flushed and Merab giggled at this. "You think he noticed me?"

"What? He practically gawked at you the entire night. You and Jonathan are the attractive ones in the family. He would have to be blind not to like you."

"Oh, Mer thank you! I love you. I wish I had your confidence," Michal said, and gripped her sister's hand affectionately.

"Don't be greedy. You can't have everything," Merab snorted. "At least David's hair has darkened; it's not that fiery red it used to be. He's taller too, isn't he? At last his beard has thickened in."

"Don't pretend you don't find him attractive, Mer, I know you better than anybody. You can't lie to me," Michal said.

Merab pursed her lips as she thought. "I have to admit he's got nice arms. A soldier's muscles, enough for any girl," she admitted.

"You know that our daughters will soon be old enough to wed. I have thought of a few suitable men," Ahinoam said, sitting beside her husband. She allowed him to caress her, and smiled as she thought of the pleasures from the night before. It had been too long since she had slept so peacefully, with Saul next to her.

Saul was quiet for a moment and then spoke without looking at his wife. "I have promised the soldier who slew Goliath my daughter's hand."

Ahinoam raised her eyebrows in surprise. "David? I hadn't thought of him," she said. Ahinoam noticed her husband glancing anxiously at something and then his eyes moved steadily across the room, as if he were following the current of air. He seemed restless suddenly.

"Yes. If only I had known …" Saul said and caught his words as he met his wife's eyes. His own eyes turned cold suddenly, and then glazed over. Ahinoam sat up from her seat and touched Saul's arm. When he didn't react, she stiffened. She could never forget that terrible stare, and then it would start.

The thought of seeing her husband in that state again tormented her. She remembered the first time it had happened. She had thought he would kill them all. He had torn off his clothes and run around naked, dancing and rolling on the floor like those prophesying priests, though he was more malevolent. He screamed and raged and she had to send their children out of the room. Then he had fallen silent and had been sullen and depressed for days on end. The fear she recalled made her shiver suddenly.

She hadn't seen her husband in many months and she adored having him home, but she could not bear to see him like that again.

Quickly she rose and hurried out of the room. As she cried silently, she wondered if Saul had even noticed that she had left.

David thrummed the strings of his kinnor and Saul immediately stopped his wild prophesying. He turned a baleful eye on David, and his mad expression became one of terror.

Every move the officer made irritated him. Even his attractive features appalled him now. Saul despised him. He glared at David and when he saw the concern in the younger man's eyes, his anger became uncontrollable. Saul thought about it all again, and swallowed the reality of it indignantly. *Again, he tries to trick me with his sweet music*, Saul thought, and became deceptively calm. He sat on his throne with his family around him, and listened to the music, breathing hard.

Saul gulped and his skin crawled when he suddenly remembered Samuel's words. He had chosen to forget what the prophet had said to him that night, with the Amalekite king dead at his feet. He felt his entire body go numb with the realization.

"The Lord has rejected thee from being king over Israel," the words resounded in his mind. He had never told anyone, not even his wife, keeping it inside of himself for many years, and though he battled with it, it had slowly eaten him up.

Then he heard David's music again and he clenched the spear in his hand. "So you think you would replace me?"

His knuckles were white around the wooden shaft, his face twisting in mute rage. *Everything he does puts me to shame,* Saul thought, as he stared at David. *The snake slithers into my trust, and then he even makes me ashamed for mistrusting him.* Saul bit his tongue, barely tasting the blood in his mouth.

His guile is sickening, Saul thought, a dark vein standing out on his temple.

"He's going to take my kingdom from me," Saul roared, red-faced as he jumped up from his seat and hurled the weapon at David. "I'm going to pin you to the wall."

With deadly precision, the weapon shot past David, the metal tip cutting the skin on his triceps as he dropped from the small wooden chair. David rolled onto the floor and scrambled to his feet, not feeling the blood trickling from the deep cut.

Bewildered, he turned to face the charging king. Saul screamed savagely, spittle flying from his twisting mouth. He snatched his spear from the floor, and when he saw Jonathan move to stop him, he struck him with a sweeping hand across his face. Jonathan lost his balance and fell backwards. Merab shrieked in terror as her father lunged toward David, pointing the spear at his chest.

David, unarmed, waited for the king. Everything around him seemed to happen slowly. Saul's muscles contracted for the connecting blow, already anticipating the spear pressing into soft flesh. David spun on his heel at the very last moment and the spear missed him by the width of his tunic. Saul stumbled and tried to regain his balance by stabbing his weapon into the floor, but he had put his full weight behind the attack and with a clatter, the spear slipped from underneath him and rolled away as Saul fell, knocking the wind from his lungs.

Horrified, David glanced back at Saul, gasping, blood dripping from his fingers. Without a word, he fled the room.

Frantically Saul looked around at his family. They had all seen what he had done; their horrified expressions making the air feel thick around him. Michal and Merab cried and ran from the room, covering their faces. When Saul met his wife's eyes, he could not bear what he saw there. She stood rigid, the color drained from her face.

What had he done? Would his family hate him for it? he thought frantically.

Slowly, Jonathan moved to his father, wiping the blood from his mouth, and when he put his arm around him, Saul broke down. He fell to the floor, the coldness spreading through his legs. He moaned weakly as he wept, his throat sore from his harsh screaming.

Jonathan sat beside his father who was sprawled on the cold floor of the palace and sighed with sudden grief at the sight of him. Saul lifted his head and glared at him, making Jonathan feel a knot in his throat; his blue eyes looked almost black under the dim lamplight.

"Did I hurt him?" Saul asked, almost in a whisper. Jonathan could not sense any emotion in his voice and it made him even more careful. Jonathan shook his head.

Suddenly his father grabbed his tunic, and jerked at it powerfully. "I'm not mad, Jonathan. You have to believe me," Saul whimpered.

"I can't remember striking him. I blacked out. It wasn't me. What's happening to me, son?" Saul asked frantically. Saul knew that he could never do whatever had just been done to the son of Jesse. He would lose everything if he did—his family, his crown, his mind. What he had seen in the faces of his family was worse than a knife to the heart.

He clutched at Jonathan's tunic again in a tight fist. "I have been keeping a secret, Jonathan. A secret so powerful that it has destroyed me." Jonathan saw his father was shaking, and he feared what he might tell him. His eyes had become soft, almost vulnerable.

"You mustn't tell anyone. Nobody must know. Promise me, Jonathan."

"You have my word," Jonathan said, glancing at his mother. She didn't move.

"Samuel told me that the Lord has torn the kingdom from me," Saul confessed, his voice shaking from the raw emotion of the memory.

Clouds formed against the steel blue sky as David rode on his mount away from the city. He was the great man, Saul's officer, and yet he had to flee from the royal palace like a criminal. His body was tense from the shock of the night before, and he smelled of the horse's sweat. He hadn't slept and though he was tired, his mind would not rest.

He had run from the palace, uncertain if he should go back. As he walked the streets, the people began praising him again, forming crowds around him, and he feared that Saul would come after him. As quickly as possible, he made his way out of the city. He had sat most of the night outside the walls, thinking about what had happened. He thought about returning home, to his father's farm, but he couldn't imagine himself living a farmer's life. He belonged in the military with his brothers. Jonathan had pleaded with him to stay and assured him that his father regretted the attack. It was a sensitive matter and he wanted to spare Jonathan his shame.

David put his head in his hands, wondering why suddenly the king despised him so. What had he done? He was loyal, he would never strike God's anointed, and yet the old king had tried to take his life. He kept seeing Saul's wild eyes, the spit stringing over his dark beard as he screamed. The image haunted him and he felt numb. David swore loudly at his weakness. *I haven't done anything wrong,* he kept telling himself, lowering his eyes to the yellow grasses moving gently in the breeze.

He was irritated at his train of thought. "Stop lying to yourself!" he grunted, shaking his head slowly. Samuel had anointed him king over Israel. He would have Saul's crown whether he wanted it or not. It was God's will.

He had to admit that he had dreamt of being king ever since that day with the prophet, but he did not know it would be like this. He had only been seventeen.

I didn't request to come to the palace to play before the king. I was summoned, David said to himself.

And how could I have possibly refused? he asked himself, pushing his fingers through his hair. *It was Saul who insisted that I stay with them, not the other way around.*

"How could I have denied a king anything, and live to tell about it?" he said looking at the clouds, lifting his palms as if speaking to God. With time, Saul and the royal family had come to love him and he did care for the king and his wife. As long as he had known the king, Saul had always been a slave to paranoia and had never been as other men. His bearing and pattern of thought had always seemed strange to David.

But he vowed he would never harm Saul.

David's fingers touched the pommel of the iron sword Jonathan had given him. It gleamed against his brown saddle and he wondered if he deserved to carry it with him. It was a testament of his loyalty to Jonathan. *How would the prince react if he knew the truth?* he wondered, feeling depressed. He could not bear to lose his friendship, though he knew it was inevitable. One day they would know his secret. If only Saul had obeyed God's orders.

David felt like riding away to never return. But he realized that by doing that it would make him appear guilty of the alleged crime.

But to some degree, I am culpable, he admitted ruefully to himself. He groaned miserably as he wished he knew what to do.

David lifted his head to the heavens and whispered a prayer to Jehovah, the only God of Israel.

"Let Your will be done."

CHAPTER TEN

Jonathan froze as he saw the bleak stone cave face. His chest closed up and when he felt his hands sweat, he realized he was clenching his fists. His skin crawled as waves of sensation spread across his body.

"Wife," he whispered. He moved his fingers across the letters cut into the rock, scraping his skin as he felt it repeatedly. He closed his eyes and looked away, but still he could not take his fingers from her name. The past month hadn't made things easier. It had been rough for all of them, with his father's dark moods, and the attack on David.

He paused for a moment, and then spoke to her as if she were there beside him. "This is my last day of mourning, Achsa. I have to come say goodbye. Why did you have to leave me? I need you, wife." Silently he stood there, barely moving. "We were great together, weren't we, wife?" he said, smiling emotionally. "Mephibosheth—that's what I named our son. Mephibosheth's eyes are changing color. They are going brown, like yours."

Jonathan's fingertips grew cold, but he would not remove his hand from the icy rock. A sudden gust of wind blew against the cave face, making his black cloak snap around him. He shivered, his thick woolen halug and fur proving useless against the coming winter. And when Jonathan looked up at the sky, clouds had formed and thunder flashed in the distance. The sun was setting and he frowned as he realized that he had been standing there the entire afternoon.

"I need you," he whispered again, and eased his fingers from her name. He turned to leave, knowing that he would never return to her grave again.

* * *

"I can't hurt him again, Abner," Saul said bluntly. "I don't want him near me anymore. To be honest, he frightens me now, cousin. He's not the pleasant young man I loved so dearly. He's a warrior now, a strong leader, and I don't know if I can stand to watch my people love him more and more every day."

Abner took a sip from his golden cup, and wondered how long Saul's calm would last. What he had seen that night was pure hatred and jealousy.

It had to come from somewhere, Abner thought. What does the king know that he isn't telling anybody?

"They adore him, cousin," Saul said softly.

"And they should," the general said casually. "He's a valiant man, Saul, the slayer of Goliath, the victor of battles, but they love you more. Do you really think they don't remember you? What you did for them? You are their leader, their fighter-king who freed them from the Philistines." Saul thought about it, and a small smile stole across his face. Finally, some support from his family, although Abner did not even know it. Saul relished it quietly.

"There are two ways to keep him from you. Either promote him to captain as Jonathan insists or have him killed," Abner said. They shared a silent glance.

Saul shook his head, "No, Abner, the people of Israel and Judah love him. I cannot harm him. They will have my crown if I do."

"Then only the other remains; you must make him a captain, then he'll be in fatal danger waging war continually and you will see very little of him."

The general watched Saul think for a moment. The prospect of giving David more power stuck in his gut, but he realized what Abner said was true. He would be in more peril and could be killed.

"I know the rumor that David will be captain is already widely believed, but I must still make it official," Saul said frowning. He drank deeply from his cup, emptying it, trying to forget.

"David has shown that he deserves his rank, I think. He has done many things for Israel. I have complete trust in Jonathan. If he thinks David is fit to lead, then so do I. Look how well he commanded his cohort and how brilliantly he succeeded in the Philistia incursion. His men respect him and he leads them fearlessly. He will do the same with a regiment of sixteen eleph," Abner said.

"Let it be done," Saul said, irritated at Abner's high regard for the son of Jesse, and he held out the vessel to one of the servants who lifted the large clay container and filled the cup with red wine.

Abner raised an eyebrow at this, wondering when Saul would stop. It was Saul's sixth cup, and although he was on his fourth, he had diluted his drink heavily, not wanting to lose his wits. Saul's speech had begun to slur on his fifth refill, and Abner knew that the effects of Saul's drinking was causing the king's honesty. Abner found it empowering to know his every thought.

"I'm curious, my king. Wouldn't you rather have him close to you and truly be in control, than send him away and ignore his increasing fame? If you don't know about it, Saul, that doesn't mean it's not happening."

"No. I don't know if I've ever told you this, but I can't stand to be around him. He scares me, cousin. When he nears me, my throat closes up and my chest grows tight. I am always fighting for calm when he is around me and I feel a weight on my neck, as if I can't look up at him," Saul confessed. Abner nodded, attributing the statement to the inebriating wine.

Saul understood that God was with David, and had departed from him, but he could not confess it. How could a king acknowledge such a thing? David terrified him, and he felt again that there was nothing left for him. Nothing mattered anymore. He thought again for a moment of what David had that he didn't, and the thought tore him up inside.

"That is where you and I clearly differ," Abner said quietly.

"Do you think David is pretending to be something he's not? You know how to read people, Abner. Does he secretly desire my crown?" Saul sensed a tiredness washing over him and he felt the heaviness of the entire world weighing him down.

"Who doesn't, Saul?" Abner said wryly. Saul shot a glance of worry at him, and the general found himself smiling suddenly. "I have kept my eye on him for some time now, and I haven't noticed anything that left me with suspicions. In fact, I think he truly loves this family. I didn't want to tell you this before because of your ill temper, but I don't think it would be a wrong decision."

Saul breathed in deeply, his face reddened by the wine.

"Cousin, your confidence is enough for me, then. You know I trust you, even perhaps more than I do Jonathan, and I rely much on your opinions. You are my blood," Saul said and met Abner's eyes. "It is decided then. Make him my captain of a thousand, Abner. I will see him as seldom as possible," Saul said nodding. "But still, I want you to keep an eye on him. Jonathan won't do it as you will; he's too fond of David. You are the only person I can ask this."

"You are a good man, Saul," Abner said with complete conviction, placing his hand on Saul's shoulder, gripping it affectionately.

Saul chuckled softly at this, asking himself silently if it were true.

"Now forget about him, and let us talk as we used to, as if I weren't king and you a general of Israel," Saul said warmly, copying Abner's gesture. "We have come a long way, you and I. The wars we have won. The men we lost on the battlefields. The nations we have conquered—Moab, Ammon, Edom.

"The Amalekites," Abner added with a crooked smile.

"The kings of Zobah," Saul continued, looking into his cup.

Abner chuckled. "Now those were wars, cousin. We stained the earth red with our enemies' blood," he said and slapped his hand on the stone armrest.

Saul was tired of it all, Abner knew.

"It was another lifetime ago. Do you think it was worth it, Abner? The lives we took, the wives widowed, the sons and daughters we made fatherless. Oh, how different it all could have been, cousin, how very different," Saul said shaking his head clumsily. "You could have been a rich farmer, and I a good father. I would have been in the fields right at this moment, I suppose, if Samuel hadn't…. We would have been other men, not made hard by the carnage of wars; no scars, no broken bones."

"No freedom. Philistine guards taking whatever they wanted from our houses, killing our sons, not allowing us weapons to defend ourselves," Abner said, and paused to give effect to the words. "My wrist would still be working without pain, but we would be back in another Egypt—slaves to a heathen nation."

Saul's thin smile showed Abner his mood, and he tried to look serious as he spoke, though the corners of his mouth turned up. "No doubt you would be pushing Achish's royal waste from the palace in a stinking cart."

Saul laughed. "You old dog, as tactless as ever."

"And if it were anybody but you that called me a dog, I would have cut out his tongue," Abner replied with a broad smile, showing his yellow teeth.

David and Jonathan relaxed on the soft cushions on the floor and David filled the goblets with wine from a heavy earthen jug.

"Do you remember old Ziph's face when I told him his breath smelled like feet?" David said and they burst out laughing at the memory. Jonathan had just taken a sip from his cup and he snorted in an attempt not to spray wine all over the floor. "His one eye winked uncontrollably from the anger. I think he grunted insults instead of speaking them." Jonathan swallowed what he had in his mouth, quickly laughing at the image of the man.

"He was still my senior officer back then, and I think if he could have brought himself to speak, he would have had me whipped," David continued through hearty laughter.

"You had to run from him like a scared puppy," Jonathan added, catching his breath.

David's smile faded. "Now that's not funny. I wasn't scared —I was clever. I wasn't about to just stand there and let him hit me, and I couldn't have struck him back, could I? It would have been mutiny."

"I think it's hilarious," Jonathan said, slapping his knee as he doubled over. David could not keep his face straight, and chuckled.

"I haven't laughed so hard in months," Jonathan said. David looked thoughtful.

"Thank you for convincing your father that I wasn't trying to take his crown," David said. "It's insane."

Jonathan stiffened slightly and then spoke as if he hadn't heard. "How could I not, David? I care for you as if you were my brother. I want to kill my brother sometimes, but I never do."

"Your father is a great man, Jonathan. I still can't believe he made me a captain." David smiled, the guilt over his words easing a bit.

The prince lifted his cup. "Here's to your captaincy, David. You will be great," he said and downed the contents, smacking his lips.

"It's going to be an adventure, my friend. The garrison won't be the same with us both there, and me a captain now. Those unfortunate soldiers," David said, feigning worry comically as he shook his head. Jonathan snorted again.

"David, enough! Give me a chance to breathe," he said placing his hand on his aching abdomen. "I've recently heard a rumor that your father has never committed a sin in his life," Jonathan said, arching an eyebrow.

David grinned at the statement and it caused him to miss his loving parents keenly. "Indeed, he is a good man and has raised me well. He is more devout than the priests, I assure you." His expression was nostalgic. "Our house is greatly blessed."

A knock at the door brought him from his musing, and David went to open it. Unconsciously, he stepped back when he saw who it was. "Michal," he greeted her, clearing his throat. The sight of him made her anger fade and she entered the room and went over to Jonathan.

"Brother, I pray you, it is late and you're keeping me awake with your howling," she said, feeling David looking at her.

"I apologize, sister. We shall retire soon," Jonathan said, noticing the way David was staring at her.

David was very attracted to Michal, and he wanted to take her in his arms and kiss her. He had noticed women before but had never felt like this, and his feelings had become stronger over the past month. They had been sitting together at dinner every night, and they spoke whenever possible, but he had to mask his emotions. With his turbulent relationship with Saul, he didn't know if it would be prudent to court his daughter. His throat was dry suddenly and he realized he was staring.

"Sweet dreams, David," Michal said, as she turned, smiling, and with a lowered head, hurried out of the room. David closed the door, as if in a daze.

Jonathan frowned slightly at what he had just witnessed and walked over to David slowly. He watched David's face for a reaction as he spoke. "I think my sister has feelings for you."

David could not control his expression and Jonathan chuckled at the revelation.

"Of course. You're in love with her!" Jonathan said pleasurably.

"What? Not Michal. Me, never! Not Michal. Why would you say something like that? Never, no," David stammered.

Michal walked in her mother's garden outside the palace walls, through the wet grass as the sun rose steadily above the horizon. She took in a breath of the crisp air. Her skin had been massaged with oil and her hair bound behind her back with a simple gold band. Layers of white silk draped her young body and a deep purple cloth hung across her shoulders.

All the scents calmed her and she twisted a dark tendril of hair as she visualized walking along the banks of the river Jordan. As she closed her eyes, she imagined her feet squishing over the mud and she could see the colorful sails of the small fishing boats on the silver water. She smiled as she wiggled her toes, almost feeling the wet earth push between them.

It was becoming a ritual for her—every morning she would think of another place that she knew she would probably never see. She had lived a secluded life locked up in her father's fortress palace, so she created these worlds in her mind from what she had heard from the servants or the people of her city.

Michal opened her eyes and heard the birds twittering in the trees. She shivered suddenly as her hand brushed against foliage and cold water splashed on her skin. She laughed and swiped her fingers across the leaves, then held her veil aside and sucked the liquid pleasurably. Ahinoam had insisted that she and her sister Merab wear the light cloth over their faces now that the men were home. They were of marrying age, she had said, and it was only proper for unwed women to cover themselves. Men are lustful beings.

She came out of her reverie as she saw David, and dropped her veil instinctively. He didn't see her, and she thought of hurrying the opposite way. Then David met her eyes, and she could see his surprise.

She felt nervous and uncomfortable at seeing him.

"Why are you here? This is my mother's private garden," Michal said, sounding quite regal.

"Your mother said I could come here. I wanted to be alone to pray and this seemed the perfect place. I apologize if I scared you, my princess. I just finished awhile ago, and was admiring the tranquility and splendor of this place," David said in a soft voice. He looked deeply into her eyes, and added confidently. "Though a garden has never looked so splendid as with you walking in it."

Michal was astonished. She had never been courted before, but she had expected more. *He has just called me splendid,* she thought, almost disappointed. *I have heard that so many times, from men, soldiers, servants, and even women, and the first thing he says to me is how splendid I am. Men.*

She smiled shyly, giggling softly into her hand, as her servants had told her to do. If you want any man's attention, they had advised, caress his ego and make him believe that whatever he does is flattering.

"You flatter me, my lord," she said. He made her heart pound suddenly as he brought his hand to her veil, and she flinched.

"It's all right, I won't hurt you. I have to see your beauty again or I would surely pine away. Since I saw you for the first time that afternoon, you are all I've been thinking about. Your laugh, your smile, your scent," David whispered into her ear, and she allowed him to lift the veil from her face. "All these days and nights of speaking to you like I felt nothing for you, while inside I thought my heart would break. All this time I had to pretend. And I won't do it any longer, I can't. Even though we live in the same place, you are miles away. I know you feel the same way."

Michal closed her eyes and sighed when his fingers touched her skin. "David, I have longed for you to speak to me like this," she admitted and realized she was shaking. She looked at him and her words caught in her throat.

"It has been unbearable," he said softly, his voice almost a breath. Slowly David pressed his lips against hers and she could not control herself any longer. He held her body against his, and she gently touched his bulging biceps, his strength making her wish he would never let her go.

A muffled cry made Michal jump back, and she saw one of the servants looking at them down the narrow stone pathway. Fear crept across her face and she felt her eyes sting with tears. She shot a glance at David and he turned pale at her expression. She shook her head delicately as she turned slowly, crying.

The servant hurried away, and Michal ran after her without a word to him. David could hear her sobs as she raced away.

"Wait, I pray you. Stop!" Michal called after the servant. The woman turned to face her, but her expression was hard and she frowned at the princess.

"Please, I beg of you to keep quiet. If my father should hear of this, he would see David exiled, or worse, killed," Michal whispered, tears streaking her cheeks. The woman's face softened and she touched Michal's skin through the veil.

"Why did you do it then? If the king should hear that I had kept something like this a secret, I could be chased out of the city. I have a husband and children, love," the servant said.

"Nobody else saw it. This has never happened before, and I swear it will not happen again until I am his wife. Please don't say anything," Michal pleaded.

The woman hesitated, and then spoke firmly. "If I should ever hear of this again, I will tell the king. Do you hear me, child?" Michal nodded with relief, and the servant stared at her, then turned and left the garden without a word. Michal dried her face with her hand underneath the veil.

Merab combed Michal's hair, humming sweetly. Michal had not spoken a word almost the entire evening and silently stared at the various shallow makeup and scent containers, thinking of what had happened earlier. A fire burned on the hearth, keeping the worst cold out of the room. The wood crackled and snapped in the flames, and Michal listened to her sister's singing as she thought about what had happened between her and David.

"What's troubling you, Mic?" Merab asked, bringing her from her fretting. Michal sighed, and when she wanted to turn in her seat, Merab stopped her with a hand against her shoulder.

"Wait, let me fasten your hair. There we go," she said, and then pulled Michal from her seat and onto the low stone bed built into the wall.

"You haven't spoken a word," she said, folding Michal's hands in her own. Her sister looked at her for a moment.

"David kissed me today," she whispered.

"What? How could you let him do that? I don't believe this. After everything mother has told us," she said louder than she realized, gasping.

"Keep your voice down!"

"What was it like?" Merab asked suddenly, moving in closer with anticipation. She smiled with her sister.

"Contrary to what I've heard, it wasn't very nice, actually," she said, and saw Merab's face drop.

"What? That's not what I wanted to hear, Mic. You're lying aren't you," she said, narrowing her eyes.

"No, I speak the truth. His beard scratched my face, and he smelled funny," she said.

"Well, you know men hardly ever bathe," Merab said.

Michal didn't seem to hear, and she continued. "Though having him so close to me was like something out of a dream." She sighed and fell back onto the bed, spreading her arms out.

"I'm so jealous. Things like this always happen to you," Merab said and bounced to her sister's side. "Tell me about the kiss. I want details."

"It wasn't much, honestly."

"I don't believe you. People wouldn't make such a big fuss about it, if it weren't much," Merab said.

"He pressed his lips against mine and held me to him, and that was it," Michal said shrugging.

"Like we kiss father?" Merab asked frowning quizzically. "Is that it? Nothing more?" Michal nodded and they were quiet for a moment.

"A servant saw us and I ran after her. She was going to tell father. I've never been so scared in my life," Michal said and lowered her eyes.

"Did you persuade her not to?" Merab asked, her expression showing her sudden concern.

"Yes."

"No wonder you were so quiet. You're thinking she might still go to father. You see why this is dangerous?" she said and took Michal's hand affectionately.

"Yes, I know. I won't let it happen again, not until he takes me as his wife. He said he loved me, Mer. Do you think he would ever have enough courage to ask father? Will father even say yes?"

"Well, we'll have to make it happen, won't we, Mic? Like we women always have to do with the men in our lives, and the best part is that they don't even know we're doing it," she said, pursing her lips. "And don't worry about the servant woman. I'll make sure she knows her loyalty is toward you." Michal smiled at her sister and embraced her.

"What will I ever do without you, Mer?" she said over Merab's shoulder.

Merab was serious again. "I have to know this Mic, please be honest. Would you have let him defile you, if the servant hadn't found you?"

"No, never! I'm not a harlot. What do you think of me, sister?" Michal said shrilly without thinking, her mouth falling open as she sat up straight. "Besides David wouldn't have; he's too religious. He told me that in Bethlehem, his family prays an hour each morning and then again every eve."

"Don't fret, I knew you would say that. I just had to ask. Though Michal, you have to admit, David loves women ... more than most men. Everybody knows this."

"Oh, Mer, I adore him. You should read the psalms he writes, and when he sings with that mesmerizing voice ... I can't move, and I lose myself in his powerful eyes."

Merab touched her sister's shoulder lovingly. "He does have a strong will and a commanding personality. People are just irresistibly drawn to him, even the king and princes of Israel. And we've all heard him sing in court, sister," she said, and smiled. "You are blessed by his love, my precious Mic."

David wondered what Saul wanted with him at that hour of the night as he walked through the palace fortress, the gleaming limestone floor reflecting a twisted, soft image of him across the streaks of red and brown cutting the polished surface.

Again, he realized how immensely he disliked Saul's home, and only lived there at the king's request. Over the years, he had almost grown accustomed to the massive, cold statues that lined the walls, but now the heavy shadows cast by the flickering lamplight made them seem malevolent. He knew it was against God's laws to have them, but Saul could never have been persuaded to remove the stone idols.

He thought then about Samuel. He had only seen the old man once and that was when the prophet had anointed him. David knew the truth about Saul, unlike most of his people, but he would not whisper gossip into other's ears. It was not his secret to tell.

David frowned at what Saul had done so many years ago and shook his head. How could he have deliberately disobeyed Yahweh, the only living God? He could only imagine Samuel's wrath at this, and he shuddered.

He cared for the old king, but wondered if he ever made offerings to God or even prayed to Him. He had never seen him in the temple or making a sacrifice unto the God of Israel. This was something he could not accept. David never spoke of it with Saul, for fear of losing his respect for his king, but if anything could ever destroy David's devotion to Saul, it would be that.

The winter had been insufferable, with tense days and forced polite dinners. Although Saul treated him well, David knew that things would never be the same between them again. At least the king had shown his good will by making his captaincy official.

Michal made the days fly with her childish giggle and delightful smile. He loved her, and after what had happened in the garden, he knew she shared his affection. They hadn't kissed again, but their conversations were filled with flirtatious gazes and laughs. They were playing a dangerous game, he knew, but he did not care. David had told only Jonathan about their kiss, and though they had had a stern discussion about it, he was happy for him and had teased him ever since.

He thought of taking her a gift. An iron ring, perhaps?

David entered the wide door of Saul's court in the center room of the palace and was happy to see Ahinoam sitting beside the king. The atmosphere would not be as uncomfortable with her there. As always, Ahinoam was elegantly dressed and looked radiant. Her scarlet trimmed and tasseled ketonet fell to her ankles, revealing the shape of her legs. Her hair was loose over her shoulders and she had an ivory flower pinned above her temple.

Saul motioned him closer with a straight face, and David bowed before the king. He kissed Ahinoam's hand and stepped back to face the royal couple. The queen smiled warmly at him.

"David, I have not forgotten about the promise I made," Saul said coldly without any prelude, feeling the sting of past emotions again. "I have discussed it with my wife, and we have agreed to give you my eldest daughter Merab to wife. All I ask is that you be valiant for me and fight the Lord's battles."

David couldn't hide his shock as he sank to the floor in a bow before Saul. His mind was racing. He didn't want Merab.

Why now? he thought in mute rage. He could not help but think that Saul had heard about him and Michal and was doing this only to spite him. He forced his eyes shut.

"Who am I? And what is my life, or my father's family in Israel, that I should be the son-in-law of the king?" David asked in an attempt to dissuade Saul without looking up at the royal couple. Perhaps the monarch was being genuine and truly wanted to bless him with his eldest daughter. But the coincidence was just too great.

"It's not about you, David, or about your bloodline; it is me keeping my word. I'm not a dog. I follow through on my promises," Saul said, wanting to hurt the man. "You have done many things for me and Israel. You deserve it, captain. Because you did not remind me of my vows, I know that you are true to Israel and to this family."

I won't strike David down, but rather let the Philistines do it, Saul thought, and bared his teeth in a grin. His plans for David's destruction were coming together nicely. This was something he had learned from his cousin, and Saul marveled at his own skill. Everybody thought that he was kind-hearted toward the young captain. Even Abner was convinced and Saul knew that his family loved him more for it.

"Then let it be so, my king. I thank you for your goodness. Your name will be praised throughout Israel," David said despairingly, though he tried to control his voice. Saul's eyes bored into him suddenly. *Is he mocking me?* he raged privately; *how dare he mock me?* When David rose to his feet, Saul smiled deceptively.

"I want you to return to the encampment tomorrow morning and begin your duties as captain. I have already made the arrangements and a servant is gathering your belongings as we speak. Ahinoam will arrange everything and we will send for you when it is time for the marital ritual," Saul said and grasped David by the upper arm. "I need you to fight bravely for me, David. Slaughter the Philistines and lift Israel's name high."

The king released his grip and sat back on his throne. "I know you will do this, David. The men under you admire you for it."

"You are too kind, my king. I will do what you ask, I swear it." David said and bowed his head.

"Now leave us," Saul said, without looking at him.

"If I may ask a question, my queen?" David said.

"Of course, David. What is it?" Ahinoam asked, and David's lips pulled into a tight smile at her grace. He wondered for a moment if they could see his displeasure.

"Does my wife-to-be know of this arrangement?"

"No, not yet. We have only just decided and it is too late now to tell her. She has long since retired to her bedchamber. I will inform her tomorrow morning, and my husband shall announce it publicly in his court shortly after," she said kindly.

"I thank you again. Have a blessed night, my king and queen." David stepped back, bowing three times before turning to leave, fighting not to show his anguish.

Ahinoam chuckled at David's humbleness. "He will make a good husband, Saul," she whispered.

"Indeed, wife. He will," Saul said distantly, staring after David.

***

David stood hesitantly before Michal's chamber door. It was hours later, and he could not sleep. He took a deep breath, as if he readied himself for physical pain. He looked down the cold corridor, and when he was sure nobody was coming, opened the door as quietly as possible, edging inside.

"Michal," David whispered loudly, in an attempt to wake her, but not wanting her to take fright and scream. In the sudden darkness he could not even see his hands before his eyes.

"Michal, wake up," he called again, and this time he heard her sit up in her bed.

"Is anybody there?" she asked frightened, staring into the darkness.

"It's me, David," he answered quickly, feeling his way through the room. "Where are you?"

"David, what are you doing here? If anybody should catch us, it'll be your head," she whispered, seeing David move slowly towards her, with his hands outstretched. "Watch out for the ... chair." David stumbled painfully over a stool, and grunted as softly as he could, rubbing his sore flesh. Michal giggled into her pillow.

"Michal, come with me," David asked as he came to her bedside.

"What's going on? We can't go anywhere at this time of night," she said questioningly.

"Michal, do you care for me?" he asked abruptly. He could finally see in the darkness, and he took her by the hand and lowered himself to his knees. "Do you love me, Michal?" She was silent for a moment.

"Yes, I do ..." she said and David broke into her sentence.

"Then come with me. I am leaving now, and will wait for you where we kissed. Dress warmly. It's very cold outside." David left as quickly as he had come and Michal jumped out of bed, excited and puzzled.

David waited tensely for her outside, thinking of that first kiss. The garden was a mass of shadows, moving in an icy breeze under the dim moonlight, and he could smell rosemary leaves in the air. Different birds hooted and called in the night, and he shivered from the cold. She was taking so long, he had begun to think she wouldn't come, but he would wait for her until dawn if he had to.

He could hear her coming long before he could see her, and he smiled at her stealth.

Michal saw him standing in the white light of the moon. He had never looked so striking. She felt nervous suddenly. What would happen when they were together, alone, covered by darkness? And then she realized how much she loved him. It was beyond childish infatuation and she would give herself to him then, she knew. The thought of it made her shiver.

David finally saw her, and gaped. She had dressed her hair splendidly and her face was clean and free of makeup. She did not have her veil, and David ached over what he knew.

"I thought you weren't coming," he whispered into her ear as Michal wrapped her arms around him. She felt his breath in her neck, and closed her eyes at the sensation, taking in his scent.

"How could I not? The excitement of this escapade is making me silly," she said blushing into his shoulder, and when he put his strong hands around her, her breath quickened and she felt as if she could faint.

"I adore you, Michal," he said, and kissed her passionately. He felt her start with surprise, but she did not pull away.

David pulled her into the dense foliage. She followed him without resistance. Michal smiled when she saw he had brought bedding with him and had made a small pallet for them. Her heart raced suddenly, and she could not breathe. It was going to happen, and she feared the uncertainty.

David lowered her onto several large cushions on thick blankets spread out onto the soft earth, and lay closely beside her. He kissed her again fervently.

After awhile, Michal moved her hand nervously down to his belt.

"No, don't. I love you too much, Michal," David whispered, bringing her hand up to his face. "Just lay here with me, my love, and let me hold you." He wrapped his arms around her, and she felt safe in his embrace. Even the thought of her father discovering them did not scare her as she lay with him.

David wrapped a blanket around them, and he kept her warm. They did not speak, and David savored every second he had left with her.

Michal was awakened by the raucous calls of the wild birds. She yawned, stretching her arms. She jumped up when she remembered where she was. The sun was shining through the trees, mottling her skin with light. She was alone, and she fumed briefly at David. How could he leave and not wake her? Everyone must be looking for her by now. How could he be so callous?

She quickly wiped her face with her hands and smoothed down her dress, composing herself. As she fussed, she noticed an iron ring on the end of the blanket, with a stem of lavender through the center. A small letter was beside it, tied with thin string.

She covered her mouth in excitement, giggling as she snatched up the precious jewelry, not even noticing the flower. She turned the metal in her fingers, knowing it must have cost a fortune. She jumped up and down like a little girl. She slid the ring onto her finger and admired it in the morning light. David was everything she wanted in a man.

She took the parchment and unrolled it gently. She bit her lower lip as she read the few words. She could hear his deep voice in her mind, as if he were reading it to her himself. In it he pledged his undying love and told her never to forget this. That was all and it was enough. Michal pressed the note to her breast and spun around, giggling quietly to herself.

After a moment, she tried to tidy her hair and then rushed out to the cobblestone pathway. She would come to fetch the blankets when it was safe to do so. As she was leaving the garden, a servant woman found her.

"Here you are, princess. The household has been looking for you all morning," she said excitedly. Michal only smiled and lifted a lock of hair from her face. She hoped the women could not see that she had just awakened.

"I have exciting news, m'lady," she said laughing, and Michal chuckled at the woman's delight. "The king has given your sister Merab to the Captain David ben Jesse to wed."

"No, it can't be. There must be some mistake!" Michal said in such a way that the servant could barely understand. She paced backward, covering her face in horror, her eyes gleaming with tears. "It must be a mistake."

Chapter Eleven

*M*ichal sat in her window, tugging at a curly tress as the winter winds blew over her, turning her skin almost blue with cold. After the news, she had fled to her room, and thought she would never go out again.

She had been raging at David and Merab for their cowardice. *How could David not tell her? He had held her through the night, but did not say a word. How could Merab accept the proposal, and not say anything?* Michal snorted at the thought that Merab called her sister.

She took the small note and read it again as she had done a hundred times before. Tears had stained it and some of the letters had run down the parchment in a watery trail. She was nobody's fool, Michal thought suddenly, crushing the papyrus in her hand. She threw it out of the window and with that, cried again.

The princess had fallen asleep when Merab entered the room. She saw her sister curled up in the window and froze. Streaks of tears were visible in Merab's makeup and she edged closer, wondering what she would say.

"Michal," she whispered, shifting the blanket from her face. Michal opened her eyes, and glared at her. Her eyes were red and the sight made Merab take her hand from her sister.

Merab swallowed and took a sharp breath. "Mic, I'm …" she started.

"Don't call me that," Michal said stonily, and sat up from the bed. She would not look at her sister.

"Michal, I'm sorry for all this," Merab said. "You are behaving like a spoiled little girl again. Do you think I want to wed David? I love Adriel. Don't you know that? Or are you too caught up in your own selfish sorrow to remember? He is also a soldier, sister. And unlike David, he has a rich family. He's a better husband for me … but I know my duty," she said scornfully in one breath. "What will you have me do, refuse father's will, and be shamed for the rest of my life? I should have known that you would be so self-centered as to expect that from me. And David? Father could have had his head if he had insulted the king with a refusal. He loves you, sister, but father has sent him to war. He didn't."

Michal turned and sank into Merab's shoulder, sobbing wildly. Merab felt terrible for speaking so harshly. Her sister must have been hurting more than she was, Merab knew. She wasn't as mature, and had a gentle heart. Affectionately, she put her arms around her shaking sibling, and shushed her softly.

"Please, Mer," Michal whispered. "You have to resolve this. I pray you, sister, I love him."

Michal was on David's mind, and he was in a foul mood as he trotted into the encampment on his horse. He had been a coward, but how could he have told her? He loved her too much to see the pain in her eyes. It was better this way, he told himself repeatedly.

The guards above the walls had immediately recognized him and ordered the wooden gates thrown open. The soldiers saluted him as he rode into the large fort. In one of several letters to Captain Ehud, Saul had mentioned David's new rank, and the word had spread fast throughout the camp. He gave a quick smile and acknowledged them with a wave of his hand.

The interior had changed so much over the past months that David felt he had ridden into a different fort. Every ranking officer now had his own small wooden quarters. Wood workers and metalsmiths had workshops, and wisps of smoke flagged their many forges against the cobalt blue sky.

The largest rooms on the second floor of the original mud brick building, now standing at the center of the encampment, were turned into lavish royal quarters for Prince Jonathan and General Abner. Another spacious room was converted into a campaign room. The smaller rooms on the ground floor were reserved for the three captains, along with a small kitchen where special meals would be prepared. The high walls and gate of the old fort added extra privacy and protection for the leaders of the Israelite military. This sturdy building was now the heart of the garrison.

David heard the heavy gates close behind him as he rode deeper into the fort. He stopped the first man that walked past him. "Prince Jonathan and General Abner will be returning two weeks earlier. Inform the garrison-master," he said, turning in his saddle. "Where are the stables?"

"Straight ahead, sir, on your left," the soldier said dutifully, indicating a neat pathway of pitched white tents.

David brought his horse to the stables and gave it to the young groom. He stroked the beast softly, whispering in its ear, and then watched for a moment as the young man led the animal to the trough. David loved the magnificent creatures. Horses were very rare throughout Israel and only the richest and most powerful men owned them. They were mainly bred for the royal household and for the military—for captains and officers. Only after coming to stay with the royal family did he first touch their silky coats. He smiled at the memory.

He cared deeply for the animals and learned to ride within a week. David remembered the pain he had endured those first few days. He had broken his arm when he had tried to ride one of the wildest stallions. Nevertheless, he had been determined and as soon as the bone had healed, he had tried again. After only a few days, the horse was eating out of his hand, and he cantered through the busy streets of Gibeah, alive with his achievement, although the stallion allowed only David to ride him. It was that very roan horse that Saul had given him and it had been his companion ever since. He chuckled softly as he scratched his thick beard and then left the stables.

David entered the pale building and with a wide smile greeted Ehud, though he had to remind himself not to salute the captain.

"Why wasn't I informed of your arrival?" Ehud jumped to his feet, and clapped David on the back. "I've heard that I now greet you as an equal. Did you know that Captain Ludim had to retire many years early because of your rise in rank?"

David looked at him guardedly, not sure how to answer.

"The old lion was delighted at the news. He has already left for his hometown, to his family," Ehud continued. "It's good to see you again. It has been a long month, a lot has happened."

"I noticed," David said, frowning at Ehud's slurring. "I barely recognized the place. I had to ask three times before I found you. If I hadn't seen it with my own eyes, I wouldn't have believed it possible." Ehud laughed and David only smiled at him, his mind preoccupied. Ehud indicated to David to take a seat and summoned the servant who brought two cups of hot wine.

"I can see that the winter did you good as well. You have a full beard now; at least you don't look like a youth anymore," Ehud said, trying not to smile.

David had never known him like this before. They sat on cushioned wooden benches, and talked as friends.

David entered the small wooden building and found his brother Eliab sitting on the floor with three young men he did not know. They were laughing and the men were speaking to him, an officer, as if he were a simple soldier. David frowned at this and looked at their faces. They had strong features and he seemed to recognize something in each of them, although he could not think what. Was he supposed to know these men? They were quite young. Their laughter died suddenly and they jumped nervously to their feet. David did not shift his gaze.

"Brother? I didn't think I would see you for months still," Eliab said as he rose from the floor in surprise when he saw his brother standing there in silence. He moved over to David and wrapped his large arms around him, lifting his youngest brother from the floor in his embrace with no effort. David could not help but laugh as he dangled. He had missed them all so much and wished they had been with him through the difficult weeks. He had needed them then.

"Eliab, I'm sure you could crush a bear with your grip, but please, I still need my lungs for awhile," he grunted through a chuckle.

"Still as witty as always, I see," Eliab said, grinning. "It's good to have you back, little brother. Or should I say captain?"

"Who do we have here?" David asked and looked at the three men again. Two of them lowered their eyes, but the tallest one kept his eyes on David.

"These are our nephews. They're Zeruiah's sons. The eldest is Joab, then Abishai, and then Asahel. Father asked that we recruit them now that they are old enough. In your absence, I thought it good to agree. I ran it by Captain Ehud, and here they are," Eliab said in something like a fluster. He spoke quickly as if he were explaining his actions. "I have trained them along with Gibbôr and father had taught them tactics and discipline, as he did us. They're quite the young soldiers," he said.

David evaluated them, as the oldest came up to him. He stood taller than David, and only nodded, challenging him silently.

David smiled at this. "Summon the captains to the battling pen. I will size them up as warriors myself."

The leaders of Gibbôr rooted for their captain as David and Joab and his brothers circled in the arena, testing each other. Joab was arrogant, David knew. The only way to establish his authority was to beat them in front of the entire regiment.

Without warning, David launched a fist at Joab's jaw. The young man grunted as he dropped. The three brothers scattered, and Eliab laughed in amazement.

David heard Eliab shout something as he darted towards Asahel and faked a blow with his left arm. When Asahel tried to block, David slapped him with his right hand. Spittle flew from his mouth and he almost spun as he fell into the mud. Without stopping, David grabbed Abishai by his tunic and threw him into the brown slush. He evaded a blow from behind, but Joab was skilled enough not to have put his entire weight behind the punch, and did not lose his balance when he missed. Before he could turn around, David struck him behind the head with a backhand that made him topple forward, and he staggered. David was playing with them.

Before he knew it all three brothers had surrounded him, and he anticipated their attack.

"You trained them well, brother," David shouted, catching his breath.

"Well enough to win against our old uncle," Joab goaded.

David smiled. "Let's finish this, boys." Eliab admired the three brothers' determination when they came at David again.

Suddenly, David struck Joab square in the face, breaking his nose.

"Not again," Joab cried, blood spurting over his face as he stepped back moaning in pain. David sprained Asahel's wrist with ease as the man grabbed his tunic and tried to punch him. His nephew screamed. Abishai reversed and mumbled something and then David knocked him unconscious. David took a deep breath, as he looked at the three men, useless in their pain.

"Good fight, David!" Eliab said and moved to Joab, who was covering his nose with his cupped hands.

"You were right, Eliab. Quite the fighters," David said as he straightened his tunic, and fixed his wild hair.

Eliab looked at him amazed, and then a deep laugh exploded from his throat. "I thought for a moment you were going to smite them."

"Let me see, Joab," Eliab said as he turned to his nephew and gently removed the man's bloody hand from his face. He frowned at the sight of the purple nose pointing in totally the wrong direction. "Doesn't look too bad. You'll live," he said, patting him on the shoulder.

Thick droplets of blood dripped from Joab's chin, and the taste of blood in his mouth was sickening. He mumbled something in response, glaring at David. Eliab moved to Asahel and whistled when he saw his inflamed wrist.

"That's really going to hurt tomorrow, lad," he said almost laughing again.

David regarded his cheering men. "Do we like them, soldiers?" he asked, turning. The crowd shouted approval.

"Yes, I approve of them Eliab. I can definitely imagine them as warriors of Gibbôr," he said. Eliab placed his hand over Abishai's mouth to see if he were breathing fine. He could not contain his laughter any longer as he looked at their miserable expressions, and snorted.

"Welcome to the military, men."

"Eliab, send them to the physician and then you and I will have a cup of wine. What do you say, brother? All this fighting has made me thirsty."

Eliab shrugged. "Joab and Asahel, salute your captain," Eliab said amused. Grudgingly they did, and Asahel whimpered when he turned his hand too much.

"Joab, I trust you haven't forgotten where the physician's quarters are," Eliab said as he followed his brother out of the muddy pen.

"Well, he's definitely Uncle Jesse's son," Joab said and spat out blood and saliva.

"Yes, my hand is the proof. He is undoubtedly *your* uncle," Asahel replied.

<hr/>

Abinadab entered the campaign room and found David's entire council seated at a stone table in the center of the spacious room.

"You're late," Eliab said and waited as his brother took a seat. David stood at the window and gazed out over the dark fort through the lattice, and finally decided that he would make his nephews officers and include them in his council. He could smell saffron and sage on the wind combined with the tantalizing odor of roasting lamb that the cook Nepheg was preparing for them on the spit. He took a deep breath. Wax torches cast moving shadows on the fort walls and small fires warmed the soldiers as winter still hung over the highlands. David enjoyed the cold breeze that bit at his exposed skin.

"Bring them in, Eliab," David said still looking out at the night sky, rubbing the beard on his neck. Eliab went to the door, and called for the three men. Joab and his brothers entered the room stiffly, bandaged and swollen. They knew that the entire council would mock them and they did not look the members in the eyes. They saluted David's back and sat down at the table. Asahel felt out of place and uncomfortable in the presence of such strong men and he felt his throat itch, but decided not to clear it with the room so still. This was something unfamiliar for them all. It was a new world with different rules, and they had learned the hard way.

Pelet stopped talking in mid-sentence and listened to his captain. David did not sit, and walked slowly, circling his council.

"Joab, my father has educated you on tactics. Tell me what you would do if you were surrounded by savage Philistines," David asked and met his eyes. Joab thought for a moment, and then smiled.

"I simply wouldn't have let them surround me, captain," he said.

"Ha! If only he moved as fast as he talked, then he wouldn't have gotten his nose broken, *twice*," Pelet said and the council laughed. David did not show his amusement, and shifted his eyes to Abishai.

"When you're surrounded it's usually finished if you can't keep it together, but I suppose I would have my men form a tight circle and cut our way outward," Abishai said flustered. David noticed it and narrowed his eyes as he wondered. He was silent for a moment.

"Joab, Abishai, Asahel. I've decided to include you in this council from henceforth. The councilmen have all agreed," David said without preliminaries. "You will be commanders of an eleph each and then officers over a hundred when I feel you are ready. I expect you to behave according to your rank. This is a war gentlemen; your youthful times are done."

Abishai's mouth fell open, and Joab smiled confidently.

"Tonight I want you to listen only. Observe and learn," David said and smiled. "Now that's decided, shall we begin? I want names, men. Eliab will you start?" He turned to face the men he knew best, sitting around the stone table.

"Well, I have given this some thought, and I have known the brothers Jediael and Joha for some time. They have fought loyally for King Saul for many years now. I've seen them in battle many times, and nobody is more fierce," Eliab said.

Shammah spoke next. "Ithai, the son of Ribai of Gibeah. He smote more Philistines than all of us combined." David nodded in agreement, remembering the names, and looked at Abinadab.

"I think Sibbicai, the Hushathite. He was the one who held my back when Philistines surrounded us, and he did not run. Together we slew certainly near fifty men. He is brave and strong," he said with conviction. The council smiled at this, and Joab snorted.

"Do you want another broken nose?" Abinadab snapped and Joab's grin died on his face.

All of the men mentioned their candidates and the hours passed as they discussed those mentioned in depth. Every character flaw, heroic deed, skill, and virtue were brought to light. Finally, as the moon lowered in the distant hills, David had a long piece of leather scroll before him with the list of names inscribed on it. He read through it again and then nodded, satisfied.

"I have decided that my brothers will be my chief officers, and the rest of you will be my officers over a hundred," David said and grinned at them as they cheered. Eliab beamed at his youngest brother. It was a good choice, he thought, to make them part of his council. Large chunks of the logs in the fireplace had burned to white ash and glowed weakly as the fire died.

"Tomorrow will be a good day, gentlemen. And I, for one, want to get some sleep," David said with a yawn. The council rose from their seats and David greeted each man with a soldier's handclasp as they saluted him one by one. He folded the leather parchment and placed it inside his belt.

David and Eliab looked at the men of the Gibbôr regiment. Eliab had trained them right through the winter and each stood to attention in front of their captain. David gazed across the wide square of his Mighty Men. He would choose his leaders from among them and each of his soldiers yearned to hear his own name. They had all fought valiantly for him, burning the garrisons, and fighting the Philistines. An anxious silence spread among the warriors as David thought about his decision again. He and his council had already discussed the matter and after a moment, he assured himself that he had chosen the right men.

"I stand before you not as a captain, nor even a leader, but as a man and a warrior. Each one of you has shown your loyalty and courage to me more than once. We have lost some of our brothers in the bloody months past, but we became stronger from it. We remember them still." All eyes were on David as he stood firm, fully armored, with his red and white striped cloak rippling behind him. Dark clouds rolled in the near distance, and beams of weak gray light mottled the black soil. The air smelled of rain as he continued. "Our great king has given to Gibbôr a thousand men, and now more than ever we will cause raw fear in the hearts of our enemy." David paused as he waited for the storm of cheers to die down.

"All here deserve rank, each and every one of you. However, I shall only choose the best and the bravest from among you. I have written down thirty names," David said, nearly shouting so that his voice boomed over all thousand armored men standing in the pale yellow fields surrounding the fort. Eliab handed David a folded leather scroll. He felt their eyes on him, the men seeming frozen in the wide column, waiting for his words. He moved his eyes across them and then looked at the leather scroll, although he already knew all the names.

"My brothers Eliab, Abinadab, and Shammah are my chief officers," David said. As one, the men thudded their fists against their chests three times. Then David read the names aloud of the new officers and they emerged from the lines and stood before him and his brothers. David looked at his officers. Their faces were those of lions and he had chosen them for their skill, and sharp minds. His chest swelled with pride. His officers.

"Honor these warriors," he roared and the soldiers broke into a loud salute. David stood like a warrior-king before his regiment in his gleaming bronze armor, his cape snapping behind him in the cold wind. Thunder rumbled in the distance and the rain began to fall.

Chapter Twelve

Achish was already sweating under his layers of fat, though the days were still cold. Ladiah smiled seductively at the Philistine king, though he disgusted her more than anything she could imagine. She trailed her finger gently along the black spiral tattoos on his fat chest, as she bit his ear suggestively. She found every inch of the man revolting. He was no equal to Saran, the officer whom she had loved once and had to watch die, and she would think of him every time she was with Achish. If she had known, however, that his death would bring her such riches and fame, she would have killed him herself a long time ago.

Over the months, she had seduced the king and tricked him into believing that she adored him and now she was a queen. She had convinced him to take her from his harem and let her stay in her own bedchambers. From there she had been free from the eyes and ears of the jealous wives and could do as she pleased.

Although she was the king's favorite, he did not call upon her too often because every time, he had to order his physician to make him a tonic to cure his impotence. A few nights a month with him was the small price she was paying for her new life.

She had been a harlot once and now they called her a courtesan, although Achish didn't know that she entertained other men in her private quarters for healthy sums of money. She smiled as she thought what an idiot he was.

Ladiah remembered how he had raped and hurt her in the beginning, and felt like biting off his ear. But that was all past now.

Achish gasped at the sharp pain of her teeth. She laughed sensually, and the king grinned at her, pulling her on top of his large stomach.

"Get out—all of you," Achish grunted, barely able to contain himself. He was caressing Ladiah and she was kissing his thick lips as the slaves hurried out of the room.

Achish grinned in pleasure, and Ladiah took pride in how good she was.

The doors of the room flew open as the five Sérèn of Philistia marched into the room. Achish threw Ladiah from him, and hastily sat up, livid with rage.

"How dare you come in here? I ordered everybody to stay out," he barked, red faced. Ladiah slowly covered herself, enjoying the men staring at her. The air was pungent with burning aromatic cane incense.

The Sérèn were the council of co-rulers, princes of Philistia, and when the five lords stood together, they could easily overpower a king. They ruled each of the five main cities in Philistia, and had to pay an annual visit to Achish to show their respect and pay him his share of the taxes. After they had been inaugurated, they would simply be referred to as the Sérèn of their city.

"No, Achish. You listen to us now," Sérèn of Ekron said belligerently, pointing his finger at the obese king. He could swear Achish had gotten fatter over the winter, if that had been possible. He saw from the corner of his eye that Ladiah was staring at him, but he ignored her. He had had enough of her the night before.

"Why haven't you organized a counter attack on the Israelites? They own our trade routes, burn our garrisons at the borders of my city, and guard the highlands as if they belong to them. And you do nothing. You are weak, Achish. Your father would be ashamed."

Ladiah placed an olive in her mouth, and wet her lips with its juice, teasing the prince. She had enjoyed his frequent visits to her, and flushed as she thought of them. The man had the stamina of a bull.

Achish was mottled with anger, a vein pulsating in the middle of his forehead.

"How dare you!" Achish grunted, his spit splattering over his double chin.

"How dare I? How dare *I*? You are throwing away our glorious country, and you think to reproach me?" Sérèn of Ekron screamed, his eyes boring into the king. "If you don't do something soon, we will see you dethroned. Now get off your fat behind and try to act like a king. Pig!" The prince spat at Achish's feet and turned on his heels. The other four lords were rigid with shock and after a moment of uncertainty, bowed disconcertedly, and followed Sérèn of Ekron out of the room.

Ladiah had to stop herself from laughing and when Achish glanced at her, she feigned disbelief. Achish shook with uncontrollable anger and Ladiah did not dare say a word.

"Leave me, Ladiah," he snapped without looking at her. I will show them what I can do, he thought, his gorge rising, but first I will teach that misbegotten Ekron some respect.

The princes walked down the corridor. Sérèn of Ekron was still fuming.

"That was harsh, don't you think?" Sérèn of Gath said, still taken aback by the Ekron's insolence. "You *spat* at the king of Philistia. Perhaps you should have been more tactful; there might be dire consequences, do you not think? You should've showed some obeisance."

"*Bow*? Before *him*? I'd rather cut off my own hands. I have his whore-queen every night, and now you tell me to respect him. He's not fit to be king," Sérèn of Ekron snorted.

The princes stopped when they heard Ladiah call after them. The woman walked gracefully to the lord of Ekron and whispered in his ear so that the other men could hear. "Will you visit me again tonight? You're upset and I know just how to lift your spirits."

The men chuckled lustfully. Sérèn of Ekron pulled her to him, placing his hand on her hip, and moving it up slowly as he spoke until his hand had disappeared underneath the many folds of silk. "Go wait for me there, I'll see you later, woman." Ladiah sighed and smiled artfully as she bit her lip. Carefully she pushed him aside and walked casually away. "You men are welcome to join us. You know the price."

Rizpah entered the room tentatively and Saul smiled at the young woman. She would give him new sons, he knew, and he would enjoy getting to know his concubine.

Ahinoam despised the woman who walked into her private chambers, even though she had never met her. How could Saul be so cold, she thought fuming; he said he loved only me.

When he had told her three nights before, they had fought about it. She had screamed at her husband, and Saul had struck her, sending her to the floor. "You will respect me, Ahinoam," he had shouted, and the queen closed her eyes at the memory. Her hip had turned a dark purple and it was painfully sensitive.

Tears filled Ahinoam's eyes, as she clenched her jaw not to let her emotions show. She touched her face where he had hit her, and winced at the sore flesh, but at least a mark did not show. When she glanced at Rizpah, she saw that the girl was looking at her, and Ahinoam's eyes went hard, as if she could kill her with only a stare. Rizpah lowered her eyes to the floor, ashamed.

The queen did not say a word. Her husband had become a different person, and though she had refused to believe it in the past, this had forced her to finally accept it. They had been married for nearly thirty years, she reminded herself, shaking her head unconsciously.

She glared at Saul's concubine. She did not know her name yet and she did not care to, either. Saul was her husband, he loved her, and she had given him six children. But now that she was old, he had signed an agreement with a rich merchant for his daughter, who in her eyes was practically a child. *The man I married would never have hurt me so much*, she almost said aloud, and her throat closed up.

Rizpah came to his throne, and bowed before him, kissing his feet. Saul took her hand and gently pulled her up.

"You do not need to do that, Rizpah. This is your home now, and you are my mistress," Saul said and kissed her hand. Ahinoam's mouth twisted at the word and her knuckles turned white as she tightened her fists. Rizpah shivered and the king smiled at her warmly. "My servant will show you to your chambers. I hope you will be happy here." His new concubine bowed her head silently, and left with the servant, feeling the old queen's eyes boring into her back.

After Rizpah had left, there was a silence between husband and wife.

Saul sighed and spoke first. "I am sorry about the other night, my love." He reached out to touch her, and when he saw his queen stiffen, he pulled his hand away.

"Will you never forgive me? You disrespected me with your tone and I won't have it," Saul snapped and he closed his eyes to control his temper. Never before in his life had he struck a woman, and he had told himself that it would never happen. Audibly, he let out a slow breath before continuing.

"It is my right as king to take as many concubines as I desire. And you won't deny me it, wife. You will not."

Ahinoam refused to look at him.

"I must strengthen my bloodline with more sons, and you are past your child-bearing years. I need more sons, Ahinoam. My bloodline must wear the crown for many generations. Do you understand that?"

The queen rose from her seat and walked to the door without speaking.

"Ahinoam," Saul shouted. She turned and looked at him, her expression stripped of all emotion. "It is my right as a man. I have been faithful to you for many years. You will be kind to the girl, Ahinoam. Do you understand me, wife?"

She bowed her head dutifully and walked elegantly from the room.

That night Ahinoam had to endure the most difficult hours of her life. Saul had been with his concubine since she had left her husband earlier that afternoon, and she had been standing before the door for longer than she would admit, secretly listening to what they were saying to each other. She had tried many times to leave, but found herself rushing back to the door every time.

When the servants told her the news that Saul had gone to his concubine and not to her, it had broken her. It took everything she had not to storm into the room and choke the girl with her own hands.

It was late at night, and she could now hear him making love to her. Images of them together haunted her and she felt sick. After days of raging and resenting him, tormented by the memories of everything they had survived in the long, lonely years of his kingship, and all the things they had made together, she finally allowed herself to cry. Saul might as well have killed her; the pain would have been less at least.

Silently she ran from the palace, sobbing bitter tears. She could not tolerate being in the same house with the man she was forced to call her husband, and she hurried to one of her sons' abodes.

The atmosphere in the palace changed subtly after Saul had announced Merab's marriage to David. It was as if everybody knew of Michal and David's love and nobody would speak of it. She and her sister never smiled, and the last discussion Merab had had with the commander Adriel plagued her mind. It was a strange thing to live in the palace with her father and brother there. Saul appeared relaxed now that David had gone, and hadn't had another fit of rage or bout of depression.

Merab paced the length of her chambers, wondering how she would let her father know what was happening. She knew she couldn't say it to him directly, though a man could, and she thought about Jonathan. He could surely succeed, but would he be willing? She pursed her lips as she thought, the only sounds in the room coming from her footsteps slapping softly against the cold limestone floor. It would be easy to persuade her father that Adriel was the better man for her. He came from a rich family, and was also brave in the wars against the Philistines, although he was still a commander and not a captain like David. Merab gasped as she thought of using her father's mistrust of David to her advantage, but shook her head as she realized that it would make things very difficult later on to get her father to give Michal to David. She could tell her mother the truth, and perhaps she would make a difference. Even if she sided with her husband, her mother would have to be told, nonetheless.

Merab grunted in frustration. She would not just accept the king's decision. She would have to be cunning in her manipulation, she told herself.

The days were becoming warmer as summer neared and Jonathan already missed the cold days of winter. He knew he would soon return to the garrison and he welcomed it, although he would never grieve his family by letting them know. He sat alone in his chamber looking distantly at the large, bleak stone bricks, with a hot drink of goat's milk infused with crushed rosemary, honey, and downy peppermint leaves to help him sleep.

Jonathan sat up from his seat when he heard his door open slowly. He had allowed Akkub, his personal servant, and the rest of them to retire, and the palace had been quiet for a long time. When he saw a cloaked figure enter, he touched the hilt of his sword instinctively, pulling the end of the curved blade an inch from the sheath.

Merab lifted the hood from her head and Jonathan rose from his seat when he saw her. What did she want with him at that time of the night?

"Merab, I thought everyone was asleep. What are you doing here?" he asked.

"I apologize, brother. I knew you would be awake and I saw the light coming from your door," Merab said. She was sweating underneath the woolen garment and she saw her brother frown at her secrecy.

"Is there something wrong?" he asked, narrowing his eyes suspiciously at her. His sisters had changed considerably over the years; they had become women, although he could still tell when they were being wayward.

"Actually there is. It's Michal," she said, and kissed the prince's hand. "She's been depressed ever since … Jonathan, it would break her if David and I were married."

"And you don't want it either, do you?" Jonathan said and indicated to her to sit down.

She took the cup from his hand to see what he was drinking, and smiled when she smelled the honey. "You and I are brother and sister. We both can't sleep at night," she said.

"This is true; we are the ones who fret long after the others dream, sister. Where would they be without us?" he said with a chuckle, taking the goblet from her and downing the last of the honeyed drink. "What do you suggest we do about Michal? We can't possibly go against father's word."

"No, but you can convince him," she said quickly.

"Me? Mother could also do it," he said. He pushed his fingers through his dark blond hair as he remembered and continued. "Mother is still not speaking to father. She's taking the news of father's new concubine badly."

"What did you expect?" Merab snapped, showing her own bitterness for a moment. Jonathan pretended not to hear.

"Can you think of any possible reason that would make father go back on his word?" Jonathan asked.

"Make father believe that Adriel is a better choice for me—or rather for him. He comes from a wealthy family, with rich merchants and powerful connections. He is a loyal and brave fighter. Father will see it our way, Jonathan, I know it. Will you help Michal? Will you help me?"

The prince laughed at her suddenly. "You are a crafty one, aren't you?" Looking at her, he enjoyed seeing his sister's nervous impatience as she waited for him to consider it, and he teased her with his silence. "Fine, I shall mention it to him, but I'm not so sure that it will work. I will discuss it with Abner and hear what he has to say. Between the two of us, you shall soon be the wife of this Adriel." Merab embraced her brother and smiled coyly over his shoulder, elated with the victory.

"If father should ever hear of this treason it will be the end of us, sister. So keep quiet about it. Do not breathe a word."

CHAPTER THIRTEEN

Saul was deep in thought about Adriel the Meholathite and he marveled at Jonathan's astuteness for suggesting it. Adriel's family was rich and powerful in many ways and if he agreed to marry Merab, Saul would have those resources available to him as long as the families were bound in marriage. He would ask a considerable bride price and make sure that Adriel's family remained loyal to the crown. It was a splendid thing, he mused, and it gave him pleasurable spite that he would go back on his word to David. Now he would have to have David killed by other means, he thought maliciously, clamping his jaw.

Merab entered the room and Saul smiled warmly at her as she came to him and kissed his hand. She looked like a queen, dressed in white silk, draped in many layers over her ankle-length ketonet. He could see the outline of her face behind the moving veil, and he touched her hand lovingly as she sat beside him on a lower, padded stool.

His courtier announced the man and Saul sat stately on his throne, squaring his shoulders. Merab was smiling underneath her veil and she lowered her face when the man she loved entered the room, followed by a line of servants.

Adriel moved to the king and bowed before Saul, kissing his feet. He was a tall man, with broad shoulders and a long face with thin black hair. Merab remained watchfully silent.

"Blessed be the king of Israel," Adriel said in a deep voice. He rose from his knees and bowed his head as he stepped back from the king.

"You are accepted in my court, Commander Adriel," Saul said. "Give me the covenant so that I may read it."

Adriel's servant brought the commander a tightly rolled leather parchment and Adriel handed it to one of Saul's many courtiers with another deep bow.

Saul unrolled the thick document and began reading without a word or expression to show what he was thinking. In this official contract, Adriel showed his willingness to wed the princess, suggested how he would propose to Merab, and most importantly, the bride price he would pay. As Saul read, he caught Adriel smiling at his daughter. The price for any woman in Israel was usually very high, and for the princesses, five times or more the normal charge. Only the richest families in Israel would have been able to afford Saul's daughters.

The king tried not to react when he saw the weight in iron that Adriel was willing to pay; it was far greater than what he had required for his eldest daughter.

Those in the room were apprehensive and after a moment, Saul folded the scroll and returned it to his courtier. He did not say a word, and Adriel moved anxiously to a long table and poured wine into a ceremonial golden cup. He knew his family wouldn't be able to afford an ounce more. He sipped at the cup and then handed it to Merab, who was still smiling. The entire court looked at the king.

"Adriel, I require something else from you," Saul said and Adriel waited tensely. "I want you to swear your family's allegiance to me and my crown. When I require anything from your family, within reasonable limits of course, I expect it to be done without question."

Adriel thought about this for a moment. "I am my father's eldest and our family's representative. I have the power to agree to such terms, and I announce to this court that when Merab becomes my wife, it will be as the king has requested." Saul nodded and Merab lifted her veil and drank from the jeweled cup. The people let out a great cheer and Merab ran to Adriel and embraced him. She was betrothed; it was official now.

Adriel wanted to kiss her then, but resisted under Saul's watchful eyes, knowing it was forbidden.

"I have brought gifts for you, my love," Adriel whispered into her ear. He signaled with a wave of his hand and all his servants brought in gleaming treasures. The court applauded and the royal musician began playing on a flute.

"Soon, my beloved Adriel, you will have me soon," she whispered and rested her head on his shoulder.

David read the letter for the third time, sitting on the floor of his cabin with his legs folded underneath him. He did not know if he should be furious at Saul's actions or thankful that he could now marry Michal. Was this an attempt at sedition? *He would not react to their evil incitements as they had hoped,* he told himself bitterly. Perhaps Michal had persuaded her father to let them wed. He decided that was most probably how it had happened, and that it was a blessing. *Did Saul know about their relationship?* he wondered. *Would the king even consider such a proposition?*

David tried not to let the herald see his thoughts, because he knew that Saul had instructed the man to note any reactions. David disregarded the man and after rising to his feet, he folded the letter and placed it on an oblong table against the wall.

"So it is done then—the marriage ceremony?" David asked.

"Yes, Captain. The princess has already left the palace and is living with her husband, the commander Adriel," the herald said, keeping David's stare.

"I would like you to take a message to the princess Merab. Tell her that I wish her and Adriel have a blessed life together, and that I am truly happy for them," David said and removed a small coin from a cotton pouch, and flicked it at him with his thumb and index finger. "Here is a quarter of a shekel for your trouble."

The herald looked surprised and caught the spinning metal midair. "Yes, captain. Any words for the king?" he asked.

"Yes, tell King Saul that he will be blessed by this union and that I bear no discontent. He is the sole ruler of my country, his will is also mine, and his decisions are accepted as well as respected," David said simply, and walked out of the cabin. He had had enough of the man.

The herald hurried after him and spoke at his back. "I will carry the message swiftly, Captain David."

"Good, now return to Gibeah. I have business to attend to," David said and walked on without looking back.

His dark shadow twisted and shifted on the reddish stone floor of the throne room as Saul paced the length of the hall slowly. Despite his efforts and his fear, now David's fame had grown nationally. Even the Philistines recognized that name. He knew that his people adored the captain. *How can I not notice their stares and their dying conversations, the whispers when I walk by?* he asked himself. *They won't speak highly of him in front of me because they know.*

Several braziers and stone lanterns burned along the walls, making the place bright with quivering flames, though Saul thought it was still too dark. He had not seen Ahinoam in over a week and was frustrated at her absence. She was his wife and belonged at his side. He frowned with mute resentment.

Rizpah, Saul's concubine, was late with her monthly blood and the days passed slowly for him as he waited eagerly for the physician to tell him that she was with child.

Saul stopped walking when he heard sandals slapping against the cold limestone flooring above the soft sound of his shuffling. He faced the tall doors, and when Jonathan entered, he relaxed slightly, essaying a smile.

"Are you well, father?" Jonathan asked, and sat with his father comfortably on soft cushions.

"Do you know where your mother is?" Saul asked.

Jonathan nodded slowly. "She's with Malchi-shua."

"That woman ... " Saul said and Jonathan broke into his sentence before his father could say anything that would make him resent him.

He gripped his father's hand encouragingly. "She'll come back to you, Lib. We're all she has. Give her time. She'll return home when she has accepted Rizpah." Jonathan called his father by an intimate term—meaning *master of the house*—and Saul was surprised to hear it. His sons had not called him that since before they were young men. He sighed and smiled when he realized how much he depended on his eldest son.

"What can I do for you, my son?" Saul asked, grasping Jonathan's shoulder affectionately.

"Father, I have come to speak with you about my sister. Have you noticed the change in Michal?" Jonathan said.

"Jonathan, I'm busy ruling a kingdom. I can't be bothered with their ever-changing moods."

"It's more than that, father. Michal is in love with ..." Jonathan said and the name caught in his throat. He had Saul's attention immediately. "I didn't want to tell you, but Michal is hurting, and now that Merab is gone she is even more alone. I hear her cry every night, father. She thinks her pillow deadens her sobs."

"Is it David?" Saul asked in a measured voice, looking fixedly at the floor. Jonathan was taken aback by his father's question.

"How'd you know?" he drawled.

"So it's true, then?" Saul said almost to himself, and when the corners of his mouth lifted, Jonathan was surprised. "I've known about it for days now, Jonathan. Believe it if you will, but it was Rizpah who told me. She heard Michal crying his name late at night, and she asked me if it was the captain David ben Jesse. I couldn't believe it, and began asking my servants if they knew anything. Word came to me that a servant woman had seen them kissing in your mother's garden. I'm not angry, Jonathan."

"You never cease to amaze me, Lib," Jonathan said stunned. He had not expected this, and he laughed. "What will you do?"

"I didn't want to think about it. I needed to be certain," Saul lied brazenly. He had thought about it for days and he knew exactly what he would do. "Will you drink a cup of wine with me tonight?"

Jonathan understood his father's need to change the subject and rose to his feet. He poured the wine into goblets and handing a vessel to his father, sat on the cushions again.

They talked through the night as they did before the time of his dark moods and raging fits and Jonathan found himself hoping that the father that had raised him was returning to them.

Saul was alone again after his son had retired, and he sat watching the moving shadows fearfully, imagining the black, sulphuric beast of his dreams rising from the darkness. Suddenly, he saw the shade of a man stretching over him and he stumbled up from the cushions with dumb terror. He looked around and saw his spy dressed in a servant's plain linen halug, standing behind him in amused silence.

The king swore softly. "Where did you come from? How long have you been here, Zidka?" he snapped and closed the large doors of his court.

"Zidka has come from the bitterness of your heart, king, and I've been here long enough to admire that performance with your son. If I didn't know better, I would have believed it," the man said and fingered the red scar across his cheek, his eyes almost black. He grinned mockingly as he continued. "Why so many lanterns and braziers, my king? Afraid of the dark?" Saul gave him a glance that made him remember his place.

"What news of David?" he asked eagerly, bringing his mercenary spy deeper into the room. Zidka waited for a moment before answering. "Nothing, my lord. He was calm, as if he were reading any other letter. I coaxed him as much as possible without becoming obvious."

Saul swore and began pacing again. "Return to him and tell him that I have declared that on this day he shall be my son-in-law for a second time."

"Zidka could have slit his throat easily under the cover of night. Nobody would have found him until dawn, and by then Zidka would have been over the walls and back here to give you his head," the spy said confidently in fluent Hebrew, though Saul could hear his Philistine accent with certain words.

"No, I can't do that. There's a small chance it could lead back to me, and ruin everything. I won't take that risk. But I have a better way, Zidka," Saul said, pursing his lips. "My daughter will be a snare to him—and your people are going to smite him for me."

"The king is pleased with you and all of his servants love you. That's why now is a good time to wed Michal," Zidka whispered in the captain's ear. The sudden closeness made David slide his sword partially from the scabbard, anticipating a dagger coming from the herald's tunic. He looked at the man in surprise and could smell aniseed on his breath. Zidka noticed the blade, and the corners of his mouth turned up at the sight.

"Does it seem to you a simple thing to be the king's son-in-law?" David said, frowning. "I'm a poor man and little esteemed. I couldn't in all my days afford the bride-price." He hesitated, before pushing the kidon back in the scabbard, although he still kept his hand around the hilt, standing in such a way that the herald could see him do it.

Zidka stepped away and bowed, feeling the cold blade of his nine-inch dagger inside his tunic press against his skin with the movement.

"I will bring your words to the king, captain," Zidka said and David wondered at the man's subtle accent, and thought that he was a Philistine mercenary, although he couldn't be sure. He only stared at the herald as he stepped back to the door in three more bows, moving into the sunlight. The light shone on his back in such a way that David could make out the vague trace of a curved blade underneath his thin, translucent tunic and knew that he hadn't been wrong in his precaution. He didn't trust the man, and would not relax until he had left the garrison.

Eliab entered the room and David smiled at Zidka. "Officer Eliab will show you to the gates." Eliab wanted to say something, but he thought better of it, and his expression turned stern as he looked at the character standing beside him. Zidka nodded with a dutiful smile, and left with the officer.

Zidka would kill David without any payment from Saul, the assassin thought. *Zidka would do it for pleasure.*

The Sérèn of Ekron was returning home after spending the night with his whore-queen, and he swore under his breath when he did not see his slaves at his small palace. He would whip them himself, he vowed silently, and increased his pace. The first light of dawn washed the pale cobblestone street and he could hear the city begin to wake.

The prince slowed when he saw that there were no men on the walls and he feared that they were dead. He rushed into his home, vowing to cut open any man who dared harm his family.

The palace entrance was closed. He had to press firmly on the decorated doors before they finally swung slowly open on the hinges. The place had a strong odor and was deathly still. The rich silk drapes undulating in the wind were the only movement. He drew his iron sword and paced vigilantly through the empty house. Where was his family? He felt he couldn't breathe and his hands were shaking.

He gasped and his body went stiff when he saw a flow of blood dripping down the marble stairs. He followed the trail until it merged into a large puddle seeping from underneath a heavy stone door, and he could smell the stench coming from the room. The fear of learning what was causing the stink of death held him. He could not move. His heart was racing in his chest and sweat ran into his beard, turning cold in the draft.

Dark blood stained his leather sandals and he could feel the cold liquid ooze between his toes as he finally stepped closer and opened the door.

The prince stumbled back at the sight and when a full wave of the pungent air hit him, he doubled over retching. All his slaves and guards had been massacred in the room, and the walls and furniture were smeared and spattered red. The broken bodies had been piled in the center of the large room and fleshy limbs were strewn across the filthy floor. The room looked like a battlefield and he screamed savagely.

He fell to his knees, knowing that he would have to search the chamber for his family. As he rose, his eyes fell on the bed in the corner of the room. He gagged when he saw that a man had been savagely disemboweled and stretched across the bedding. The Sérèn covered his mouth with the back of his hand as his stomach lurched.

Suddenly he heard a terrifying scream coming through the window and he raced outside. Was somebody still alive?

"I have to save her," he said through heaving breaths. "She knows." He could hear more shouts and he ran faster than he thought possible, searching the gardens. The scream came from behind the outer walls, in the streets, and he darted around racing for the gate. He hoped he could face the man who did this. He would laugh as he cut him open.

The Sérèn tore around the corner and sprinted along the wall until he realized he was heading toward the other exit of his estate. The prince fixed his eyes on a male slave, holding a young woman, with three others looking horrified.

The slave girl, traumatized by what she had discovered on her way to the market at the city-center, cried into the man's shoulder, and he comforted her, his eyes not able to move from the hanging corpses.

"Don't hurt her, you animal. I'm going to kill you!" the Sérèn roared at who he believed was the slaughterer. The slave began to run when he saw the wild Sérèn come at him, but it was too late. The prince of Ekron did not even see his mutilated family, nailed broken and lifeless to the gates. He struck the fleeing man down with one blow to the side of the head and fell on him. Viciously, he hammered him to death until the bones in his fist broke from the blows. It did not seem as if the Sérèn of Ekron even felt it as he panted over the smashed slave. Spittle had thickened in his mouth and he spat it onto what used to be a face.

The disheveled prince glared at the women with red eyes and they shrank back. He kicked the man one last time and when he approached the women, appearing malignant and evil, two ran from him. He snatched the remaining woman at both shoulders and screamed at her, shaking her. "What happened? Where is my family?"

The slave girl could not speak, looking pale with shock at the bloody man. Tears washed her face, as she managed to lift her arm shakily and point to the black gate.

The Sérèn of Ekron's eyes fell on his family, and his hands slipped from her.

He fell to his knees below them and when he touched his eldest son's cold twisted feet, he wept.

Others gathered around the gates, but he did not see them. He moaned in such a way that the slave could not understand what he was saying.

As the Sérèn looked up at their bodies, he could see the emblem on Achish's ring imprinted in their skin and he bit down on his teeth in madness as he realized that the king had personally beaten his family to death.

His sight turned to blackness and he could no longer remember anything.

CHAPTER FOURTEEN

hree scouts finally approached him through the long winter grasses. David had sent them out to the nearest Philistine garrison, and he had been waiting for days in the field for their return.

"A cohort marches, captain. There are more than one hundred. I estimate close to three-hundred," the scout hissed. David nodded and the man took up his place with his band of fighters.

David rushed through the fields and gave Pelet the signal. "They're coming; ready the men," he said to Eliab, and clapped him on the back.

Saul had informed David that he did not require any bride-price for his daughter, but wanted David to bring him the foreskins of a hundred Philistines. He had given him two weeks to accomplish this. David and his brothers had discussed their tactics and decided that to move the entire Gibbôr regiment would be unnecessary and expensive. They had chosen a hundred of the best slingers, javelin throwers, and swordsmen, and rode out across the Philistine borders into Gath. It had been a long week in the enemy fields, with only cold rations and no fires to warm them at night. The early morning gusts and frost were the worst part for the men, and David had to keep up their morale with promises of new ranks.

The loose formation of Philistines marched along an overgrown dirt pass, fully armored and deadly. Gibbôr had to hide in the dry grasses from their searching scouts, and David was thankful that they had missed them, although a soldier had been inches from discovering one of his men.

For some tense moments he could hear the cohort of soldiers marching before he gained sight of them, and suddenly he felt uncertain.

They outnumber us three to one, even though we have the element of surprise, he thought tensely. They could easily lose the battle, but he had prayed to God for success and he believed in his fighters. He resolved to fight.

With a deep roar, David came from the grassland, spinning his sling above his head and shooting a stone at their officer. The missile crushed his skull and he went down with a piercing cry, his tarnished copper helmet useless. The air crackled with small stone projectiles and Philistine bodies broke in agonizing pain. Several javelins arched through the air, tearing into leather and flesh, blood spattering.

Without their officer giving orders, the Philistines began to panic and would have retreated if a commander did not rally them. David had ordered his slingers scattered across the fields, and the Philistine commander could not form a defensive line against them. They were surrounded.

They had dealt a crushing blow and David did not hesitate as he gave the order for the melee. Israelites came from the thick grass closer than the Philistines had expected, and broke through their shields with heavy blows. David kept shouting orders as he hacked at a Philistine, twisting away from a descending sword.

Slowly, the Israelites tightened the circle, stabbing through bloody armor.

"Retreat!" a commander screamed and ran, dodging blades and spears, but one of David's men stabbed him in the back with a kidon. As the Philistines dispersed, the killing became easier. David did not keep his blade still for a moment and ordered his men to kill everyone in the rout before they could alert their garrison. If not, they would have hundreds of warriors hunting them down before nightfall.

It felt like mere minutes as his men hunted down every fleeing man, cutting them to pieces. Within an hour, they had won.

Waiting for a number, David had tried to clean off as much of the blood as he could. He had helped dress many wounds and he grunted as the deep cut on his thigh burned underneath temporary bandages. Eliab stood beside him and they were both quiet. His brother's eye was swollen and crimson, and David saw red stains form on the strips of linen covering a laceration on his chest. The scene was desolate; his men were black with blood-soaked mud and nobody spoke.

Pelet brought the number to David. "Two hundred and eleven Philistines dead, not including the routed corpses in the fields, and thirty-two of us killed. All the wounds have been treated and cleaned as thoroughly as possible, but we'll have to make haste for the garrison, or the physicians will have to amputate limbs tainted with the sickness of the flesh. If fever doesn't kill us first."

"Thank you, Pelet. You fought bravely, and we had a good victory." Pelet didn't have any wounds, but had several bruises already turning purple.

David nodded and moved to where he had left a large linen bag and picked it up carefully, trying to spare himself as much pain as possible, although he could feel the cut bleed again under the tight bindings with his every move.

As he walked, he pulled a dagger from his bronze belt, and stopped at a Philistine, staring hesitantly down at the body. Curling his upper lip in disgust, he began harvesting the foreskins.

Eliab ordered the men, and without a complaint or sound, knives were unsheathed.

Under an amber moon, David came for his bride. A breath of air chilled his bare skin in the late hours of the night as he walked through the dark streets of Gibeah with his three elder brothers, Jonathan, his nephews, and Pelet at his side. They carried clay oval vessel lamps for him, lighting the way.

A week prior, according to the agreement, David had delivered the foreskins to Saul in front of his entire court. He had seen fear in the old king's face, then hatred. Saul had been reserved and seemed vexed as he announced David's marriage to Michal publicly, and then dismissed David coldly without the expected festivities or ceremonial wine drinking. David had bowed respectfully, and then left the royal court eagerly. He had not seen the king since, but had heard that Saul had screamed with rage moments after he left. He had dwelt on the matter for days. Word of the forthcoming royal marriage spread like wildfire through all the regions, and the son of Jesse was hailed as a prince of Israel.

Now as his marriage was imminent, David imagined the sight of his bride, clothed in traditional marital attire. He was anxious as he moved stiffly out in front of the groomsmen, although he enjoyed the emotion of tense expectation melded with euphoria. It was almost unreal. David was dressed in an embroidered crimson vesture hanging to his ankles and bound at the waist with a thick leather belt. His hair had been oiled back and his skin massaged with scented emollients. He looked like a prince among his company of eight men.

For the first time in years, he did not have his kidon at his side and he felt awkward without its weight on his belt.

As they approached the walls of the estate, David unlocked the gates with a large bronze key, under the favorable eyes of the watch-guards, and walked down the side of the fortress palace. David brought the silver mouthpiece of the traditional shofar to his lips and blew the ram's horn loudly, notifying the women that he was coming.

Suddenly his palms were sweating when he saw her looking at him from underneath a stone arch-window, the light of a dim lantern washing her shapely figure.

Michal. She was his, finally.

The princess was splendid in her apparel, dressed and laced with gold and white. Every piece of cloth had been embroidered. Even her veil glittered with tiny red cornelian gemstones and fine beads of silver and a delicate meshed circlet held up her hair, braided and twisted into a knot. Sheer purple silk flowed from the golden headpiece. Her skin shimmered with gold dust and her cheeks were powdered rose and her lips painted vermillion. The rims of her eyelids were black with kohl and her nails had been colored orange-red with henna dye.

David blew the horn again and when he saw his betrothed leave the lattice window, he began unconsciously pressing and rubbing his hands together as he waited nervously.

A line of bridesmaids came from the palace in pure white, glowing in the dancing light of their olive oil lamps. When Michal came out last, David realized he was holding his breath and inhaled deeply.

Without a word, the princess came to him and he took her hands and kissed them tenderly. Michal could hear the weeping of the women at her back. She smiled at her husband and, in a joyful procession, they left for the ceremonial wedding chamber that Jesse had prepared for them, as was the custom. The residents of Gibeah came from their homes and lined the streets where the couple walked, playing melodiously on large rattles, whistles, and kinnors.

The house was full of guests when David and Michal entered, and Michal laughed blissfully.

David looked across his company, and they all nodded to him, their eyes bright. Michal laughed when Eliab urged his brother into the marriage chamber with a brisk wave of his hand.

David smiled at Michal lovingly and led her into the large room. When they closed the doors, they could hear a loud cheer.

David pulled his bride to him, and kissed her passionately. She had cleaned her teeth with aniseed and her mouth tasted of the warm, sweet licorice. She wrapped her arms around his back and David moved her to the bedside. He looked deeply into her eyes and felt his heart quicken.

He took his time undressing her, kissing her skin in such a way that his lips barely touched her. Her lustrous hair flowed over her shoulders and the heat of her skin and closeness of her lithe body excited him. Michal caressed his body and watched curiously as he loosened his belt. She unfastened two fibulae on his shoulder and his robe fell to the floor. She had seen his muscled torso and brawny abdomen before, and she touched the war scars on his body delicately.

She trembled when he lifted her dress from her.

She took his hand into hers when he began untying the straps that held her inner tunic, stopping him with nervous hesitation. No man had ever laid eyes on what was beneath her protective garments and she was untouched by their hands.

David kissed her again and she allowed him to loosen the cotton slip, gasping softly as her undergarment fell to her ankles. She stood awkwardly before him, virginally covering herself with cupped hands.

David lowered her onto the bed. Michal could feel his warm body as he began to make love to her, and although she was too tense to enjoy the experience, she loved David with all her being.

She touched his face and watched his intense green eyes, her breath quickening.

Pain shot through her at the moment of consummation and she clenched her jaw against the sensation and cried out softly. Despite the burning and stinging, she would not let him know it, but allowed herself to moan at the uncomfortable soreness. David groaned with pleasure and was done.

He opened his eyes and looked at her, their breath hot against each other. He kissed her brow and Michal could see the love in his eyes as she pressed her lips against his.

David got up from bed and moved to the door. Michal felt strange, almost defiled and dirty. She could not understand her emotions. She loved him, she told herself, sitting up and trying to hide the slight show of blood on the sheets.

David knocked once and a voice came from the other side.

"Our marriage has been consummated," he said to Eliab through the narrow cracks of the wooden door, and he could hear him make the announcement. The guests let out a great cheer, and began celebrating with food and drink.

Husband and wife remained together in the chamber for seven days as the guests feasted, and only after a week, would they emerge and have a final celebratory meal with their friends and family.

David turned to her, but Michal could not look at him. He came to the bed and she shied away, trying to cover her body. David frowned at this, trying to understand. He put his hand at the back of her neck and stroked her cheek with his thumb. Michal shifted her eyes to him, and his adoration made her feel slightly better about herself.

When David brushed a lock of hair from her face, she kissed him deeply, and suddenly sank into his embrace and cried softly into his bare shoulders. He could still smell the lavender in her hair as he rested his head on hers, and he closed his eyes, fighting tears.

Chapter Fifteen

Jonathan was happy to be returning to the garrison at Elah
Valley, his soldiers, to his life there, and the familiarity
of war. They were weeks late in returning, but they had
been delayed with everything that happened during the five
months in Gibeah.

He felt the gentle wind brush the soft fur of his halug
against his skin, and he smiled warmly at his father and mother
standing on the wide steps of the palace. He could hear his son
gurgling in his mother's arms and he wondered if he would
see the child again before he could walk. It stung at his heart
fiercely.

The prince's eyes fell on the shy woman standing by
the wide doors. He could not hate Rizpah; she was merely
a participant in her father's and the king's transactions. He
nodded to her but she lowered her eyes. He felt sorry for the
girl. He could only imagine what she must have gone through
at the fortress-palace, and he knew she would still have to
endure a great many things. Jonathan knew he could not
resent his father for claiming his right to another wife, though
the pain it had caused his mother was a different matter. If he
ever had to marry again, he would never have more than one
spouse.

Michal rushed from the house and flung her arms around David, holding him close. She cried as he kissed her intensely. It would be months before he would see her again, and for the first time David understood the wretchedness the royal family must have felt so many times before when they left for war. They had only been together as husband and wife for a week, and he would miss her terribly. Jonathan had suggested that he stay with his new wife for the first year of their marriage before returning to the military, as was the law. His pining for his new wife would create a sense of longing among the ranks for their own loved ones, and that would be bad for morale, Jonathan had said.

But he was a captain before a husband.

David glanced at Saul and saw the king's eyes gleam dangerously. He gasped softly at the deadly stare. Finally, he had seen the bare and complete truth.

David was puzzled at the shifting expression until he realized it was fear he saw, noticing the king trying to repress it. Saul smiled deceptively and shifted his gaze to Abner, hoping that David had not seen the look on his face. But David had seen the hate in his eyes, and knew that he had to leave Gibeah as quickly as possible. In an instant, it became horribly clear to him. No matter how much he wanted to, there was no denying it—Saul longed for his death.

Michal quickly composed herself, drying her tears with her hand, and then embraced her brother firmly. She whispered eternal gratitude in his ear and after she had kissed his hand, she hurried to the roof to wave them farewell when they rode from the city, as was their custom. David watched his wife run into the house and then climbed onto his mount stiffly.

Jonathan had known that his brothers wouldn't be there, and he sighed with the reality that he hadn't been wrong in thinking the worst of them.

Saul had decided that he would remain at the palace, and regular letters from Abner would keep him informed.

The many events of the past winter had made Jonathan tired and he would not spend a day longer in Gibeah than necessary. It had been the longest months of his life. So much had happened—his father's attack on David, both Michal and Merab had wed, David was a captain now, and a prince. He had ridden out to the garrison and had returned to deliver the fleshy bride-price for Michal to his father. Saul's disposition grew worse every day, and for once, Jonathan would not have to write the letters telling of the king's illness, but receive them.

So many things in the city still reminded him of Achsa, and his family had become strangers to him. It would be good for him to break away. He needed it. He also knew it was strange for him to feel this way.

He mounted his horse and with a final wave, circled the horse tightly, and cantered towards the city gates.

The soldiers had already gathered there, and he was anxious to meet up with them. Abner and David were silent, and he understood why. It would be months before they would see their loved ones again, and he sighed inwardly with nostalgia. Jonathan heard his sister call out to them from the flattop roof, and he waved to her a final time. David gripped the pommel of his saddle and turned in his seat, gazing at his wife.

The soldiers were well rested and in marching formation when they reached the heavy arch of the town gates. They were the finest warriors in all Israel: one hundred of the best from Saul's nucleus of three thousand war men—his ben-hayil. Their well-oiled armor gleamed and their old weapons had been melted down and recast, and were impressive at their sides.

As Jonathan marched them at an easy pace, he did not look back. Everything that had happened at the palace during the terrible winter would remain there.

David brought his horse alongside Jonathan's white stallion. "Would you mind if I ride out with the scouts, brother? I need to think for awhile," he asked gazing out over the golden hills in the distance.

"If that is what you want to do, I will not stop you, my brother," Jonathan said. "You know you can talk to me, if something is troubling you."

"I know, Jonathan. You and my brother are the people I trust most. Let me first understand what it is that is unsettling me, and then I will speak to you about it. I think I'm going to ride out to the fort on my own. I will see that the men prepare for your arrival."

Jonathan nodded and knew better than to press the matter. David would come to him when he was ready.

David took a deep breath and with a sharp sound spurred the gelding into a gallop.

The garrison was a greater comfort than he had imagined and he rode in with more confidence than he had two months ago, nodding at the saluting watchmen. Without looking at the young man, David ordered a servant to inform the garrison-master that their prince was returning. Without thinking, he cantered his horse through the network of pathways and buildings to the stables, his leather armor burning his skin in the heat of the afternoon.

He wondered when he would see the walls of Gibeah again—the coming winter perhaps?

If he had his way, he would have taken Michal to Bethlehem, his birth town, to see his sons come of age on the stony, green valleys below the rolling hills, oblivious to Saul's dark moods, and away from the king's private hate and murderous schemes. It was a dream, he knew.

David had barely been at the garrison an hour when a soldier, running to him, brought him out of his musing. The man, covered in a light film of dust, saluted him and stood to attention. David recognized him; it was one of the mercenary-spies he had sent into the city of Ekron before he had retired the first time to Gibeah for the winter months.

"What news, soldier?" David asked. The man looked nervous.

"Their armies march, my captain. The entire military force of Philistia is coming for us," he said anxiously, focusing his eyes on his captain.

David shouted orders as he began walking. "Sound the horn! Inform the captains and tell them to gather in the campaign room. Dispatch heralds to the towns and cities. I want every man of fighting age and capable of waging war at this garrison before the sun sets tomorrow."

Weeks had passed with deliberations and preparations. Spies had delivered information about numbers, and David and Jonathan had privately discussed geographical elements and tactics, and had planned strategies and arranged the forces.

The sun scorched the rocky Elah Valley and the horizon seemed to quiver as heat radiated from the dusty earth. Scattered stones and rocks shone under the burning rays and David stank from his own sweat gleaming on his skin. All of his men were damp and hot as they stood in rectangular formation.

Their eyes were focused into the distance, waiting. They could hear the battle horns of the approaching armies echoing through the hot air, and the power of their march would have made any soldier shrink. But not Gibbôr. Not his Mighty Men. David would have their rank if they cowered; they would be disgraced and relieved of their duty. The years of killing, all the adversity and sacrifices, everything they had fought for would have been gone in an instant of cowardice.

David stood in front of his unit and looked down the line of thirty-seven captains, standing like statues in the killing heat. He was clad in a bronze breastplate and a chain mail skirt. David glanced back at his officers. They had faces like lions and their fierce expressions reassured him. He guessed where his brothers Nethaneel, Raddai, and Ozem were in the ranks. They were already esteemed commanders. Having all six of his older brothers with him always gave him a sense of bravado.

His nephews appeared calm and he wondered if they would hold through the attack. They had never been in the midst of battle, and it could be a terrifying place, he knew. Joab had a glint of aggressiveness in his eyes, and David smiled at the man. He was the only one of the three he would rely upon in the heat of battle. It was his tenacity and grit that made him like the young officer. They were of one blood, and he would make them generals when he became king, he told himself. He set his jaw against a pang of guilt, but suppressed it as he swept his gaze along the torrid Elah Valley.

He recalled over two years ago when the two countries had faced each other exactly where they stood now. How immature he had been then. *I am a different man now,* he thought. He could see the wild killers shouting at them across the distance in his mind's eye and he felt his heart race with excitement. With God's aid he had slain Goliath, and his countrymen loved him for it. He had fought and won many great battles since, and now he had come full circle as a captain, treasured by the twelve tribes. A prince of Israel. The turpentine trees and shrubs seemed to wilt under his gaze.

Then he heard the call again; they were close.

David closed his eyes as he took in the rich scent. "Slingers ready," he cried out so that the entire Israelite military could hear him. The other captains repeated the order one after the other and he heard the soldiers emerge from their units behind him. David would not wait for the Philistine's negotiations. He would strike abruptly when they did not expect it.

"Slingers, march!" he roared. As one, over a thousand men marched across the burning sands and formed a wide line at the bottom of a steep ridgeline. Dead grass covered the highland and the men loaded their leather strips with clay bullets and lowered themselves into the dense fields.

A single Philistine horseman rode along the crest and was joined by four others. They scouted the Israelite defense force. Their horses whinnied and reared as the men shouted back a report in Semitic to their captains, then disappeared behind the mountain.

There were tense moments as David waited for the Philistines. The Israelites could hear their savage screams and war horns, and David searched the faces of his men for any traces of fear. He screamed out over the valley and Gibbôr let out a roar. The men hammered their spears against their shields and the crashing sound filled the dry air.

Finally, a line of silhouetted figures appearing across the stony crest silenced the Israelites and the Philistines shouted wildly, their shadows falling over the hidden slingers. Their armor and weapons shot flashes of light across the valley, and still David waited.

His men were silent behind him. He looked at Ehud and lifted his fist up to the captain. Ehud returned the signal.

"Units ready!" David shouted, and waited for the rest of the captains to repeat the order. He brought a curved shofar to his lips and blew on the golden mouthpiece. The sound of the ram's horn went unnoticed by the Philistines, but the slingers came from the grass with loud screams.

Before they could react, the sky became dark with raining clay pellets and the front lines of the Philistines dropped away in a wave of death. The slingers were quick and intermittently launched hundreds of projectiles again, and then swiftly retreated sideways before their enemies could recover and retaliate.

Within moments, however, Philistine missiles rained down on the last of the escaping Israelites, killing many on contact. The Philistine's masses of hardened warriors surged over the highland, their spears upraised. David could imagine the panic his captains must have felt as the thunderous din of the sudden Philistine charge deadened his orders to halt. His stratagem was working and David beckoned them to him, grinning.

He ordered his men to hold their positions, feeling numb with the anticipation of the strike. David gauged the distance of the assailing warriors, feeling the tension build among his ranks as the enemy stormed, but he knew they would not dare falter. He held his hands up signaling them to wait.

David wondered briefly at the limited size of the enemy, fearing that Achish had reserves and would deploy them in strategic attacks.

"There have to be others," David whispered. There was no way he could get to Jonathan, he knew. He trusted that the prince had also noticed the Philistine numbers and would act accordingly. *Jonathan will send out scouts,* David assured himself. The thought was soon lost.

With another blow of the shofar, archers stepped from the lines of infantry, and nocked their bows. David had to time the order perfectly. If he called it too early, the arrows would fall short, and if too late, the Philistines would hurl their spears.

Suddenly the crest turned black with horses and David had to think quickly. He had not expected cavalry so soon; they would devastate his infantry if they were to reach them. At that moment, the warriors came into range and he brought down his arm in a wide swing.

Hundreds of wooden shafts quivered through the air. The dead Philistines fell to the ground, and warriors stumbled over their fallen comrades, breaking bones, screams cutting through the chaos.

"Again!" he shouted lowering his hand with the command, and more arrows brought over half of the ascending masses down. After a final flight of bolts, David ordered the archers back.

"Infantry! Shields!" he roared as Philistine spears arched through the sky tainted with red. Iron thudded against hard leather, some tearing into Israelite flesh, others embedding themselves into the baked earth. David cursed under his breath, as he saw the cavalry turning left. They were trying to flank him, and it could break his forces if he did not act.

It had taken all of his will not to order the third of his men that he had hiding in the fields, reserved for flanking the enemy, to retreat before the horses. He fretted over how many of them were being trampled to death by iron hooves.

The Philistines crashed into the Israelite units.

David slashed open a throat, and turned on his heel to block a sudden thrust at his side. He pushed his kidon forward, cutting into the large man's abdomen. The man grunted and fell forward.

David hacked left and right, sending men down with deadly precision. Metal clanged as a blade sliced against his bronze shoulder, and he rounded on the man and killed him with a twist of his sickle-sword.

From the corner of his eye, he saw Asahel pressing back two men, and with a quick jolt stabbed a warrior in his thick beard. Blood splattered his armor, and he focused on the remaining fighter. David rushed in when he saw a man aim for Asahel's back, and he forced his blade into the fighter's ribs. Asahel turned when he heard the scream behind him and saw his enemy dropping to the ground. David simply nodded to him, and then was gone in the swell of battling soldiers.

David blew three short notes on his shofar and with that, his hidden army moved from the grasses and began stabbing into horseflesh. He could see the cavalry breaking through the side of his units, and he was lost again in fighting.

His arms were burning and he felt as if he could not go on. He drove his sword through leather, and the man died on his blade.

David could not believe it. The entire enemy force was dead. He gazed around the tired Israelites, grabbed his horn hanging at his side, slippery with blood, and blew the victory sound.

The warriors screamed in passionate triumph. Gibbôr began chanting his name through the cheers and soon the entire army was calling out to him. It was an unbelievable experience.

David could not see the look of resentment on Ehud's face, his lips moving in silent indignation. He had also fought with them, he grumbled, he had been a captain far longer.

David was brought from his idle enjoyment when he understood suddenly why the Philistine offensives had been so small. He felt his stomach drop at the realization, and he gasped in horror.

"Have the captains meet me in the campaign room, now," he ordered a strong fighter, and left him as he ran to Jonathan astride a horse on the outskirts of the battlefield.

Ehud's anger swelled inside of him at the newly commissioned captain's authority, and his knuckles turned white as he gripped the hilt of his sword.

"It was a ruse," David said to the council of bloody captains and they broke into rowdy objections. "I believe ..." But the men continued shouting. David raised his hands for silence. "... I believe we have only defeated a decoy force, meant to deceive us into mustering our forces and leaving our cities defenseless. With this victory, they had us thinking that we have won once again. They are playing our egos like a kinnor and we fell right into their snare. They will attack again, and with all of our men assembled here in the Elah Valley, they will walk straight into our cities." The men discussed this among themselves noisily, and David searched their faces.

"What makes you think this?" Jonathan asked above the discussions, and their voices died suddenly.

"My informant told me that the entire Philistia force was marching out against us. That would mean far more than tens of thousands of warriors, but according to my scouts, we fought roughly nine thousand. Where were the rest? It was only a detachment. Think about it," David said to Jonathan, and then paused to let the captains consider his words. "This battle was meant to distract us while they march around us. They're going to attack our cities."

The council of captains gasped collectively, and only then did David see their faces flush with alarm.

"If they have our cities, they have our families, our land, ... our lives. They will force us to give them back the trade routes and the highland passes," an old captain said suddenly, standing up from his stool.

"They will have us under an iron heel, slaves to their mercy," another said.

Ehud glared at David through narrowed eyes. "Is this informant a Philistine?" he asked.

"He is, Ehud, and what of it?"

"How do you know Achish didn't buy him over? A king can be very persuasive when you are captured for treachery," Ehud asked, his eyes cold.

"His loyalty is beyond questioning," David said, and Ehud broke into his sentence.

"Why? Why is he beyond questioning, David?" he said menacingly and rose from his seat. "Is it because he is the spy of the great David ben Jesse? The killer of Goliath, the conqueror of Philistia." He rapped his knuckles on the low table.

"Captain Ehud, contain yourself or you will be dismissed from this council," Jonathan snapped. Ehud lowered his eyes to the table, taking a deep breath as he calmed himself. He knew that his outburst was a display of weakness, and he regretted his anger.

"Bring him in for questioning then, if that will soothe your animosity. I won't object." David said evenly. "My men have fought valiantly, and they wait for me outside. I don't know about all of you, but I will take my regiment and march to Bethlehem. I will defend my birth town, if it isn't too late already. Talk all you want, it will serve you nothing. But if we do not act, we might again suffer under Philistine tyranny before the winter chills our flesh." David did not wait for a reply, and left the men debating heatedly behind him.

David stepped on the head of a Philistine corpse and pulled his sword from the chest. He looked out over the open lands of Judah, shaking with exhaustion, closing his eyes as he caught the scent of the wild flowers over the stink of butchered flesh. David's body was covered in cuts and bruises and he did not know how much of the blood on his skin was his own. Many of his men hunched onto their swords, were covered in gore. They were too tired to cheer, and eventually, without David's command, began searching the battlefield littered with bodies for their own dead, as the sun set on the horizon.

Finally, after months, they had won.

After a heated and swift debate, Jonathan had commanded that each captain march at double pace in the hope of catching Achish's' armies. David and three other captains were dispatched to the lands of Judah, and it was on Israelite soil that he had fought with King Achish. He saw the fat king for the first time then, standing on a chariot in the distance and he had laughed at the sight of him. The man was as large as he had heard.

That day the armies had battled for almost an entire day, losing roughly six eleph of warriors. They routed the Philistines as darkness fell, which made it impossible for David to pursue them into the black night. He knew he would fight the king again; it was what he would have done.

By dawn, David had sent out trackers and as he had believed, Achish had regrouped his men and marched deeper into Judah. David made haste to follow, and after trailing them at a grueling pace, they waged war for the second time only a few miles from the city of Hebron.

The Israelites had outnumbered the Philistines two to one, but the enemy was fierce in combat, and it would have been only a narrow victory if the old war veterans of Hebron had not come from their city and flanked Achish's forces. After that, it had been total slaughter. The king had fled at the head of small group of cavalry and David sent a group of riders after them to make sure they had returned to Philistia.

David moved among his men, clapping the warriors on the back that he had seen fighting valiantly. They were his family, he said to one man, and then he began searching for his officers. It would be a long night before they had sorted out the dead, and he would not rest until he knew that the fat king had left Israel.

Another summer had passed and the trees were brilliant shades of brown and gold, leaves wafting across the plains on dusty palls. After months of marching and waging war, he prepared himself to return home to his wife—and to Saul and his blind hatred. But not before he saw his parents; it was a much delayed visit.

It would be an interesting winter, he told himself, chuckling, and then he heard Pelet call out to him.

CHAPTER SIXTEEN

"I have spoken to all my servants, Jonathan. They will smite David before he steals my crown." Saul said sadistically, and enjoyed the shock he saw on his son's face. "I won't be surprised if they assassinate him tonight."

Jonathan could not speak and the hate in his father's expression made him cautious.

"All my servants had the same reaction when I told them," Saul continued. "What about this man makes you all adore him so? If I could, I would kill him with my own bare hands, but he's loved by all Israel. The masses would see me dethroned for my evil deed, and we wouldn't want that, would we, Jonathan?"

The king was quiet for a time, his wild eyes boring into the prince. He leaned in closer, and Jonathan flinched, though he held his father's intense glare.

"Jonathan, prove to me that you came from my loins. Show me that my blood flows through your veins," Saul whispered, and was silent for a second. "Murder him for me, Jonathan. He won't expect it from you. He trusts you, and your dagger will be like poison on honeyed dates. He will love the sweet taste, and when it's too late, the venom will make his mouth foam, and his body jerk, and he will *die*," Saul said smiling deviously at the image.

When his son did not react the way he imagined, he snapped at him, sitting forward on his throne. "He is going to take your inheritance from you, Jonathan! He will take my crown, and you and your descendants will be commoners. Do you understand that?"

Jonathan lowered his eyes. "How can you ask such a thing of me?" Jonathan had seen his father's hate grow since he had tried to kill David. The notion that David would dethrone him had never left Saul. To Jonathan's shock, he had learned that his father had privately harbored the consuming emotion of an ominous paranoia, and it had festered and swollen with time until it finally spewed bitterly from him. The king would not think rationally any more and was dominated by his rage and resentment, fueled by David's ever-increasing fame and success.

"That is why you are weak, Jonathan," Saul sneered viciously. "Get out of my sight."

Jonathan stared at his father in surprise. Feeling the sting of Saul's words, he rose and bowed. "As you will, my king." Saul ground his teeth and felt like slapping his eldest son. Saul hated all who dissented with him, and he was cruelly vocal in his bitterness.

You are paranoid, Jonathan thought sadly. *David would have killed you by now if he wanted. You cannot prove your accusations, father. David is a good man.*

The prince left without another word, slowing his pace, hoping that his father would call him back. Jonathan paused briefly as he reached the door, and when he was not summoned, he sighed in disappointment, and left the throne room purposefully.

Michal slept beside David, the sheets partially covering her naked body. He gazed at her, and then pulled the soft cloth over her shoulders. She was his wife, and it still seemed unreal to him.

He rose from the bed and before dressing, he moved to a clay jug and washed his body with icy water. Despite the blazing fire on the hearth, the room felt cold now that he did not have the blankets to warm him. Shivering, he dressed in thick woolen garments and wrapped a fur cloak around his shoulders. He made sure that Michal was warm and then left, looking at her again before leaving their home.

It was a fierce winter and the cold tore at his skin. Rain clouds threatened the city. As David rounded a corner, suddenly a man called out his name in a rough whisper and moved into a filthy side street. As he turned toward the voice, David unconsciously gripped his kidon, his fingers numb with frost, and waited for the man to appear from the darkness. The flames of torches greased with animal fat flickered in the cold breeze, and the moving shadows and sound of dripping water gave his surroundings an element of danger.

"David, it's me, Jonathan," the voice came again when the prince noticed David's hand on his hilt. He was hiding in the black alleyway and called him into the darkness. David let his hand drop from the sword, frowning. Why would the prince of Israel want to meet him under the cover of night in such conditions?

Slowly he walked to his brother and when Jonathan grabbed his upper arm, he knew it had something to do with Saul. Jonathan's stare made him flinch slightly.

"Saul, my father, wants to kill you. David, I pray you, take heed until morning, and hide yourself. Stay in a secret place," he said and increased his grip, hurting the captain's arm. David stared at him.

"I will speak to my father about you. And what I find out, I will tell you. The barley fields, tomorrow afternoon."

Jonathan walked past the captain, as if nothing had happened. David stared after the prince until the gloom of the street swallowed him.

He looked over his shoulder to make sure nobody had seen them, realizing the peril he was in. Abruptly, the place he felt safest, became unsafe for him, and his stiff fingers did not leave the hilt of his sword as he left.

"Do not sin against David, your servant, father, because he has not wronged you. In truth, his works have been extremely beneficial to you, my king," Jonathan said, heedless of the light rain falling on them.

Saul snorted at the words like a small child, and looked across his lands. The coldness seemed to abate Saul's temper and Jonathan pressed the matter.

"He risked his life when he slew the Philistines, and the Lord wrought a great salvation for all Israel. You saw it and you rejoiced with us, father," Jonathan whispered, and waited for the king to look at him. "Why then will you sin against innocent blood, to slay David without any reason?"

Saul sighed and his eyes changed. Jonathan verbalized some of the many conflicting thoughts raging in the king's own mind, and to hear his eldest son voice his private arguments made him realize what he had been doing to himself, to his family. He was miserable in his depression, and he nodded, clenching his jaw as he held back tears.

"It is true what you say, Jonathan."

Jonathan saw his father's shoulders droop and when Saul looked at him, he could see guilt in his eyes. He embraced his father, comforting him with gentle clapping on the back.

"I swear, Jonathan, as the Lord lives, he shall not be slain," Saul said shivering. "I have been through a dark time, my son. A dark time."

"You are a good king, Lib. And you are going to be a father again soon," Jonathan said relinquishing his father's hold. Saul smiled at the words, and stroked his son's hair. "Love your children with Rizpah as you loved us, father, and let me care for the rest. I am loyal to you first, my king. And when I know that any man wants to harm our family without cause, I will tell you, and we will have his head."

"That is why you will be king after me, Jonathan. Not your brothers, not your sisters' husbands. You are my light. Have I ever told you that?" Saul said and he saw Jonathan stand taller. The prince could not speak, though Saul could see the rapture in his eyes, and he chuckled.

"Will you not say anything?" Saul asked, clasping his son's shoulder.

"It is a great honor, my king," Jonathan said and prostrated himself before Saul on the cold earth. "But it is too soon to make such a decision. You still have many years on the throne, Lib. And when you are old, and you still favor me, only then will I wear your crown."

When Jonathan called out to David in the barley fields, the rain had cleared and the sun shone weakly through rolling clouds. The earth was clean and Jonathan breathed in the distinctive smell of rain and wet grass. His tunic was black with mud. Under the thin sunlight he was freezing, his lips blue.

David appeared, and Jonathan walked up to him thinking of his father's words. He was cold, and his skin around his jaw was a light purple. He was quaking with the cold, and they were both wet from the rain.

The sight of him made David expect the worst. *Saul is after my blood,* David decided, and felt his world crumble around him.

As the prince neared him, he said, "My father has called back the order on your head. You are safe, my friend."

"What did you say to him?" David asked, kissing Jonathan's hand.

"I said that he shouldn't sin by killing you because you are innocent, my brother," Jonathan said plainly, drawing out the word slightly, and he looked at David with deep affection. "And that you have done many things for Israel."

David laughed, and slapped Jonathan on the shoulder. The prince took the blow without a word, and chuckled.

"Come, I will take you to him. It is high time you two reconciled. But first, some dry clothes and a hot meal before a scorching fire. I think he needs some time to reflect."

Saul shook his head involuntarily as he saw David. He had thought about what Jonathan said, but though he wanted to believe it, he couldn't. Even in the few hours since they spoke, he had felt his old thoughts and emotions return. He had nothing left but his hate and misery.

Although he pretended for both Jonathan and the son of Jesse, he remained suspicious of David. He remembered Samuel's words again, and they weighed down on him like lead.

"My lad, come to me. I am truly sorry for all that I have done to you," Saul said, his voice breaking with emotion and he opened his arms in a wide embrace. David gripped him powerfully. It seemed that the old king had forgiven him.

In all your days, you shall not have it, David, Saul thought privately as he crushed David to him—*never. I'll have your head first.*

David's breath quivered through his lips as he fought with his thoughts. He could never tell them about Samuel, he resolved. David glanced at Jonathan over Saul's shoulders, and the prince saw his face was heavy with guilt.

Jonathan narrowed his eyes, frowning with sudden suspicion.

Eliab and his brothers sat closely together around a brazier, turning their hands above warming flames that were consuming the dark logs. The tent shook with heavy rain beating against the stout canvas and the air seemed to freeze as it left their lips.

"Will this tent never become warm?" Abinadab said and wrapped a woolen cloak around his body, holding his hands closer to the fire.

"Stop your complaining, brother. If you want to sweat in the middle of winter, go home and make love to your wife. You chose this life, and I don't remember you grumbling so much when you got your monthly wages," Eliab said taciturnly, and Shammah laughed.

Abinadab curled his lip, and dismissed his eldest brother's words with a grunt. Eliab's lips turned up at the reaction, and he leaned forward into the escaping warmth of the fire.

A cold breeze nearly killed the flames as a messenger, drenched from the rain, stepped into the tent. All three men reacted with shouts for him to close the flaps behind him, instinctively pulling fur and wool tighter to their skins against the biting wind.

The man was blue around the lips and trembled as he saluted Eliab and the commanders. He looked longingly at the fire, and Eliab nodded. The messenger threw off his wet tunic and huddled naked before the glowing brazier until he could control his shuddering. After his skin had dried, Eliab gave the man a halug and a blanket, and he quickly dressed.

"Do you have a message for us?" Eliab asked.

"I have parchment from Prince Jonathan, Officer Eliab," the man said and produced a folded leather goatskin from the pile of wet clothes. Eliab took the letter and felt the wax seal. Jonathan's bulla was clearly imprinted and he touched the impression of a palm tree, frowning.

"Is my brother David ben Jesse well?" Eliab asked still looking at the white signet.

"The Officer David is fine. The parcel is of utmost importance and I was given orders to deliver it to you, Officer Eliab, and none other."

Eliab burned to read it, but decided to wait until the envoy had left. "I shall read it later, when I am alone," he said and pushed the thin leather behind his belt, although he knew it would trouble him until he knew what it said.

The men ate bread and dried fruits together and washed down the meal with mulled wine. After an hour, the rain had lessened and the messenger left them with a salute and made his way to the quartermaster.

"Read the letter, brother," Abinadab said anxiously, moments after the envoy, sheltering underneath a hide cloak, had run into the light rain.

Eliab pulled the parchment from behind his belt and read it silently.

He gasped suddenly.

"He knows David's secret," Eliab said in accents of dread, his eyes wide. Shammah and Abinadab gaped at him. "Prince Jonathan knows that the prophet Samuel anointed David king."

With his hands clasped behind his back, Jonathan paced across his room, irritated at the contents of the letter he had gotten from Eliab. He looked at the papyrus scroll and curled his upper lip with indignation, grunting at the parchment as if it were alive.

Why did David not trust him enough to tell him about the anointing? he asked himself, warming himself against the cold of the new day before a wide fireplace. It was almost too much to bear. He tightened his grip until his knuckles whitened. Would he confront David? He did not feel his hands go numb as he thought. Jonathan feared his temper, and he closed his eyes, calming himself as he let a rush of air through his lips.

When David entered the room, Jonathan composed himself with a deep breath and hid his emotions behind a strained smile.

"You summoned me, my prince," David said bowing. "It's a great day. Shall you and I and Michal take a walk through your mother's garden?"

"I want to speak to you about a serious matter, David. This is not the day for meandering walks," he snapped. David was uncertain what had happened. He had never known the prince to be so irate.

Jonathan sighed and raked his fingers through his hair. He thought for a moment and then spoke, appearing calm. "Is there something that you want to tell me, David?" Jonathan turned dark eyes on David.

"Nothing specific," David said shaking his head lightly after thinking for a second. "Why do you ask, my prince?"

Jonathan set his jaw in frustration. "David, you say you love me as a brother. But then you keep a terrible secret from me." David's face dropped, and he struggled not to show his anxiety.

Jonathan couldn't know, he told himself. The air was thick between them suddenly, and he felt nervous sweat break out on his skin. "What do you mean, Jonathan? I have my secrets just as you have yours. Does that mean that you are not a friend?" David said regaining his confidence. He would not be intimidated like a frightened little roe deer.

"I received a letter from your brother, Eliab. In it, he writes … no, you read it for yourself," the prince said and snatched the papyrus sheet from the cushion where he had thrown it.

He knows, David almost said aloud, taking in a sharp breath. His heart raced.

Jonathan held the torn document in his face. "Read it," he ordered. David took the papyrus from him slowly, and began reading with something like fear.

David closed his eyes, and sighed softly. He couldn't believe that his brother had written to Jonathan and told his secret. Jonathan knew.

When he opened his eyes, the prince's rage seemed to vanish at the sight of his anguish. Eliab had killed him emotionally with his betrayal.

"You lied to us, David! You lied to *me*, your friend, your prince," Jonathan hissed. "Our friendship is nothing."

"That's not true. I love my lord like my own brothers. You know this."

"Do I, David?" Jonathan was silent. "You know what really kills me? My father was right about you all this time, and I believed you over my own father. My own father! What does that make me?"

David suddenly had a seizure of fear. Did Saul know? If that were true there would be guards storming into the room at any moment. He stiffened at the realization, and felt claustrophobic. He would be hanged.

"I haven't told anybody, David," Jonathan snapped into the silence, as if he had heard David's thoughts, and looked away, painfully. He could hear David breathe out with relief.

"What will you do, my lord?" David asked, managing a steady voice, although a dark vein stretched across the skin of his neck, and he shuddered with emotion. Jonathan did not answer, turning his back on the captain.

"What will you have me do, David?" Jonathan said harshly. David's betrayal was a terrible thing.

He waited a moment to give more weight to his words.

"I am to be king after my father," Jonathan said acrimoniously. "Would you smite me in my sleep, when I'm king?"

David exploded with resentment. "Do you think I planned this, Jonathan? Do you honestly believe that I befriended you so that I could *kill* you in your sleep? I didn't want it to be like this. If I wanted you or your father out of the way, I would have murdered you a long time ago." David said emotionally. "I am sorry that is what my lord thinks of his servant. How could I have told you? I feared that you would react this way. I'm sorry, Jonathan. You must believe me."

David turned to leave and Jonathan imagined seeing tears. He looked after him sadly, and said softly. "David, wait." Jonathan sighed. He did not know what he was feeling. Everything was different now. He was certain of nothing.

David stopped, but did not turn to face the prince.

"Your brother did not write to me first," Jonathan said and David turned slowly. "I tricked him into admitting the truth."

"How?" David stood erect, looking at his prince.

"I figured it out, it wasn't that difficult. You should've seen the guilt in your face when you embraced my father so tightly that day ..." Jonathan said and he took a deep breath before continuing. "My father told me how he and the prophet Samuel parted ways. It was a shock to me when I first heard of it. He told my father that he would anoint another, and that God would take the kingdom from him—*rend*, he said. God had rent the kingdom of Israel from him. I took a risk in writing to Eliab, and it was immoral, I know. I wrote to him, saying that you told me everything."

David looked at him guardedly, his eyes moist with tears.

"You have to understand my feelings. I won't be king, David," he said sternly, stepping forward. "Nor will the throne pass to my family."

He looked away, the muscles on his jaw standing out, clenching his teeth.

"Such is life, captain. Such is life," Jonathan said despondently. They were quiet for a long time, and then he spoke again. "I will keep your secret as if it were my own, David. You are Yahweh's chosen. I cannot deny that, nor disobey His will. But allow me to mourn my family's loss."

David nodded solemnly.

"You have found favor in father's sight again, and I can't tell him the truth. He would kill you if he knew. It would drive him to madness. It's a burden that I must carry," Jonathan said almost to himself, and sank into the multi-hued pile of silk cushions.

David kneeled before the prince.

"I need to be alone, David; I cannot look at you now." After a moment, David left miserably.

Jonathan ladled wine into a goblet from a rounded clay container standing beside the warm brazier, and downed the tepid drink, lost in his thoughts.

ספר דניאל

CHAPTER SEVENTEEN

*M*ephibosheth teetered around the throne room naked. In the heat, the child would not keep his clothing on. He would tug and pull at the silk garments, whining and complaining until his servant undressed him and he was free to do as he wanted. His perceptive eyes missed nothing as his tiny hands tried to touch everything that caught his interest. The boy rocked with laughter as his nursemaid took him and tickled his protruding stomach. Ahinoam kept a watchful gaze on Jonathan's son and the woman running after the boy. She sat beside Saul with her hand on his knee, entertained by the courtiers' blatant adulation.

Rizpah sat on cushions on the floor; she was a concubine, and could not sit beside the king. She held her baby son on her lap, but would often let him crawl around the large room. Saul's youngest child was the center of attention. The courtiers gushed and smiled at the prince overtly, and Rizpah glared at the sycophants when they did. She touched her belly, thinking of the new life inside of her, although her pregnancy did not show yet.

Ahinoam ignored the concubine completely.

It had been over a year since the king had ordered David killed, and for the most part, it had been a good one. Saul had

215

not seen the captain in six months and although he would not admit it to anyone, he enjoyed the time away from David and his own constant scheming. The Philistines were warring with his country again, and he received weekly reports of the ongoing battles. They had launched another frontal assault over the valleys merging into the Judean ridge. It was a tense time, and he longed to be there. It was a custom for him to lead the battle, to give fierce orders, and he missed the late nights sitting around a table with his council, designing stratagems. He was getting old and was tired, he had decided, and the nostalgia of it all made him restless.

Saul had not dreamt of the evil spirit for many months and he believed that he was rid of it. He touched his wife, although he knew she was a different person. She had been cold and aloof since Rizpah came to the palace. He smiled at her, and Ahinoam managed to return the gesture, though faintly.

His mind drifted and he struggled to focus. The endless words of the courtier before him melded with sudden silence and the room began to spin. Leaning forward, Saul placed his feet more firmly on the floor, and gripped the warm stone of his throne to make it stop. He felt nauseous; sweat streaking his face. The images of the others twisted and churned, and he could hear disturbing laughter in rolling echoes. He was trembling, and could smell sulphur, and then it was there. Saul could feel the hilt of his sword. It was as if he could not control his hand, and his fingers clenched the kidon.

I'm going to stab myself, he cried out in his thoughts, the realization, causing him to gnash his teeth. The demon was controlling him, he feared, its black eyes penetrating him. It took all of his strength not to pull the weapon from the scabbard. For several insane seconds he had been more terrified than he had ever thought possible, and he felt his power fade. The evil spirit grinned at him brutally, and laughed, showing yellow fangs.

Saul went terrifyingly cold when the thing screamed at him savagely and then in an instant, it was gone.

His skin was dry, and his breath steady. He was on his throne and he could feel his wife's hand on his thigh. Another courtier was speaking to him, as if nothing had happened. How long was he gone? He felt drained and his head ached.

"David ben Jesse will seize your kingdom. Murder him while you still can," the courtier drawled in a harsh whisper, his eyes like a snake. Saul stiffened, his skin crawling. The man erupted into laughter.

Saul jolted as he awoke from the disturbing dream. Was he truly awake or was he still dreaming? His wives smiled at him, and the courtiers looked at him strangely.

Ahinoam was touching his face tenderly. "You dozed off, husband, and then you began sweating. Were you dreaming?" she asked.

"David—no," Saul said weakly. His eyes glazed over "Everybody leave—get out!" Saul shouted frantically as he gripped his throne.

The courtiers and servants left hurriedly, glancing back in curious dread. Ahinoam nodded at the nursemaid, and the woman snatched up the children and took them to the garden, far from the king.

He had almost lost consciousness, and if Ahinoam hadn't gripped his arm, he would have blacked out. Her steady gaze brought him back, and he could breathe again.

Saul had a bitter taste in his mouth and with a deep, quaking sigh he relaxed, and sagged back into his throne. Sweat broke out on his skin, and he breathed in weak shallow breaths.

Ahinoam caressed his skin and whispered strength into his ears.

Rizpah stared at the father of her son. He was as pale as death, and she could not react. She had become fond of the king over the past year. He had been kind and caring, and so encouraging that she had come to terms with the arrangement between her father and the king of Israel. Seeing him in that state was worse than physical pain. She had only heard of his wild fits from her ladies maids. Was it happening now?

Ahinoam's sharp voice brought her from a daze as she shouted. "Stop gawking like a mute, you silly girl. Pour me some water and bring towels. Now!"

Rizpah hurried from the room and with shaking hands poured the fluid into a large bowl, and brought it to the queen.

Saul moaned as his wife sponged his hot skin and smiled at her feebly. She took his hand in hers and gripped it affectionately, willing back her husband's strength.

The day had gone before Saul came around. Rizpah had lighted the lamps, pressing back the darkness from the room, and was sitting anxiously at his feet, stroking the cold flesh of his legs. Ahinoam wondered at the fact that the concubine had not left her husband's side despite everything, and she began to understand that the young woman loved the king.

When Ahinoam had shouted at her earlier, it had been the first time that the queen had spoken to her since she came to the palace, and Rizpah relished the fact privately. She longed to have a relationship with the old queen. They were family in a strange way, she thought, shrugging delicately, if not by law or blood, at least through Saul.

A servant rushed into the throne room.

"Captain David has returned from the war. Hail David ben Jesse! He slew the Philistines with a great slaughter, and they fled from him," he said. He was euphoric.

Ahinoam cried out in pain as Saul tightened his fist around her hand. His eyes became distant, and then not even his queen could stop it. He screamed and tore off his robes as he began prophesying.

Saul was sitting naked on the streaked floor with his back against a wall, his legs stretched out before him. He was silent while David played on the kinnor. Memories of the last time he played for Saul in his troubled state flooded David's mind. He kept his eyes on the old king, anticipating another attack.

The music soothed Saul and he was silent where he sat.

Suddenly, Saul reached for a javelin. David could not believe it, and his body tensed as he sprang to his feet. He instinctively locked his eyes on the troubled king.

Saul grunted and hurled the spear at the captain. David turned from the projectile easily, and ran from the palace.

Saul collapsed and lost consciousness.

⚜

There was a terrible silence in the Philistine court as Achish moved sluggishly around the room. Large green plants gave life to the grand stone chamber, and massive statues of pagan gods lined the walls, their expressions cold and unemotional. Colorful silk in varied hues draped the ceiling and hung before large square windows in artistic splendor. Two slave girls moved beside their master fanning the king with palm fronds. His layers of fat quivered as he paced.

"What do you suggest we do, Sérèn of Ashod?" Achish broke the stillness, looking at the prince from the corner of his eye.

"The Israelites may have won the war, Lord Achish, but we are far from defeated," he said reverently, stroking his dark beard. After the unfortunate death of the prince of Ekron, the four Sérèn treated the king with great respect, which Achish relished inwardly. He had them by their necks, he thought.

"They have conquered our forces," Sérèn of Ashkelon said. "We don't have the men to wage a full scale war. We'll have to weaken them by random raids, choking them slowly like the great python."

"We are not scavengers or snakes. We are Philistines, Ashkelon."

"Yes, my king, what you say is true. We are a proud nation," Sérèn of Gaza said quickly. "But the Israelites still control the Judean ridge. They have erected strong garrisons at the mouth of the ridge. They occupy every fort in the highlands and man them well. They have the trade routes and...."

"Enough," Achish snapped. "I hear what you are saying, Gaza."

"We must think about strengthening our defenses," Sérèn of Ashkelon said. "If Saul is cunning, he will march to our cities and he will succeed. If we do not act, we could all be paying taxes to the Israelites."

Achish rounded on him suddenly, glaring at him as he considered the prince's words. The Sérèn of Ashkelon retreated under the king's penetrating eyes and bowed his head.

"We cannot have that." Achish drawled. "We will attack in spring, with the harvest. We will smite their men and rob their threshing floors."

***

King Saul had summoned Zidka. His family was around him, and Michal pleaded with her father.

"I pray you, Lib. Please don't kill my husband. I will die," she screamed and knelt, pulling at Saul's tunic. The muscles of his jaw stood out as he clamped his teeth with the sorrow he felt for his daughter. He was like a statue, inexorable, his eyes hard. Michal wept at his feet. Over the months, his jealousy and fears had slowly dominated and dangerously consumed him.

Saul did not look at her and she sank onto the floor again, wrenched violently with sobs. She shouted, hitting the floor with her fists. "I love him, Lib. Please!"

Ahinoam led her daughter out of the room, glancing back at her husband with disgust. He turned away from them coldly.

It can be no other way, Saul knew. He had to kill David while he still could. Only then would his throne be secure, and he would know peace again.

"You dog," Michal shouted at the Philistine mercenary as he walked past them. She spat at his feet, and it took some restraint for the spy not to slap her.

"Philistine slime!" she screamed, and with a final, contemptuous glance, he turned the corner and was gone from their sight.

"You should put a leash on that daughter of yours, my king," Zidka said, looking at the entrance, expecting the distraught woman to come tearing back into the throne room with her nails sharpened, like a fierce feline.

"I am in a foul disposition, Zidka," Saul snapped, his eyes dark suddenly. "Do not ever speak of my family again."

Zidka lowered his gaze, and bowed. "What may I do for you, king of Israel?"

"Get a few men and slay David ben Jesse," Saul said.

"Ah, finally. Zidka will have his head," the Philistine mercenary said with a Philistine accent, and smiled as he straightened from his bow.

"No, father, don't," Jonathan said and took Saul's arm. The king glared at him, and thought he would kill his son right then. Jonathan shivered under Saul's murderous gaze and released his father's arm.

"You cannot enter any man's house against his will after dark. Even you, my king," Jonathan stammered. "It is the law of our people. You know this, father. The people will stone you alive if they should hear of it."

Saul thought for a moment. "Yes, what my son says is true," he said, touching his beard. "Watch his house, and at first light, smite him."

Zidka bowed again and paced back to the entrance.

"Zidka. Be my hawk. Keep him under close observation, and when the time is right, swoop down on him like a falcon on a rat," Saul ordered his assassin.

He turned to Jonathan. "Stay with me for awhile, my son. We haven't spoken in months," he said and smiled deceptively, his eyes wild.

Michal entered her home illuminated by a flame flickering on the twined wick of a bronze lamp. She breathed anxiously and tried to search the dark hall for a moment before shutting the wooden door. She had nowhere to look for her husband, and it was evident that she had been crying. Suddenly the flame died.

Fear crept over her as she wandered through her home.

A rough hand gripped her face out of the blackness behind her. When she felt cold bronze press against her throat she was convinced that it was the Philistine assassin, and screamed in terror, the sound muffled by his hand.

"It's me, wife," David whispered. "Did you see anybody follow you? Are we alone?"

The smell of his skin made her relax, although her tears flowed over his hand. Michal nodded and David eased his grasp. She was shaking. "I'm sorry, wife. I thought it was ..." he said, feeling her face gently in the dark. Michal flung her arms around his neck and kissed him.

"I love you, husband, but you must leave tonight," she said, urgently. "If you don't save yourself now, tomorrow you'll be slain." David stiffened in her embrace, and she kissed him again, sobbing.

They sank to the floor, still holding each other.

"There are men outside, watching. My father has sent them to kill you," she said softly, and David dried her tears with a thumb. He pressed her to him.

"We can go to the elders of the cities. Surely the people will speak," David said and Michal silenced him when she pressed her fingers gently to his lips.

"They will do nothing, husband. Truly, not all of the voices of Israel together would deter my father. You know this. The king will never stop," she said and shivered as she sobbed. "I pray you, husband, escape tonight." David nodded, and she slid her fingers from his face and kissed him passionately. She did not know when she would see him again. She wept into his chest at the thought, feeling desolate inside, fearing the days ahead. She might soon be a widow, and she would die of grief, she told herself.

David shushed her, and lowered her onto her back, feeling the coolness of the stone against their skin against the heat of their bodies.

"I adore you, wife," he whispered, and held her trembling body close to his own.

They made love on the gray stone floor one last time.

David touched his wife's face tenderly as he sat on a windowsill above a black alleyway, and embraced her. They kissed, and he could taste the salt of her tears.

David took her arms in a soldier's hold, nodded to her, and slowly slid from the stone sill. Michal grunted as the square edge of the stone pressed agonizingly against her abdomen as David hung from her and carefully lowered his grip down her arms. She let him down as far as she could physically manage, the yawning darkness below waiting to swallow him up. Her hands began to sweat.

Then he let go. With a quiet flutter of his silk tunic, David plummeted to the cobblestones. The soles of his feet burned, despite his protective leather sandals. His ankles were stiff from the impact. David lowered to his haunches, silent in the darkness, listening for any foreign sounds.

Michal searched the streets for approaching men, and when she did not see any light or movement, she gave her husband the signal. She could not see him in the street below, although she knew he was looking at her. She kissed her hand and waved into the black of night. Without a sound, he was gone, and she was alone. Slowly she pulled the shutters closed.

As the first light tinged the sky, Michal realized that they would soon come. She gathered herself. All she could think of was her husband. Did he get out of the city safely? Was he alive?

Above the six pillars that supported the second story floor and divided the living area from the storage room stood a stone image in their sleeping quarters. Michal slowly dragged the heavy object next to their large bed as she and her husband had discussed. The rough stone broke the skin on her hands, but she ignored the pain. With a final grunt, she pushed the solid sculpture, and it toppled over, sinking onto the soft bed. After placing it in a suitable way, she used a pillow of goat's hair as a head and covered the statue with blankets, altering it as best she could to make it look like a sleeping man. She remembered how David had hated the image and did not want her to keep it. It was against God's laws, he had said, and she bit her lip with the emotions welling up inside of her.

Michal went to the door, and waited.

The sudden knock at the door sent a shock through her body as she sat holding her legs bent and pressed up against her chest. She was almost frozen with fear and when fists hammered again, she rose. The pounding became insistent and a husky voice shouted for the door to be opened. As she opened the door, Zidka looked at her ruthlessly. The savage eyes and unsightly scars on his face made her recoil.

"The king has ordered us to slay David ben Jesse. Stand aside, m'lady," Zidka said.

Michal did not answer and when the Philistine lifted his hand to push her aside, she snapped at him. "Do not dare touch me! My husband is ill in bed; you cannot come in." She glared at the men. "It is our law." He tried again to enter.

"I am a princess of Israel. If you come into this house, I will see you hanging of the end of a twisting rope before this day is over. Now leave."

The man had the eyes of a raptor and she knew better than to enrage him further. With a heave, she slammed the door shut.

Michal pushed her back against the door, and covered her quivering mouth with her hands. They would be back, and then she would not be able to stop them. At least she had bought her husband a few more hours.

The pounding on the door came again in less than an hour, and this time she let them in without a word. It would have been useless to waste her breath, she knew. Her father was the king and he wanted her husband dead.

"The king has ordered that we bring the bed to him with David in it, so that the king can kill him," the men said as they rushed into her private chambers. She waited tensely.

Zidka came from the room, his eyes boring into her. "You will explain this to your king, princess," he said, and grabbed her upper arm. Michal tried to resist, but when he jerked her, it felt as if her muscles would tear in his grip.

Saul sat forward from his throne when Zidka entered the room with Michal. The sight of the Philistine dragging his tearful daughter, made him insane with rage.

The king could not stop the images flashing in his mind from his childhood, when the heathen soldiers would slap and jerk women and men around in the streets. Everything he had fought against during the years of his reign was happening right in his own throne room. Saul clenched his fists. He would not tolerate such actions. His emotions raised him from his throne and he waited for the Philistine to stand before him.

"My king, there was a stone image ..." Zidka said and Saul hit him square in the face, breaking his nose. The Philistine stumbled back, moaning as blood dripped over his chin.

"I told you, Zidka. Never disrespect my bloodline or any Israelite, ever," Saul screamed. Zidka covered his nose, casting a deadly stare at the king, and spoke something in Semitic so fast and unclear that Saul could not understand.

"Give him forty lashes." Two burly men dragged Zidka away, screaming.

Saul glanced at another man, and spoke to him, appearing calm. "What is the meaning of all this? Where is David?"

"When we came to the bed, sire, there was a stone image under the clothes. Zidka then brought the princess to you, my king," the messenger said, and bowed. Saul looked at Michal, slack jawed, the pain of betrayal showing in his eyes.

"Why have you deceived me so, my daughter? You helped my enemy to escape?" he asked, barely managing a composed tone.

Michal fell to the floor and pressed her face against her father's feet. "He told me to let him go or he said he would kill me," she whimpered tearfully.

Ramah was a small town within a day's walk from Gibeah. Gray light filtered through thick clouds, as David lowered his headdress over his brow and lifted the cloth over his face against the veil of sand riding the heavy gusts. Silently he made his way through the busy beaten-earth streets and yellow mud brick houses, not wanting the inhabitants to notice him.

The prophet was an elderly man with swarthy skin and stringy gray hair coming from underneath a fine linen miter wrapped around his head. Samuel, the prophet and judge, had a thick beard with patches of gray reaching his chest. He was richly clothed in official attire with blue, purple, and scarlet folds of delicately twined cloth woven with gold string. His cloak was completely embroidered.

"I knew you would come, David ben Jesse," Samuel said and David kissed his hand. He smelled of incense. "Come let us retire to Naioth."

David had so much to tell the old prophet that he did not know where to begin. As they walked to the area of closely built houses for the prophets living in Ramah, he told him everything that Saul had done.

David looked at the man who had secretly anointed him king with something like awe. He felt nervous around the old man. The power of God was strong on this righteous man; David could feel it emanating from him.

"You mustn't worry, David. The Spirit of Yahweh is on you. I will tell you what is to come," Samuel said, looking ahead of him as they walked, fabric surging and snapping behind them. He was still physically strong and carried himself like a powerful warrior. "Saul has many informants across Israel, even in the Philistine cities. By tonight he will know you are here."

David suddenly looked worried, and Samuel took his arm in a firm hold, the wind gusting around them. David was amazed at his strength, noticing that the prophet was slightly taller than he was, and had broad shoulders beneath the linen robes. He could only imagine what a sight Samuel must have been in his youth.

"Saul will send messengers after you, but the Spirit of the Lord shall come upon them, and they will prophesy along with all the other prophets. Again he will send men, and even a third time, but they shall all do as the prophets do," Samuel said as if reading the words from a scroll. He had David's complete attention, and his face broke into a web of characteristic wrinkles. He continued, and David felt safe with him. "Then Saul shall come to the great water well in Secu, and he will ask after us. He will be told that we are at Naioth. The Spirit of Yahweh will be upon him then and he shall also shout and dance as he prophesies until he comes to Naioth, before me. Then he will strip off his clothes, and he will speak of things not known to him. Saul will lie down naked all that day and all that night and the people will ask among themselves if Saul is also one of the prophets. All these things will come to pass, my king."

David was startled by what Samuel had called him.

"What's wrong, David? You have been anointed as king over Israel. Saul is no longer ruler. God has chosen you. *You* are king, David. Why should I not call you so?" he said openly, shrugging delicately, and David lowered his gaze from the man.

"It is then that you must go to Prince Jonathan in Gibeah and he will help you, David. You must tell him that you will hide in the fields until the third day. Saul will miss you when they sit down to eat. Jonathan must say to his father that you have earnestly asked leave to go to Bethlehem, for there is a yearly sacrifice there for all your family," Samuel said and waited for a moment before continuing. "If Saul says that it is well, then you shall have peace, but if he is very wroth, then know that he is governed by evil."

"Why would Saul ask such a thing? Why would he ask why I'm not at the dinner table, when he himself has come to Naioth to kill me?" David said, frowning quizzically. The winds died suddenly.

Samuel was silent for a moment as he thought and then sighed softly.

"After Saul's rejection as king, I mourned for him, David. It was a terrible thing for me. You shall understand one day," he said. "An evil spirit from the Lord troubles Saul. He is not himself, David, and he hasn't been since before you went to his court. He does things and does not remember. That's why you were summoned to his court—to play for him on the kinnor. So that the evil thing may depart from him."

"I have been at his court for almost eight years, Samuel," David said, shaking his head.

"And you were only seventeen when I anointed you," Samuel added.

An unexpected gust blew sand into David's eyes, and the men pressed their faces into the folds of their arms. "It is a sad thing," David almost had to shout over the blowing sand stinging them.

"Indeed. If only he had not rejected the word of Yahweh," Samuel said, and for the first time David could hear a tinge of emotion in his voice. "Now you understand, king."

David nodded solemnly.

They were silent as they walked up a stony slope covered with green shrubs made pale by a film of dust. David wanted to ask the prophet what would become of Michal, but decided against it. He retreated into his memories, and the corners of his lips curled up gently.

"Do not be concerned about things to come, David. You're wife is unharmed and will be safe. Saul will not hurt his family," Samuel said, bringing David from his musing. He knew what would happen to Michal and he could almost feel the pain that husband and wife would endure. He clenched his jaw as he envisioned their turbulent relationship and frowned ruefully.

Samuel patted David's shoulder, knowing that the few years ahead would be a fierce time for the young king. It would be the worst he would ever know. He would pray for him, he decided, increasing his grip, willing him strength.

"You are young and powerful, David. Yahweh is with you," Samuel whispered into the rush of murky air deadening his words.

CHAPTER EIGHTEEN

Eliab, his brothers, and nephews were putting their men through battling formations and fighting techniques.

Eliab had not seen his wife and family in over two years and he missed them intensely. To forget the pain and the longing he kept himself busy with the men until it was too dark to continue by day, and at night, he fell into a deep slumber from exhaustion.

Gibbôr was the fittest and fiercest regiment in Saul's military.

Joab came running to Eliab and Abinadab. "Officer Eliab, I have a letter from Captain David, and it's extremely urgent," he said, clearing his throat. "I did not recognize the boy who delivered the letter. It was not Uncle David's usual messenger." Eliab held out his hand, and Joab gave him the furled parchment.

He was quiet as he read the cryptic note, and shook his head questioningly as he finished. "Is this all? Was there nothing else?" he asked.

"That is everything. He gave me nothing more, uncle," Joab said. Everything about the letter was off, and he knew by Eliab's expression that something was wrong.

"Well, what does it say, brother?" Abinadab asked, leaning over to try to look at the scroll. Eliab handed him the paper and rubbed his sweaty beard flat with his palm.

"Saul wants my brother dead," Abinadab said, deep in thought. His hard eyes became distant, and he spoke almost to himself. "He fled from Gibeah and wrote to me from Naioth. He wants us to meet him on the road leading south from Gibeah, an hour's walk from the city Nob. In six days."

Eliab frowned worriedly as he said softly, "He might have to leave Israel."

Doors swung open and one of his people was escorted into the throne room. A chilling draft entered through high open casements. His stomach was bare against the icy air but Achish did not seem to be cold underneath his layers of bulging fat. He had a gleaming skeletal cranium in his hand and drank a sip of steaming wine from the polished brim.

He had been in a stressful state since Israel had routed him a second time. His armies were considerably reduced, and he would have to think of something to break the Israelite forces. He would not let them invade his lands.

What would his late father have done? he thought, slurping the hot liquid and lifting his eyes to the man standing before him. Achish wondered about the scar across his face. His eyes were like those of a carnivorous cat, his pupils like diamonds inside hard brown circles. The king took another taste of the strong drink.

"Who dares come before the king? Name yourself immediately," Achish said without looking at the man.

"I am Zidka, my king," he said and did not shift his eyes from the large monarch sitting with the skull-bowl. He admired the idea for a moment.

"What do you want, Zidka?" Achish snapped and still did not meet the man's eyes. Zidka wanted to smile at this. He had seen this reaction too many times to remember, and he loved the sense of power his abnormal eyes gave him over weaker men.

"I come from the court of Saul ben Kish, my king." Zidka said in a husky voice.

A sharp glance from the king made him lose his voice. He could see intense anger and Zidka stepped back, bowing. The welts on his back stung fiercely, but he did not show his pain.

"Explain yourself hastily, before I have your head." Merely hearing the name of the Israelite king had enraged Achish, and he felt like having the man whipped just for mentioning it. He set his jaw and scowled.

"I have come to give you information, my king of kings. I have been a mercenary in that court for months, and I have heard and seen enough. I will tell you everything," he said coming up from his bow, "if my liege would be so generous and reward me accordingly."

He bowed his head.

"You traitorous Israelite dog!" Achish said vehemently, and Zidka jerked his head up. "You think I'm that ignorant. I know what that king is trying. You speak my tongue and now you want me to trust you. You will run to Saul as soon as I have given you something to tell your king. I spit at you." He spat red saliva, colored from the wine, onto his chest.

Zidka flinched. "No. I'm of Philistine blood. I betray them. I can tell you of their strategies. I have heard much in the shadows of Saul's court," Zidka said staggering backwards. "Did my king know that Saul is mad? He sees things that no other eyes do."

Achish smiled suddenly.

"You see this head-bone, servant?" Achish asked, and Zidka barely nodded in acknowledgment. "You should know that this is the skeleton that protects the flesh of a man's thoughts."

Achish arched his eyebrows questioningly at Zidka, and continued. "This man was also a traitor. He stormed into my palace and wanted to kill me with his dagger." Zidka's eyes widened suddenly.

"Do you see how small the rounded part of it is?" Achish asked and lifted the vessel for him to see. Zidka did not move. "It proves that he did not think much; he did not deserve his title. Do you know to whom this belonged?"

Zidka shook his head slowly. "I do not, my king."

"It was the Sérèn of Ekron, who dared affront me, the king of Philistia. And I made his head into a drinking bowl, so that I may always remember him. The bone gives the wine an interesting taste."

"My physician says that I have the perfect shape. I have a brilliant mind, he told me," Achish said and felt his head.

His eyes bored into the smirking traitor. "I am sure you must also have thought about coming to me several times— and thoroughly, I would hope," Achish said and motioned his guards closer with a nod of his head. "Your skull would make a deeper bowl, I think. I would drink longer out of it." Achish took another long sip.

Zidka gasped in sudden terror, falling backwards. He jerked violently when two firm hands grasped his arms. Skilfully he pulled a blade from his tunic, and stabbed one man three times before the guard fell to the floor. Zidka pulled his arm frantically from the other grip, and raced to the fat king. The scabs on his back had torn open and were bleeding. His tunic turned red from the fresh blood.

Achish choked on the warm wine. Zidka screamed as he ran, raising his hand toward the king. He could almost feel his curved blade tearing into his soft heart. Two more men grabbed him, and dragged him away from their king, leaving a smeared trail of blood behind them.

Achish realized he was panting, and placed his hand on his tight chest. He grunted and lifted his yellow bone-cup and drank quickly, trying to douse the discomfort with the wine.

"You fat goat!" Zidka roared, his face contorted with agony and fear. "You will be the reason that Palestine dies. You will kill my people. You are not a king. You pig—bastard!" Zidka's voice faded as he was pulled away and Achish smiled as he mused, holding the bowl to his lips.

"What have I done, Jonathan? What is my injustice or immorality? How have I sinned against your father that he wants to kill me?" David asked intensely, clenching his jaw.

"God forbid that you should die. My father does nothing either great or small without telling me about it. Why now would my father hide these things from me? It isn't so," Jonathan said, shaking his head.

"I swear to you, your father knows that I have found grace in your eyes, and he knows that if he reveals this to you Jonathan, you will be hurt. But truly as the Lord lives, and as your soul lives, there is but a step between me and death," David said, and turned away from the prince, scratching his beard. He sighed, and Jonathan placed his hand on David's shoulder, turning him around.

He looked David in the eyes. "Whatever your soul desires, brother, I will do it for you."

"Tomorrow is the new moon and I'm supposed to sit with the king at the dinner feast," David said after a moment, "but if it is right by you, let me go so I can hide in the fields, until the evening of the third day." He continued, frowning slightly, "If your father asks where I am, then tell him that I had earnestly asked leave of you to return to Bethlehem, my city, for there is a yearly sacrifice there for all my family. If he says it is good, your servant will have peace; but if he is angry, then be sure that he is determined by evil to hurt me. If it is so, you must deal kindly with your servant. Keep my secret, I pray you. My prince, remember the covenant that you made with me before the Lord. If you think that there is iniquity in me, slay me yourself. Why then take me to your father?"

"Far be it from you, David. If I certainly knew that evil was determined by my father and he wanted to smite you, wouldn't I tell you, my brother?" Jonathan asked almost in a whisper.

"Who will come to warn me if your father answers you angrily?" David asked. Jonathan exhaled slowly.

"Come, let's go out into the fields," he said. David followed him, understanding that Jonathan wanted to be away from spies.

After they had gone into the grasslands surrounding the city, Jonathan began, "O, Lord God of Israel as my witness, I will question my father in the days ahead, and if his attitude toward you, David, is good, then I will send word. However, if my father wants to do you evil, and I don't warn you of any danger, then may Yahweh smite me. I will tell you that you may leave safely. And may the Lord go with you, like he has been with my father."

David was silent.

"And you will, not only while I live, show me the kindness of the Lord that I won't die," Jonathan said and stared at David before he continued passionately, "and also, you will not cease your kindness toward my house, forever."

David wanted to speak, but Jonathan silenced him. Jonathan removed a short dagger from his belt, and slashed his palm. He handed the blade to David, and watched as he slid the edge across his flesh. With a penetrating stare, he held David's bleeding hand tightly, mixing the blood of his house, making a solemn pledge with David ben Jesse. The prince continued. "When the Lord has cut off the enemies of David from the face of the earth, may our covenant still be unbroken, and if it isn't, God will punish you," he said emotionally. David swore again, because he loved Jonathan like his own soul.

Jonathan lowered himself onto his haunches and gently rubbed sand in the wound, wincing at the sharp pain. The dirt would cause a prominent scar; a permanent reminder of their covenant made before the Lord. David did the same, and then took Jonathan's hand in a soldier's grip.

"Tomorrow is the new moon, and you shall be missed when your seat is empty," Jonathan said. "After three days, then you must go quickly, and wait by the stone of Ezel. I will shoot three arrows beside it, as though I shot at a mark, and I will tell a lad to go find the shafts. If I expressly say to the boy, 'The arrows are on this side of you,' take them and come, because there will be peace for you, and no harm, as the Lord lives."

David nodded.

"But, if I say to the young man that the arrows are beyond you, go your way, because the Lord has sent you away."

Jonathan held David in a firm embrace. "And as touching as the matter is of which you and I have spoken, know that the Lord is between you and me always."

"For all time, my brother," David whispered.

*

Saul sat in his chair against the wall, as always, with Abner at his side. The king had not said anything about David the day before, and Jonathan wondered if his father would mention him. The atmosphere was thick and the men ate their breakfasts in silence.

"Why did the son of Jesse not come to eat yesterday or today?" Saul broke the silence, and looked at his son from underneath arched black eyebrows.

Jonathan explained to Saul from across the wide table as David had advised.

Saul smashed his fists onto the table. "You son of a perverse, rebellious woman! Now I know that you have chosen the son of Jesse and are disgracing yourself and that mother of yours." Saul scowled at his son and Jonathan stiffened. "For as long as the son of Jesse lives, you shall not be king. Your kingdom will not be established."

Jonathan tried to feign shock. He had known this for months, and the idea stung his heart. He felt bitter resentment seep into him, as if his father's odium was an infectious disease. The prince suppressed the thought, clamping his eyes shut. He told himself that it was God's will, and that he had made a covenant with David. It could be no other way, he decided.

"Now send a man and fetch him to me. He will surely die," Saul said through gritted teeth. Jonathan did not do as his father ordered, and Saul lowered his hand to his spear instinctively. Jonathan saw the gesture and gasped. Would his own father spear him? Jonathan stared at Saul resolutely, frowning. Abner chewed his food slowly as he watched. He would not interfere, he decided, it would be safer, and he pushed another bite into his cheek, as if nothing were happening.

"Why must he be slain, my king? What has he done?" Jonathan asked, finally answering his father with a note of anger.

Saul grunted sullenly and without warning, cast his javelin across the wide table suddenly. Abner's jaw dropped, the food nearly falling from his mouth.

Jonathan ducked away underneath the tabletop.

The prince arose from the table in fierce anger, and knew that his father was determined to slay David. This had been the second time his father wanted to kill him, and it was almost too much to bear; a pain worse than death. He glared at the old man, and his eyes became distant for a second as he remembered. His own father had ordered him to be killed many years ago, when Jonathan had eaten when his father had ordered a fast, although he was unaware of the edict. When Saul had heard about it, he was furious. If Jonathan's men had not stood with him and pleaded with Saul to let their captain live, he would have died that day. It was a long time ago, before David came to the court, before Samuel had reproached his father, and he had buried the memory and the pain, deep within.

He refused to look at his father as he left the king and his general at the table in mute resentment, and strode to the palace.

The prince was grieved for his brother David because his father had done him shame, and he did not eat meat on that second day of the month.

～♔～

It had happened exactly as the prophet Samuel had said, David thought, as he waited in the fields outside of Gibeah in the late hours of the morning. The wind was blowing and thunder cracked in the distance. The air was pleasant with the smell of rain. He resisted scratching his skin, as the grasses scraped his exposed legs.

Jonathan had made a covenant with his house in those same fields. The night before, David had seen the new moon in the sky after the monthly festivities, and he prayed to God silently.

He jumped to his feet as he heard Jonathan approach, and hunched over behind the large boulder. The minutes dragged tensely as he waited for the prince to launch his first arrow.

"Run, find the arrows that I'm shooting," Jonathan said to the lad who accompanied him. As the boy ran, he shot an arrow ahead of him.

With a soft whistle, the arrow pierced into the ground. The moments were terrifying.

"Isn't the arrow beyond you?" Jonathan cried out to the boy.

How could this happen? David thought miserably. He would have to run for his life, like some bandit. He suddenly thought of his brothers in the army. He knew Saul would remember them, and they would be killed. His family would lose their lands and his parents would be tortured for information about where he was hiding. He would never see his wife again. It was too much for him. The world around him began to spin, and he felt his strength leave him. Slowly David sank to his knees, pulling at his beard violently as he rested his head against the cold stone. His senses were dulled by his raging thoughts.

"Hurry, Oreb. Haste, don't tarry," Jonathan shouted to the lad searching the fields. The boy had not known of the arrangement, and Jonathan feared that he would see David hiding behind the boulder. The child snatched the last of the arrows from the ground and raced to his master.

"I have decided differently, Oreb. The weather is foul. Carry my artillery back to the city. Go, and I shall meet you in the palace, soon enough," the prince said. The boy nodded enthusiastically and set off at a jog.

Jonathan knew David was watching him.

As soon as the lad had gone, David rose out of the field toward the south and approached him. The sight of the broken man made Jonathan clench his jaw.

David fell to the ground on his face, and bowed three times. Jonathan doubled over and together they kissed each other's cheeks as a single tear rolled into the prince's combed and oiled beard.

David took Jonathan's arm in a soldier's grip, and when the prince returned his grasp, he wept. The prince cried with him, placing his hands on his shoulders. There was nothing he could do, and it broke him.

Finally, David could not restrain his emotion, and he sobbed loudly. Jonathan simply held him.

"Go in peace, my brother," the prince whispered, managing a steady voice as David released his hand, "We have both sworn in the name of the Lord, that our sacred promise will be between you and me, and between your seed and my seed, forever."

David nodded, and managed a tight smile.

He rose and left wretchedly through the swaying grasses that seemed alive from the moaning wind. David did not look back as he walked, drying his tears with his tunic.

Jonathan looked after him for a moment and with a sigh, turned, and walked back to the city.

CHAPTER NINETEEN

avid pushed aside the large embroidered linen hanging at the door of the tabernacle and entered the long expanse of the courtyard. Twenty pillars with brass sockets supported the fine-twined textile walls. Inside was a splendid square tent, with colorful sails of blue, purple, and scarlet with a covering of badger skins and red dyed ram's leather. Gold pillars made of shittimwood supported the massive structure.

Although David had seen it many times before, he found himself gawking like a youth at the regal holy place. There was nothing else like it in the entire world.

He waited as a man in ceremonial apparel approached him, seeming afraid.

"Why are you alone? Why is there no man with you?" Ahimelech, the priest, asked hesitantly.

David understood this immediately, and leaned in closer as he whispered. "The king has sent me on business and told me to let no man know about what he has commanded me," he said, and he could see Ahimelech relax slightly. "And I have told my men to wait for me at a certain place." David swept his gaze across the room. They were alone and he continued.

"I need five loaves of bread, priest, or what there is to give."

"I have no common bread, but there is hallowed bread, captain ... if the young men have, at least, kept themselves from women. You know they cannot eat of the loaves if they are unclean."

"Truly, priest Ahimelech, we have been kept from women for the past three days, since I left Gibeah," David said. "And the bodies of the young men are also holy. We are always ritually purified when we go out on a mission, and especially on a secret task for the king."

Ahimelech thought for a moment and went into the tabernacle. David was nervous and agitated because he had to wait. He had decided to leave Israel, and the sooner the better. Everything was so uncertain, and he tried not to think about it. It would drive him insane, he knew.

Other eyes peeked from inside the holy place, watching intently. The man made sure that nobody noticed him overhearing the conversation.

Ahimelech returned and gave David the hallowed bread, tentatively. Only the priests were allowed to eat the bread, but it was for a higher cause and he forgot his concerns.

David glanced down the side of the colorful tent again, and saw a man staring at him for an instant. When the man realized this, he pulled his face back.

David frowned, and then remembered the face.

"Doeg," David said to himself softly so that the priest could not hear.

"Do you have a spear or sword for me, priest?" David asked as he turned his eyes from the opening in the tent to the holy man. He saw Ahimelech's wariness at this request, and explained quickly. "I didn't bring my kidon or weapons, because the king's business required haste."

When David was in Saul's city he had to keep himself hidden for fear that someone might inform the king. He had yearned to go to Michal, but he knew that his house was being watched, and so he kept himself hidden in the fields, as Samuel had instructed him.

The priest looked at David for a moment, and then spoke guardedly, his eyes showing his hesitation. "The sword of Goliath the Philistine whom you slew in the valley of Elah." He waited for a moment and then rushed his words as he decided that David was a good man. He admired the young captain and he could feel a holy energy coming from him that he had only felt flowing from the high priests. "It is here, wrapped in a cloth behind the ephod. If you want it, take it, because I have no other."

"There is none better anywhere. Give it to me," David said smiling, knowing that he could finally be on his way. He was eager to leave, and he imagined seeing Saul's men ride after him. He had to leave, he resolved.

"I pray you, priest, before I leave inquire after God for me."

"You just lied to a priest," Eliab said, and took some round bread from David.

"Only the first part, about my being on the king's business. The king's my enemy, and I had to do it, or else we would starve on the way to Gath," David said as they walked. Abinadab, Joab, and Pelet were silent beside them, as they put the bread into their skin bags.

"It was an innocent lie; nothing will come of it," Joab said, watching David tear into the brown loaf hungrily. He had not eaten for days and was ravenous.

"Is there even such a thing—an innocent lie?" Eliab said, and when David did not answer, he knew better than to continue the conversation, and he broke off a piece from the round cake and pressed it into his mouth.

They were heading to Philistia, into Gath. It was his brother's only escape.

Eliab did not want to admit that he was now in just as much danger as David was; Saul would have had their heads if they stayed at the garrison. He prayed that Shammah, Abishai, and Asahel made it to their families in time to warn them.

David looked around at the men, and nodded solemnly as he realized how much he needed them with him. At first, he did not want them to go with him into enemy territory and he had ordered them to leave, but Eliab adamantly reminded him that he was no longer a captain, and insisted on going with him.

He would not let his youngest brother walk into dangerous exile alone, Eliab had said, and David was content that he had decided to go with him. He knew he would come to depend on his elder brother; he would need all of them in the uncertain time that loomed ahead of him.

⟨⟨⟩⟩

They did not know exactly when they crossed the border into Philistia, but they knew that they hadn't been in Israel for days.

They sat in a field surrounding the massive capital of Gath, watching as Philistines walked the winding road to the city and children played in the grass near the gates. Horses pulled drays and soldiers marched on top of the double stone walls. From outside, the city was enormous and David was silent as he studied it. He had never been so deep into Philistia. Hunger made them all uncomfortable.

"You will wait for me here," David said suddenly, not looking at his company. Eliab wanted to speak but David continued, silencing him. "I will not hear a word, brother. I won't endanger your lives. I cannot. I will go in alone and you will remain hidden."

David was silent for a moment with his fears. "If I don't return, know that I am dead and flee from these lands."

Eliab sighed away his resistance, and his silence was acknowledgment enough for David. He looked across at them, gripping Pelet's arm firmly. "You have been a brave soldier, Pelet. You are blessed, my friend."

His officer forced a smile and nodded.

"Eliab, Abinadab, make sure father and mother are safe. I hope you can forgive me."

"There is nothing to forgive, David. We don't blame you," Abinadab said, his voice breaking.

Enough of this nonsense," Joab snapped. "Nothing is going to happen to you. We will wait here for you, and we will see you soon. Now go. I'm getting hungry, and a warm plate of food would go down nicely right now." The men gawked at him. Pelet struck him on the shoulder.

David chuckled, and took his nephew in an embrace. "I knew you would say something like that."

"God be with you, brother," Eliab said.

David crawled out to the wide beaten road, leading to the gates of Gath.

It took all David's courage to walk to the city, through the crowds of Philistines. His heart pounded, and his tongue stuck to the roof of his mouth. He prayed silently for strength and protection as he trod through the heavy stone gates.

Achish was sitting on the wide portico of his palace with Ladiah by his side, caressing her as she listened to his courtiers reading monotonously from numerous scrolls. He regarded his citizens lazily as he sat back into soft cushions, six women fanning him. His queen placed a grape in his mouth, and he kissed her.

Slowly, he stroked Ladiah's hair with his round fingers. She giggled shyly, and he grinned at her.

Ladiah stiffened when she saw David.

She could never forget his face, and that night at the garrison played back in her mind. She sat up straight with a fear she could not understand, placing her hands on her slightly protruding belly, instinctively trying to protect the child growing inside of her. She was safe with her king, she knew, but still pressed herself tightly against Achish.

After what happened to the Sérèn of Ekron, Ladiah had gained a new opinion of her husband. He was the type of danger that one never realizes until it's too late, like a poisonous snake that bites suddenly from beneath the wild grasses. She had decided that she would cease her adulterous ways and when the time came, she allowed Achish to impregnate her. If she gave him a son, then she would be his queen forever. Daila, Achish's last concubine, who had threatened Ladiah, had died mysteriously in her sleep and her secret with her.

The king frowned at his wife's behavior and noticed three guards approaching with their swords pressing against a man's throat. He focused his attention on the captive. Achish thought he recognized him, but was not sure.

"My Lord, this Israelite has requested an audience with you. He says he is the foe of your archenemy, Saul," one of the guards announced, bringing the sword to David's neck. He could feel the cold metal scraping over his Adam's apple as he swallowed nervously.

"And that makes him my friend?" Achish muttered, rounding his lips. David felt as if he could breathe again as the guards lowered their blades and released him, shoving him forward aggressively. His expression was unreadable.

"Is this not ben Jesse, the king of the land?" one of the king's servants said as Achish regarded David, pursing his lips. "Don't they sing one to another of him, 'Saul has slain his thousands, and David his ten thousands'?"

Achish's eyes widened as he finally recognized the Israelite, and then narrowed to small slits. *David.*

The king's eyes bored into the Israelite and he almost ordered him killed and his body hung at the city entrance, when he decided he wanted to torture him first. He would open his throat himself, he decided. David saw the malice in the king's eyes, and the color drained from his face. He would have to do something, or die. His breathing became erratic, and he blinked away the sweat stinging his eyes.

Achish frowned slightly.

David squinted suddenly and he began to laugh raucously as he feigned madness. Achish sneered and looked amazed at his courtiers. David made vulgar signs and began speaking gibberish.

The Philistine king's eyes flared with disgust. "Look, you see the man is mad. Why did you bring him to me?" Achish said.

David screamed violently, spittle dribbling onto his beard and he scrabbled at the doors of the gate. Finally, he sat down with his legs folded underneath him, humming like a child, pulling and twisting his lower lip.

"Have I need of madmen that you bring this Israelite to play the insane in my presence? Shall this Israelite come into my house?" Achish screamed at his guards, pointing at David. They became flustered under his stare. "Take him from my sight and throw him out of the city. Our laws protect him. I cannot slay him if he is unstable … and he evidently is."

David was dragged away, saliva bubbling from his mouth. Achish shivered when he heard David cackle disturbingly.

CHAPTER TWENTY

It had been weeks since Shammah and his three brothers had come home to their birth town and he relished the days spent with his family. The farm where he had grown up opened the floodgates of his memories, and despite the reason for his return, he longed to find a wife and finally begin a family of his own. It was only a dream, he knew. Since his return, he had become increasingly bitter about the years spent fighting in Saul's wars and now the vengeful old man wanted the house of Jesse dead. He had lost so many years.

Now David and his brothers had fled into Philistia and each passing day fed his fears that they were dead, that the king of Gath had hung their corpses on the city gates.

His sisters and their husbands had also come to the farm on the border of Bethlehem. He had rarely seen Zeruiah and Abigail over the years. Their husbands were strangers to him. His sisters had grown old and Zeruiah had gray streaks running through the heavy black curls hanging over her shoulders. Her concern for her eldest son showed in her tight face, and she rarely spoke. Abigail's son, Amasa, had grown into a young man since he had last seen him. He had broad shoulders and a strong figure, clearly inherited from the house of Jesse. Shammah noticed he had large hands and knew he would make a fine swordsman.

Shammah had not been together with his entire family since before he left for war when he was still a young man. His father would not rejoice in the reunion and the atmosphere was thick and dismal.

In the distance, a lone horseman sped to the farmhouse, trailing a bleak pall of dust behind him. Amasa saw him first and shouted for his uncles. The men gathered outside. Zeruiah and Abigail rushed from the house, hope gleaming in their eyes.

"Get back inside. We don't know who he is," Jesse ordered. Zeruiah stood on her toes to try to get a glance at the cloaked figure.

"Now, daughter. Leave." Abigail pulled her sister inside. It was too much for her to bear and Zeruiah finally broke down. They could hear her crying inside, but the men did not shift their eyes from the approaching figure. Was it a messenger from the king, summoning them to appear before him?

"Do you think it might be Eliab or Joab, father?" Shammah asked. Jesse was silent, and they waited anxiously.

Shammah fingered the concealed hilt of his kidon and noticed from the corner of his eye that his father did the same. He could almost smile at this. His father's hair was silver and his skin weathered with age. Deep wrinkles, like the lines of a fishing net, scored his skin and flesh swayed underneath his thin arms as he moved. Jesse had fought many wars over the years and the way he held his kidon was proof of the deadly skill he possessed.

His father was not too old to die fighting, he thought, and it was a good thing to see; it gave him a sense of courage.

"It's Joab, father," Shammah cried, and smiled in relief.

Zeruiah rushed out of the house before all the other women and ran to him, dust caking the streams of tears falling down her cheeks. He was alive, and she praised God.

Joab slowed his horse as he came to his mother, and she grabbed one of his legs, pressing it against her body.

"I feared you were dead," Zeruiah sobbed, as Joab dismounted. His horse breathed wildly, its sweated coat gleaming in the light.

"I have urgent news for the family, mother," Joab said and embraced her. He had missed her this past year. He wiped away the dirt from her face, and then held her again.

"Uncle David is hiding in the cave Adullam. We must go there, mother; all of us, before Saul comes to have his revenge," he said walking his horse. "Tell the women to take only what they need. We must make haste. We must travel under the cover of night."

Zeruiah's son was alive; she did not care about anything else. She was not concerned with giving up her home, her belongings, or her life. Gathering her skirts, she hurried past the women, calling them into the house as her son embraced his father.

***

The market was unusually quiet. Whispers traveled along the few groups of gossiping servants. The air was dense with heavy dust, which covered everything. Even the jewelry did not shine, although the merchants polished the rare items ceaselessly.

Michal meandered through the many stands and spoke a few cordial words with the sellers, admiring their merchandise. She tasted the earth in the air and brushed tendrils of wavy hair from her face. She had to narrow her eyes suddenly against a strong gust, and then she decided it was a foul day for the markets.

The princess thought of David constantly. *Where is he? Is he safe? Did he have food in his belly?* This made her days long and her nights terrible. Jonathan had told her how he had helped her husband escape and she knew that she would never see David again. Michal hated her brother for keeping such a secret from her until her husband had gone from Gibeah. She could have seen him again, although she understood why Jonathan had done it. It was a good thing, she decided. She would have run with her husband, if she had had the chance. The princess could not mourn her husband publicly for fear of her father. She had lied to him, to save David's life. At first, the king had been suspicious, and only after she had scoffed at David before all his courtiers did Saul seem to trust her. She was aware he had somebody following her, watching her continually. She had seen the man following her before, and was afraid at first. One afternoon she decided on a whim to confront him in the markets and threatened to scream and say he tried to dishonor her if he did not speak. Her father's servant told her everything.

Michal was tired, and her movements were listless as she walked back to the palace. She could smell the pungent odor of seafood from the fish-gate on the wind, and she curled her lip slightly.

"David has fled to Gath." Michal heard a voice from behind a stall and she froze. When the two women saw her, they stiffened and were incriminatingly silent.

"What did you say about my husband?" Michal asked impetuously. She could see that they were nervous and she lost her temper. "Tell me. What about David?"

"My princess, I have only heard rumors …" the servant stammered, looking away. Michal slapped her palm against the table, sending some of the artifacts to the ground. Her hand burned, but she glared at the women. "If you don't tell me, I will tear open your throat with my teeth," she shouted, and saw the woman's face whiten against her black hair. She swallowed nervously.

"David fled to King Achish of Gath. I don't know what went wrong, but I hear things went bad, and he barely made it out alive," she said quickly. Michal gasped into cupped hands, her eyes brimming with tears. "He is hiding in the cave Adullam now. Everybody knows this, and I hear many people are going to him, my lady. Everyone who is in distress or discontented, even those who are in debt left the towns days ago. There are rumors that they would make him king."

Michal was like a pillar of stone. She did not react, the women could hardly see her breathe, and then a single tear streaked her face.

"I know nothing more," the woman said and dropped her head in shame. "It saddens me that you had to hear it from me, my princess."

"Here is a coin for your services," Michal said gratefully, her voice quivering slightly. She placed a small brass coin on the table gently and left without a sound. The women looked after the princess, wordless in her wake.

Michal's mind was racing and her emotions were tearing her apart. She wanted to go to David then. She wanted to leave everything, and risk her life to see him again, to hold him. Would she betray her father for the love of a man? It was a terrible choice. She shook her head and covered her mouth tightly with her hand, stifling a sob.

It was a strange thing to see his people there, inside and around the cave Adullam. David swept his gaze across them. They had trickled to the cave over a period of three days, leaving the harvest behind. He had asked Pelet to count them. There were four hundred men over the age of twenty and they could all handle a kidon or spear. Even some of his officers and fighters of the Gibbôr regiment were there. He still did not know how they had heard about it, but he vowed that he would reward their loyalty when he could.

Such news always spread fast, he assumed. He could smile when he looked at his father sitting with him in the cave along with his brothers. It was a great relief to have them with him again. His mother had danced and sang when she saw him, and he had laughed for the first time in the month since he left Gibeah. His father had embraced him and he was shocked to see how old they both had become over the years he had been away at Saul's court. They spoke for hours about everything that David could imagine and, for a brief period, he forgot his circumstances. His entire family was together for the first time in five years.

"Your mother and I are too old to live in the forests and wilderness, David," Jesse said and David sighed, understanding that it was true.

"Where would you go? I need to know that you are safe, father," David said. "I won't leave you anywhere."

"Moab?" Jesse suggested, raising his eyebrows.

"We're not on peaceful terms with Moab, father."

"Saul isn't. Our house is," Jesse said taciturnly. "Your great-grandmother came from Moab and when Shammah first brought news of you, I sent a servant to the king with a message."

David was stunned.

"You knew about this, brother?" David asked Shammah. His brother only shrugged and David looked at his father again. "Will you be safe there?"

"We will be out of the reach of Saul. I survived decades before we brought you into this world. We will be happy there," Jesse said and smiled at his youngest son. David gripped the weak hand of his elderly father and chuckled. "I know."

They shared a silent moment.

There was a letter on her bed. Michal looked at it with dread, her hands shaking. She did not know who brought it or how he achieved it, but somehow she knew it was from David. Her throat closed up at the thought and she could only manage to stare at it.

Finally, she mustered her courage and sat quietly on her bed. She gazed at the folded piece of parchment for minutes before lifting it carefully. The letter was rough between her fingers, and she stroked it before finally untying the thin cord around it and holding it in the dim light of a decorated oval bowl lamp.

It read:

> My beloved wife,
>
> I long for you when the night air is cold and when the days are hot. Time is so much crueler without you by my side. I have found myself running from my own country. I do not know what God will do for me, but I must press on. I have escaped to the cave Adullam and I wait for my family to join me. Please come to me, Michal. I need you to come to me. I will wait until the new moon, only a few nights from now. If I don't see you before then, I'll know it was impossible for you to make the journey. This is my last letter to you.
>
> I adore you, Michal.
>
> Your faithful husband

Michal pressed the letter to her chest and clenched her jaw with killing guilt.

"I cannot come, dear and glorious husband," she said as if he could hear her. When she closed her eyes, tears rushed down her cheeks, and she sniffed, wiping them away. Michal rose from her bed and walked to a brazier warming her chambers, feeling the waves of heat against her cold skin. She looked at his writing one last time and kissed the papyrus gently. Then, she dropped it into the coals. The letter took flame instantly, and the edges shriveled and curled, and then blackened until there was nothing left. Michal realized that she was shaking, and she could not raise her eyes from the burnt ashes of his written words. A sudden gust surged the cloth at her window, and dark pieces blew from the fire in a fluttering trail away from her. Michal held out her fingers slowly in the rush of icy air, as if she could touch her husband, catching some of the cold embers.

"I adore you also, husband," she whispered desolately.

"You sent for me, Samuel," Gad said as he kissed the old prophet's hands, the sun beating down on Samuel's skin as he sat outside his small home in Naioth. He smiled at the young man standing before him in a rich blue tunic with an embroidered shoulder cloak. Gad was one of his most promising disciples.

"David has escaped to the cave of Adullam. I want you to go there, and stay with him. Be a prophet to him, Gad, and show him God's will," Samuel said in a husky voice, and coughed suddenly into his fist. He lifted the drinking bowl filled with water to his lips and emptied it, soothing his dry throat. "I am old, Gad; I cannot go with him. That is why you must. I relieve you of any duties to me, and all I ask is that you continue your holy calling as David's prophet."

"I will do as you ask," Gad answered simply and bowed his head respectfully.

"God is great. May He be with you all your life," Samuel said, and gripped Gad's arm in a silent farewell.

"God is great," Gad repeated, and after a brief moment, turned and left.

There wasn't a trace of a cloud in the sky and the black night seemed alive with glittering stars. David gazed at the heavens, sitting around a flickering flame, amazed at the works of Jehovah. The new moon lightened the endless grass fields around Adullam, which rustled softly in the gentle winter breeze.

Each family had made fires to keep warm, but David sat alone above a ridge so that he could see all around the stone precipice while he waited anxiously for his wife.

With a sigh, he pulled the badger skin tighter, and searched the distance again for her.

Pelet came to him in the early hours of the morning. David had not slept for days. Blue circles had formed under his eyes, and he was weak with exhaustion, but every time he wanted to sleep, his thoughts and fears kept him awake.

"She will come, David," Pelet said softly and placed his hand on his shoulder. David shrugged, and stared into the dying flames. He was quiet, and Pelet did not have the words to speak. He could not stand to see his captain like this, and he resented the princess for the pain she was causing David.

"I will keep watch for her. Why don't you sleep until the sun rises? It's going to be a long day tomorrow," Pelet said and sat down beside his leader on a thin reed mat. His skin was blue from the cold and he bent forward into the heat of the smoldering fire. David nodded, and wearily curled himself onto his small carpet.

"Wake me when she comes, Pelet." As soon as he spoke the words, he was asleep.

It was a slow trek to the mountainous lands of Moab. It had taken David nearly eight days to cross the border and then three more to reach the city of Mizpah. David was frustrated with the pace, and had to remind himself that he was not leading a regiment of fit warriors, but civilians. He could have made the crossing in three days, he told himself, but he would not leave anybody behind.

There was no trace of Saul or his men, and this concerned him. Why wasn't Saul following him? The first few days were the worst, when David had to order double pace when they traveled around the region of Gibeah and the borders of Benjamin, Saul's tribe. He would not relax until he reached the first plateaus of Moab. They would be safe there.

David was in a sensitive mood for days, and though he tried not to think of Michal, he did constantly, mentally stoning himself, raging at Saul. Torturing himself with images of her, he fought with himself not to become bitter. He lived in mute anguish.

Mizpah was a small town, heavily protected by double stone walls and heavy wooden and brass gates. David and his parents could enter the city, but the rest of the Israelites had to set up camp outside of the walls. The royal city was attractive with large houses architecturally unique to the region, and a massive well in the center of the town. The king's palace was the largest structure in Mizpah with massive engraved wooden pillars against the walls that supported the second and third stories, and a lush green garden surrounding it. Hundreds of slaves moved around the royal grounds all dressed in plain gray tunics. David and his parents were invited into the palace with great hospitality.

The Moabite king was a short, slender man with hard masculine features. He had red ridges on his skin, which to David looked like ritualistic scars of some sort. He was dressed in fine silk and had women, almost entirely naked, dancing around his throne waving many-colored cloths in a carnal fashion to the rhythm of musicians playing on flute-like instruments and small hand drums. When the king noticed David's and his parent's discomfort, he smiled broadly and ordered the performers out of the throne room.

"Your message was a great surprise to me, Jesse ben Obed," the king said plainly in a deep voice, taking a cup of wine mixed with milk that formed a thick soup. He waited as the slave held a tray for Jesse and his family to take goblets. Jesse understood that it would have been rude not to accept the king's hospitality, and they all took a brass vessel. Jesse bowed his head to the young king. David smelled the heavy drink for a moment. It had a pungent odor, but he closed his eyes and tasted it. It had a bitter, almost sour, flavor although it wasn't so unpleasant that he could not finish it.

"You are welcome in my court and my palace," the king said. "Is this the great captain that Saul pursues? He has a strong spirit, I can see."

"Thank you, king of Moab," David said and lowered his eyes to the floor.

"Enough of these pleasantries. I will have your parents eat from my table and live in my city if we can come to some kind of arrangement. I will be generous; after all, you have Moabite blood in your veins," he said and David met his eyes.

"A good king is always quick to speak his mind," David said with a smile.

"When you are king of Israel I want to know that our two nations will be at peace, and may even trade."

"If there is no bad blood between us, it shall always be so, lord of Moab," David said reservedly.

The Moabite king looked David squarely in the eyes as he spoke. "May there not be, in all our days, descendant of Ruth." David kept his gaze as the king continued. "Jesse, it is my honor to have your house sit at my table, and you will be accepted among my people."

David smiled finally and lowered his head. "It is a great thing you do for us, and I shall remember it always."

"Let us have some food and drink," the king shouted and the room filled with slaves.

The strong afternoon sunlight dappled Saul's skin as he sat underneath a tamarisk tree on a low hill looking out over Gibeah with a javelin in his hands, his hatred for David overpowering him. The king tightened his grip on his spear, his flesh white around the wooden shaft.

"Hear now, you Benjamites. Will the son of Jesse give every one of you fields and vineyards, and make you all captains of thousands and hundreds, that all of you have conspired against me?" Saul sneered at his officers standing around him, bristling. His eyes were cold and glared dangerously. "None of you told me that my son had made a covenant with the son of Jesse."

Saul's servants were quiet, and could not look him in the eyes. He was their king, he was of the same tribe as they, and they would hate David if he ordered them to.

Their silence confirmed Saul's suspicions that they were all against him. He raised his voice in anger as he continued. "And there is none of you who is sorry for me or tells me that my son has stirred up my servants against me, to lie in wait and try to assassinate me?" Saul scowled at Ehud, his captain over a thousand, and the man knelt.

A burly man with short black curls stepped from behind the tight arch of men and bowed his head respectfully before Saul. He took a deep breath and then answered the brooding king. "I was detained before the Lord and I saw the son of Jesse come to Nob, to Ahimelech the son of Ahitub."

Saul did not say a word, and his eyes gleamed violently.

The man continued with a note of caution. "Ahimelech inquired of the Lord for him, and gave him provisions, and also gave him the sword of the Philistine Goliath."

What is your name, servant?" Saul asked.

"Doeg, I'm an Edomite, my great king. I'm your chief herdsman," the man said and prostrated himself before Saul.

"Doeg, you assert this is true?"

"I do, Lord Saul," Doeg said. Saul's face flushed and he grunted, his hand shaking with malevolent passion. He had had enough and something in him took over. He did not think reasonably, and jealousy and evil revenge possessed him. He became insane.

Saul screamed savagely, spittle catching in his beard, "Call Ahimelech and his father's entire house, and the priests that are in Nob." The king snapped the spear in two. There was nothing left for him and he surrendered completely. He was exhausted, and mentally and emotionally spent. Saul could not take the depression any longer. It had ruined him. He could not stand to compare himself with the son of Jesse, and wondered what he lacked that David had—all of the virtues that he did not possess, God's blessings, the love and loyalty of his own country. Saul was driven by pure hatred. In an instant, Saul felt depression come over him in a suffocating wave.

Something died in the king that day, and he lost all sense of reality and restraint. He only lived to kill David, and secure his crown. Only then could he be content.

Chapter Twenty-One

David sat around a large fire banked by heavy stones in the wilderness of Moab, with his newly appointed council of ten men. David had chosen his three eldest brothers, his nephews, Pelet, and two of Gibbôr's officers that had come to him from Saul's ranks. The winter nights in the foreign land were colder than David had ever experienced and he thought no fire would ever warm him, the icy air seeping through layers of fur.

"David, God has spoken to me," Gad said powerfully, and waited until David's council of men had quieted down. He did not move; it was as if he were made from iron. "We must go back to Israel at once. Into the lands of Judah."

The council was silent, looking at the prophet, their breath forming into white air from their lips. "It would look suspicious if we stayed in Moab. Our own people might think we are guilty of something that we run from our birth lands," Eliab agreed solemnly.

"Where in Judah, prophet?" David asked, his eyes distant as he contemplated the young man's words.

"To the forest of Hareth."

"If it is the will of Yahweh, we shall go," David said, nodding slightly. "Pelet, sound the horn. Get the men ready to move. We depart at first light."

The throne room was a cold, dreary place. Saul had all the plants and color removed, and now all that remained were his plain wood and ivory throne and the massive earth statues against gray stone-block walls. Nothing was splendid to him anymore, and anything that was lovely to others, he could not stand to look at. He wanted the world to be as miserable as he was. A large fireplace dimly lit the room along with few bronze bowl lamps burning with olive oil. A brazier by his throne provided warmth against the night breeze hissing through the high, oblong windows.

Doeg stood somberly in a dark corner.

The king slumped miserably on his throne. His hair was filthy, his beard unkempt, and his sweat acrid on his skin. A servant entered and bowed before Saul. "The priests of Nob have arrived, my king."

Saul's eyes went hard and he waved the man away.

In a silent procession, the holy men entered the chamber, their faces grave. Saul watched them like a lion stalking prey.

Eighty-five men stood in a semi-circle before the king and Saul observed them with a penetrating gaze. Ten footmen entered the room last and when they closed the doors, the priests tensed visibly. The room became suddenly claustrophobic.

Saul brushed his filthy hair back from his face and sniffed, staring at Ahimelech who was standing in front of the priests. He did not bow, keeping Saul's bloodshot gaze. The king's skin was pale in the dimness and the light reflecting on his face lent him a murderous aspect.

"Hear now, you son of Ahitub," Saul said.

"Here I am, my lord," Ahimelech answered.

"Why have you conspired against me, you and the son of Jesse, by giving him bread, a sword, and inquiring of God for him? Just so he should rise against me, to lie in wait, wanting to assassinate me?"

"And who is so faithful among all your servants as David?" Ahimelech began.

Saul broke into the priest's words with a brutal scream, gripping the armrests of his throne, his knuckles white. "You will not speak that name in my presence." He pushed himself forward like a frenzied animal, showing his teeth.

"Who is the king's son-in-law, and goes at your bidding, and is honorable in your house?" Ahimelech continued resolutely, seeming undisturbed by Saul's behavior. He drew in a slow breath. "Did I then begin to inquire of God for him? Yes, I did. Don't accuse your servant of anything, nor anyone in the house of my father, for I knew nothing of this matter."

Saul rose from his throne and waited before he spoke. There was a terrible silence and nervous sweat broke out on some of the priests' faces. He swept his gaze over them and then smiled maliciously at Ahimelech. "You shall surely die, Ahimelech; you and your father's entire house."

The priests gasped in stark terror. Ahimelech's features were hard, scowling at the mad king. He would not let him see his fear. Saul laughed at the strain he saw on the priest's face.

"Turn and slay the priests of the Lord," Saul ordered his footmen blasphemously. "Because their hands are also with David, and because they knew when he fled and did not tell me."

Ahimelech began to chant. He was not afraid of any man, and he would not cower from death.

Bewildered, the footmen watched their king, held by indecision. They could not smite the servants of Jehovah, but they knew Saul could have them killed for not acting on his orders.

The other eighty-four priests began intoning a dramatic Hebrew hymn with Ahimelech.

Saul's soldiers refused to murder the holy men. Saul frustrated, tugged at his hair, groaning irrationally.

"Doeg, kill the priests," he roared.

The muscular man came from the shadows like an evil spirit. He did not say a word, but his eyes made the men shrink away from him as he stepped forward. He pulled his kidon from his scabbard in a flash of yellow light and without hesitation slit the first man's throat in a clean slash. The man dropped, but the priests knew there was nowhere to go, so they continued there humming, not looking at the killer, their bodies painfully rigid. Doeg's hand quivered, his blade dripping with blood. He clenched his teeth as he increased his resolve.

With a loud cry, he attacked those wearing the linen ephod, hacking at their flesh like a mindless creature. He stabbed at chests and stomachs and opened throats with his blade without seeming to stop. The singing, tinged with the screams of dying men and painful groans of death, did not quiet as Doeg swiftly murdered the priests.

Finally, corpses surrounded Ahimelech, his legs dripping with the lifeblood of his fellow men. He closed his eyes valiantly, and then the sword was thrust into his back. He cried out in pain, gripping the gory tip of the blade protruding from his stomach. Moaning, he sliced his fingers as he fell from the blade, dropping into the pool of blood.

The room was silent and Doeg was aghast at what he had done. His kidon slipped from his fingers weakly, his body shaking violently as he struggled to breathe. They were all dead.

Saul smiled evilly and lowered to his knee beside the still Ahimelech, his robe staining dark. He slowly dipped his fingers in the thick liquid, and he stared at the red tips.

Screams filled the morning air as Israelites ran from their homes in the priestly city of Nob, frantically trying to escape the footmen slaughtering all that breathed. Women held their children as bronze cut into their flesh. The men tried desperately to defend their families, but Saul's force was overpowering.

A small boy ran through the narrow alleyways, covered in blood. He had watched his mother die as his father carried him away, frantically running from a soldier. Now, all he could think of was his father's expression after he had fallen on him when a killer had speared him. The child had slithered out from underneath the weight of the corpse and raced away not looking back at how his father was beheaded. He did not cry. His eyes were hard and his face tight with horror. He rounded a corner not knowing where he was fleeing. The shouting and screams faded into the background, his mind blank. He did not see anything around him, just the high maze of stone alleyways he sprinted through.

He just had to keep running, he told himself.

Suddenly he crashed into a tall figure looming over him. A strong hand covered his mouth and the child felt his heart pound. When the man pulled him closer to his body, he went numb with fear. He was crying hysterically, and his face was glowing from the heat. He struggled, kicking and writhing in the man's firm grip.

"I don't want to die," he piped into the hand that kept his mouth shut, muting his terrified voice, shaking his head violently. Images of his parents' contorted faces as they died flashed into his mind, and he lifted his eyes to the strip of steel blue sky above the buildings.

"Please, Yahweh, don't let him hurt me," he prayed desperately and then he was jerked from his prayer.

"If you want to live, keep quiet. If they hear us they will come," a deep voice whispered harshly and only then did the child look at who was holding him. It was Abiathar, the priest Ahimelech's son. A man and a woman were with him who he did not recognize. The Israelite boy broke down bawling.

He would not be slain; he rejoiced and he thanked God through his sobbing. Abiathar held the child, rocking him slowly, keeping his mouth covered. After a moment, he picked him up and they hurried down a deserted path that led to a dark, dead end.

Abiathar put the child down for a minute and told the boy to be silent. The lad nodded, some of the color returning to his face.

Abiathar and his servant moved heavy earthenware pots away from against the wall, revealing a small wooden door in the ground. He quickly lifted the secret door and lowered first the youth into the gaping blackness, then the woman, and his manservant. Silently, he pushed all of the several vessels as close against the wall as he could manage. Abiathar had to pull in his stomach as he slipped down between the clay vessels and the coarse stone bricks scraping him. After he fell through the square door in the floor, he closed it gently.

They were in a small room, with no other way out. The air was thick with dust and they were in total darkness.

Ahimelech had shown his son the hiding place moments before he left for Gibeah and told him to save as many people as he could, but to get out of the city if something were to happen. He did not understand what his father had meant then, but now the facts fell into place in his mind. It was too much for him to handle at once. For the first time he realized that his father must be dead and he wept softly. The woman held the youngster firmly in her arms. Now they had to wait, and time seemed their enemy.

Abiathar did not know how long they were in the hole. It felt like days. They had to hold each other in an attempt to stay warm. They shivered with the bitter temperatures and weariness, and he knew that if they were to doze off, they would not wake. If it hadn't been for the blanket in the hidden room, they would not have survived. They drank water sparsely from five clay jugs. The cramped room was almost a furnace in the afternoons.

The city was deathly quiet.

"Stay here with the boy and the woman," Abiathar told his manservant and opened the hatch. Slowly he climbed through the door and gingerly walked down the small street. He did not hear a sound.

The air stank of decaying flesh and he felt like vomiting.

As he approached the main street of the city, he heard growls and he froze. He did not know what the sound was. Could it be soldiers still lurking around the streets? He carefully edged from the alleyway.

Abiathar gasped, his face paled in shock at what he saw. His birth town was strewn with the bodies of men, women, and children, their blood staining the streets. It struck his heart like a stone.

The sight of infants still wrapped in swaddling cloths, their skins purple and black, would haunt him forever.

Saul had even killed the livestock and asses—nothing was left alive. The king had placed the city under a total ban.

Black swarms of flies buzzed over the bodies, and he could smell disease brewing in the heavy air. A pride of lions had entered the city from the wilderness and was tearing into the broken carcasses. A young lioness jerked at a discolored limb, giving the arm a sickening appearance of life. Vultures stalked around the feeding beasts, trying to get scraps of skin and bone. The sight was too much for Abiathar and he doubled over, vomiting on the filthy cobblestones. He moved back cautiously, his eyes wide with revulsion as he wiped his mouth with the back of his hand.

"We did nothing wrong," he screamed, his eyes gleaming with tears.

He had to get to David, he realized. His father had made him swear that he would escape the city and flee to David.

It was if he were seeing everything from outside his own body. Everything he did felt mechanical and dominated by the plaguing images of his people.

The forest of Hareth was a good place for David to hide from the king. It was a densely wooded area and full of deer and small animals to hunt. The woodland floor was covered ankle deep with leaves and was constantly moist from the winter rains. Strong sunlight filtered through the thick canopy of leaves and branches in rays of moving light, mottling the ground. The air was cool and crisp, although it smelled of moldering vegetation.

David walked alone through the temporary camp. People moved about as if they were in a busy city. Children played, their voices happy, and he smiled at them. The Israelites were gathering food from the woods and the women had already begun lighting fires in anticipation of the cold night.

David thought about Michal occasionally although he tried not to because it always left him in a distasteful temper. Over the weeks, his desire for his wife had diminished and he found himself seldom dreaming of her. He was inured as much as a husband could be to his wife's absence.

Asahel, Joab's youngest brother, brought David from his musing as he placed his hand on his uncle's shoulder. David started at his touch.

"You have to come now, uncle. Saul has slain all the inhabitants of Nob. The priests are dead." David reeled at the news, his eyes widening incredulously. Guilt hit him like a blow to the stomach. He would not believe it.

Abiathar looked like death had touched him. His eyes drooped with dark shadows underneath and blood and filth caked his skin. He could barely stand up straight.

"What has Saul done?" David asked with a slack jaw, distraught by the man's appearance.

"David, the king murdered my father," Abiathar said, and his voice broke with his surging emotion. He clenched his teeth against the feelings welling up inside of him, and he tried to stop himself from weeping. He looked away, as if ashamed of his weakness. "… my father and eighty-four priests wearing the linen ephod."

David gasped. Fresh remorse shrouded him now that he saw the son of Ahimelech. David knew he had to comfort the man, but he could not bring himself to do it. He wanted to speak, but the words caught in his throat.

"He came to the city with hundreds of soldiers and they slaughtered everyone, even the young children and the women. I saw infants rotting in their mother's arms. I can still smell their stink in my nose, and I …" Abiathar rushed his words and then wept bitterly. "I managed to save three people: my servant, a woman, and a young lad," he finally continued. "We buried only the closest relatives of the people that had escaped with me—what was left of them anyway. I still have their blood on me. The rest of the dead we burned. We watched Nob blaze behind us as we came here. I only managed to save the ephod, and I brought it here," Abiathar wiped the tears from his eyes with his fingers.

Abiathar stared before him as he saw the images flash painfully in his mind again. He was silent for a moment and then continued. David could hear a note of frenzy in the man's voice. "David, when I ran through the side streets of the city

I had a glimpse of Saul. He was insane, howling like some animal. He laughed as his men killed our people. I did not wait to see anything else."

"He's a tyrant," Abiathar added, compressing his fists as he shuddered.

"No, Abiathar listen to me now. I ..." David said suddenly, hanging his head, searching for words, "... I knew that day when Doeg the Edomite was there. I had known that surely he would tell Saul."

David looked Abiathar in the eyes and took him by the shoulders. "I have caused the death of all the people of your father's house," he said emotionally and dropped to his knees. He kissed Abiathar's feet.

Ahimelech's son could not speak. He closed his eyes as he tried to calm down.

"Did you stab my father?" Abiathar asked abruptly, his voice desolate.

David jerked his head up, looking at him in surprise.

"No, you did not; this Doeg creature did. You did not cause the death of anyone, David," Abiathar said before the son of Jesse could answer.

David rose to his feet, and embraced him. "Stay here with me, Abiathar, and fear not, because he that seeks my life seeks your life. But with me you shall be safeguarded."

Chapter Twenty-Two

Teams of oxen bellowed as they pulled drays loaded with trading goods into the city of Keilah of the tribe Judah.

The city had large stone walls with heavy wooden doors and wide beams to bar the gates.

The drivers studied the port sullenly. A man glanced behind him, checking underneath the linen cloth covering his wares. An Israelite woman noticed that one of the men had a large scar across his forearm, and she wondered about it for a moment. When the driver saw that she was looking at him, his eyes gleamed dangerously. She stepped back uneasily from the cumbersome beasts as they slowly tramped past her, and ran off, holding against her body a small bundle of material that she had purchased from the market.

Suddenly the first driver shouted and snapped the reins, bringing the bulls to an uneasy halt.

"What do you have to sell?" the market overseer asked, patting the sweaty coat of a bullock. He looked up at the muscular man and his eyes widened as steel cut through his abdomen.

He doubled over, and a sandaled foot kicked him from the blade.

"Now, men—attack!" the carter shouted and jumped to the ground. Linen rags were thrown from the carts and hundreds of Philistines emerged. Women screamed and scattered with their children into the nearest houses where they locked the doors and began barring the entrances.

A guard came at the Philistine leader. His kidon was blocked, and the large man punched him in the gut. More Israelite combatants came at them in waves. The fighting men kicked up clouds of dust, and the sounds of battle raged.

David had organized the four hundred men with him into ranks, and his newly selected officers had trained them for weeks in the concealing forest of Hareth. They practiced battle formations and the melee as well as weapons exercises and ranged attacks. David was shaping them into Israelite warriors, his band of skilled fighters, his apiru. David had heard that Saul dissolved Gibbôr and the men that remained loyal to the king had been initiated into existing regiments. But David had been determined to keep the unit perpetual. Soon after, he inaugurated only the fiercest and bravest men that were with him into an elite fighting force. Gibbôr was reborn—David's Mighty Men.

David was dueling with the kidon against Jediael, one of his council members who had come to him at the cave Adullam from the decommissioned Gibbôr in Saul's army. Sweat was dripping from his bare arms and chest as he parried every attack. Jediael was panting, his muscles burning as David blocked his sword with his wooden shield, and he was now on the offense. David hacked with great precision, his blade thudding into the hardened leather. Jediael stepped back, rustling through the undergrowth, when his back knocked suddenly against a tree. This threw off his aim and he missed a blow with his sword, and froze as David pressed cold bronze against his neck. With a gentle slide of his hand, David nicked the skin.

He smiled at him. "I drew first blood. I win . . . again," he said, rolling his eyes. He lowered his blade, chuckling.

Without warning, Jediael launched a series of fierce strikes at him, grunting as he felt exhaustion grip his body. David had to defend with all of his skill, and his council member nearly slashed him. David's face twisted in determination and in one movement, ducked below a high swing, and smashed aside the impeding shield with a grunt. He creased Jediael's throat with his kidon again. He was careful not to make it fatal.

Jediael groaned at the stinging wound and felt the trickle of warm blood from his neck, staining the edges of his tunic red. "Want to try that again ... when I'm looking?" David whispered into his ear, and kicked him down into the leaves.

"Get that cleaned or disease might taint your flesh," David said. The glance Jediael gave him made him burst into laughter and he helped his chief-officer to his feet, standing on his blade to make sure that Jediael did not attack him again. Jediael smiled dutifully at him. "I'll be back in a moment, after the physician has bound this little scratch you accidentally managed," Jediael said. "Now I'm furious, and then I always win."

David snorted and he saw the corners of his chief-officer's mouth curve up. "You will learn your lesson sooner or later," David shouted after him.

Several of his men were still fighting in pairs, and wiping the sweat from his brow, David studied them. After a time, many men had drawn first blood and only two teams were still at it. An officer raised his hand to call a halt, understanding that the fights were becoming dangerous. He feared that the men might fatally injure one another.

David stopped the ranking soldier and moved closer to the struggling men. It was a good show. The men had particular skill. He folded his arms on his chest as he watched, entertained.

Slowly the other fighters formed a wide circle and began to cheer the men still battling it out.

Finally, David decided it was enough and began applauding. The crowd's roar died away and the four men stopped, panting heavily as they rested their palms on their knees. Everyone began to shout their names rowdily, clapping their hands.

Eliab touched David's shoulder from behind and spoke into his ear. "We must convene the council; I have news."

David nodded and demanded silence with a show of his hands. He waited for them to quiet down.

"The warrior that can beat all four of these fighters in a duel, I will personally make a commander," David said, and turned on his heel. He left to the approving shouts of the men.

"The Philistines fight against Keilah. They're robbing the threshing floors as we speak," Eliab said as he sat in front of a large fire, alongside the nine councilmen.

"Call Abiathar, and tell him to bring the ephod," David said, sweeping his gaze around the men. He began pacing around the circle of baked earth covered in mounds of soot and ashes from the fire of the previous night. He placed his foot on one of the charred stones rimming the fireplace.

Abiathar brought the priestly robe. It was a sleeveless vest of fine twined linen with scarlet, blue, and purple interwoven with gold wire, and had a square breastplate hanging in front of the chest. It was embedded with twelve precious stones, each representing one of the tribes of Israel, with each name delicately engraved on them.

On the shoulder pieces were two onyx engraved with the names of the children of Israel.

The artifact seemed to shine in the dim light and they could feel a holy energy flowing from it that made their skin tingle.

David watched as Abiathar pushed his head through a mailed hole in the robe and hung it upon his shoulders. The priest adjusted the golden plate against his forehead, fingered the Hebrew letters *"Holiness to the Lord,"* inscribed into the gold, and exhaled a quivering breath. The rich blue garment undulated above his knees and the many golden bells fastened to the hem rang sweetly with Abiathar's movements.

Abiathar closed his eyes involuntarily and began a low chant. He could no longer feel the leaves of the forest floor scraping and itching against his skin or smell the damp air of the lush woodlands. His breath was gone suddenly and he could hear the echo of the bells as if in the distance.

He felt himself in a light so pure that it made the blazing sun look faint. His nostrils filled with the overpowering scent of roses. It was as if he were a visitor in a new celestial body and he found himself thinking instinctively, *"Shall David go and smite these Philistines?"*

All around him boomed an omnipotent voice, *"Go and smite the Philistines, and save Keilah!"* It was like the roar of a thousand waterfalls and the words resounded deep inside his mind, almost at the core of his very being. Then he returned to Hareth. He could hear the birds of the forest and he could smell the distinctive odor of the moist vegetation. He knees wobbled as if after great exertion. He swallowed and closed his eyes as he felt his strength returning.

David waited anxiously.

"We march for Keilah, men," Abiathar said.

David lay on his back, sunken in the forest bed as he contemplated the works of Jehovah. Everything that he feared seemed simple and even the thought of Michal did not hurt him. Wind whispered through the heavy branches of the trees, swaying them rhythmically. The gray light of the afternoon presaged the coming rainstorm and David frowned at the thought of the late rain. It was nearly summer. He took in a lungful of the rain-scented air, welcoming it. He loved when the heavens opened and showered the earth.

The day had grown cold and he wondered when his brother would call him to lead the men to Keilah. He had decided that the women and children should remain hidden in the safety of the woodlands.

He would march his four hundred men south.

David heard the dried plants and twigs crush under heavy footsteps and he rolled over and turned his head to see who was approaching. Eliab rustled through the foliage and lowered to a knee beside his brother.

"The men want to speak to you, brother," he said sternly, and rose and walked away. David got up from his bed of leaves and hurried after him.

"What's this about, brother?" he asked, nearly running to keep up with Eliab's long steps.

"They're afraid," Eliab said abruptly glancing at him with a flash of irritation. David knew his brother could not stand cowering men. To him it was unacceptable and he strode like an angry bull.

David walked beside him in silence and when they neared the group of waiting men, he placed his hand gently on Eliab's shoulder. "Calm yourself, brother," he said.

"They had better be careful. I would shout at them what I think of their fear," Eliab grumbled.

"You will calm yourself, Eliab. Agreed?" David demanded authoritatively. He could see the anger in his brother's expression subside as he slowed his pace suddenly and David walked past him determinedly.

A large group of men watched as their leader approached and he could sense their anxiety grow as he marched towards them.

"What is the problem here?" David asked in measured tones, looking at the bearded men. They moved uneasily as a faint murmur escaped from them.

"We are already afraid here in Judah; how much more then, if we go to Keilah against the armies of the Philistines?" a voice shouted from the crowd. Cries of agreement rent the quiet air.

David stared at them, his expression unreadable and then, he nodded silently.

"If I inquire of the Lord again, then you will follow me?" David asked, raising his eyebrows. The men whispered among themselves and then one of the taller men in front of the host of Israelites voiced their collective concurrence. David smiled confidently, and he summoned Abiathar again with the ephod.

Abiathar stood chanting before the men with the embroidered and decorated garment hanging over his shoulders. The encrusted jewels gleamed with soft flowing light as he moved, the bells chiming gently. The men were completely still, watching in anticipation. The moments seemed to stretch endlessly.

Then Abiathar opened his eyes and slumped weakly. As one, the group moved closer. David held his hand up for them to halt and he could hear them press against each other, as he focused his attention on the priest. Abiathar inhaled deeply as he straightened himself. He was grinning as he cleared his throat. There came a few hushes from the men, summoning silence.

"The Lord has answered me," he spoke loudly so that they could all hear. "The Lord answered me and said, 'Arise, go down to Keilah. For I will deliver the Philistines into your hand.' Glory to Yahweh!"

The crowd came alive with wild shouts and confident cheers and David roared over them, waving his tight fist in the air, "We march for Keilah!"

David's woolen halug was heavy with rain and his skin was blue from the morning cold. His thighs and forearms were splattered with dark mud as he crawled on his knees through the beaten wild grasses, the silvery raindrops hitting against his leather armor. Water flowed from his soaked beard and he licked his trembling lips. David had to will his body not to shiver too wildly from the cold.

It was the perfect time to attack the city. Thunder muted their movements and the violent weather covered their approach behind a natural watery veil.

His men were close behind him.

To get a good shot, David had to creep closer for a clear view. Strong gusts blew the curtain of rain aside and David could suddenly see six large men guarding the closed gates of the town. He motioned four other slingers to his side with a wave of his dirtied hand beside his head.

In deadly silence, five stones flew, striking three of the men. They coughed and grunted, their sounds of pain deadened by the squall. They dropped into the mud.

David could see the other men search through the downpour and then as one, they turned to hammer at the door. More stones struck them and David hit a man at the base of his skull. His head jerked against the wooden gates and he splashed into a puddle. With another sign, David and his men rose from the grass like steam from a cauldron, and hurried for the walls. His muscles were slow to react in the freezing temperatures; his mind tired.

David hammered at the large gates with all his strength, feeling the soft flesh at the side of his fists burn from the impact.

He waited and then knocked again. "Open the gates," he shouted in Semitic Philistine.

He untied his hand-axe from his bronze belt and readied himself. It took awhile for the gates to creak open and as soon as a man peered outside, David struck at his neck. Blood spurted across his hands and the man cringed and contorted as he managed to run back into the city, grasping the wound.

Twenty hands grabbed the massive doors and forced them open. An Israelite screamed, as a steel blade cut off his fingers gripping the wood.

David rushed around the partially opened gates and met two fighters with their swords drawn. Quickly he severed an arm and spun to cut the second man, a massive brutish Philistine.

David slipped on the wet stones, perilously falling winded before the huge Philistine. The man sneered and David's eyes widened as the slicing blade came at his face.

He rolled aside and heard the blade clang against the cobblestones. This time he felt his hair pulled from his scalp. It burned fiercely, but he could not think about it then and snatched his blade just in time to block the assailing sword. David turned and hacked at a leg, his kidon embedded in the bone.

The man screamed and David rose without a weapon. He had hoped the Philistine would fall and then he could arm himself again, but the colossus didn't. He roared and as David came to his feet, the man punched him square in the face. He could feel his nose snap and rain sluice away a torrent of blood, although he could taste it in his mouth. His sight darkened as he staggered back, dizzy, tiny flashes of light piercing the terrible numbing blackness.

Where were his men? David willed himself to remain conscious, as he anticipated the Philistine slicing him open.

In his frenzy, the warrior rushed forward and when he put his weight on the broken bone, he came down with a crash. David regained his sight, though his head throbbed horribly, and he saw the man fumbling at the bronze lodged in him.

Eliab dashed past and stabbed him in the heart.

Most of the Philistines had nodded off from the sleep-inducing cold and the Israelites caught the enemy off guard. Four hundred men charged through the city with flailing weapons. It was a massacre.

Chapter Twenty-Three

Saul rubbed his forehead with his thumb and sighed. He had a throbbing headache. His royal harpist strung the strings of a kinnor and began to play.

"That's enough," he snapped and sent the young man away with a wave of his hand. The few swaying flames of bronze bowl lamps gave the room a menacing atmosphere.

"Why isn't that potion working?" Saul demanded of the physician standing beside his throne. He gripped his head tightly as another pang, more intense than the previous waves of pain, stabbed at his pounding head. The king's sight blurred and he felt nauseous, moaning as he writhed on his throne. He broke out in a cold sweat and lost consciousness.

Cool water dripped across the king's face as a servant girl pressed a soaked cloth against his forehead. Saul realized what was happening and flung his eyes open. He gave the woman a backhand slap, sending her to the floor.

"How dare you touch royal flesh without permission," he screamed coming from his chair. Saul stared after her furiously as she ran from the throne room holding her burning cheek.

"It was to wake you, sire. I ordered it to break your fever," the physician stammered.

"I'm fine, leave me," he shouted. He hurled the wet rag into the old man's face and sank into the thick yielding cushions of his stone chair.

"Y-yes, King Saul," he bowed and could not leave the room soon enough. For a moment he thought about joining the son of Jesse in the wilderness. He was no man's dog, not even a mad king's, he decided, clenching his jaw in frustration as he stumbled though the cold, bare corridors of Saul's fortress-palace.

A courtier entered the large room and prostrated himself before Saul. He felt the king's eyes bore into his back and he feared for a moment that the insane monarch would spear him where he lay.

"What do you want, little man?" Saul sneered through gritted teeth, holding his hurting head. "The pain—get me some water."

Saul's richly dressed servant walked to a clay pitcher and ladled room temperature liquid into a small drinking bowl. Saul drank deeply. The cold stung his head and he grimaced as the water dripped from his mouth and down his beard.

"It's too cold, you goose!" he roared and smashed the ceramic vessel against the man's skull. Blood ruined the courtier's silk tunic as he gripped his bleeding ear. The wound burned and he ground his teeth as he pulled a bloody piece of pottery from his flesh. Warm blood flowed down his neck and he staggered back as he looked at the shard in his hand. Shaking with fear, he glanced up at Saul.

"Didn't I ask you why you came here? Stop gawking at me."

"A soldier came to me, Lord Saul, from Keilah. He said that David and his followers are there in the city. Philistines raided ..." he said and Saul leaped at him, grabbing the courtier's neck in a choking grip.

"Haven't I ordered that no man shall mention his name in my presence? Does nobody ever listen to the king?"

The short man groped desperately at Saul's rough hands. He tried to scream, but his voice was hoarse and he groaned as he felt his lungs grow tight.

Saul drawled harshly. "I will make you obey me, you and all Israel."

The courtier reached desperately for Saul's face and scratched him, tearing his skin. Saul did not even blink. His own blood dripping across the bridge of his nose infuriated him and he pressed down on the man's throat more tightly.

The flesh collapsed under his grip and the body went limp.

God has delivered David into my hand, Saul thought suddenly, *because once he entered into a town that has gates and bars, he is shut in.*

"David ben Jesse," Saul intoned as if singing a song, repeating the words, as he began dragging the dead courtier away. He sat the body behind his broad throne and wiped his face dry on his sleeve, biting his lip as the cloth stung the lacerations.

"Call Doeg," he shouted, and two guards entered. They hesitated for a moment at the sight of their king, and then one spoke. "You're bleeding, my king."

Saul shot him a glance that made the man reel. "I did this to myself. Look," Saul raged and sank his nails into the side of his face. He began jerking at his beard until he held a hand full of black hair in his fist. He showed it to the guards, his eyes cold and dangerous.

"Do you have anything else to say? I ordered you to summon Doeg. I will not tell you again!" he screamed, spit flying from his mouth.

The man started from the room, disturbed. Saul paced the length of the room, mumbling with delusions, blood dripping from him. His sandals smeared the veined floor with streaks of red and he shook as if freezing.

Doeg entered the room, panting from his run. He gasped at the sight of Saul. It was as if the air around him was black, and violent negative energy was pouring from him. The king's clothes were dark with gleaming stains of his own blood and he lurched from one end of the room to another. When Saul looked at him, a chill raced down his spine.

Doeg bowed. "You summoned me, my king," he said managing a steady voice after his initial alarm.

"I want to ask if you will do a small deed for me," Saul said in a deranged, uncertain voice.

"My king?" Doeg asked.

"I knew I could rely on you. Look behind my throne."

Doeg rose from the hard floor, feeling a slight ache in his kneecap. He moved to the royal seat with something like fear, shifting his eyes constantly toward the menacing king with growing distrust. He leaned behind the back of the stone structure.

Doeg looked into the glassy eyes of the dead courtier, shrouded in shadows, and had to restrain himself from stumbling away in horror. He had known the man well and he gritted his teeth when he thought of the courtier's three little boys.

He would never speak to the widow again, Doeg promised himself.

"I want you to get rid of him. Push him through the windows and bury him outside in the fields," Saul said without meeting his henchman's eyes. "If anybody hears about this, my good servant, you will share the same grave." The king's voice was cold and unemotional, and Doeg understood the certainty of the threat. His throat closed up, his breath erratic. Finally, he managed to look at Saul, and he nodded.

He could only keep Saul's stare for a moment.

Doeg heaved the drooping body over his shoulders with a grunt. It took all of his strength to raise the corpse to the high casement ledge and he searched the darkness below. There were no guards and reluctantly, he rolled it out. The body fell lifelessly and hit the stones at the bottom with a deadening thud. Doeg slid out from the window, hanging from the ledge for a moment, and then was gone.

Saul studied the creeping shadows for a while as he contemplated his actions. He strode out of the throne room and then summoned his three sons to his bedchambers where he would have Rizpah clean him.

They would go to war with him, or die if they refused, he thought. His people would go to Keilah to besiege David and his men.

The baking sun had dried the earth, and David felt the promise of summer. He was thankful that he and his people would not have to be cold again for at least six moons. His broken nose had been set and would heal quickly. Physicians had bandaged and treated his scalp with ointment where he had lost a patch of auburn hair.

His muscles ached the day after the battle and he slouched in a cushioned seat as the Israelites of Keilah danced and sang before the fighters. Women fed them from what remained of their winter stores and he smiled, enjoying the festivities. Music filled his ears and he wished he had brought his kinnor as he tapped his leather sandal against the beaten-clay floor of the small portico where he and his council relaxed in the shade.

"You know Saul will hear that we're here," Eliab whispered, away from a servant girl's eavesdropping.

"Yes, I know," said David calmly, as if not troubled by the words. Eliab gaped at him.

The girl glanced behind her nervously, her face tight with anxiety.

"Why are you so relaxed about it? We must leave this place as soon as we can. They have begun harvesting and the farmers have already winnowed the grain on the threshing floors, enough to fill many wagons. Let's take the Philistines' cattle and the supplies the governor has promised us and leave this place—before Saul catches us. You know he will destroy the place to get to you."

"Do you think the men of the city will deliver me up into his hands?" David asked softly, not looking at his brother.

Eliab looked sadly at him. "You are always trusting and seeing the best in people, little brother. Not everybody deserves such trust."

David nodded with a slow sigh.

The girl looked around cautiously and then bent to David's ear. "I can't stand this any longer. You must know," she whispered, and smiled winningly as if she were saying something pleasant. David turned his head to her awkwardly, surprised.

"Please, I beg you, laugh. Nobody must know what I tell you." David chuckled uneasily.

"I am Keturah and my husband has forbidden me to speak to you. He has gone to tell one of Saul's soldiers that you are here. He thinks you are a traitor. I don't believe this," she said, giggling misleadingly. "He warned me that he would divorce me and have me stoned for my unfaithfulness if I told you. You must leave Keilah." She laughed again as she stepped away.

"You were right, brother," he said still smiling falsely, though his face was stern with sudden realization, his expression unnatural. David rose to his feet. "Ask Abiathar to bring me the ephod. I need to inquire of the Lord what will happen." He disappeared into the quietness of the house.

Keturah's eyes widened and she pleaded with Eliab. "I pray you, cover the holy garment. If my family sees this Abiathar bring it to David, they will know. I will be shamed in this town."

Eliab grinned at her and winked his acknowledgment. She blew air audibly from her lips and then bowed submissively, as if he had dismissed her. She joined in the dancing. Eliab stared after her for a moment. She was young and reminded him of his daughter.

Abiathar inquired of the Lord for David.

The priest found himself in that wonderful, peaceful place of light again.

"O Lord God of Israel, your servant David has heard that Saul seeks to come to Keilah, to destroy the city for his sake. Will the men of Keilah deliver him up into Saul's hands? Will Saul come down, as your servant David has heard? O Lord God of Israel, I beseech You; tell your servant."

"He will come down," God answered in a rich rolling voice, like roaring thunder.

"Will the men of Keilah deliver him and his men into the hand of Saul?" Abiathar asked in awe.

"They will deliver him up."

The small bells around the hem of the linen robe tinkled between the alternate pomegranates of blue, purple, and scarlet.

Abiathar opened his eyes calmly. "The Lord God has answered my question," he said with a soft gasp. "Saul will come and Keilah will betray you, son of Jesse."

"Grease the torches. We leave at dusk," David ordered.

***

"Ben Jesse has escaped from Keilah, my king," Jonathan said, lifting a cup to his pale lips, not showing his elation. Glacial eyes scowled at him from beneath heavy eyebrows. The prince kept his father's glare.

"You warned him didn't you, my beloved son, crown prince of my kingdom?" Saul said angrily through gnashing teeth. "You stab me in the heart with your betrayal. I have given you life and riches and this is how you show your love? Bah! You are not of the house of Saul."

His father's words hurt, but Jonathan kept his countenance tranquil and sipped the cool dark wine. Licking his lips, he said, "I did not, adored father. I have been here in the palace with you, tirelessly planning the siege of Keilah for days. Have I not shown my support, father? Have I not been the son you commanded me to be—a ruthless prince?"

Jonathan regretted his words acutely, and dropped his head. The warm day pressed down on them in the throne room like a heavy cloak, smothering them. Sweat trickled down the sides of his chest, dampening his cotton tunic with dark patches.

"I have done nothing these past days to receive your cruel accusations," the prince said distantly, searching his father's face for even a trace of love. The reddish brown scabs against the pallor of his face made Saul look diseased. A spot of white scalp mottled with tiny sores, gleamed in his silver hair.

"I will not be made a fool, Jonathan. Do you hear me? Never!" he cried suddenly, rapping his fist on the armrests of his throne. He leaned forward and glowered at his eldest son. "If you want my trust again, earn it."

Saul's two sons watched wretchedly, their awkwardness clear. Jonathan stared sadly at the man whom he physically resembled so much, although spiritually was so completely at odds with. Jonathan could only manage to bring his father's hands to his lips and he kissed them tenderly.

Saul did not yield and his eyes gleamed with anger.

"Tell my people we will forbear to go forth against Keilah," he said darkly. "But I want him found. I shall seek him every day until I have his traitorous black blood on my blade."

It was a devastating thing to see their father in that state and there would be tense and trying months ahead, they realized.

"Summon my commanders and council. We begin our campaign immediately," Saul ordered. Jonathan rose in silence, bowed his head submissively and started from the room.

His royal guard had escorted one of his spies into the throne room. The man bowed humbly before him.

"Hail King Achish!" he cried, and prostrated himself in front of the magnificent throne. Achish smiled smugly.

"I have news, my king," the informer said loudly, and rose from his knees. "From Gibeah, the city of Saul."

"Well, what is it, you dog? Tell me," he said impatiently.

"Saul has declared David ben Jesse a traitor and an enemy to the crown. He has taken all the Israelite forces and is scouring their lands for him. The towns and garrisons are scarcely manned."

"So it was true—that *was* the infamous ben Jesse in my court. But he was mad, I saw it," Achish mused, stroking the roll of skin hanging below his chin with the back of his fingers. "When?" the king asked, and the man wilted.

"Seven weeks ago, oh great king," the man stuttered briefly when Achish shot a disquieting glance tinged with controlled anger at him. He then steadied his voice. "I could not come sooner without arousing suspicions. It would have been suicide."

"You have brought me great news, slave. My treasurer will reward you aptly," he said without looking at the man, and gestured him to leave his court.

The Philistine king grinned viciously. "My time for revenge has come sooner than I anticipated." He chuckled inwardly.

CHAPTER TWENTY-FOUR

The warm winds sang over the golden dunes of the desert Ziph, raising palls of pale sand. The wide horizon seemed to dance in the surging heat, shimmering in the thick air. The stony mountains of the wilderness of Ziph, strewn with shrubs and succulent plants, were a desolate and bleak place. In the distance, a small dense wood climbed the stretching foothills of the highland.

David and his brothers sat in the cool of a shadow cast by a crude canvas awning. Gentle breezes covered them with a film of dust. The burning sun had turned their skins a golden brown. They were dirty, sweaty, and their throats were parched.

Many more followers came after David when he freed Keilah, and Saul's ill temper grew with each day. At last census, there were six hundred men of warring age. They lived in strongholds and the men created makeshift defenses and guarded the borders like eagles searching for prey. Lookouts in camouflaged clothing, caked yellow with dried cracking mud, hunted the vicinity and at night, under the cover of darkness, they would run out wide and scour for any approaching forces.

David knew that Saul was searching for him. His scouts had seen Saul's armies march close to him many times before, but David had fled before he was discovered.

David believed God would not deliver him into Saul's hands, and he thanked Jehovah abundantly in his prayers.

A girl stepped into the shade of the shelter and gazed at David with a seductively innocent smile. Her hair was a deep shade of brown, lustrous, and flowing over her shoulders. The desert breeze moved tendrils across her delicate face. The men gaped at her. Her skin was like soft silk, her fringed linen ketonet flowing over the contours of her body.

David caught himself gawking, entranced by her gorgeous features. He looked away flustered, his face flushing with sudden guilt as he thought of Michal.

She is young, he told himself. Irresistibly, he slowly shifted is eyes to her again and swallowed nervously when she lowered her gaze shyly, biting her lip. Her eyes were light brown with a tint of green, flecked with gold.

The young woman bowed before him and he sat up straighter when she touched his feet. He caught her scent of rosemary oil on the wind and he closed his eyes as he savored it, then it was lost in the strong odor of the arid desert.

She is more breathtaking than Michal, he admitted with a strange pang of betrayal inside of him.

"My mother has sent me to serve you for the afternoon and fan you cool, David ben Jesse," she said softly. Everything about her made David dumb. He had to remind himself to speak.

"What's your name," he asked.

"I am Bathsheba, my lord," she said plainly. His eyes, forceful with authority heightened her private infatuation, though she behaved herself better than the men, she thought. She bowed her head. "I am the daughter of Eliam ben Ahithophel."

David's face changed with pleasant surprise. "Your grandfather is a wise man, Bathsheba. He has spoken many good words to me. I plan on asking his advice again. And your father is a brave man. I have heard only good things."

"You are too kind," Bathsheba said and unconsciously batted her eyelids at him.

David took a deep breath. "Tell your mother I thank her for her thoughtfulness," he drawled, regarding her every movement. He returned suddenly from his wandering mind and spoke quickly, shaking his head slightly. "My brothers are thirsty, you may fill their cups."

Bathsheba only nodded. After she filled the cups and gave them to the men, she stood beside the man she secretly adored and waved a wooden fan to cool him. She swept an amorous gaze over his tanned skin, along his broad forearms and brawny legs stretched out before him, and imagined touching him. Her face reddened.

Bathsheba was dragged from her reverie when a man encrusted with filth ran at them.

"Saul is here! His men are at the foothills. They came from behind the clouds of dust," he cried. David's council jumped up wildly.

"How did he find us?" David groaned, noticing the scout's eyes were rolling in fear as he panted hoarsely. "We run for the woods. Now!"

♛

Jonathan knelt beside a small mound of human waste. He broke off a piece and felt it between a finger and thumb. The inside was still wet and it smeared his skin. He took burning earth and sanded off the remains, cleaning his skin.

"How long ago?" Saul asked sternly, sweeping his gaze around, searching for any movements. Jonathan hesitated.

"Maybe a day or two, father," he said. He was lying. As he rose, he noticed small irregular indentations leading to the south and he knew they were footprints, partially blown away by the winds of the wilderness. David was in the woods.

Jonathan looked at his father suddenly, and realized that he was showing his concern. He blinked away the expression and got himself together before his father met his eyes.

"Do you see any trail?" Saul asked frowning at his son.

"No," Jonathan said as he explored the area with his eyes, shaded by a hand. "Wait—there."

Saul snapped his head around and looked at where his son was indicating. They were sweltering in the fierce sun and sweat washed their exposed skin. Dust clung to their moist skin and Jonathan narrowed his eyes against desert sand stinging his eyes.

"Where, tell me?" Saul snapped.

"There's a rough trail in the sand; do you see it, father? It forms a narrow line."

"I see it," said the king irritably. Saul hated his surroundings.

"That is caused by hundreds of feet walking in a column. The winds have blown them in such a pattern. We should go south, my king. We are on their heels; they are in the woods, I swear it." Jonathan swallowed nervously and Saul's eyes filled with angry comprehension.

"I don't believe you," Saul roared and slapped the prince's face. "You dishonest, ungrateful son. You try to lead me away from your precious David. I'm not blind. I won't fall for your treachery!" Jonathan fought the surging anger inside him and glared at the old king. He clenched his jaw. He did not dare look at his father and he focused on his dusty feet.

"Believe what you will," he said bitterly.

"The son of Jesse wouldn't be that stupid. He wouldn't hide when he can run. He knows that small clump of trees wouldn't protect him," Saul told Ehud, his Benjamite captain over three thousand.

"We march north, in the opposite direction … away from the woods," Saul sneered. Jonathan feigned dread and Saul turned from him, chuckling vindictively. He walked away, his gait showing his rage. Ehud followed like a mindless minion.

Jonathan glowered after them and then slowly the corners of his mouth turned up.

The prince bent underneath a low branch, the rough bark scraping against his skin. In the blackness of the night, the woods were a dismal place with pale glowing vegetation, moving in the wind howling through the tall trees. Jonathan searched vigilantly before taking every careful step so that he would not crackle the dried vegetation of the thin woodland bed or snap twigs as he crept in silence. Leaves fluttered from above him, gleaming in the soft moonlight rays. He could smell smoke and he knew he was close.

The prince had taken his horse and disappeared from his father's camp. He had covered his tracks and hidden several times to wait and see if he were being followed. The moon had reached its zenith when he finally tied the reins to a low tree and crept into the woods.

It was deathly quiet.

Suddenly, he heard an owl hoot and take flight noisily. Now Jonathan knew they were watching him. He stood straight and raised his hands into the air with a sigh.

"I know you're there," Jonathan said softly and heard someone behind him. The prince decided not to move. Cold bronze pressed against his throat. Jonathan stood rigidly, leaning away from the blade nearly cutting his skin. A man's beard scratched his neck and he could smell his sweat.

"Not a word," the man whispered menacingly into his ear and twisted his dagger threateningly. Six men emerged from the shadows with pitch-black hair and their faces and hands covered in soot. All he could see were the whites of their eyes, glaring at him.

"Tell me what you want or I will bleed your veins," the man demanded harshly, and moved his blade again.

"I have come to speak with David. He is my brother in a covenant before the Lord," Jonathan said quickly. He noticed that the man was holding him entirely wrong; it was not a soldier's way. Only then did he realize that the man was gripping his weapon too tightly. They were novices; recruits, no doubt, Jonathan thought. He tried to look for hiding slingers or archers, but in the dark it was no use.

"So that you can kill him," the dirty soldier said and when he moved his blade again, Jonathan became angered.

Before the man could react, the prince had his hand on the man's forearm and pushed the blade from his neck. He forced his elbow into the soldier's ribs and the hold constricting him eased with a painful grunt. Jonathan twisted his body and moved around to the man's back. Faster than the scout could think, Jonathan had his hand on the man's throat. In a second, the scout's own weapon was pressed against his chest.

Jonathan was suffocating him.

"If you want him to breathe, step away," Jonathan said clearly. The man scrabbled at his grasp, choking. "I am not your enemy."

Slowly they backed away.

Jonathan eased and the man coughed violently. "That is how you hold a foe," whispered Jonathan.

A rough jerk brought David from his slumber. He looked up at the blackened face of his scout and he sprang to his feet.

"Prince Jonathan is here, David," the man said. "Should we bring him to you?"

David's eyes widened. "Immediately," he snapped.

When he saw the prince, he embraced him strongly, laughing into the darkness.

"Why have you come, brother?" David asked. "It has been long."

"Over a year, my brother," Jonathan said and clapped him on the shoulder. He thought David looked appalling. His hair was stringy with filth and dirt smeared his skin.

"I fear I cannot stay. I just had to see you again," Jonathan said and put his hand behind David's neck, affectionately. "Don't fret, David. The hand of Saul, my father, shall not find you. God is with you. You shall be king over Israel and I shall be next in rank to you. My father knows this. He is not the man he was, David. I understand now why he can't be king and why it must be you." It was difficult for Jonathan to admit it.

David could not speak for strong emotion. "You are a true prince, my brother," David said and enfolded him again vigorously with one arm.

Jonathan took his knife from his belt and halted for a moment when he heard swords pulled from scabbards. David frowned at them, and the men eased. The prince regarded the long scar on his hand and remembered that day in the fields outside of Gibeah. He cut his palm along the old scar. "I make again a covenant this night with the house of David with all here to witness," he said. David took the blade from him and did the same. They pressed their bloody hands together in a tight grip, and they swore before the Lord.

"Brothers and friends," they said together. They both took dirt between their fingers and massaged it into their wounds, silently enduring the uncomfortable pain of the scarring.

David fleetingly considered asking about his wife. Was she still his wife? He didn't know anymore. He decided against it; he would not cause himself fresh torment. The grueling months in the wilderness had been soul-deadening enough. He could not handle hearing that Michal still loved him. Would they ever be together again?

"Will you return to your father's camp? If Saul sees your wound he will, know," David asked as he sliced a piece of his tunic. He winced as he bound the gash tightly, and watched as the rag stained with his blood.

"I will return to my house. I have written to him imploring him to stop this madness," Jonathan said, also wrapping his laceration. "I will not be part of this anymore. If he wants to smite me, then let him try."

David looked concerned. "Don't be foolish, Jonathan."

The prince chuckled. "I have been foolish all along, my brother. It is time I do what is right. I know my father, David. He will give up the hunt when he realizes that you have completely escaped him again. He will tire of it soon. The king will return to Gibeah and send out spies and a notice to the cities of Israel and Judah requesting your whereabouts. Be well, David. I don't know when I will see you again," he said, smiling warmly, and grasped David's good arm in a soldier's grip. "Strength, my brother. Yahweh protects you."

David nodded solemnly. "Farewell, my prince. Remember your servant always," David said.

They looked in each other's eyes for a moment and then the prince turned slowly and left. He did not glance back, and David gazed at his back until the black shadows consumed him. Then he lowered his eyes.

"God be with you, my friend," he whispered.

CHAPTER TWENTY-FIVE

A group of Ziphites stood before Saul, still loyal to his crown. It was a warm day in Gibeah, and the men sweated nervously before their king. They had come to appease Saul, hoping for his esteem, or even to be given rank or reward.

Saul dried the perspiration in his black beard and ordered a man to speak.

"We believe that the son of Jesse is hiding in our territory in a stronghold in the woods on the hill of Hachilah, which is on the south of Jeshimon, my king," the Ziphite said respectfully. They had seen David in the regions of Ziph and had come to inform the true king of Israel and Judah with news of the absconder and his band of warriors.

Saul's eyes came alive at the news and he rose from his throne. He had longed to hear such information. David was again in his grasp. The Ziphite continued, not looking at the king. "Therefore, my king, do as your soul desires. Come with us, and we will help you seize him."

He gripped the man firmly on the shoulder, staring at him. "Blessed are you of the Lord, because you have compassion on me. Go, and make sure once more. Find out exactly where he lurks and who has seen him there. I've been told that he deals very subtly. Return to me with conformation and then I'll go with you. If he's in the land, I will search him out throughout all the thousands of Judah."

✦

"David, I fear that the Ziphites have gone to Saul and that they will surely lead him to us," Eliab said softly. David hung his head, sighing wearily. Their clothing was tattered and yellow with age and their sunken faces showed their starvation.

"Brother, do you know this for certain?"

Eliab nodded, seeing the pain in David's eyes. His brother had been betrayed numerous times and it was like the beatings of a whip. David loved Judah and Israel and their disloyalty was worse than physical torture.

"When?"

"I don't know, David; hopefully not soon."

"How many times more?" David whispered to himself, closing his eyes. They were exhausted from the many months of running from the troubled king. They sheltered in strongholds and lived from day to day, eating seeds and roots, and a few fruits, only indulging in the luxury of having meat on the monthly thanksgiving festivals before the new moon appeared in the sky. It was a perilous time.

"We must disappear, brother. We can't stop running, ever," David said with sudden realization. "There are caves in Maon, on the plain south of Jeshimon."

"To the caves then?"

"To Maon."

✦

"Saul is coming! He has found us, sound the horn!" David shouted to his men, his eyes wide and his voice echoing through the massive cave. His men sprang to their feet, and began racing to prepare for escape. The flames flickered in the prevailing damp breeze, the tension palpable.

How did Saul find me? David reeled in anguish. *I thought we would be safe here.* He did not know how Saul had heard that he was in the wilderness of Maon, living in the rock on the plain of the south of Jeshimon, but all he could think of was to get as far away from the king as possible. Children cried as their mothers snatched them up and most of their possessions were left behind.

As David turned to leave, the color drained from his face. He had not realized that Saul was so dangerously close. He could see Saul's forces marching, their scores dappling the horizon further than his eyes could see.

They were here. Saul would finally have him.

David's body shook with dread and he spun on his heels and screamed. "They're here, leave everything. Run!" As the men and women rushed from the cave, David heard the horn of war wail through the afternoon, shattering the silence. He recognized the signal. The captains had ordered the men to march at double pace.

David had seen Saul's armies too late and he knew he would not escape.

Saul could imagine David's blood on his hands as he gripped the reins of his horse. He knew he had him and he laughed at the feeble attempt to flee. He scanned the land as he rode and watched David running behind the mountain. He grinned viciously. The fact that David was fleeing from him fueled his desire for the chase.

The earth shook as Saul's men marched to encompass his enemy. Within a day, at most, he would have him.

David could hear Saul's marching warriors on the other side of the crags and he feared that the king's forces would surround him. His mind was raging with possible outcomes. He ran with his people, ignoring his burning lungs.

How would he escape? It seemed impossible. Unconsciously, David began praying.

"God will not allow my capture, my death," he said his desperate prayer aloud, repeating the words several times. David refused to believe it and though he was terrified, he prayed again, forcing from his mind the sudden flashes of negative images of his broken body hanging from a tree.

"Be merciful to me, O God!" he cried, bathed in sweat as he bolted from capture and imminent death.

Saul observed his men riding around the mountain and he knew he had caught David; there was nowhere he could run. He could not break away. Now it was only a matter of time, Saul thought clasping his hands in anticipation.

Suddenly a rider approached the old king.

The messenger brought his horse to a stop in a cloud of desert dust and greeted the king with a tinge of dread.

"A message from the Prince Jonathan, my king. The Philistines have heard that my king has marched our armies against the son of Jesse. They have crossed our borders … an army to be reckoned with, sire." Saul's eyes widened at the news and the muscles of his jaw stood out. Saul knew that if he waited even an hour it would shift the odds to the Philistines. If they lost power over the highlands and the mouth of the Terebinth Valley that led to the Judean ridge, then Israel would be vulnerable against attacks and raids. "With respect my lord, if you do not march now, the cities of Israel will certainly burn."

Saul screamed savagely, shaking with anger.

Two short notes on the war horn cut through the clamor of the marching men. It caused temporary confusion and brought the hunting warriors to a slow halt.

David recognized it instantly and he gasped at its meaning. Again, the horn sounded and suddenly the riders turned their steeds and galloped back. The soldiers turned and David could see them marching away. He fell to his knees and weakly lifted his hands to the clear blue sky, blinking tears from his eyes, washing the coat of dust from his face in streaks.

"Yahweh is merciful," he shouted and wept with overpowering relief.

They were gone and he did not care about the reason. The Almighty God of Israel had delivered them.

CHAPTER TWENTY-SIX

avid woke that morning from a deep sleep. He had not slept as sound since he had left his wife and fled from Saul that night in Gibeah. David and his men had left the plains of Maon in celebration to Yahweh many moons before. David had named the place, 'Sela-hammahlekoth—*The Cliff of Escape*.' That day was still raw in their minds and David had lived in constant fear of the inexorable king since.

That morning seemed different to David, the air tasted fresher, and the sounds of the wilderness of En-gedi appeared clearer. The place was a desert oasis with waterfalls, two large streams for fresh drinking water and bathing, and natural pools. Date palms grew in abundance, which was a great source of sustenance for them. They had feasted away their malnutrition on the fruits for months. They washed their clothes in the fresh water and they appeared decent once more.

Saul had been waging war with the Philistines for ten months. David had survived a cold winter and had been absent from the cities during the Passover and Pentecost festivals that marked the grain harvests while he lived in strongholds, planning with his council. The men were strong from training, the women sang often, and the children played again. Many people had secretly come and given them food and freshly woven clothing, even blankets and other crucial supplies, like fat for cooking, and spices and honey for sweetening cakes.

"How goes the war?" David asked, pushing a stick into the dying coals of the fire. A dim ray of golden light fell over his tunic, dull with age as embers wafted into the cold air, glowing in the light.

"Saul has fought wisely and the enemy strength is waning with each assault," Pelet said, and looked at Eliab, who sat quietly studying his brother's face.

Bathsheba bas Eliam strolled across the stony terrain and smiled at David, lowering her eyes as she blushed. David had thought of courting her many times before, but the events and worries of the past had kept him occupied. She was now of marital age and the temptation was strong.

"That one loves you, David," Eliab said with a strange expression on his face. "I can see it in her face and by the way she acts when she sees you. When you're not looking, her eyes follow you everywhere."

"I dare say she's more radiant than Michal—my beloved Michal." David said, not feeling the guilt he had known before. When David looked for Bathsheba again, she was gone.

"Where will we go from here, David? The war won't last forever," Eliab broke into his reverie. David sighed and nodded.

"I cannot think of it now, brother. We must remain hidden. I pray that when Saul returns home, he will have forgotten about us."

Eliab and Pelet were awkwardly silent, knowing that David was being overly optimistic, but David did not notice as he thought of the nubile Bathsheba.

That night, among the activities of the camp, David went looking for Bathsheba. He found her dreaming idly beside a campfire, her feet covered with her ketonet and her legs held against her body. He watched her silently for a moment and then sat down beside her.

Bathsheba was flustered. David laughed at this, gazing at her intently. Bathsheba was nervous, but she managed to look into his eyes. It made her heart beat faster and she did not know what to say to him.

"Why is such an exquisite flower sitting alone? It cannot be that no man has any interest in you," he said softly. When she smiled shyly, lowering her head to her knees, David felt sudden attraction.

"It's not that they don't; I almost have to beat them away with a stick," she said in an innocent voice. "I simply enjoy the little time that I have to myself, away from their flattery and seductions."

David nodded and rose. "I didn't realize. I will leave then," he said, but she took his arm gently.

"Stay, I pray you. I have wondered enough for one night. Your presence makes the night more pleasant." David felt awkward suddenly and had to fight for calm. She was intoxicating, her eyes showing her strong personality. He sat down clumsily and had an uncontrollable urge to kiss her tender lips, gleaming in the soft light of the fire. David almost leaned in and kissed her when he realized what he was about to do. He sprang to his feet. He would not touch her unless they were married.

David did not like the effect the woman had on him and he kissed her hand gently. "I apologize. But I have things I must tend to," he said, noticing the shadow of rejection on her face. She tried to speak, but he turned and left quickly.

David sighed, despising his lust. He could not betray Michal, he thought; she was still his wife. After so long, he still loved her. Although the law permitted him to have more than one wife, he wouldn't do anything to cause his beloved spouse any pain. He remembered how Jonathan had told him how his mother Ahinoam had felt when Saul had taken another wife. *I'm not like that*, David thought frowning, trying to convince himself.

He was troubled by fresh guilt. He resolved to avoid the irresistible Bathsheba, and forget her.

Following almost a year of defending the highlands, Saul had beaten back the Philistine horde and Israel grew in power. But during all of this time, the son of Jesse plagued him. After David had expelled all the Philistine outposts, Israel still controlled the hill country of Judea and for the past years, they had had the Jezreel Valley and its valuable caravan routes. The cities experienced a fragile peace again and they celebrated and praised God.

Saul returned home and enjoyed his family. He had a feast to celebrate his victory and he had forced himself to forget about David that night.

The following morning Saul summoned his council and began preparations for another campaign against the son of Jesse. The people of Israel had shown new loyalty for Saul after his successful war against Achish and this would add credibility to his hunt.

"Where is he, Ehud?" Saul asked with a terrible gleam in his eyes.

"I knew that my king would want to know, so I had my informants inquire after his location before we returned to Gibeah. They tell me that he has gone east; he is in the wilderness of En-gedi," Ehud said, feeling an odd sense of satisfaction.

"We are of the same tribe, you and I, Ehud—the Benjamites. We understand one another," Saul said with a smirk. The captain bowed his head.

"Gather my ben-hayil. My fierce warriors will hunt David on the Rocks of the Wild Goats. He won't slip from my grip again. I will find him. And I'll destroy him and all that have aligned with the son of Jesse."

David stood outside a cave and gazed into the night. He had heard that Saul had won the campaign against the Philistines and he wondered when the king would come for him. He swept his gaze around the wilderness of En-gedi, at the hundreds of natural caves where his people sheltered from the elements. It was a peaceful scene with the winds blowing over the desert, the stars piercing the black heavens. David could see the spring from where he stood and the green foliage of his surroundings. He had discovered a trail that, after an hour's trek, brought him high enough to have a magnificent view of the Dead Sea and the mountains of Moab. It was a perfect place to pray in solitude. When he looked at the massifs of Moab, he often wondered about his parents. He missed them. David could feel the first chill of another winter as he remembered how long it had been. In the fall, as always, his father would have been harvesting olives from their few trees if they hadn't had to escape to Moab.

"Three years," he whispered into the biting breeze, shaking his head. He had grown accustomed to this life, but still he longed for civilized living. He touched his frayed tunic and felt the coarse wool between his fingers that had darkened with use.

He thought of all the things his loved ones had given up for him. He had not seen his parents since he took them out of the country. His brothers and their families, their sons, his nephews, carried swords and were willing to fight his battles. How much longer would he have to run? He could not do it for much longer, he admitted. He was exhausted with constant stress and fear. He was emotionally spent.

David's heart longed for his wife, although he had begun thinking that they would never be together again. He remembered how he had betrayed her with the feelings he felt for Bathsheba bas Eliam.

Was his beloved Michal safe? He wished he could touch her skin, hear her laugh, look into her adoring eyes. David would not speak to anyone about what he was thinking.

I cannot burden them further, he told himself; *it is a weight that I must carry.* With the roar of the waterfalls in the distance and the wild birds crying into the night, David needed comfort and hope. He sank to his knees and sought guidance from Yahweh.

***

Phalti, the son of Laish, stood beside a fluted granite pillar before the king. He was a short man with broad shoulders and a brave fighter. Silver streaked his sable hair and the men were silent as they waited for Michal. He fingered a long scar on his forearm unconsciously, thinking of the princess. Saul regarded the man with pride and he studied his movements, heedless of the coldness of the night coming in through the large windows.

The king wondered where his defiant daughter was and sighed impatiently. He still had many things to do before he left on the campaign against David ben Jesse in two day's time.

As the sun lowered to the horizon, the stone floors gleamed bright with reflected light. Leather sandals slapped against the floor in the corridor and Saul's daughter entered the room with grace.

Michal had been living in a prison of fear of her father since she helped her husband escape Gibeah years ago. She had become a taciturn woman and her life was a lonely, bitter existence. She never mourned her husband publicly and she lied to her family constantly.

The young princess had matured into womanhood and she was breathtaking. Her silken hair flowed over her shoulders and many layers of bright colored, fringed clothing covered her lithe body. She smelled of scented oils.

Her eyes were emotionless and she bowed dutifully before her father, ignoring the man gawking at her. "You sent for me, father?"

She glanced at the man, wondering about him for a moment.

"This is Phalti ben Laish, my exquisite daughter. His family is from Gallim. We have negotiated and I have decided that you shall be his wife," Saul said simply, as if speaking about the changing season. Michal stiffened, and her mouth dropped open. She shot a glance at the strange man, but could not bring herself to speak. She was married to David. Her father was breaking the law. She belonged to David. Her emotions welled up as her father spoke. She had thought that nothing could bring her to that frantic state again.

"You will be his spouse in every way, do you understand me, Michal? You will beget him strong sons and you will see to every wifely duty," Saul said, untroubled by his daughter's expression.

Michal stood like a statue, a tear gleaming on her cheek. She could not imagine making love to another man. How could she bear this brute any children? *He is not my husband,* her mind screamed. She belonged to David. Her breath trembled. She would never be legally married to this man, not until David divorced her before the town elders.

She would be an adulterer.

Michal was startled when Phalti took her upper arm, and she wanted to pull away from his touch. His hands were rough and she met his eyes. They were kind and gentle, but a sense of loathing filled her entire being. She blinked more tears from her eyes. She bowed her head delicately and watched as the king, a great man, but never a father poured wine the color of blood into a jewel encrusted goblet. Phalti took the vessel from the king and supped the drink. He handed her the vessel. Michal hesitated, but knew that it was futile to object. She sipped, refusing to look at the men. Now she understood why her mother was such a pillar of a woman. Over the years she had hardened from men's cruel domination. Michal understood her duty, and in an instant, she unconsciously adopted the graceful cold posture of her mother the queen.

Without a sound, she allowed the man to take her from the room. She did not look back at her father before they left. She was dead inside, her heart a desert.

The earth shook with the force of three thousand men marching over the Rocks of the Wild Goats. Saul had left Gibeah and weeks had passed since his campaign began.

The cold air bit at their skins and Saul's robe snapped gently in the winds. Rays of weak light from gathering rain clouds mottled the harsh terrain. They trooped past a massive sheepcote, one of many, and the shepherd guarding the gates fell to his knees before Saul as he rode past. He could hear the sheep bleating in the distance. Thunder cracked threateningly.

After many long hours, Saul began sitting uneasily in his saddle and regarded the foul weather for a moment. With a hand signal, he ordered his captains to call for an hour's respite. Two long notes on the ram's horn brought his men to an organized stop, and Saul dismounted effortlessly. He snapped a command to his servant and entered a cave to cover his feet. While he was inside no man was allowed to enter.

David and his elite fighters crouched in the sheltering darkness of a grotto, nervously watching the soldiers waiting outside of the many natural caves of En-gedi. Did Saul know they were there? The chirps of the cave crickets and the sounds of flowing water in the cavern deadened their nervous breaths. If Saul found any of David's many hidden men, they would all be flushed out and he would be killed. Then Saul stepped inside and walked right toward them. David felt a consuming urge to run, but he calmed himself, and remained still, studying the old king.

Saul was temporarily blinded by the sudden darkness and he moved slowly, feeling his way around as he entered deeper, searching for privacy.

The king undid his robe and threw it aside in a heap and squatted, relieving himself. David and a few of his men watched silently and unseen.

"Look, God said that he would give your enemy into your hands so that you may do to him what seemed good to you," Eliab whispered into David's ear, his voice barely a breath. David glanced at his brother, and then watched Saul again as he thought.

Like a stalking lion, David moved in the shadows. Gingerly he slid a small blade from his belt and crept toward the pile of clothing on the rough cave floor. Saul seemed busy with his thoughts and did not see David cut off the skirt of the fringed silk robe. Stealthily, he crept back deeper into the grotto, unnoticed by his enemy. It was done.

David held the smooth cloth in his hand as he sat on his haunches beside his men. Guilt struck him suddenly like a stone. He had shamed the king of Israel, God's anointed. He could have cut Saul's throat easily, he knew. It would all have been over; he would have become king. He fought with his conscience.

"Why didn't you slay him, brother? He's relieving himself and you were right behind him. He's vulnerable and unarmed." Shammah asked quietly, gesticulating at the king. Pelet drew his sword and stepped toward Saul. David grasped his arm, stopping him.

"The Lord forbids that I do this to my master. I won't stretch my hand against him because he's God's anointed," David said, and the men gazed at the king. David could not see their expressions, but he knew they would stay because he willed it. He would not allow it. "If I kill him now, it would set a precedent for a man to murder me when I'm king." The men did not respond.

Saul finished and dressed, his eyes just beginning to see in the blackness. He left humming.

On a whim, David got up from his knees and walked after Saul. His men tried desperately to stop him, but he ignored them. He had had enough and he would end it now. If he were killed that afternoon, it would be the will of God.

The sunlight stung Saul's eyes and he shaded his face with a hand. He thought of having a light lunch and then he would continue. Ehud, the king's captain, gasped as he saw the monarch's attire. When Saul realized this, he looked down at his robe in blank terror. He immediately knew what must have happened.

"My lord, the king," an emotional voice called from behind him. He immediately recognized it. Saul went cold and turning on his heel, glowered at the cavern entrance. A man walked cautiously from the darkness, his hands in the air, holding a part of his shredded garment. Saul stiffened at the sight of him. David!

Quickly David stooped, pressing his face to the ground.

Saul could hear many men nocking their bows and swords being pulled from scabbards. He could not understand why, but he hesitated to give the order. Coming out in the open was suicide, Saul understood. He could have David's head and he would be rid of all his fears. The house of Jesse would never sit on his throne. But why would his enemy show himself? His mind was racing, his eyes boring into the prostrate man.

"Why do you listen to the men who tell you lies that I want to do you harm?" David asked loudly, his voice reverberating through the low gully.

Wild goats, which had began grazing on vegetation watchfully, dashed suddenly to safety at the noise.

"Today, you've seen how the Lord has delivered you into my hands in that cave. Some bade me smite you, but I spared you. I told these men that I would not put forth my hand against my king, because he's the Lord's anointed," David continued, shivering with dread. An arrow or a blade could pierce him at any moment, he thought anxiously.

Saul could not speak for the inexplicable waves of emotion. His face twitched as he fought tears.

"Look, my father, see the skirt of your robe in my hand," David continued, gripping the colorful cloth, waving it at the king. He took an uneasy breath. "Because I cut your clothing and didn't kill you, know now that there is neither evil nor transgression in me, and I haven't sinned against you. Yet, you hunt me and try to slay me. The Lord judge between me and you, and He will avenge me of you, but I shall not harm you."

David swept his gaze across the hundreds of fighters, armed, and aiming at his heart. They seemed strangely passive, their eyes not as hostile, and when he looked at Saul again, he saw the pain of the king's past actions in his aged face. David clenched his jaw, still feeling the tension between his shoulders. He felt the breeze cold against his skin, as he said, "As says the proverb of the ancients, 'Wickedness proceeds from the wicked.' But I won't injure you."

Saul did not lower his gaze from the young man.

David was a king, Saul admitted, trembling. He felt empty and terrified suddenly. It was a difficult thing to admit, but he was tired of fighting against it. He had hounded David for years, and the man had done nothing wrong. He wanted to kill an innocent loyal fighter because of his own useless fears.

Saul's shoulders drooped as he recalled Samuel's words, those awful few words that had haunted him for so long. He was done. A tear flowed into his silver beard as he remembered his love for the strong and passionate David ben Jesse.

David's powerful voice broke the silence again. "After whom has the king of Israel come out? Whom does he pursue—a dead dog, a single flea? The Lord be judge and arbitrate between you and me, and He will defend me and deliver me out of your hand," he said and let the cloth slip from his grip. Dust rode on the breezes and it shrouded the king momentarily. Instinctively, David held his breath.

Saul was silent.

"Is this your voice, my son David?" Saul asked, and wept. "You are more righteous than I, because you have rewarded me with good, whereas I have done evil to you. And you have shown this day how morally you have behaved toward me. The Lord delivered me into your power and you did not smite me."

Saul wiped away his tears and walked to David. The man was thin, and his clothes were old and worn out. He had no weapons, Saul noticed, and he wept again. David's eyes were bright above an unkempt beard.

"If a man found his enemy, would he let him go away unharmed? That is why the Lord blesses you for what you have done to me this day," Saul continued, and touched David's face roughly. He breathed harshly, his expression intense suddenly. The king was silent, as if in pain. "And now I know that you will surely be king."

David's jaw dropped slightly at the words, and he lowered his head.

"… and that the kingdom of Israel shall be established in your hand." Sharp whispers pierced the afternoon in reaction to his words, but Saul could not look away. More tears washed his face. He was finally free.

Everybody will hear it after today, he thought with mixed feelings. It was a bittersweet thing. He bit his upper lip as he closed his eyes, a king vulnerable and exposed. He waited for the reactions to fade. When he looked at David again, Saul's eyes were gentle, gleaming with emotion.

"Therefore, swear now to me by the Lord, you will not cut off my seed after me and that you will not destroy my name out of my father's house."

David couldn't speak and gripped the king. "I swear it, my king," he whispered, nodding. A few drops of cool water fell from the sky, stippling his clothing, and he could smell the rain in the air.

He watched the astonished men, their bows lowered, their blades sheathed. He looked at them with new eyes; it was a strange thing for him. "This I promise," David shouted for all to hear. Powerful energy coursed through his veins. He stood tall, despite his miserable appearance, the wind touching his skin as sweetly as the caress of a lover, his long hair swaying in the winter breeze. David could not think of anything else. They would someday be his men, his ben-hayil. He savored them and he stood before them. A king.

David turned to Saul and embraced him. Saul did not say a word, but simply nodded.

Saul mounted his horse and galloped away without a backward glance. He wanted to go home and be with his family, meet his newborn son, and play with his toddler. He would celebrate his wives and the sons and daughters he had with Ahinoam. Now he would return to them, not as a king, but as a father and finally, a husband.

The army left the Rocks of the Wild Goats, and David stared after them, stunned at what had happened. He could only praise Yahweh, because He had delivered him. The men and women came from the caves and excitedly gathered around David. They were safe again, but David knew that men wanting his blood would soon poison the king's mind.

He would see Saul before long, he knew, but he would not think of it now.

David noticed Bathsheba bas Eliam in the crowd of people and she looked more radiant than ever before, despite her poor clothing. Her eyes were hard and full of pain and he feared that her adoration had turned to hate after he had kept himself away from her. He felt for the girl. If they had only met at a different time, he could have taken her as his wife. He would have loved her. Only she could possess his mind and thoughts so. As he kept her gaze, he could see tears flow down her face. She turned from his sight and was lost among the crush of people. He wanted to run to her and take her in his embrace, but he thought of Michal and resisted the intense urge, dutifully dousing the passionate fire he felt for her.

With a roar of thunder, the rain poured down and the men got themselves up to the holds.

Days later, David heard that Bathsheba's father, Elim, had given her to wed one of his brave fighters, Uriah the Hittite, and it stabbed at his heart. She would come to love her husband, and he would forget her, he promised himself.

CHAPTER TWENTY-SEVEN

A woman sat on the floor, washing her husband's feet. Gently she took a cloth and cleaned the soles, using pressure to clean the heels. She hummed sweetly as she worked. Suddenly the man belched rudely. She closed her eyes, pausing from her task. When she took too long and he felt the chill on his wet skin, the churlish man kicked water onto her, striking her on the chest with his foot.

"Who told you to stop, woman? I am the master of this house. Wash me!" he screamed. She placed his feet back into the water and rose in a stately way. He grabbed her by the hair, and jerked her down to his face.

"Where do you think you are going, Abigail?" he snapped. Abigail groaned at the pain of her scalp, and grasped his hand to ease the pain.

"I am richer than any other, wife. I've three thousand sheep and a thousand goats. So don't think you're special. I could afford many wives in your place. Now get out of my sight." He released her, and she started out of the room. Nabal kicked the wooden basin, sluicing the floor with scented water, and swore obscenely.

Abigail hurried into her bedchambers and as she closed the doors behind her, she broke down. *I'm a good wife,* she told herself. *I don't deserve his cruelty.* She cried into her tasselled silk ketonet and wiped her tears on the soft sleeve, thinking of leaving him. But she knew his heart. She believed that he would accuse her falsely of adultery and would have her stoned alive. He had threatened her many times before.

Her father had given her to this crass man of the house of Caleb for a liberal amount of money. At the time, he had thought Nabal to be a good man. In the beginning it was a good marriage; he treated her well. It was only after he earned his wealth that he changed, although to others he had always been a rude and unkind man. Biting her lower lip, she wept bitterly.

Her handmaid came from the water closet and when she saw her mistress crying on the floor, she rushed to her. Abigail tried to hide her face from her servant, but the young girl was persistent, and Abigail met her eyes.

"Has he hurt you again, mistress?" she asked with a note of anger.

"Oh, Ahinoam, he pains me always. He is evil in his doings. If he despises me so much why does he keep me?" she asked, tearfully.

"Your exquisite countenance feeds his pride. He has what many men want and he knows this," Ahinoam whispered as she took her mistress's hands into her own, and helped her to her feet. "M'lady, it saddens me to see you like this. We should feed him poison and then you will inherit all of his fortunes, which he always boasts about so profusely."

Abigail's face changed suddenly. "I won't have such talk in my house. Do you hear me, Ahinoam? Never again," she snapped, and the servant bowed her head.

"Yes, mistress. I was merely jesting. I apologize."

Abigail dried her tears with her hands. She smiled at her and touched her face gently. "You care for me, Ahinoam. Don't think I don't notice what you do for me. You are a good companion, and I appreciate you. Hiring you was the only good thing my husband has done for me."

Abigail walked passed her and slowly removed her accessories and put them away in a small cedar wood jewelery chest. She loosened her hair and tilted her head back, working her fingers through the golden curls. She removed her richly embroidered silk ketonet and gave it to Ahinoam. "Despite everything he does, Ahinoam, I do love him. He hasn't always treated me like this," she said, almost to herself. "He still cares for me. I have to believe this. Don't take that away from me, I pray you."

Ahinoam nodded delicately, pressing her lips into a thin line. "The sheep shearing festival begins in two months; then he will be in better temperament."

Abigail fingered the fragrant wood ornament case for a moment and then turned and walked into a small adjoining room. She heard her husband screaming at the servants for wine and she loosened the fibulae holding her inner tunic at her shoulder, letting the cotton shift slip from her body. Her husband would be drunk again that night. After removing her undergarments, she stepped into a large washing container. She was a sensual woman, with a curvaceous body, large blue eyes, and flowing blonde hair.

"Ahinoam, bathe me and comb my hair and scent my skin," she said, staring at a hazy reflection of herself in the polished brass mirror. "Eve approaches, my dear handmaid. I must beautify myself for my husband. He will retire to the bedchamber before long."

⟨♔⟩

Curtains billowed before the large windows in the breeze. An old man lay in his bed covered with animal fur. Coals smoldered in the small hearth beside the low stone bed. He was still.

His son entered the room with a ceramic cup of hot goat's milk and spices. Feeling the breeze in the room, he closed the shutters. He called out to his father softly, and moved to the bed. His father seemed so peaceful in his sleep that he almost did not want to rouse him. Shivering from the winter chill, he called to him again.

When he touched the elderly man's shoulder, he felt the coldness of death on him and then noticed the pallor of his skin. He fell back, dropping the pottery vessel on the floor. Yellow milk splattered his ankles, and fragments of clay stung his skin. He shouted his father's name terrified, but there came no reply. Gently he laid his hand on the aged man's chest and held his other hand above the thick white beard to try and feel his breathing. The lungs were still, and he knew that the prophet had died peacefully in his sleep. His father had passed.

He stumbled outside, his face tight with grief, and ran through the town to a physician, wailing loudly. He fell to his knees and threw sand over his head and tore his clothes.

"The prophet Samuel sleeps with his fathers," he cried.

David stared at the boy who delivered the message. David held his face, covering his mouth in disbelief. His beloved friend had died.

"You say he went peacefully?" David asked, pressing his hands into his beard.

The young man nodded. "All Israel mourns him. He will be buried in Ramah."

David sighed. "I thank you for your words. Yahweh be with you."

The messenger hesitated for a moment. "King Saul has banished all wizards and those with familiar spirits from the land now that our great prophet sleeps with his fathers. Those that are found in the cities after the new month festival will be put to death. None are to be spared."

"I thank you for your words," David said and the man nodded, "Our king has done a great thing, casting out witchcraft from our holy inheritance, Israel."

David watched as the messenger left, then spoke to his brother, his voice strained by his emotions. "We cannot be there for the burial ceremony, Eliab. We must stay clear of the cities. The great prophet shall be sorely missed."

Eliab clenched his shoulder, not saying anything, feeling anguish himself. Samuel was Israel's spiritual leader, and he was a guiding light in all of Israel and Judah.

"Those who want to leave are free to do so, I will not stop them. Order a month for lamenting. And then, we head for the wilderness of Paran. Saul mustn't know where we are."

David sat beside a crackling fire, holding his hands to the quivering flames, which were eating at the black wood. He could hear the goats bleating in the night. He was alone after many days and finally had time to reflect. Gazing out at the mountainous horizon, at the beauty of the heavens, he considered God's splendid creation. For that moment, it brought peace to his troubled soul.

He did not understand why, but for the past few days, he could not stop thinking of Michal. Images of her and their marriage tormented him and he feared that something had happened to her. The thought of it gave him a sinking feeling inside.

He seldom wrote to his parents, but they seemed content and safe where they were. *I will bring them back as soon as I am able*, he said to himself in a whisper.

Saul's words echoed in his mind again, *"I know that you will surely be king."* He saw Saul's intense expression in his mind's eye, and could feel the king's grip against his jaw. Had Saul known about his anointing all this time? How, and who had told him? Was it Jonathan? David rejected the thought from his mind. His beloved friend wouldn't have betrayed his confidence. But Saul did know. The realization made him sympathize with the old king.

If only he had listened to the voice of Yahweh, David thought shaking his head; he would not have suffered so. The cold bit at his uncovered skin and he leaned into the fire again, rubbing his hands briskly. The smell of the blazing logs was a comfort to him, and he remembered how Samuel had anointed him. It had been so long ago. Thirteen years, he mused with a soft sigh. He had learned and done so many things in the past years, he had grown so much.

A cold breeze blew dying cinders into the air, and he turned to see his eldest brother standing behind him, looking at him with a grim expression. The darkness, partially beaten back by the light of the fire, gave him a forbidding appearance. David stiffened at the sight.

"Eliab, you frightened me," he admitted. Eliab gave a weak smile and lowered himself to his haunches. "What's wrong? Is it Saul?"

Eliab could hear a note of anxiety in his brother's voice, and he moved beside him, and knelt on one knee. "I have terrible news, brother," he said and paused, looking at the flames.

"Eliab, what's happening?" David demanded.

"The words to say this, David, escape me," Eliab hesitated, and then spoke as gently as he could. "Saul has given Michal to another man."

David sprang to his feet, his face incredulous. His fists tightened, and he shook with sudden rage, the muscles on his jaw standing out visibly. The news had struck him like a blade in the heart and he could not breathe. He glared at his brother, his face flushing red, his eyes wild.

"David, I ..." Eliab tried to speak, but David spun on his heel and bolted into the blackness. Eliab had been afraid that the news would drive his brother to act dangerously. He wanted to run after him, to comfort him, and to make certain he did not do anything irrational. But he also understood that David had to be alone. He could not help him.

Eliab smashed his fists into the ground, helplessly.

♛

The month of lamentation had passed slowly for David. He had been desolate and aloof, only regarding his men with distant glances when he came from his bitter thoughts. He never spoke, always feeling the pain and misery. Michal was his wife, but the king had given her away, as if she had belonged to him. He did not sleep at night, always thinking of her, and this made him irritable most of the time.

He was broken.

David prayed often but the anguish remained, eating at him from inside like a worm in a persimmon. He had allowed himself thirty days to mourn both the prophet and his beloved Michal, and not an hour longer.

Finally, he could begin to understand what Prince Jonathan had gone through when he had lost his spouse. It was a terrible thing, but he knew it had made him a stronger man. He thought of his dear friend often, and had considered writing to him many times, but thought better of it.

On the final day, he had washed for the first time and burned his filthy clothing of bereavement. He came from his crude tent a new man, hard and emotionless, and he forced himself not to remember his grievances. David knew he would never forget her; she would be with him through all the difficult days ahead. When he was finally made king he would send for her, he promised himself. They would be husband and wife again. The thought made it easier for him to forget.

A scout approached David through the crowd and bowed a knee before him. David did not like it, but his brother had insisted that he allow the men to bow before him, their future king. He still had to grow accustomed to it. He quickly looked at the people busy around him to see who was watching. The man hailed him, and David ordered him to stand.

"What have you seen, Hushai?" David asked, knowing most of the men's names.

"There are shepherds in Carmel guarding thousands of sheep and goats," he said quickly. "What do you want us to do, David?"

Touching his red beard, David thought for a moment. The wool would make warm clothing and the meat would last for days. They had not eaten meat for many weeks, and he could almost taste it in his mouth.

"There are many scavengers in this wilderness, aren't there?" David asked smiling.

⁂

Three of Nabal's servants sat at the crude gates of a sheepcote scanning their surroundings, as the sun set in a sky blazing red. The rocks gleamed with warm light and the wild grass swayed in a gentle evening breeze. Soon it would be dark and they would have to be vigilant. They had heard of the traitors roaming in the wild, like carnivores looking for flesh to devour. They feared them silently, hoping that they would not be overpowered in the darkness. They were few, and could easily be killed by hardened fighters.

A man lit a torch smeared with animal fat and fixed it to the wooden gates. Many other watchers patrolled the dense thorn-branch fence, listening for any threats. It would be another long night. At least the shearing festival would begin soon and they would celebrate for weeks.

Suddenly the guards saw a group of rugged men walking in the distance. They could not see if they were armed and they feared for their lives. The three shepherds looked at each other nervously and silently they resolved not to try to stop them. They weren't willing to die for their cruel master.

They waited for the large group of men to approach. Their expressions were fierce and their bodies marked by battle scars. One man detached himself from the others and walked toward them, smiling suddenly. The man was tall and handsome, and had a glint of authority in his eyes. He was not a man to insult.

"Blessed evening to you, good servants," Joab said, holding his hand close to his weapon at his side, ready for an attack. "I come by the orders of my uncle, David ben Jesse. I am no foe gentlemen, I swear it." Joab could see them ease slightly, and he lowered his hand from his kidon.

"We come to inform you that while we shelter in the wilderness of Paran, we will keep watch over your flock. Two hundred men will patrol around you at night and by day until we leave again." The shepherds smiled broadly and kissed Joab's hands. They would be safe for the remaining weeks until the shearing.

❦

Nabal walked with heavy steps as he inspected the servants shearing his many sheep. He had a throbbing headache from enjoying too much fermented drink the night before. He never relaxed and always fretted about the simplest things, except when he was drunk. Nabal hated people who gave of their fortunes to the wretched poor; he had worked for his success and he would not share it with the cursed lazy and deprived.

The scents of spring were in the air and the earth had dried after the winter rains. The morning air was cool on their skin and the smell of the wool, the slicing sounds of the metal scissors made him feel pride, and for a moment, he was content, though he did not show it.

Nabal scowled at the men, flexing his large biceps unconsciously. His servant, a young man with a new beard, walked dutifully behind him, not daring to speak unless spoken to.

On the horizon, ten strong men came dressed in miserable clothing and Nabal regarded them as they approached him, and wondered if they were servants. Then he remembered that the so-called ben Jesse and his band of men were hiding in the wilderness, and he was instantly alert. He had heard what King Saul had said to this David, the son of Jesse, the famed and beloved captain, and he thought it absurd that an enemy of the crown should receive such words.

I won't be so generous, he thought, clenching his fists.

Nabal was like a giant statue as the men walked up to him in the morning light. Nabal wore silken yellow and red garments embroidered with gold, and had jeweled rings and an iron blade hanging from his broad leather belt. He was as tall as Eliab, with curled black hair, and he glared at the ten young men, who now stood before him, his eyes like those of a madman.

The messengers of David bowed before Nabal and their leader spoke reverently. "We come and speak to you in the name of David. Peace be unto you both, your house, and all that you have."

Nabal did not respond and wanted to kick the man for his audacity. How dare they come before him and speak to him without permission as if he were a poor man? His anger was palpable as the silence became suddenly awkward.

"I've heard that you are shearing. Know that your shepherds who were with us were not hurt, nor was anything stolen from them all the time we were in Carmel," the messenger said, and rose. He felt uneasy under Nabal's stare, and shifted his clothing as he paused uncomfortably. "Ask your young men, and they'll tell you. That is why we ask now that you receive us kindly. We have come on a good day. I pray you, give of whatever you have to David and his servants."

"Who is David?" Nabal sneered. The men looked at him, affronted by his demeanor. "And who is the son of Jesse? There are many servants these days that break away from their masters." He looked at their faces and spat at their feet. Nabal's servant glanced at the men, and then at his master. He was unarmed and would not interfere, and he stepped back two paces.

The men paced backwards, frowning, wishing they had brought their swords. The man thought he was somehow above them, a king or nobleman. His arrogance was insulting, but they remained quiet, only looking at the muscled colossus as he continued rudely.

"Shall I then take my bread and water and my animals that I've butchered for my shearers, and give it to men whom I don't even know?"

The messengers had heard enough, and the leader turned on his heel and left without a word. They would tell David every offensive word. Nabal stared after them, quiet in his rage.

⁂

The messengers came into the fortified camp and walked straight to David who was playing on his kinnor. David knew that something had happened when he saw the young men troop towards him. He rested the musical instrument on the ground, and rose to meet them. He frowned as he saw their expressions. He understood what had happened even before they spoke. He had seen it several times before, and he was furious.

The messengers bowed and David simply nodded. He listened quietly as they told him what had happened. His green-flecked eyes were hard, and gleamed dangerously.

After they had spoken, David thought on his actions, clenching his jaw. His men had gathered around him to hear, watching him, waiting for their leader to reply. David walked for a short while, pursing his lips thoughtfully. The heat of the afternoon beat down on them and David blinked sweat from his eyes. Hospitality demanded that Nabal feed any traveler, David told himself. The man is rich and could easily afford the small request. He wasn't asking for a handout; his men had protected his servants and his livestock, and their vigilance had been extremely beneficial to Nabal. The insult was too great.

Finally, David spun on his heel and said, "Surely, I have in vain protected all that this man has in the wilderness, so that he missed nothing of everything that belonged to him. And now he has requited me evil for good."

He looked at his warriors who surrounded him, and when he met Joab's eyes, his nephew nodded and David continued. "God do so much and more to the enemies of David, if I leave alive all that belong to him by the morning light, as much as one man."

Eliab gripped his shoulder powerfully in support. "Every man, gird on your sword!" David shouted. He would cut out the man's tongue for abusing the anointed of God.

The men fastened their kidons and David took the sword Jonathan had given him years before, after he had slain Goliath. He thrust it into the air, and the men roared.

❦

The house at Carmel was busy with servants preparing for the great annual feast. Many measures of grain had been ground in basalt querns for bread and cakes, and hundreds of loaves had been baked in tabuns—small clay domed ovens. Animals were slaughtered for grilling on fires, and varied fruits and vegetables had been harvested and prepared for boiling. Beer had been fermented and strained of its sediment and poured into large vessels. Nabal had tested each of the many large bottles of ale fermented for the shearing celebration.

Abigail was busy allotting tasks to her servants to prepare for the return of the men. They would be hungry after the day's work, and liters of drink would flow right through the evening to slake their thirst. She had wrapped her long hair in a cotton cloth to keep it out of her face, and only wore a simple ketonet with a twisted fabric girdle and comfortable sandals for the day's work.

Nabal's servant ran into the room, panting. He did not even greet Abigail in the proper manner, and rushed his words. "Noble mistress of the house, I bring dire news."

Abigail covered her mouth in dread when she immediately thought that something had happened to her husband. He had many enemies, and his murder would not have been a surprise to her.

"What has happened to him?" she demanded, stepping closer to the man. Ahinoam was there immediately and supported Abigail at the shoulders, expecting the worst.

"Our lord is safe, m'lady; do not fret," he said, and saw the dismay ease from her expression.

Abigail exhaled with relief, pressing her hands over her heart. She snapped at the man. "Don't be a mute. Speak servant, what is it?"

"Our master has acted foolishly, noble mistress," he said. He looked at Ahinoam, standing beside the lady of the estate, and then continued. "David sent messengers out of the wilderness to salute our master, and he railed on."

Abigail touched her delicate face, concerned. "David ben Jesse, the king's son-in-law?" she asked. The man nodded.

"Oh, dear Lord, give me strength," she whispered.

"These men were very good to us, we weren't harmed nor did they steal anything from us all the time we were with them in the fields." Abigail shook her head, understanding what her husband had done. She hated his foul moods and evil ways.

"These men were a wall to us, night and day, the entire time we were keeping the sheep," he said and waited for a moment before continuing. "Now that you know, consider what you will do, because this could be disastrous for our master and all his household, because you know he is such a son of Belial, such a wicked man, that none can speak to him."

Abigail knew that the man spoke the truth, and with a seizure of fear, she realized that she would have to do something to save her husband and their household. She would have to go to this man looking for her husband's blood, and appease him.

"Ahinoam, have some of the prepared food and drink laid on asses, two hundred loaves and two bottles of wine, five prepared sheep, five measures of parched corn, a hundred clusters of raisins, and two hundred cakes of figs," she said quickly. Ahinoam tried to remember it all and then hurried out, calling for the lady-maids.

Abigail turned to Nabal's man. "Let the servants go before me, I will come after them," she said with in attitude of alarm. "Good servant, my husband cannot know of this. Do you hear me?"

"M'lady," he bowed his head, and left her to her thoughts.

CHAPTER TWENTY-EIGHT

The past seasons, Saul had been caught in a dark, mental prison. He had become isolated in his own house, a cold, distant man. The king was often troubled by nightmares and would wake bathed in cold sweat. He did not make love to his wives any more, and had not seen his sons or daughters in eight months. The old, miserable man had not spoken one word since he came from the Rocks of the Wild Goats, only brooding in his private chambers. His thoughts of old threatened him, and he fought not to be enslaved by them again. Gradually he had fallen into a severe depression, and the events of the past rankled as he wasted away.

His wives had begged him to utter a single word, but they always left disappointed. He ignored all who came to him, only regarding them with unhealthy eyes, as if he were the only man alive in a dreary, pitiless world. Queen Ahinoam had summoned the physician to Saul, who had diagnosed him with only a foul temperament. The king was healthy, though clearly distressed. It seemed to them as if their husband had aged years in the few months since his campaign against the son of Jesse.

His small private room stank of old air and he was shrouded by darkness, the only light yielded by a pitiful flame struggling to burn in a single stone lantern against the wall. His skin was acrid with sweat, and his eyes were wild and sunken in dark circles. Saul held his head in his hands as he sat on a small stool, plagued by the murders he had committed, the deaths he had wrought—the guard Tilon, his courtier, and the priests at Nob. The things he had said and done to Jonathan and his loving Ahinoam were things he could never take back.

I've lost all control during the years, he told himself; *I don't know who I am anymore.* Saul had practically given his throne to David, in front of his men, for all the world to know. It was a bitter thing to him, and he cursed his feeble mind. He could not face his people. He told himself that he was disgraced in their eyes. Jonathan and Abner were forced to take over his kingly duties and this convinced Saul even more that he wasn't needed. He was not a king anymore; just another hoary old man, wretched in his old age. He hated himself.

His wives had ordered a young man to sit with him in his room, and never leave his sight. Saul despised the lad and threw him out of his chambers numerous times daily, but the young man had been forced to return or suffer the wrath of his queens.

Abner entered the room and the servant rose dutifully, and bowed. Abner barely nodded, and the young man took up his seat again.

He kneeled before Saul, who only glanced at him. "Cousin, this has to end. You cannot be weak at a time like this. Your country needs a king, a strong leader. If the Philistines hear about this, they will attack," Abner said, touching the king's arm. "In all your days, cousin, will you not forget? You're stubborn, Saul."

Saul shot an enraged look at the general. Abner knew well how to get his cousin to react, and he found satisfaction in the anger he saw in Saul's face. Saul lowered his eyes again and turned his head from Abner, still silent. Abner sighed softly.

He knew what he had to do, though it grieved him. It was the only way. Israel needed their king—*he* needed him.

Strengthening his grip on Saul's arm, he said, "Saul, I have news about the son of Jesse." Saul tensed, and Abner knew he had Saul's attention. He continued quickly. "He has been conspiring against you again, my king. You were right when you proclaimed that he would be king. He will be."

Saul stared stonily at him. He was reacting precisely as Abner had hoped. "If you don't hunt him down and stop the threat to your kingdom, he will take your crown and destroy your name, and your seed. You will disappear from the history scrolls and the world will forget you ever existed," Abner said in a rough whisper, and he saw Saul think. The thought must have been terrifying to him.

Abner rose, the corners of his lips turning up.

The manservant sat uneasily on his simple folding stool, looking out of the small window through the decorative lattice, pretending not to listen. The night was splendid, and the smell of fermenting grapes on the summer breeze during the two month harvest was invigorating.

Saul suddenly spoke. Old emotions assaulted him, and in an instant, he finally surrendered.

Saul changed before Abner's eyes.

"*'I know that you will surely be king,'*" Saul remembered, sitting up from his wooden chair, clenching his fists, and then sinking back into the cushions.

The young man shot his head around and gaped at the old king and the general. He had spoken. After a moment Saul looked at him, and he rose from his seat and stepped closer. "My king, is there anything you need?"

"Send for my son Jonathan now, or feel the blow of my fists, boy." Suddenly everything he had struggled with the past months was overpowered by desperation and fresh anger. Abner had planted the seed, and it grew quickly.

The servant bowed his head and started from the gray stone room. As he hurried through the corridors of the palace he ran into the queen, who snatched him by the arm.

"Where are you running off to? Where's my husband?" she snapped.

"He has spoken, my queen. I must call Prince Jonathan." Ahinoam gasped and without a word, hurried to her king, calling for Rizpah. The other queen came from her quarters, startled, and followed without question.

The women rushed into the small room and Ahinoam paused momentarily when she saw Abner, fearing what he might have done. She lowered herself at Saul's feet. Rizpah stared at Saul, her hair falling across her face.

"Husband?" Ahinoam said, looking, searching the king's eyes.

Saul touched her face and kissed her forehead. A tear wet her face and she smiled. She had resented him the past winter for his abstraction, but it had been a lonely, cold winter without him.

"I'm not well, wife. I need Jonathan. I will be my old self after I have seized that son of Jesse. We will speak soon," he said, not realizing the pain those words caused her. Ahinoam snatched her hand from his, and with a cold stare rose. She glowered at Abner, her eyes violent. She had never liked Saul's cousin. Her husband could have forgotten about David, and they would have been happy. She made Abner feel uncomfortable, and he cleared his throat self-consciously, but did not look away.

Ahinoam slapped the old general and enraged, stormed from the room. Rizpah left after her silently; she had not expected more.

Saul rose and began pacing the room. His itching scalp and filthy hair irritated him suddenly, and he would have his servants bathe him as soon as he had spoken with his son. He had to protect his name, his family, and his crown.

"You should have taken his head when you had the chance, Saul," Abner said coldly, refusing to feel guilt. He had simply done what was necessary.

"No, David should have killed me in that cave when Yahweh gave him the opportunity," Saul said looking out of the window. "Find him, Abner."

Abigail rode watchfully on a gray mule behind a procession of servants with food, the beast braying monotonously. Ahinoam was beside her as always reassuring her as Abigail wondered about what she was doing. She feared her husband's rage, but she did this for him, whether he would believe it or not.

She thought again about what she had heard about David. He had been chased from the palace, but Israel loved him, and the people spoke of making him king. But that was long ago, and Saul's recent victory over the heathen Philistines returned to King Saul a new loyalty, although David was still on the tongues of many. He was the great captain. She remembered what a woman had said his name meant—*Beloved of God*. She thought about Princess Michal and how mercilessly her father had given her to another man. David was a fugitive, she told herself again, shaking her head, but Saul himself had announced that David would one day be king. Things did not make sense to her. What didn't she know? Everything stirred in her mind, and she was uncertain how she would react to this famed son of Jesse.

"I've heard many things about him," Ahinoam said smiling, bringing Abigail from her fretting. Abigail only shook her head at her maidservant's playful expression.

Abigail is clearly resistant to meeting him, Ahinoam thought. "Apparently, he's extremely handsome, with intelligent eyes, and a commanding air about him." Her eyes became distant as if dreaming, and she wet her lips. Abigail frowned at this.

"Rumor has it that he loves more passionately than he fights. Evidently he understands us women and knows how to please us," Ahinoam drawled.

"You shameful lass," Abigail snapped, bringing her handmaid from her musing. "The man wants my husband's blood and here you are longing for him in your dreaming. Holy law forbids sexual dissoluteness. You dishonor me with your immorality, girl." Ahinoam understood that her mistress was anxious about the pending meeting with David.

"Mistress, I am still pure. I have not let a man touch me," Ahinoam began when Abigail interrupted.

"Good, then stop behaving like a cheap harlot, you silly girl."

"I apologize, m'lady. It is true that I do not think before I speak," Ahinoam said and lowered her eyes to the ground. She walked silently beside Abigail, feeling the pain of her mistress's sharp tongue.

Suddenly as they reached the ravine, many men marched down toward them. Abigail's servants called out to her and she stiffened visibly at the sight of them. Her heart pounded, but she willed herself forward. *You have to do this, Abigail; you cannot be weak now*, she told herself, and rode to meet them, overcome with dread. Abigail forced herself to breathe, trying to think of what she would say to the prince of Israel.

She would be completely humble, she decided.

As they came closer, she noticed a man standing before them and she wondered if he were the famous son of Jesse. He was more attractive than Ahinoam had said, with a red sheen in his brown hair, and a square, masculine face. He appeared taller on the hill above her, and she knew she would submit to his authority, despite his rugged appearance and wild hair and beard. When she looked into his eyes, she became nervous.

They were a dazzling green, powerful and intelligent. She had never felt like this before, and she could not understand it.

As the man walked from the group of fighters down toward her, she realized that it was David. She got off the animal quickly and modestly fell before him in a bow, touching her face to the ground at his feet. Swathed in rich silk attire dyed with indigo and lilac, Abigail's skin was scented with oils, and her hair bound with a golden clasp behind her neck.

"Upon me, my lord, let this iniquity be upon me," Abigail said, and David was surprised by this strange woman. She had broken down all of his hostility in an instant with a single act. He did not know how to react and he looked at her silently. She was comely, her lips full and moist, her eyes hazel with delicate tresses of golden hair hanging over her shoulders. David felt an immediate attraction, though he refused to show it. *Nabal was cunning to send this enchantress to him,* David thought. He would not have listened to a man, although the idea of sending a woman to do a man's dirty work vexed him, and he frowned.

"I pray you, let your handmaid speak and hear my words," she said sensing his rage, and David relented somewhat. "I pray you, don't regard my husband Nabal, this man of Belial, a wicked man, because he is what his name means and folly is with him. But I, your handmaid, didn't see the young men that my lord had sent. Now therefore, as Yahweh lives and as your soul lives, in view of the fact that Yahweh has withheld you from coming to shed blood and from avenging yourself with your own hand, may your enemies, and they that want evil for my lord, be as Nabal. And now this blessing, which your handmaid has brought to you, let it also be given to the young men that follow you, David. I pray you, forgive the trespass of your handmaid, because Yahweh will certainly give you a sure house because my lord fights His battles, and evil has not been found in you. And when a man pursues you and seeks to kill you, God will protect you, as someone guards a treasure. And

He cast out your enemies, as a stone from a sling." She rushed her words desperately, her eyes pleading with him.

David was speechless at the woman's loyalty and love for her husband. Abigail met his eyes, and he admired her grace. He marveled at her intelligence, and he realized that she spoke the truth. He allowed her to speak, drinking in the sight of her, listening to her as a man would to a priest. Her gentleness made him forget all his anger.

She is a rare woman, David thought.

Abigail did not allow him to speak as she continued, pressing her forehead against his feet. "And it shall come to pass, when Yahweh will have done all of the good things He promised you, that you shall be ruler over Israel. Then you wouldn't have to feel grief nor suffer regret in your heart because you had shed blood needlessly or that my lord had avenged himself. When God has dealt well with you, please remember your handmaid then." She exhaled. She had said what she had come to say, and she waited for David to speak. The silence was palpable with tension. She did not look up at the man.

David had never heard a woman speak with such passion and understanding. He said her name in his thoughts.

"Blessed be the Lord God of Israel who sent you to me this day," David said finally, looking down at the delicate figure bowed at his feet. Then Abigail looked up and their eyes met. "I thank you, woman, for your sensible advice, and blessed be you, because you have kept me from murdering a man and taking my own revenge. The Lord God of Israel has stopped me from hurting you. If you hadn't hastened to meet me, then there would have not been any man of Nabal's left alive by the light of tomorrow morning."

Abigail kissed his hand and rose to her feet gracefully. They did not speak, but only looked at each other. The rage had left his eyes; they were now gentle, yet confident, and she swallowed nervously. Abigail realized that her heart pounded.

She was shaking. She was attracted to the rogue prince of Israel, and it scared her.

Abigail called for Ahinoam, who came quickly.

"My lord, I have brought food and drink for you and your men, in gratitude for your protection of my husband's herds," Abigail said. David was silent, his eyes always on her, and she wondered at this. Ahinoam bowed before David, smiling pleasurably. "This is my loyal and beloved handmaid, Ahinoam." David looked at her fleetingly and nodded, then stared at Abigail again. She could not meet his gaze and she spoke to her woman servant. "See that these good men receive what I've brought," she ordered, and hesitated to look at David again. She fought her attraction. She was a noble, Abigail told herself; she would not behave like a common girl.

She curtsied and turned to leave when David suddenly took her arm. His touch flustered her, and she lowered her eyes away from him.

"Go up in peace to your house. I've listened to your voice, and will do as you've asked," David said, and he let her go. She turned without a word, hurried to her mule, and mounted elegantly. She rode away with a line of her servants behind her, feeling David looking at her. She glanced back at him a final time.

David stared after her as she slowly descended into the ravine, and then she was gone.

⚜

The sky had darkened by the time Abigail saw the estate looming in the distance. She dreaded seeing her husband again. *What will I tell him?* she asked herself. The nocturnal fowls called in the night, and the air nipped at her cheeks as she rode uncomfortably on the braying beast. She imagined his wrath at the news, and she feared what he would do to her.

She gathered her strength as she entered through the gates. It was a large estate with many outbuildings, stalls, and even horses, although only Nabal was allowed to ride them.

Abigail slid from the animal and nodded, allowing a servant to take it to the stables for feeding and grooming. Nabal's wife looked at the house for a moment. Every step to the door brought her closer to her husband's judgement. She touched the handle and paused, praying for strength. Sighing, she opened the creaking door and slid inside, terrified.

Her ears were suddenly filled with laughter and the merriment of men and women. The house was warm with many fires and pervading smells of roasted meat and spices filled the rooms. Hesitantly, she walked into the massive room at the center of her house where guests were entertained, and she was relieved at what she saw. All of their servants were sitting at the large table, feasting like kings on what had been prepared earlier that day. The odor of heavy drink lingered in the place, and when she looked at her husband, she knew that he was very drunk. The sight of him saddened her.

Nabal tore off meat with his teeth and began chewing, his eyes red. His beard was disgusting with pieces of food and smeared with sauce. Suddenly, he roared with laughter, revealing the food in his mouth, waving a cut of grilled lamb around and then hurling the meat at a reveler. Taking a goblet of wine, he held it up in the air and announced a toast to his workforce. There was loud cheering, and Nabal downed the contents of his drink, red wine spilling onto his beard, staining his tunic. Abigail smiled at this. There was no music, and she assumed that the musicians had long since stopped their playing and were now merry with the rest of them.

Abigail stared silently at her husband and decided that she would speak to him in the morning. She left unnoticed.

The following morning, Abigail woke early. She bathed and scented herself, and beautified herself for her husband. She bound her hair splendidly and dressed in a revealing ketonet that accentuated her curves, and then prepared breakfast for her slumbering husband herself. After the festivities of the night before, she found the servants useless.

Nabal woke in a foul mood, feeling sick, and refused to eat after the night's drinking. He forced himself to drink the milk and cool water she had brought with his meal, finding that it eased his discomfort.

Abigail gathered her wits and took a deep breath before saying his name. "Nabal."

Abigail saw his eyes slowly come to her, simply staring at her. After a moment, she spoke carefully. "The day before, your manservant came to me and informed me of what had happened with the messengers of David ben Jesse. I,..." Her words caught in her throat when Nabal glowered at her suddenly. He did not like that name, and he despised it even more when it came from his wife's lips. She had his full attention now, and he was deadly silent.

Abigail continued, though inside she felt like hunted prey. "I hastened to him, husband ..." she confessed. Nabal gasped, his eyes round and then he screamed at her, throwing the vessel of yellow milk on the floor. His eyes were murderous.

"Tell me what you have done, woman," he croaked, his face dangerously red. A vein stood out on his brow, and he shook with rage.

Tears came to Abigail's eyes, but she explained quickly. "He was going to shed all of our blood, husband, after you insulted him." Nabal choked at her words, groaning as he swallowed down his burning gorge. He couldn't get his words out.

"When I met him, he was on his way to my lord's estate with warriors. I gave him and his men bread and wine, and meat and ..." she stammered. Nabal took her silk ketonet in a quivering fist. He lifted his hand and Abigail cried out, cringing from him.

Nabal grunted with pain suddenly and his eyes rolled back in his head, veins jutting from his neck. He hissed as he struggled to breathe, and saliva gurgled from his mouth as he doubled over, jerking with severe spasms. He dropped from the bed, his face blue. Nabal clamped his teeth tightly and blood dribbled from his lips as he bit his twisting tongue.

Abigail screamed for the servants, but none came. She fell at her husband's side, whimpering, not knowing what was happening to him, touching his face gently. He was burning up. Was he dying?

When foam oozed over his taut lips, Abigail became frantic. She shrieked for help.

She had to force his grip from her clothing, and looked down at him for a second, tears streaming down her face. When she saw him lose consciousness, Abigail ran from the room, crying hysterically.

Abigail sat beside her husband in his bedchambers. She touched his face lovingly, tears wetting her trembling lips. Nabal did not react to her. He was as a stone.

He has suffered from a deathly seizure, m'lady; his heart has died within him. She shook her head emotionally as she recalled the physician's words. It was the chronic and acute drunkenness, the old man had told her empathetically.

She buried her face in her hands, and shook as she wept. If only I hadn't gone to David, she reproached herself. She knew that her husband would not live long. She would be a widow soon and she would be disgraced in society.

Abigail remained at his side continuously, praying that he would wake, but he remained unresponsive. Ten days later he died.

"Praise the Lord! He has taken revenge on Nabal over my reproach and has kept His servant from evil," David said to his men who had brought him the news of Nabal's death. "Because the Lord has returned the wickedness of Nabal upon his own head."

Since the meeting with Nabal's wife, David had not thought about the woman who had commanded his attention and emotions like a war general. She was a married woman and he knew to think of her would lead him to sin. Now Abigail was a widow and the law permitted him to take her as a wife. She was a good woman, he had seen it, and she would be a good spouse to him. For a moment, the grief of Michal stung his heart, but he suppressed it. He had to find another wife; he needed a woman to comfort him and give him sons. David was silent as he thought, not showing what he was feeling.

"Tell the widow Abigail that I understand her loss," David finally said. "Tell the mistress of the estate at Carmel that I want to take her as my spouse. Bring my message to her, and then bring her to me to wife."

Surprised, the men looked at David for a moment, and then bowed. They had learned never to expect the commonplace from their leader, and that David was a man with a different, though brilliant mind.

Eliab smiled. *It is long overdue,* he thought, nodding unconsciously. *He has mourned Michal for far too long. A man needs a wife,* he said to himself. Then he realized that Abigail was now one of the richest women in Israel, and David would receive her fortune when they married. His eyes widened at the thought. David would become the richest man in Israel and Judah.

The messengers left and Eliab clapped his brother on the shoulder. David finally smiled, and the men let out a great cheer.

CHAPTER TWENTY-NINE

Abigail still felt emotionally raw after the funeral of her husband. She would wear black for a month as the law required, and she would not bathe, nor scent her skin, nor smile.

She thought about her marriage with Nabal and shook her head as tears welled in her brown eyes. *It was a hard marriage,* she admitted suddenly. *It is better that he is gone.* As soon as she realized what she had thought, she covered her mouth in shock at her disrespect for her deceased husband. She wept bitterly, and sadly allowed herself to confess that it had been true.

She would have to find another man to wed when her days of mourning passed. It would not be a difficult task. She was rich and attractive and she promised herself that this time she would not let a man choose her husband for her. It would be her prerogative and she felt a sense of pleasure at the thought. Perhaps she would not marry again. She would never have sons, and she would be alone and disgraced by society, but she would be her own person.

Ahinoam entered the room then, and Abigail wiped her tears, feeling vulnerable suddenly. She frowned at her handmaid who never knocked and seldom left her to her thoughts.

"Mistress, lessen your tears, because I have news from David ben Jesse. His servants are outside," she piped, and moved excitedly to Abigail's bed. She took her hands in her own, and looked into her mistress' hazel eyes. "He's going to ask you to wife him."

Abigail gasped and jumped to her feet. She blew her nose, and the thought of it made her heart race. David was a man among men, she knew; he had a good soul. If Ahinoam spoke the truth, she would not think twice about going to the mysterious man that she had met in the ravine. She saw his stunning eyes in her head and everything she had heard, both good and bad, flooded her mind. She could not think, and for the first time in her life, she gave her handmaid an imploring gaze, pleading with her to tell her what to do.

"Well, don't let the men wait," Ahinoam spoke quickly, waving her mistress from the room. Abigail pulled down her black veil, hiding her austere face, and composed herself as best she could. Ahinoam smiled at her and Abigail giggled nervously, taking her hands in a tight hold. The maidservant embraced her and watched her leave. If the rumors were true, Abigail would one day be a queen of Israel.

Ahinoam hurried after her.

Three of David's men were waiting in the vestibule and when Abigail came to them, they bowed.

"Messengers of David, you are welcome in my house," she said, and they rose to their feet.

"My lady, we bring a message from David," a man said simply, and when she nodded, he spoke swiftly. "David has sent us to fetch you to him to wife, my lady."

Abigail stiffened when she heard the words. It would happen. She blinked as if coming from deep thought, and lowered her eyes from the men. And then on a whim, she decided nervously to accept.

"Look, let me be a handmaid to wash the feet of the servants of my lord," Abigail said and knelt before them, pressing her forehead on the floor, feeling the cold stone against her skin. Ahinoam fetched the container with scented water, reserved for that purpose, and placed it beside her mistress. The men smiled nervously.

Abigail washed their soiled feet one by one and dried them with cotton towels.

"There are things that I must do, and then when the time comes, after I have finished my mourning and my business here at the estate, I will send for you again and you shall bring me to him," she said gracefully, and the men thanked her for her hospitality. "Ask of my staff anything that your hearts desire. Stay as long as you like."

She allowed the men to enter into her home and then she turned on her heel. "Ahinoam, this is happening too quickly," she said, covering her mouth with amazement. "I must prepare myself for my new husband. Gather the servants to me; make haste. I'll have to follow my husband. I don't even know when I shall return to this place. I must find a man to manage the estate, I must pack, and there are things to be done, Ahinoam, so many things."

Ahinoam touched her face through the thin veil and looked into her eyes, "There is enough time, Abigail. Now, my lady, I pray you, forget about it all. You have a good soul, and you deserve this," she said and they embraced. Abigail remembered her promise to her lady servant, and she laughed into her shoulder.

"Now my lady, let us ready ourselves for your waiting husband."

She rode the same path as she had almost six weeks earlier, and Abigail looked at the messengers riding ahead of them. They were silent as if sensing her anxiety. She couldn't believe that she would be married again so soon. She had just finished her days of grieving and she had burned her black clothes of bereavement.

Ahinoam was at her side, as always, and she regarded the young woman. She had fine features and flowing black hair, attractive in her own way. Abigail remembered what the woman had done for her over the years; she had comforted her and was a pillar of support. Ahinoam noticed that her mistress was gazing at her, and she tilted her head, smiling at Abigail as she wondered at her exquisite mistress' thoughts. "What is it, m'lady?"

"Ahinoam, you must be brutally honest with me now," Abigail began, and saw the pleasant expression on her servant's face change subtly. Ahinoam glanced back at the four damsels accompanying them to David's camp. Without needing to be asked, Abigail ordered her ladies to walk a few steps behind them, demanding privacy.

"Are you still pure?" she asked suddenly, looking squarely into her eyes.

"Truly I am, m'lady."

"So then, Ahinoam of Jezreel, it must be, that when you lay with your husband for the first time on your wedding night, your virginal blood will stain the sheets?"

Ahinoam nodded, and wrinkled her brow slightly at the private questions.

"I haven't forgotten my promise to you, loyal friend. I have the right to give you to a man that I think is deserving of you. Do you agree?" Abigail asked, and she saw Ahinoam's face drop.

I don't want to wed any man, she thought horrified, but would not say anything. *I want to marry for love.*

Dismay gripped her, and she could not answer.

Abigail did not wait for her to respond, and continued. "Well then, Ahinoam, I am content to tell you that I intend to persuade my husband-to-be to also take you as wife."

Ahinoam's mouth fell open, and she froze in her step. Abigail rode on and did not look back at her, struggling to keep a straight face. She smiled into her sleeve, and waited for her lady maid to say something. Ahinoam's eyes were wide with shock. Then gathering her skirts, she ran after Abigail, snatched her mistress' hand and kissed it tenderly. Her eyes were brimming with tears, but her words caught in her throat. Her mind was in turmoil. She would be rich, and no longer a servant.

"Soon you won't have to dream about David so sinfully," Abigail said beaming, and Ahinoam lowered her head, her face flushing. Abigail took her hands in her own, laughing excitedly. "You and I, my dear lady, we will be the wives of a king."

Abigail stood beside David in the stony lands of Carmel, the splendid rays of moonlight washing over them. She wore a delicately embroidered ketonet for the marriage consummation, colored a rich shade of purple and indigo with the finest dyes, and decorated with lines of white, her hair bound regally with silk and iron. David, looking rugged, stood next to her, dressed in a simple silk halug with a gleaming metal waistband. He was draped with a linen cloak of dark lavender and white pattern, his dark beard kempt and his skin oiled. Small flames lit the night and the air smelled of blooming flowers and dust.

Men and women surrounded them, and all were silent as the priest Gad spoke. He told the two betrothed of their duties to one another in accordance with the holy law. He told Abigail that she must obey her husband and that he would rule over her, and that she had to support her husband by giving him children and strengthening their family. David was commanded to love his wife, respect her, and provide for her, so that she would long for nothing. When the priest was finished he nodded at them in a dignified manner.

Abigail was startled when David took her hand and she noticed that it was moist with sweat. He was also nervous, she realized. David smiled at her with kind eyes, and Abigail knew that she had not made the wrong choice.

David had not been with a woman since Michal, and he was tense as he led Abigail into his tent. He would make her his wife that night. The people watched as the light died inside the quarters and it was dark. They waited.

Abigail did not know what to expect from this man. Her heart pounded as David touched her, his hands rough against her delicate skin. She stiffened slightly as he kissed her on the neck, his beard scratching her. Slowly, he loosened the clasps that held her dress and slipped her ketonet from her. Her husband was skilled at lovemaking and she surrendered to him completely. Lowering her onto the small bed, he bent over her and she became weak with desire. Never had she experienced anything like this with her first husband. David adored the feel of her skin against him as he held his new wife close to him, their bodies gleaming with desire.

After some time, David called for his brother through the slit of the tent flaps. Eliab approached and crouched at the entrance.

"Their wedding has been consummated. They're now husband and wife," Eliab announced proudly. A great cheer exploded from the crowd and music filled the night, as the people celebrated and feasted.

The king's three thousand men of war camped on the arid plains of Jeshimon. Ziphite leaders had come before the sadistic king. It had not taken much to persuade Saul to pursue the son of Jesse in the wilderness again. They had informed him that David and his apiru were hiding in the hills of Hachilah.

Abner had been eager to assist Saul in planning his campaign. The war council had decided that Jonathan would remain behind to stand against the Philistine hordes and would send for the king and his ben-hayil when the enemy crossed the borders into Israel or Judah.

The Philistines had been threatening, yet dormant over the months, and Jonathan knew that when they marched, there would be a war like never before. It would shake the very core of Israel.

Saul and Abner would hunt the king's enemy.

All Israel had heard of Saul's proclamation that David would be king and rumors were rife in the cities. None spoke of it too loudly for fear of the authorities, but in tavern corners and shady side streets, the inevitable truth spread. Saul was a bad-tempered man who glared at his people in the streets and snapped at the citizens around him. He was determined again to search for the man who would claim his throne. Silently, he despised his weakness, and he vowed that he would not be so feeble when he found David again. His words plagued his consciousness constantly, and he raged and resented himself privily about it always.

He had given in to his old jealousy and depression haunted his moods. Saul would not rest until he held the severed head of David ben Jesse in his hands. The king lived for that moment; his every thought and every action were dedicated to that goal.

The early spring air nipped at their exposed fingers and faces as David and his men crouched dangerously on a hill above the campsite. Saul's men lounged lazily around many fires and the encampment had grown quiet as the moon made its way across the sky. Hundreds of white tents lined the stony earth, with the royal tent in a trench at the center.

The smell of the food cooking made David hunger for it. He counted the watchmen. Twenty were standing guard at the perimeter, clutching their spears beside the blazing torches.

David had sent spies to confirm the news of Saul's military camp and when they reported their findings, he and his officers stole down to the campground under the cover of night. Now they watched the activities for hours in complete silence; they could not speak for they would have been discovered.

The moon reached its zenith when David finally said solemnly, "Who'll go down with me to the camp? To Saul?" and looked at the two men standing beside him.

Before Ahimelech the Hittite could answer, Abishai, Joab's brother spoke. "I will go down with you, uncle."

David and his nephew crept stealthily down the hill and waited at the foot of the slope, listening. The watchmen had dozed off, and David shook his head at this. Saul's men had grown weak since he had left, and he thought for a moment how he would have punished the man for his slackness.

David moved even closer, cloaked in dust and filth. He came to the sleeping man and stared into his face. David knew the man. He was a soldier of the long decommissioned Gibbôr, and the sight of him in Saul's ben-hayil tore at his soul. The soldier had sworn allegiance to him, and now he hunted him. David glared at the dozing soldier for a tense moment, his face fierce, and then he was gone as silently as a breeze blowing over the desert.

The guard woke suddenly with the feeling of being watched. He scanned his surroundings quickly, feeling nervous. There was nothing. Leaning against his spear again, his heavy eyelids closed after a few minutes.

Every man was asleep, and David crept through the white tents unnoticed, his mind fixed on his movements, his breath nervous. If they were caught, they would be killed. The moon illuminated his way in soft silver light.

Then he saw him finally. Saul ben Kish.

David prayed for strength not to murder the king sleeping under the stars. He eased down into the trench, his movements only a whisper. He came beside the man who had been hunting him for years, the king who had taken his wife from him, the one who had caused him so much misery and pain. Saul's royal spear was pegged into the ground beside his head, and David took it in a firm hold, his mind raging. He felt such resentment for the old king and yet, as he slept so peacefully, David could forget everything Saul had done to him. General Abner, the son of Ner, lay beside him snoring as loudly as the bellow of an ox.

David's dark shadow was cast over Saul as he stared at the king, clasping the weapon in his fist. It could all be over in a moment. He could return home with his wives, Abigail, Ahinoam, and … Michal. He could begin a family and work his father's lands, and he would have rest for his soul.

He would be a king.

David shook his head against his line of thought. "No," he whispered. Abishai leaned in close to his captain, his lips touching David's ear. "God has delivered your enemy into your hands again this day. Now let me plunge his spear through him, I pray you; I won't have to strike twice," he said, his voice barely a breath.

"Don't destroy him; for who can stretch forth his hand against the Lord's anointed and be guiltless?" David answered as always, keeping his eyes fixed on the king, his voice emotionless. "As the Lord lives, God will smite him, or his day will come to die, or he will descend into battle and perish. Yahweh forbids that I stretch my hand against the Lord's anointed, but I pray you, take his spear and jug of water and let us go." David lifted the water skin, and took the spear from the ground.

Silently they escaped as quietly as spirits in the night. Nobody had seen them, and David knew that a deep sleep from the Lord had fallen upon all of them. David prayed silently as he hurried up the hill.

There was a great distance between David and Saul's camp, and he swept his eyes over it. Then he cried loudly into the night shattering the silence, "King of Israel!"

David saw the men react to the sudden scream. "Abner, son of Ner, will you not answer me?"

"Who are you that calls out to the king?" Abner hollered into the darkness, searching the surrounding hills with his eyes. Then he saw David standing in the distance, and he indicated to his men to ready themselves. He saw them draw daggers. The general gauged the distance; it was out of range of a spear. He swore softly.

"Aren't you a valiant man? And who is like you in all Israel? Why then have you not kept your king safe?" David shouted. Saul shot a glance at the surprised general. He shrugged, confused, shaking his head.

"Because there had gone people into the camp to destroy the king, your lord. What you have done is not good. As Yahweh lives, you are worthy to die because you have not kept your master, the Lord's anointed." Loud whispers filled the camp, and Saul's glare became savage. Abner became stiff like a stone pillar, shifting his eyes between Saul and the man on the hill, his face showing his confusion.

"Now look where the king's spear and his jug of water are that were beside his head," David roared, and lifted the items into the air for the men below to see. There were mutters when they realized what had happened. They had slept through it all and could be hanged for it.

Saul had recognized David's voice, and his fists tightened when he understood that the son of Jesse had spared his life a second time. "Is this your voice, my son David?" he asked, his words echoing.

"It's my voice, my lord, O king. Why does my lord pursue his servant? What have I done, or what evil have I committed?"

David shouted. "Now, I pray you, let my lord the king hear the words of his servant. If God stirred you up against me, let Him accept an offering. But if children of men have brought it about that you spurn me, cursed be they before the Lord. This day they have driven me out of our land, God's inheritance, and they say I should go and serve other gods, because I am not allowed to offer at the tabernacle, nor partake in the festivals. Let not my blood fall on the earth before the face of Yahweh, because the king of Israel has come out to seek a flea, as when one hunts a wild bird in the mountains."

It had happened again. David had shown generosity and no harm to him, and now he could not order him killed, nor show any cruelty toward the son of Jesse. Saul sighed, and he knew he had been wrong, but he didn't want to admit it. His rage and anger gave him a sense of power, and he did not want to surrender to the truth. He clenched his jaw, his face contorting with raw emotion. All eyes were on him again. He remembered the last time this had happened, and he recalled his vow not to be weak.

I will have to do something, Saul decided. *I'll have to apologize, let this son of Jesse come to me, and then I'll dispose of him when time permits.*

Saul swallowed down bile and then finally screamed miserably at David, "I have sinned. Return, my son David. I will not harm you again, because my soul was precious in your eyes this day. Look, I have played the fool and have done a terrible thing." Seething silently, it took everything Saul had to speak the words. The only way he could kill David was by doing it with his own two hands behind his palace walls at Gibeah.

David waved the spear above his head. "Look, the king's spear. Send one of the young men over to fetch it," he shouted. Abner ordered a soldier to retrieve the weapon.

"Yahweh rewards every righteous and faithful man," David continued, "for God has delivered you into my hands today, but I wouldn't harm Jehovah's anointed. As I have spared your life, so be my soul in the eyes of God, and let Him deliver me out of all tribulations."

"Blessed be you, my son David. You will do great things," Saul answered, his voice tainted with hatred.

David struck the spear into the earth and stared at Saul for a moment. Then he turned on his heel and left.

Saul watched him disappear behind the hill and grunted with indignation. He wanted to command his men to march after David, but he knew he would lose the little respect they had for him, and he would be a disgrace to his people. He could be dethroned. He would not allow it. He had to watch David escape again. He was bitter as he stared after him.

"Abner, I'll hunt him until the end of my days," he said softly to his cousin, and spat onto the ground.

David could hear the sound of the ram's horn crying behind him, and knew that Saul was leaving for his palace. He did not stop to look back. David went his way in silence, his men walking reverently behind him.

David was deep in thought as he strode to his hidden camp. He remembered everything that had happened, not feeling the cool air of the early hours of the morning against his skin. He heard Saul's voice in his head as he recalled how the king had tried to kill him, and had almost succeeded. He never knew if what Saul said was true; he always harbored enmity, it seemed. Would Saul truly allow him and his six hundred men to return to their homes? David sighed despondently. He knew what he had to do, but it grieved him. Saul would never stop hunting him.

I will perish one day by the hand of Saul, David thought frowning. *There's nothing left but to escape speedily into the land of the Philistines. Saul will despair of me, of seeking me in any coast of Israel.*

"So I'll escape out of the hand of Saul," David whispered through clenched teeth, his voice barely a breath.

Chapter Thirty

"Mistress," Ladiah's handmaiden called desperately with heaving breaths and Ladiah turned on the soft bed of cushions and silk, and faced the young woman. "I've news. The son of Jesse has entered the city. He's here!"

Ladiah's full lips separated, and she covered her mouth with her hand. She thought for a moment and then sprang from her bed. The queen called for her slave caretaker to tend to her infant son, and ordered her lady-maid to summon slaves to dress and paint her. She would have to be as seductive as she had ever been if she were to succeed in her task. Ladiah loosened the iron clasps at her shoulders and allowed her night shift to slip from her silken body, watching as slaves entered her royal quarters bringing many fine dresses laced with gold and colored with the finest dyes. She pulled in her stomach as a woman brought cloth to bind her, and began searching for the right words she would say to him.

She would be a seductress, Ladiah knew, and she smiled deviously.

David studied the statues in the cold hall as soldiers escorted him and his brother Eliab, his cousin Joab, and his best fighter Pelet to an audience with King Achish. The room was colorful with draped cloths and painted murals of sensual men and women in the nude. The floors were tiled with terracotta and gold, and appointed with fine cedar wood furniture. The palace made David sneer with disgust when he noticed the stone and gold-leaf images of the Philistine gods. He hated the place despite its regal interior.

The Philistines did not speak and only motioned to them with spears, although David knew they could easily overpower the four guards if he wanted it.

A deep voice ordered David to turn left to a wide arched door. He then saw a large figure, swathed in multi-hued cloths, and wearing a heavy iron crown encrusted with precious stones. The man glared at him. Achish.

David wondered if he had made a mistake in coming. He took a deep breath and mustered his courage as he stepped before the obese king. Studying his face, David noticed that he had grown older and had a savage glint in his brown eyes. His skin was covered with black tattoos of the royal names of his bloodline. Achish's beard glittered with gold dust and his eyes were dark with kohl.

"The son of Jesse," Achish said finally after tense moments of silence.

David bowed his head respectfully. "King Achish, noble son of King Maoch."

Achish scrutinized the young Israelite and sensed pride and an air of indignation, but he was not hostile. David's look was sharp with intelligence and Achish admired it for a moment, and then moved his cold stare over the miserable appearance of the man. He was rather tall, with brown hair that, in the light, had a glint of fire, and overpowering eyes of green. Achish liked his humility and he thought about everything that his advisors had told him of the Hebrew traitor over the years. *He would make a strong ally,* Achish mused. *His men are fierce warriors, and his apparent hatred for King Saul could be useful.*

"How would I know that you are truly an enemy of Israel?" Achish asked suddenly.

David did not even think before he answered, "I will deliver Israelite heads to you from the raids on their cities. Will that be proof enough, king?"

Achish touched the golden ring in his nose as he thought, narrowing his eyes.

"If you do this, you may stay with me in my city. But I will be watching you closely, you and your men." David nodded.

A woman entered that made David gape. The sight of her demanded the attention of every man in the court. She was alluring in a red and yellow streaked ketonet, tied in a knot at her waist, revealing her voluptuous form. Sleek hair curled over her shoulders and flowed down her back, styled away from her face with a metallic hairpin of Astarte, the goddess of fertility. Ladiah swayed her hips seductively as she walked to the throne. Her eyes were inked prominently with black kohl and dusted with gold and blue powder, and her lips were painted vermillion. She seemed a queen in every respect.

Ladiah was amazed that her husband had not sent the man to be hanged at the gates, and she wondered at this. As she moved past David, her heart throbbed with anxiety and as she met his eyes, she remembered the night when he had burned the garrison. His glare had been harsh and he had looked like a savage war-god. They had escaped into the night and she had stopped to look back at the blazing fort. The memory made her shiver, but she kept her composure. She recognized Pelet standing behind David and she could feel his blade at her neck again, rubbing the skin gently where he had pressed the knife. The queen shifted her eyes to her husband; she could not stand to look at the rogue prince of Israel.

Ladiah lowered herself before Achish and kissed his feet. The king pulled her to him, and they kissed. Then she took her place at his side. Now she had a new sense of power and could look at David. Her eyes bored into him, and he appeared simple to her, like a beaten man.

"You do not remember me, son of Jesse," she asked fingering a tress of hair.

"I do not, queen," David replied, and bowed his head for a moment. When he looked up again, he noticed some of her features and then he recognized her. She was one of the whores he had allowed to escape. Unconsciously, his jaw dropped. Ladiah smiled at his reaction, and placed her hand on her husband's fleshy leg.

What was she going to do? David wondered fearfully as he tensed.

"He does, my queen," Achish said, with a questioning gaze.

"He was the one that brought me to you, husband. And now you have a son, an heir to your throne," she said and looked at David from the corners of her eyes.

"I am indebted to him, my lover," she whispered into Achish's ear. "Please, repay my debts, give him harbor, and let my bond to him be done." The king was quiet for a moment.

"David ben Jesse, I proclaim you safe in Gath, and free in my city."

David bowed his head. "I thank you, good king," he said. "If I've now found grace in your eyes, then give me a place in some town in the country that I may dwell there. Why should your servant reside in the royal city with you?"

Achish narrowed his eyes at the request, immediately suspicious.

"Please, husband, he frightens me; give him what he asks. I cannot have him here with us in the city. I will become austere, and you wouldn't want that, would you? Do it now my lover, quickly, then I will call for the physician to mix you a tonic, and then I can show you the full extent of my gratitude," Ladiah breathed into his ear wantonly. "Send spies if you have to. Decide, now my lover." She knew her husband could not resist her, nor deny her anything when she made the right promises, and behaved according to his desires.

Achish suddenly called for his courtier and ordered him to grant David his request.

"You and your men may bathe and feast in my palace, and then when a place has been made available, you will be escorted to your new town," Achish announced, and studied David's reaction. "Now, everybody leave us."

As David and his men left, Achish called out to him, "You will honor our agreement, David."

"Indeed I shall, good king," David said.

Once outside, a young girl spoke his name suddenly and ran toward him, holding her skirts. Without looking at him, she walked past and leaned in close as she spoke softly, "My queen's debt to you is repaid in full, son of Jesse. She owes you nothing for her life." David watched after her as she hurried past and turned a corner and was gone as quickly as she had appeared.

Winds shook the trees on the hills of Gibeah as Saul and Jonathan walked through the fields. The breeze caressed their skins and Jonathan stroked his golden beard as he listened to his father speak about the past. Saul was tired, and the years of ruling Israel had taken its toll on his physique. His skin sagged with wrinkles, his hair was silver and white, but his blue eyes were as piercing as ever. His voice was calm and Jonathan was intently listening to his father's words. He had not known his father like this, he thought. His voice was composed and assured, wise in his old age.

"David has fled to the cities of Philistia," Saul said and studied Jonathan's expression.

"I've heard, father, that you have driven him out of his birth land, into a heathen world," Jonathan said, looking down at the moving grasses. He hesitated before asking the old king, "Will you follow him, to the city of Gath—to your death?"

"You know I cannot, son," Saul said, his voice tainted with sudden misery. "Why do you mock me, even now?"

"I don't, father, you hear things that aren't true." Jonathan was startled when his father patted him on the back. Jonathan met his eyes.

"We do not have the strength in men to campaign into Philistia—for just one man. I will have peace now that he is gone, Jonathan. I pray I will," Saul said as if thinking. "We will be a family again."

Jonathan was taken aback, and after a moment he smiled, gripping his father's shoulder affectionately.

I would forgive the man anything, Jonathan told himself, as he took his father in an embrace.

"You've always been my favorite son," Saul said, and a tear ran into his beard. "How can you ever forget my transgressions, my sins, my hate?"

"I already have, father. You are all I have. The noblest of fathers, the most passionate of kings."

Saul looked at his son with such ardor that Jonathan had to fight tears. The king gripped his son's head.

"I shan't be king for long. Let us enjoy the time we have together, you and I." Saul lost his voice, and he frowned. His eyes became opaque as if he knew death was coming. He was silent for a long time and Jonathan could not speak. "I'm an old man, my son." The king essayed a weak smile. He hesitated before continuing, crossing his arms upon his chest.

"I have tried to fight God's will, my boy. But when Jehovah has become your enemy, the world changes. Every word uttered has a hidden meaning and is an insult. Every action is a threat. And each breath is full of dread and suspicion. My depression and jealousy will be my undoing. I cannot change the Lord's will," Saul admitted and brushed tears from his eyes. Muscles on his jaw stood out as he spoke through clenched teeth. "It is a terrible thing, Jonathan, to be rejected by God."

"Father, He has not cast you off; you did Him," Jonathan whispered, feeling his father's pain.

"What you speak is true, my noble Jonathan. I know," Saul said, dazed, and clapped him on the shoulder and sauntered off into the moving grasslands. "I know."

Chapter Thirty-One

black suffocating smoke billowed into the air from burning houses as David's men rode through the city. All were dead. Bodies of men and women laid sprawled on the muddy soil, and furniture, baskets, and shards of broken clay vessels were scattered in the streets. The scene was desolate and the afternoon air was filled with the distant screams of citizens being slaughtered as they fled from the Amalekite city. None of the inhabitants of the lands where he attacked could be allowed to return to Achish and tell him what he had done. The king had to believe that he was raiding the tribes of Israel. David looked up at the fiery sky, at the incandescent sun and heard animals cry nervously through the chaos.

David had been living in Ziklag for over a year, and he hated the lands with their dead gods and shameless ways. His men and their families had settled in the city. Now, almost thirty thousand of his people had already come to him there with a desire to see God's will in making him king. God had given him an army that was compared to the host of Yahweh.

The Hebrews in Philistia had transformed Ziklag into a small Israel, as much as they could, and had secretly destroyed all the idols of Astarte and Chemosh, cleansing the small city in the Negev region. The houses had been painted in vivid colors and they had reconstructed the buildings and had built new dwellings. The time there was peaceful for the wives and children. As vassals of the king of Gath, it was a fair existence, but it was not Israel. They were close to the borders of his tribe of Judah, and yet were so far from their homeland.

Astride his dark mount, David stared down at the destruction and clenched his jaw. In the past months, he had attacked the people of Geshur, Girzi, and Amalek, who had inhabited the region for a very long time. He had raided their land as far as Shur, all the way down to Egypt and he had had vicious victories. He had ruined them completely, and most of their livestock and apparel were delivered to Achish as deceiving proof that he was spilling the blood of his own people. The fat Achish was convinced of every word, and delighted in his new riches. The spies that the king had sent had been silenced by extravagant bribery and violent threats to their families and loved ones. They were even threatened with death if it were demanded.

David had been delivering spoils of camels, asses, sheep, and oxen to the elders of Judah, to attest that he was loyal to Israel and to his heritage.

He knew that soon the Philistines would eventually venture to the devastated cities for the annual taxes, or to renew their treaties, and then the truth would be known. He was fighting himself into a corner, but he would never have attacked his own people. He would rather flee from the Philistine king and be a fugitive once again. It was a forbidding prospect.

"All are dead, uncle. Our secret is safe for another day," Joab said coldly, covered in the blood of his victims, his face spattered red.

"You are bleeding. Go to the physician, Rehabiah, and let him clean and bind your wounds. I need you in these wars, Joab," David said, detached, sitting rigid in his saddle. Coldly, he turned his horse, and rode from the burning city, his striped red and white cloak flowing behind him.

Now he had to act for Achish as he delivered his report to the king. Again.

Dusk had begun darkening Gath as David and his entourage of warriors rode through the gates. They were still bloodied and they stank from the two days' hard ride to the city, but they did not bathe for the sake of a dramatic appearance. David would deal with the king as swiftly as possible.

As he trotted on the wide cobblestone road that led to the palace, David rode past the massive stone statue of their goddess of fertility, Astarte, and grimaced at what he saw. Several infertile couples were making love at the feet of the sculpture on red blankets. It was widely believed that the deity made men potent and women fecund.

David gripped his reins tightly, and sped past the Philistines, raging privately with disgust. If he could, he would gut them personally for their brazen behavior.

When they reached the stone arched doorway of the royal building, the streets had cleared for the night and torches lightened the dark eve. With a swift word, soldiers allowed David and his men to enter, glaring at the Israelite who spoke to them so disrespectfully.

David and Eliab shared silent glances as they waited in the regal vestibule for an audience with Achish. They did not wait long. The palace was gloomy with quivering lamplight, and the faint sound of music haunted the corridors. A young servant dressed in a rich blue tunic brought them into the king's chambers.

Achish stood naked before them as they entered. Slave girls massaged abrasive oil over his lumpy skin and folds of flab, scrubbing his flesh with ivory combs. David forced himself to look squarely into Achish's eyes, and did not dare look at the fat king's body.

"David, my loyal servant. You have returned, presumably with rewards. I have been waiting for your reports on your raids," Achish said lifting his arms for the women to work at his ribs. Baggy skin quivered as he moved and David was instantly repulsed at the man's nakedness.

"My men are shepherding a hundred camels, seventy oxen, and two hundred sheep to your palace, my lord." David replied, managing his tone.

"Where have you made a raid today?" Achish asked, and ordered a girl to use more of the olive oil mixed with balm and coarse salt and scented with rosemary.

"Against the South of the Kenites, sire."

"You haven't brought me heads, have you, David?"

"Indeed I have," David said and took a leather bag from Eliab. He undid the cord, and lifted a gruesome head of a man with a dripping beard. The eyes drooped open and the skin was dark and sagging. Achish grinned at the sight and nodded, satisfied.

He has made his people Israel to utterly abhor him, Achish thought sadistically. *He will be my servant forever.* He chuckled.

"You please me, son of Jesse," Achish said. "I will have my bath now. Join me, David."

"If my king does not oppose, I miss my wives and they have been lonely these past weeks. I would like to return to them, have them wash me, and properly clean my wounds," David said and bowed his head.

"There is nothing like a woman's touch. You may leave for Ziklag."

"I thank you, Lord Achish." David said, turning on his heel and leaving the sight of the boorish king as swiftly as he could.

Ahinoam ran from the stone house, followed shortly by Abigail, as she heard the people singing and dancing at the return of their brave men. She held her skirts tightly, calling out to her husband. When David saw her, he spurred his horse towards her, his eyes bright. He laughed as he pulled her onto the animal and kissed her fiercely. The people cheered at the sight.

"Oh, how I've missed you, husband!" Ahinoam said, and she touched his face.

"And I you, wife," David said. He chuckled as he then lifted Abigail in front of him on the mount and greeted her passionately, before they rode to their home. It was a small place with wide lattice windows and mud-plastered walls painted a bright yellow. He had missed his two wives and the smell of bread and meat baking in the kiln that pervaded the atmosphere in the warm, pillared rooms of his abode.

David slid from his horse and assisted the women down, embracing them tenderly. He did not care for the festivities and closed the door behind them, shutting out the entire world. He would spend the night with Ahinoam and Abigail, but first he would have a bath, and have Abigail massage his aching muscles.

As David slept that night, he dreamt of the slaughter. His body jerked as he reacted to the violent images, kicking and twisting in his bed. All of the people of the many cities of the lands of the Geshurites and the Gezrites that they had killed were in his dream in a crush of terror. He smelled the blood of the women and children, and it was as if he were there all over again. Their screams echoed pitifully in his mind. David moaned, dripping with sweat as he tried to stop the killing in his dream, but he was powerless. His sword was gone, and he wore only a plain linen tunic, though it was stained with gore and mud. Suddenly Michal was there in the thick of the battle. David screamed for her, struggling through the teeming masses. Blocking flailing limbs. Pushing forward. He had to save her; he loved her. Then an Amalekite with a dark beard stood behind her, shouting savagely at David, his eyes murderous. When Michal turned, her face broken with terror, and then in a flash of light from a blade, the man pierced her with his kidon. Michal cried out and tears washed her delicate face. David roared with rage, his muscles stiff.

He awoke, still screaming.

Abigail awakened with a fright, and saw through the darkness that Ahinoam had also roused and was sitting up.

"No, let me go to him, Ahinoam," she said, as David's other wife shifted out of bed. Abigail flung the covers from her and lit a lamp from the dying embers on the hearth in their small room. She entered her husband's quarters quickly and found David breathing wildly. He was frantic and confused. She tried to calm him, and only when he looked into her eyes did he realize where he was. The room was quiet and he was home. Gasping, David searched the darkness, and then sank back in his pillows. He was exhausted.

Abigail undressed and slipped under the bedcovers and comforted her husband. She knew that he would ride out again in a few days, and she savored the little time she had with him.

David had led his men to an Amalekite town and they caught their warriors by surprise in a night raid. The heathen men had fought valiantly until the morning rays touched the wide plains in a blaze of color, their numbers diminishing under Israelite blades.

David cut through a man's muscled torso with an iron broadsword, pulling the kidon from the flesh. He waited as another Amalekite charged, and skillfully he faked a blow, and knocked the man unconscious with heavy strikes from his shield. He pierced his heart.

The clamor of battle overpowered his senses as he searched his fighting men. For a moment, he found himself looking for Michal, fearing that he might find her there. He shook the feeble thought from his brain, and saw that Asahel was fighting several men who were beginning to surround him. He rushed to his side, and broke a man's face with his small shield. Before they knew it, they were surrounded, and they fought at each other's backs. Asahel shouted the signal in Hebrew, and David bent over. Simultaneously, Asahel swung his blade over him, and sliced open his attacker's throat as David turned from underneath his nephew's strike, thrusting his blade into the Amalekite's gut. In another exchange, they sent down the final two men in confusion.

They fought together intensely for some minutes and then it was over. There were none left to kill, and with burning biceps, David sheathed his sword. Another city had been vanquished and their bodies littered the bright desert soil.

David caught his breath and blew the victory horn. His warriors exploded with shouts, and then as a wave, they struck the gates of the town, and scattered through the streets.

After many terrible hours, it was finally quiet.

Limp bodies were stacked for burning and the grass roofs were set alight. Reticently, David watched it all burn feeling sick to his stomach. He thought of his own wives and the children of his brothers. David knew that there was still a key city to break before the Amalekites could be conquered, and he subdued his weakness with a clench of his fist. He decided that he would send much more than the usual number of livestock to the elders of Judah. He would buy his way back into Israel, and into the hearts of his people.

David watched his brother jog up to him, as was almost a ritual after a battle. Eliab stood before him, panting. He was getting old and few black hairs threaded through his silver head. David admired the man for his strength of character. He had been there with him through it all; he was his pillar of strength and his wisdom, apart from prayer.

"It is done, little brother. Now only one town remains."

✶

Days later when David returned to Ziklag, royal messengers awaited him. David halted impatiently, and did not greet the two Philistine men, arching his brows as he listened to their report.

"Philistia is marching against Israel," a man said plainly. "The cities are gathering at Aphek. You are ordered to march your men there and meet with King Achish. He awaits you."

David turned to stone at the news. Achish hadn't even mentioned the notion of war to him. He could not fight against his own people. The two men looked at him guardedly, and then left as David stared after them, his mind wild.

He knew he would have to depart immediately. He would only have one night with his wives and then he had to leave them again. He missed them during his raids and he longed for more time with them.

Slowly, David rode into his city.

CHAPTER THIRTY-TWO

David led his six hundred men to the Philistine camp with solemn reservations. He could not kill his own people. It was three long days before he finally reached the site of the army encampment. White tents climbing the gentle slopes and lining the horizon surrounded the silent valley.

Disturbed at the sight, David exhaled slowly as he looked across at the Philistine gathering place at Aphek. Men in ranks of hundreds and thousands were still arriving from all across Philistia, riding into the camp as the sun set.

Scores of battle-hardened warriors worked around the many small shelters. The smell of smoke filled the air as fires were lit for the evening. Smiths sharpened blades and spearheads, and many fighters sparred in groups. Iron from Achish's fleets of chariots gleamed in the fading rays of the fiery sun. Wind blew clouds of golden dust across the scene as the battle horn of the Philistines pierced the late afternoon, sending a chill down David's spine.

David had never seen such a gathering of Philistines in his military career. Achish had summoned all of the cities together and each man capable of wielding a sword was ordered to join the army. It was a congregation of heathen killers ready to devour the cities of the earth. Fearing the outcome, he turned on his heel and made his way to the tents, which Achish had prepared for him and his men, arrayed around the royal canvas. Israel would be outnumbered.

An hour later, David entered Achish's campaign tent and froze when he saw the Philistine war council gathered around a leather map of the regions. He fought not to show his thoughts when he greeted Achish. The Sérèn leaned on the table, and when they saw David they instinctively shifted their hands to their hilts, furious at the sight of him. He was an Israelite, and even worse, a traitor. They all remembered his battle with Goliath. He could not be trusted, and they let him know it. David chose to ignore their hostility and gathered himself together as he came further into the room.

Achish put his arm round David's shoulder and brought him to the table. The men glared at him.

Achish's Israelite dog could easily stab him, the Sérèn of Ashkelon thought, and gripped his hilt again. David stared at the map, noting their strategies and military forces. What he saw vexed him. They weren't going to attempt another anterior offensive on the Judean ridge, but would try to bypass Israel's defenses instead. They would move their forces north up the coast and into the Jezreel through the middle pass through the Carmel Mountains. The Wadi Ara was protected on the east by the fortress of Megiddo. It was brilliant. Though the hills adjoining the Wadi Ara were forested, it was still distant enough to make an Israelite ambush from the Judean ridge highly unlikely, and also it was wide enough to allow his large fleet of chariots and infantry to maneuvre if they were attacked. If they succeeded, Philistines would control the entire Jezreel valley with all the valued caravan routes. If their stratagems were achieved, they could attack southward and ultimately threaten Gibeah itself. Achish would again impose his power in the area, just as his father King Maoch had done decades before.

"Know assuredly, David, that you shall go out with me to battle, you and your men. You are my vassal, son of Jesse," Achish said and indicated the map, bringing David from his thoughts. The air in the room was stifling, and David felt irritated by the king hanging over him. His breath smelled of aniseed, but his sweat was pungent and hung around him like the scent of dust in the desert.

"Surely, you know what your servant can do," David said, his mind sharp. He smiled deceptively.

"David, you have shown me your loyalty, and if you do this for me, then I will know that you are truly an enemy of Israel and I will make you keeper of my head forever," Achish said and clapped him on the back. "My personal bodyguard."

"You honor me, Lord Achish."

"All of the cities are gathering for warfare against Israel. Rest your men. We march tomorrow when the sun breaks the darkness," Achish said, watching David's reaction. David faltered, but regained his composure swiftly. "You have neglected to inform me of any of the deliberations or even the notion of war," David said and bowed his head.

"Surely you must have expected it."

David suppressed his surprise and nodded. "We will spill their blood and take their women and sons as slaves to serve Philistia." The council members narrowed their eyes at David's answer, but were silent. They would not speak in front of him.

"Your fire will inspire the men, David," Achish said frowning slightly. "Now leave. My council still has much to discuss. I will speak to you again tomorrow at sunrise."

David could do nothing more and he left, his thoughts anxious. *Would Saul expect Achish's bypass? Would Israel be ready?*

After David had left, there was an awkward silence.

"What are these Hebrews doing here?" Sérèn of Gaza asked, managing his anger.

"Is he not David, the servant of Saul, the king of Israel, who has been with me these past days of the year? I have found no fault in him since he came over to me," Achish said as he looked at the frowning princes of Philistia.

"Make this fellow return to the place which you have appointed him," Gaza said, and the four other men voiced their support. "Don't let him go into battle with us. He might turn on us in the heat of the fighting. How much better for him to win back his master's favor than by the death of our men."

"Is this not David, the one of whom they sang in dances, 'Saul slew his thousands, but David his tens of thousands'?" Sèrèn of Ashkelon asked, arching his brow.

"I hear what you say, princes. If it will put you at ease, I shall heed your advice," Achish said, rubbing his beard. "Summon David to me again."

Within moments, David stepped into the tent.

"Truly as the God of Israel lives, I know that you have been loyal to me; and I would have been pleased to have you fight in this battle. I haven't found any fault in you from the day you came over to me. But the Sèrèn don't approve," Achish said immediately.

"What've I done wrong, sire? If, as you say, you haven't found any fault in me since the day I came to you, why shouldn't I go with you, my lord the king, and fight your enemies?" David asked and glanced at the princes. Their expressions were wroth and they glared at David, silently daring him to offend them.

"I know you are as good as an angel of God. But the Sèrèn insist that you do not go with us to the battle," Achish replied. "Rise tomorrow morning early and depart with your men as soon as it is light enough."

David had to stop himself from smiling as he bowed and left. He would not have to fight; God had heard his prayers.

He would return to his wives and then he would finish his campaign against the last of the Amalekites.

David waited on a low hill outside of the Philistine camp at Aphek with his six hundred men waiting silently behind him in square formation. Standing beside his gelding, he held the reins and admired how the warm light of morning flowed over the gentle slopes, making them seem incandescent with gold. The air was dry and dust particles stuck to his oiled beard as he gazed out over the shimmering land.

Then the serenity was shattered by the fierce sound of the battle horn. David turned his head to the echoing cry and watched as thousands of Philistine warriors marched out against his country. Stones danced and the leaves trembled with every heavy step. It gave him a sickening feeling in his stomach as he thought of the days ahead. He would not fight in the battles, and that would plague his thoughts constantly. He was an Israelite, and he needed to fight in the war beside his king. Saul.

Miserably, he mounted and rode back to his heathen town, back to Ziklag.

The sun burned the earth as Abigail and Ahinoam sat and kneaded dough for the following day's bread. Ahinoam added a little water to the mixture and then spiced it with saffron and sage. Abigail mashed dried locusts to a powder in a pestle and mortar and handed it to her.

"I miss him, Ahinoam," Abigail said suddenly as she got up and stoked the coals of the fire in the small oven. "I love him. I didn't think it would happen so soon after Nabal."

Ahinoam thought for a moment. "Me also, Abigail. I wish he were here to hold me in his strong arms and kiss my neck." She blushed. Women passed their modest house and greeted them.

"Today is the day of his birth," Abigail said, her hands busy crushing seeds between the two basalt implements.

"Yes, I remembered. He's thirty years of age, strong and in the prime of his years. Our beloved David," she replied fondly.

"Soon, love, he'll be with us again."

Suddenly a scream rent the air, and then it was silent. Ahinoam dropped the dough on the stone slab as she jumped to her feet. They listened nervously. Then it happened again. More women shrieked and they heard shouts from the men and instinctively Abigail knew that they had to run for their lives. She snatched Ahinoam by the hand and hauled her away. In her flight, she tripped and fell to the ground, tearing the skin on her knees. She cried out and sped for the opposite town gates. She had to reach Gath; they would be safe there.

Horsemen charged through the wide gates of Ziklag, flailing their swords, shouting profanities and violent threats. Women cried as they tried to run from the wild men, but they were snatched up onto the mounts and blades were pressed at their hearts. Clouds of dust were kicked up in the flurry, and those who attempted to escape through the haze were knocked down or were caught by scarred foot soldiers with their noses pierced with large metal rings and their long hair folded up in dirt stained turbans.

Bathsheba was held to a naked chest and she could smell the stink. In a desperate attempt, she jerked at the nose ring. The man howled in pain as the metal tore free and blood spattered over her. She pushed the blade away and fell from the rearing horse. She did not hesitate and ran into the nearest building. She slammed the door shut behind her, and pressed her back against the hard wood. Her mind was wild as she whimpered, trying to decide what to do.

"The window," she said loudly as she thought of climbing through the small, high opening. "No, they're everywhere." Clasping her mouth with her shaking hands, she wept when she realized that she was trapped.

"Pssst ... over here; make haste!" A voice came from another room. Bathsheba stiffened with shock and jumped away from the door, staring into the other room.

"It's us—David's wives. Come hide here, child," Ahinoam whispered harshly. Bathsheba caught her breath, and rushed into the room. The women were hiding in a large concealed closet and she crept inside with them. Abigail held her, and she broke down.

As they waited for what felt like hours, they could hear women wailing and moaning, and they feared what the men must be doing to them. Abigail struggled to breathe from fear.

"It's the Amalekites," Ahinoam piped, and the other women looked at her fiercely. "David described them to me. They're raiding the town." She could not contain herself.

After awhile, the crying of the women became distant and ceased. The streets were silent.

Then they heard the door creak open, and Abigail held the mouths of the women shut, shaking with terror. Leather sandals slapped softly against the stone floors.

They're searching the houses, she told herself bitterly, *we'll be discovered*. She clamped her eyes shut, tears spilling over her cheeks. Abigail could taste the salt. When the man opened a cupboard door, she jumped. Her heart raced and she felt faint.

Then the steps receded into the other room. She opened her eyes, and gasped with relief. They would live. After a moment, the front door opened and the house was silent again. The women all moaned as they sobbed against one another.

"What is that smell?" Bathsheba asked abruptly through her tears.

Thick smoke flowed in and they stumbled from the closet. The house was white with smothering fumes.

"They have set the roof afire."

The women could not wait much longer or they would burn to death. Straws of glowing grass wafted from the crackling ceiling and hot embers dropped to the floor through the blanket of toxic air. They could feel the heat above them. Abigail assessed their options. They could barely breathe and the women covered their faces with cloth, but it did not help. Choking, Abigail could hear a beam of wood supporting the clay rooftop crack and she reacted, quickly pulling the women from the house.

Several men waited for them as they fell out of the smoldering building, their faces black and their clothes torn. The men laughed raucously and spoke in a language of which they could only understand a few words. The women suppressed their retching and gasped the fresh air, their lungs burning.

The men seized them violently.

CHAPTER THIRTY-THREE

Saul and his captain over three thousand struggled up a steep hill that would bring them above the enemy camp. The moon provided little light for them to see, but the gleam defined his muscular physique and made him look like a warrior-king again. Ehud remembered the lifetime of wars at his king's side, and despite everything that had happened in the past, he admired the king at that moment.

Weeks before, word had reached Saul of the approaching Philistine horde, and the king had sent emissaries to each of the twelve tribes, ordering the tribesmen to muster at the fountain at the Jezreel Valley. Over a period of two weeks, thousands of skilled and war-hardened Israelites had arrived at the gathering place in large groups from each city.

Saul and his council had been busy in his tent working on strategies and war tactics. The princes and Abner had chosen to set up camp just outside of the border of Israel, north of the Shechem plains. Days later, when all of the tribes had been accounted for and the numbers were tallied, Saul marched forth against the Philistines. Now Israel was pitched at Mount Gilboa and though the two hostile nations could not see each other, they could sense their battle lust across the distance. The scouts had returned with estimated numbers, and Saul had scowled at them for their lies. These men had spoken of scores of thousands of Philistines shaking the very earth.

The king could hear distant savage howls echoing over the plains as he ascended the highest peak. His feet slid on loose soil, kicking up a haze of dust. Saul inched up until he finally reached the crest, breathing heavily. His old body wasn't as fit as in his youth, and his lungs panted after little exertion. Under the cover of darkness, he and Ehud crawled closer still.

Saul gasped as his eyes scanned the endless points of lights from fires of the military camp reaching over the hills as he tried to take it in all at once. From that height, he could see everything without any obstruction.

"No, it can't be," Saul whispered incredulously through clenched jaws, his face broken with sudden fear. "Their camp runs on against the base of Mount Moreh with no horizon, Ehud."

He reversed back down on his hands and knees, and rolled onto his back, his breathing erratic. He could hear their wild cries breaking the silence of the night, and he shuddered as terror overpowered him.

Ehud was like stone as he examined the unending tents and hordes of bare-chested warriors preparing for war. As a captain, he had fought in many wars and only once had he seen such a force. He clamped his fists and moved to his king. Saul was quiet, his eyes transfixed on the silver clouds. The moonlight gave him an appearance that made Ehud uneasy. Saul realized that his heart was pounding. These men were giant, cruel killers, and were unrelenting and feral in battle.

"Ehud, go and summon the priest; we must pray for deliverance," Saul said suddenly, and then glanced at his captain. "I will remain and learn as much as I can from here. I want men scouting them constantly, day and night. I need to know every detail—numbers, chariots, cavalry, archers, and infantry. We must miss nothing, Ehud." The captain nodded and left in a swirl of dust.

"Our forces must descend from the top of Mount Gilboa," Jonathan said, and looked up at Abner from the large leather map of the battlegrounds spread over a low table. The general nodded in agreement.

"Their chariots will not ride up the steep slopes and the Philistines would have the disadvantage of attacking uphill," Abner added, fiddling with the blue clay statue resembling the infantry as he thought. "We must array our forces in an arch around the mountain—east, north, and west. But the southern hills are negotiable for vehicles; they could flank us from behind. We would be surrounded and they would choke us gradually."

"It is a problem," Jonathan said, touching his lips through his beard as he contemplated their situation. "We could send a detachment to the city Gina in the southwest, and they could protect the opening."

Jonathan had begun to show his age. Silver broke through the light facial hair on his temples and below his chin. His short curls had begun to turn ashen, and wrinkles lined his cheeks and webbed under his hazel eyes. The prince shifted the blue clay infantry to a square mark on the map that was the city of Gina. He smiled.

Saul sat on his throne lost in his thoughts, rubbing the bridge of his nose absent-mindedly. He had prayed many times, but no answer came. The war council gathered around the table as Jonathan enacted the battle.

They would spend days preparing, but Saul decided that this time he would not act of his own volition as he always had in the past. Not until he had an answer.

After a few days, Saul had grown frantic and he knew he had to make a decision. He had to know how the war would turn out. Biting his fingernails, he could not stand still for a moment longer.

"Yahweh does not answer me, Ehud, not by dreams or Urim or prophets." Saul raged at his most trusted captain as he strode purposefully around his lavish royal tent. "Any word from the prophets?"

"Nothing, my lord," Ehud said, shrugging.

"How much longer will Jehovah be silent, Ehud? What shall I do?" Saul asked with a sigh, forcing his hand through his white hair.

Before Ehud could answer, the king turned on him sharply, staring at him threateningly. "Ehud, seek me a woman who has a familiar spirit so I can go and inquire of her."

"But my king, you banished all of them from the lands," Ehud said.

"I did not ask for your words, captain. I have told you what to do. I care not how you do it, but you will do as I command. Now leave and make haste."

"My king, I've heard that there is a woman living in Endor. Not far from here, sire."

No torches burned in the silent streets around the secluded house. Saul had removed his crown and had dressed as a poor man, his clothing torn and tattered with stains and smelling of animals. The sackcloth halug scratched his skin as he walked apprehensively to the door. Saul felt weak because he had not eaten that day. His hands shook.

The king knocked and looked at the two men at his side, swallowing nervously. He did not know what to expect or what he would learn from the old hag. Saul could hear the sounds of the night fowls and he felt a shiver run down his spine.

This is wrong, he thought, touching his forehead.

The door creaked open and an attractive young woman looked at them through the narrow opening of the crude door.

The king was caught by surprise at the sight of the young woman, and he stared. She did not speak, only gazed at the men. After a moment of silence, she tried to close the door, but Saul pressed his hand against the wood, keeping it open. He said quickly, "Please divine for me."

Saul could now see her entire face as she looked at them. She was splendid with flowing brown hair and striking blue eyes. Her skin looked soft, and he could smell the scent of oils on her. Many necklaces of bone and small carved stone shapes clattered as she opened the door further. Her gaze was piercing, and she wore a simple ketonet edged with fur. "Bring up the man who I will name to you, woman."

"Look, you know what Saul has done. He has cut off mediums and spirit-knowers from the land. Why then you do lay a snare for my life, to cause me to die?" She asked, narrowing her eyes.

"As Jehovah lives, you shall receive no punishment for these things," Saul answered and held her cold glare. She hesitated and then stepped aside and allowed him to enter.

Her house was a single small room with a door at the back leading to an elongated stable. The room was filled with unholy artifacts and signs painted on the walls, with many colorful crystals and rocks. The eerie place had a strange odor, but he ignored it, as his eyes took in the rest of the building. It was dimly lit, and glimmering shadows crept across the furniture.

She indicated for him to sit on the bed, but he refused.

"Whom shall I bring up to you?" She asked, and he could see her prepare herself.

"Bring me up Samuel," Saul said firmly. She closed her eyes, and began humming.

Suddenly she fell back, screaming as if in acute pain. "Why have you deceived me?" She was terrified, and fell to the floor as she saw the prophet Samuel in the room engulfed in a fierce light. She pressed her back against the wall. The room was suddenly too small for her.

"You are Saul, the king!"

❖

Abigail gripped the bars of her cage. They were kept together like animals on a barred dray pulled behind oxen. She was exhausted from struggling, and her mind was never quiet. She looked at Ahinoam who held a young lad on her lap. His mother was on another wagon, and he had eventually fallen asleep as she held him close. The sun baked them as they jerked with the motion of the heavy cart, hurting her flesh against the metal. She had not spoken for hours. Nobody had. Their captors laughed, and prodded them with sticks, licking their lips at the attractive women.

"Will they kill us? Sacrifice us to their dead gods?" Ahinoam asked in a voice raw from screaming. Her face was sensitive from all the crying. She could not look at Abigail.

Abigail shook her head, deep in thought. "No, they won't harm us. They will do far worse," she said coldly, staring out across the desolate wasteland, "We'll be dispersed and sold as slaves to distant lands. Servants to the lusts of heathen men and the revenge of their jealous women."

Ahinoam stifled a sob, gripping the child to her.

❖

The city was ruined. The buildings had been burned, and in the moonlight silver lines of smoke still streaked the air from the destroyed houses. The scenery was desolate and the air thick with smog. A numbing quietness hung over the city. Ziklag was empty.

The sight of the city tore at David's very being. He was like a statue as his eyes took in the debris and destruction. Slowly he slid from his horse, his fists clenched.

David could not contain himself as he fell to his knees, and shoveled dirt over his head in raging agony. Had his wives been taken? Were they alive? He could not bear to think about it. A man wailed somewhere behind him, but he did not look back. The men were wild with emotion and they dashed into the city to their homes.

David sprang up from the ground and ran to his house. The door was open wide, and he stared for a moment into the threatening darkness of the collapsed house. He gathered courage and edged inside. They were gone. Silently he wept, red mud caking across his cheeks. He pulled at his hair, and sank to the floor covered with ashes and rubble.

"Why did this happen?" He screamed.

I was a fool to leave them, he blamed himself, and painfully hammered his fists against his heart. After everything that had happened, he could not handle this, he told himself shaking his head frantically. It was nearly too much for him, and he shuddered with sobs, rolling frantically in the filth.

David lost all sense of time as he lay there, his face raw from the tears. He heard his men in the streets, but he did not get up. He was emotionally spent, and he closed his eyes. The violent sounds grew louder, and David sighed as he rose, stirring up a cloud of ashes. He did not dust himself, and walked slowly out of the ruins.

He heard their words clearly in the quiet night. "This is David's fault. He was careless in riding after the Philistine king and leaving Ziklag vulnerable. The Bedouins are always lying in wait, watching for when they can seize a city," a man said. "He must be stoned to death." David tensed as he turned his head up to the heavens, and called out to Jehovah, silently encouraging himself.

Muscles on his jaw stood out as he walked to them, breathing heavily. He swept his gaze across the gathering of warriors. Their eyes gleamed dangerously with resentment, and he could sense murder in their postures. A man bowed down and picked up a small stone and clamping the rock in his fist, he sneered at David.

"Abiathar, please bring me the ephod," David said to the priest, after some anxious moments. The soldier stared at him, his eyes cold, and then he left silently. The grief and hate was palpable in the hot desert air.

They could hear the jingle of the holy garment as the son of Ahimelech brought the ephod to David. Abiathar donned the linen garment and then placed the golden band over his head. He closed his eyes and went to inquire of the Lord.

The men waited for the priest to finish. They would have blood on their hands for their families, one way or the other. If they did not murder the men who had taken their sons and daughters, they would have David's head.

David inhaled audibly, and looked at the mutinous men. Abiathar returned to the assembled group.

"I asked Jehovah if you should go after this troop," he said to David. "Shall you overtake them? And the Almighty God has answered me, and has said to me *'Go, for you shall surely overtake them and, without fail, recover all.'*"

"Jehovah has answered me favorably," David's voice boomed over the men, shattering the threatening silence. "Ready your swords, men. We will hunt Amalekite flesh tonight."

They broke out into raucous cheering, flailing their swords above their heads. David spun on his heel and raced to his horse. Six hundred armored fighters charged from the wreckage with savage passion into the darkness of the desert.

"Don't be afraid," Saul said to the witch. "What do you see?"

"I saw gods coming up from the earth," she shrilled, her body writhing.

"What is his form?" Saul asked impatiently.

"An old man comes up, and he is covered with a cloak," she said in a tremulous voice. Saul understood that it was Samuel, and the king bowed. He pressed his face to the floor as he prostrated himself, feeling the coldness of the stone against his skin.

"Why have you disturbed me, to bring me up?" Saul could suddenly hear a voice. He recognized that it was the prophet who had anointed him the first king of Israel, and he searched the room in vain for the apparition.

"I'm grievously distressed because the Philistines are warring against me, yet again," Saul said quickly with a note of fear. "And God has left me and does not answer me, not by prophets nor by dreams. And I've called you, so that you can make known to me what I should do."

Only the woman could see Samuel, and she could not look away, though terror gripped her. She moaned at the powerful sight of the man.

"Why do you ask me? God has left you and has become your enemy," Samuel said. "Jehovah has done precisely to you as he said through me. He has taken the kingdom from you and is giving it to your neighbor, to David. Because you did not obey the voice of Jehovah, nor execute his fierce wrath on King Amalek, that is why he has done this thing to you now. And, Yahweh will also deliver Israel with you into the hand of the Philistines. And tomorrow you and your sons shall be with me."

Saul fell to his face at Samuel's words, whimpering. He was weak and could not lift himself, and he lay on the floor breathing in uneven gasps, his violent eyes fixed and distant.

The woman sighed and her muscles relaxed as her body went limp. They were alone. She stared at the king lying flat on his face, and pitied him. She could not imagine what he must be thinking or feeling. After a moment, she rose and moved to his side. When she touched him, he did not respond, and she knew that he was sorely troubled. *What had he heard?*

She lifted the strands of loose hair from her face and spoke softly to him. "I have done what you asked me, and risked my life in doing so. Now, I pray you, listen to me. Let me set a bit of bread before you, so that you can have strength when you go on your way."

Saul managed to shake his head. "I will eat nothing."

The woman hesitated, and then called in his servants. They armed themselves immediately when they saw their king on the floor. She quickly stopped them, showing her hands, and explained quickly what had just happened. The men were frozen with shock. She stepped back a pace, and then told them that he would not eat. It took them awhile to come from their thoughts at the disastrous prophecy.

"Prepare the meal. He will eat," Ehud said and watched her leave through the door to the stable.

The captain lowered himself beside Saul and when he touched his king on the floor, he was startled at his coldness. Saul was pallid as a corpse and moaned weakly.

"Will you have the bread?" he asked.

Saul shook his head, and turned away from the captain. Ehud knew what he had to do. He turned the king around and slapped Saul's face. Nothing happened, and he hit him again harder. He saw his king come from his state of devastation, and he met his eyes that were wild with shock.

"You must have some bread and meat, my king," Ehud said. Saul nodded, and Ehud helped the man to his feet. His knees gave out under him, but the men caught him, and sat him on the bed.

Saul sat, as if dead, staring again at nothing. The men could not stand to look at him. Ehud could hear the witch kill a calf and he began noticing his surroundings. His face showed his disapproval.

After some time, she entered and carried meat upstairs leading to the roof. There she kneaded flour and cooked the meat and unleavened loaves in the outdoor kitchen.

Saul said nothing, dreadfully quiet in his thoughts. When the woman brought the food, they sat on the floor and forced Saul to eat.

When the men mounted their horses, Saul had gained some strength, although he was still mute. The woman watched them ride slowly into the night. They trotted down the road, into the darkness that swallowed them, to the king's death. The corners of her mouth turned up as she entered her home.

Chapter Thirty-Four

David had ordered the men to make a circular formation and they slept for a few hours. When dawn broke over the horizon, David sent out trackers to search the lands ahead. The sun had lifted from the horizon by the time his men returned. In a cloud of dust, they galloped to the formation and dismounted with a foreign man bound at the wrists, wearing only a loincloth.

As David ate fig bread, they escorted the slender man to him. David studied him, and tore another bite from the loaf. *He's clearly Egyptian, but what's he doing so far from his homeland?* David wondered. *Is he a slave?*

The day before, David had stopped at the brook Bezor to rest the few mounts and to refill all the water skins. He had been eager to march again, when men came to him and told him that they were too exhausted to continue. He had allowed two hundred men to stay behind with most of the belongings, and ordered the rest of his four hundred men to regroup into lighter and smaller units of roughly sixty-five, with his brothers and nephews in command. His group had seventy fighters.

Then the six eleph trooped on swiftly with the only five horsemen scouting ahead.

The Egyptian did not look David in the eyes. He was taciturn, and David noticed that he was shivering in the morning air. He was weak and had nearly collapsed before him.

"When last have you eaten or drunk?" David asked. The man's scalp was shaved bald, but fresh dark stippling had grown after his time in the wilderness. He had the marks of an owner on him.

"I have not had bread nor water over my lips for three days and three nights," the slave said with a thick accent. David nodded to the scout, who took a cake of figs and gave it to the dark man, and sat him down on a blanket. David gave him his cloak to warm himself. They cut his bonds, and watched as he devoured the figs greedily. David handed him his large water-skin, and the man drank deeply, water streaming down his chin and over his chest. David offered the slave raisins and allowed him to rest. He ate two clusters. Smacking his lips, he belched softly into his hands and nodded gratefully to David. They saw his spirits return. Stroking his exposed stomach bulging with food, he smiled, showing a mouth full of well-kept teeth.

"Tell us, man, whose are you? And where do you come from?" David asked and saw the man struggle to remember the words to speak.

"I am an Egyptian youth, a servant of an Amalekite. My master left me behind three days ago to die because I had fallen sick," he said gesticulating, mixing his Semitic with some Egyptian. He took another drink from the sack before he continued. The slave winced from the sting as the dry skin tore on his lips, and licked the cut as he spoke. "We raided the lands of the Cherethites in the south of Judah, and on the south of Caleb. And we burned Ziklag with fire."

David sat forward suddenly. "Can you bring us to this company?"

"Swear to me by God that you won't kill me or deliver me to my master, and I will take you to them," the Egyptian said, kneading his hands unconsciously.

Many men were dancing besides fires, howling and singing exultantly, lurching drunkenly around the temporary camp. They had been celebrating their victories, and warriors lay sprawled unconscious across the hard-baked earth.

David saw his wives in the caged wagons arranged in a circle in the center of the few tents of the officers, and he clenched his fists at the sight. The women and children were bound around the neck and ankles like animals, and he hated the Amalekite men more. He knew that his fighters experienced the same thoughts; he sensed it in their attitude.

The crest of the sun rose brilliantly from the horizon; dawn was the best time to attack. There would be enough light to see and still catch the enemy off guard. He studied the men and waited for the signal from his commanders that they were in position. Eliab and Joab had the western ridge, Pelet and Asahel had the east, Abinadab and Abishai the north, and he and Shammah the southern hills. They each commanded one hundred men. He and his family planned to ambush the festive encampment.

They were outnumbered almost three to one, but the Amalekites were drunk on wine and grain-lager.

As the sunlight beat back the shadows, he heard the calls, one soon after the other. All of the men were in place. David was flat on his stomach in the dust as he gazed over the disarray of the merry warriors. He could smell the odor of scorched meat forgotten on the fires, and hear the vigorous cheers and cries of the heathen encampment.

"We're right here, so close, and they don't even see us," Shammah said with a vindictive grin. David narrowed his eyes, gripping the ram's horn as he waited for the right moment. He nodded.

After a few more intense minutes, he could not wait any more, and he brought the siren to his lips. His brother saw the movement, and gripped his kidon. They would fight for their women, and he could almost taste Amalekite blood. His racing heart was from battle-lust as he crouched, readying himself.

David blew on the horn, the harsh sound echoing threateningly.

Hundreds of men bounded from the morning shadows and the Amalekites screamed in terror, scurrying for their swords. Fierce men poured in from all directions and the camp was crippled with confusion. Savage screams polluted the air as the Israelites slaughtered the Amalekite men.

They had fought the entire day, and now the shadows of night crept over the barren lands as the sun sank behind the burning horizon. David could not feel his arms anymore and he had more wounds and bruises then he could count. His muscles were taut from battling and his lungs ached with each breath rasping through his throat.

His blade severed a tendon and the soldier dropped. David decapitated him. They had surrounded the enemy and had fought fiercely, tightening around them slowly, killing them with dreadful precision. Some had tried to slay the women and children in the cages, but all were met with bloodied kidons. David had given orders that the women be protected at all times during the battle.

He knew it would be over soon. The enemy numbers had diminished and there could not be many more. As he cast his eyes across the disordered violence, he realized that a large group of men were escaping the kidons of his warriors. He sounded the horn.

"They are running for the camels!" David roared over the chaotic din. Bronze stabbed at Amalekite flesh, and those who could, pursued the leaders of the rebels. He watched as they vanished in a storm of yellow dust, and he was satisfied to see so many of his men chase after the camel riders.

David did not hear a brutish warlord come at him and only caught sight of his gleaming blade from the corner of his eye. Instinctively, he turned and brought his shield up to the descending broadsword, barely blocking the stab. The Amalekite struck him with his shield against the side of his face. David's eyes went dark and he was disorientated. With a wail, he fell to the trampled earth, which was littered with corpses, feeling the cold slush of bloody mud against his skin as his assailant loomed over him with blade and shield. Hearing the battling screams fade, David lost consciousness.

In the coldness of the desert, David woke in the early hours of the morning. His head felt strange, and then he remembered the Amalekite standing over him with the double-edged sword. He felt his body and inspected his limbs.

"You are safe, David," Eliab said, sitting beside him with Joab, next to a fire. "You almost slept through the entire night."

"Am I whole?" David asked fearfully.

The men laughed. "You miss nothing—apart from your ego and dignity."

David fell back onto his pillow and swallowed, having a foul lingering taste in his dry mouth. Gently, he felt his head. He was not bandaged, nor had a wound, although the flesh was sensitive to his touch.

Eliab handed him some water, and David drank deeply, quenching a terrible thirst. He licked his lips and put down the skin beside him.

"What happened after?" David asked and hesitated, ashamed.

"Shammah cut down the man before he could hurt you, and then he fought beside your body until it was over. You wouldn't be alive if it hadn't been for him."

"Numbers, brother?" David asked and held his head in his hands.

"Eight hundred dead. Four hundred escaped on camels. We lost an eleph of men, but we got back everything. Each man has his wife and ..." Eliab said when David broke into his sentence.

"Where's Abigail?" David asked suddenly, sitting up again. "Ahinoam?" Without waiting for an answer, he jumped to his feet.

"Under the awnings of the wagons," Eliab said and pointed to the formation of vehicles. David was lightheaded for a moment, but he gathered himself and ran to look for them.

He called out to her when he saw her sitting huddled beside the flames. Ahinoam sobbed his name with a note of frenzy as she saw him. She jumped up and stumbled to him.

Ahinoam flung her arms around him and kissed him intensely, touching his face. The scrape of his beard against her cheeks was a great comfort, and she was quiet as she drank in the sight of him. Tears welled in her eyes.

"You're safe, my beloved," David said. "I wouldn't have survived if something had happened to you. I feared ..." but Ahinoam stopped his words as she pressed her lips against his again. She would not let go.

I've been so afraid, she thought. She had fretted that she would never see him again.

David pressed her to him and he closed his eyes as he embraced her. Then he heard Abigail scream for him and he wept for joy at the sight of her.

David set the pace in front of his men, driving the cattle from the spoils onward. Abigail sat before him and Ahinoam at his back, and he felt their arms around him, pressing against him. They were safe and he had thanked Jehovah in his prayers. He would write psalms, he decided. They had gotten everything back that the Amalekites had raided from Ziklag, and much more from the other cities. They were rich. David had heard the men say that they were his spoils, but he would not be so selfish.

Then David saw the brook Bezor in the distance, and he could hear a great cheer explode from the men who had remained by the stream. He rode out and greeted them warmly.

There was powerful joy at the reunion of the families, and David rejoiced that he could witness it. He was alive with the victory and he fed off their joyous energy. The women and men cried, then they danced and sang, and David ordered a camp set up for the night.

Later that afternoon David gathered his men about him, and they all knew that he was about to divide the spoils. There was excitement in the air, and David sensed it as he looked around at his men.

"Jehovah has wrought a great triumph ..." he spoke loudly, and the Israelites cheered rowdily. David chuckled as he raised his hands, summoning silence. They chanted his name.

"We've looted much from our enemies, and I will equally divide this among everyone," he continued and again, they erupted raucously. It took some moments for them to quiet down, and David beamed with delight.

"No!" A man yelled suddenly and the crowd hissed, staring at him. "Because these two hundred didn't go with us, we will not give the spoils that we fought and bled to seize to any of them! They can only have their wives and children. They should take them and leave."

The people were immediately upset and some men voiced their displeasure, while others, their approval.

"Those men who stand with him were worthless and are evil," Eliab said into David's ear, and folded his muscled arms across his chest. He glared the man down.

The people looked at David eagerly for a verdict. He thought for a moment, and then his voice boomed over the host.

"My brothers, you cannot do this after what the Lord has given us. He led us into battle and kept us safe and gave us a great victory over the raiders. Not many will agree with you. The spoils will be divided equally between the men that stayed behind with the supplies, and all of those who fought bravely."

There were a few hoots among the whispers.

"And when I'm ruler, this shall be an ordinance and statute in Israel."

The following morning they returned to Ziklag.

CHAPTER THIRTY-FIVE

Jonathan waved the red flag frantically above his head, the rough material flapping in the violent gusts. Foot soldiers fought below him, protecting him.

"Stop them," he grunted through gritted teeth. Standing up in his saddle, the prince stared at the formations of the city of Gina. They were commissioned to protect the south-western hills beyond the fortified town. The slopes leading up the western rise of Mount Gilboa were gentle and were negotiable for the Philistine chariots. If the Philistine vehicles managed to bypass Saul's troops guarding the base of the mountain, the battle would be lost. Achish would charge with his chariots from behind them, and they would be surrounded.

The sounds of war raged about him. The infantry grunted and screamed, and he swept his eyes across his battalions battling downhill against the Philistine foot soldiers. They were holding. The left wing was tightly pressed against the foothills, and he knew that this would compromise maneuverability. His brothers, Abinadab and Malchi-shua, were insane in combat astride their black mounts. Jonathan glanced back at Gina and panted as he flailed the bright ensign again.

Still they did not react.

They were immobile as Achish and his hordes ascended toward them. *Did they not see him?* Achish would ride right through them if they did not fire their arrows soon.

"Launch. Launch. Launch!" he shouted over the savage sounds piercing the heated afternoon, his expression showing his anger and anxiety. His horse reared suddenly, and the prince clutched the reins. He rounded his mount to face the city.

Jonathan looked out into the distance and saw his father wielding twin swords in a skilled dance of death. He was in the thick of the fighting, his shield bearer blocking the blows for his king, and although his body was old, it was well trained, and did not give out.

Jonathan searched for Abner, but could not see him. Again he signaled, anticipating the clash of the two nations. The enemy chariots would cut through the defenses and it would be slaughter. The prince gasped in terror as he realized that his men were not going to attack, and his knees faltered as he fell into his saddle. They had seen the flag, but they were ignoring it.

"Treachery," he whispered, shaken and slack jawed, his eyes hard. The fleet of vehicles rode past Gina unchallenged and Achish did not signal an attack against the regiment. He moaned as his body shivered. As the Philistines turned a hard west up the slopes, Jonathan felt overpowering fear.

His father was right; his brothers, his men—they would all die.

He realized he would have to do something. His jaw hurt from grinding his teeth painfully with anxiety. His kidon slipped in his grip and he felt the earth tremble under the wheels of the Philistine chariots. If he sounded the horn too soon, the men would turn to the chariots and they would be hacked from behind. His only offensive against the vehicles was his archers, and they were with the Gina contingent. It was a terrible thing for him to admit that he was powerless against the host that was racing over the dark soil of the baked earth. He watched as Achish flanked his forces downward from the heights of the mountain.

Jonathan snatched the ram's horn dangling at his side. With a gasp of air, he blew on the golden mouthpiece, and the sky darkened as Philistine arrows arched through the sky.

The Israelite warriors turned at the sound. The front lines were instantly slashed and they dropped. The Philistine lines ascended the steep circular slopes and cut into more backs in a wave of death. Infantry charged to the chariots, and Jonathan ordered the launching of spears. They were surrounded. It was over.

The prince turned in his saddle, his eyes wide as he lifted his shield against the hail of wooden missiles. Arrows thudded into the wood, and his horse reared as iron tore into its flesh. The animal screamed and fell, crushing Jonathan's leg underneath it. Malchi-shua cried orders for the men to assist as he and his brother lifted the beast to free Jonathan.

The eldest prince grunted with pain, and pulled his leg free as soon as the weight eased. His face contorted as he stepped on the sprained foot, but he ignored the agony as he unsheathed his sword and was handed a shield.

The three princes of Israel waited.

The enveloping Philistine chariots as well as the infantry from the rear pressed at the left wing, until finally the lines broke.

"Retreat," Jonathan howled.

Israel fled over the mountain toward the Shechem plains, falling wounded and dying as they ran. The heathen routed them viciously.

Achish advanced.

Jonathan ran with his brothers at his side, when suddenly Abinadab fell behind. Turning, he saw his brother had been struck in the leg and was limping. Jonathan cried out to Malchi-shua, and hurried to Abinadab's side. Malchi-shua was frozen with fear and he staggered back at the sight of his wounded brother. Shaking his head, he heard Jonathan call out to him again, but he could not help them. He spun around and ran away. Jonathan put Abinadab's arm around his shoulder as he tried to carry his brother to safety. Abinadab screamed suddenly and when Jonathan glanced back, a Philistine had stabbed him through the ribs. Blood dribbled into his beard as he coughed, and he slumped from Jonathan's grasp, dead. Jonathan was wild with rage and he hit the soldier square in the face, killing him with one blow.

Jonathan bent over his brother's corpse, crying out his name, willing him to open his eyes. He shuddered as he sobbed.

An Israelite soldier gripped him and pulled him to his feet. "We must run, my prince. Live and fight another day," he said and sprinted away. Jonathan stepped back and stared down at the dead warriors scattered around him. He fled.

***

Saul sweated as he fought with his dual blades and the Philistines shifted cautiously around him. Sporadic arrows flew his way, but he ignored them and raged on. He was well armored and his man was quick with the shield. Killers surrounded them and slowly pressed the battle-hardened fighters back.

Saul gasped as an arrow shot through his stomach. He doubled over, coughing and gasping with explosions of pain, and then another arrow tore into his shoulder. Fear seized him.

"Draw your sword, and thrust me through with it!" Saul screamed to his shield-bearer who gaped at him in dumb terror. "Don't let these uncircumcised heathen kill me, and abuse me!" The pain was overwhelming. The young man stood like a stone pillar and dropped his shield weakly.

"I cannot," he said and stepped back. Saul looked around, his face expressionless. After an appalling moment, he turned his sword upon himself and fell onto his own blade. His face twisted grotesquely, his lips trembling as blood dripped from them. Wheezing, he glanced up at his servant and then his head dropped as his body sagged over the weapon.

Saul was dead.

The armor-bearer screamed as he reached out to his dead king, weeping. A Philistine rushed at him, and without thinking, he took his kidon, collapsed onto it, and died with his king.

Jonathan's lungs burned as he sped from the Philistines hunting them. He stumbled on a stone, smashing his toes. He did not notice as he ran. Suddenly, he saw a decapitated body sprawled on the ground in Malchi-shua's armor with three wooden shafts sticking out from the back and leg. Jonathan searched for the head. In a grip of temporary insanity, he saw his cowardly brother's severed head, and looked into the open, lifeless eyes staring at him. He screamed as he dragged himself on.

Archers released another wave of arrows, and with a fatal shriek, six arrows tore into his chest and neck. The prince choked as metal pierced him and he fell to the ground. Blood gurgled from his throat as he scrabbled at the wood projecting from him, unbearable pain pulsing through his broken body. His leather armor was wet with the blood seeping onto his chest. He tried to breathe and coughed a splatter of red fluid into the dust, his lungs aflame. He could hear his own breathing, and his life flashed before his eyes. Finally, his muscles relaxed and he laid the side of his face in the filth. He could not feel his body anymore. The taste of blood lingered as he batted at the dirt in his eyes. The world around him faded as the sounds dimmed, and for one glorious moment he felt enlightened. Then the life left his body, his eyes gentle and fixed.

Jonathan had passed quickly, and now men, unseeing, charged past his corpse.

As the sun set over the battlefield the last of the Israelite troops fled before the Philistines. It was over. The battle was lost.

The king and three princes of Israel died together that day on Mount Gilboa.

Abner fled, exhausted from the carnage. He was bleeding profusely from a cut on his bicep, blood dripping from his fingers. As he ran, he tore a strip of cloth from his sleeve, and grunting, he tied it around his arm with his teeth to staunch the bleeding. He could not rest; he had to warn the royal family. The images of Saul's death flashed in his mind again and he fought tears, weak from the day's battle.

The general found a stray horse that had escaped the fighting and, after a gentle approach, he snatched the reins and managed to calm the bewildered animal.

He rode resolutely for Gibeah, Saul's city. He did not know if Jonathan and the princes had died, but he had seen the Philistines rout their regiments.

I will see Gina burned to the ground for their treachery, he thought, clenching his fists, possessed by rage and resentment, and harassed by grief.

All of them must have been killed, he told himself dispirited, thinking of Jonathan. His armor was tarnished and smeared with the remnants of the battle, and he stank from the filth. He had fought for as long as he could after the left wing had broken against the press of the Philistine chariot assaults. After he witnessed Saul's suicide in the near distance, he finally fled the massacre.

Abner sped through the gates of Gibeah. He brought the tired beast to a sudden stop before the walls of the fortress-palace, and he did not look at the watchmen as he screamed at them. "The king is dead and the battle lost. Alert the people and send word to all the cities in danger. Have a group of ten soldiers fetch Prince Ish-bosheth, and guard him with your life. For he is the new king of Israel and Judah." The men staggered in shock, and then ran into the city shouting.

Ahinoam and Rizpah heard the commotion and they knew something had happened. Ahinoam covered her mouth when Abner stormed into the room. The queens sprang to their feet at the sight of the bloody general, and shrank back, shaking their heads violently. They knew.

"My lady, I'm truly sorry, but our beloved king is dead. Your sons, also," he said compassionately through clenched jaws, as tears stung his eyes.

Queen Ahinoam screamed as she pressed her back against the wall, sliding to the streaked floor. She wailed into her cupped hands, clamping her eyes shut as she rocked herself. *Her husband could not be dead,* she thought, refusing to believe it.

"We must make haste, my ladies," Abner commanded. "Danger is at our gates."

Rizpah wept bitterly and held the old queen to her, weak in their grief.

"Fetch the young princes, and meet me at the gates," Abner ordered servant girls, and they scurried out with muffled sobs. Abner had to take the queens by their hands and drag them forcibly from the room, keening and stumbling behind him.

Jonathan's young son was running around the room playing with a wooden sword. He was a brave fighter like his noble father and he swung at his nursemaid who stepped aside carefully, amused at the child's enactment. He was only five years old, but already had a firm arm from sword training. He thrust the toy into the curtains and twisted it.

"Saul sleeps with his fathers! The Philistines are coming!" came the frightful cries of the soldiers spreading through the city. Instinctively, the woman leapt to the window and opened the lattice. She listened anxiously. "Saul sleeps with his fathers! The Philistines are coming!" and terror numbed her.

Turning, she snatched the child and ran from the room. She had to reach the palace. She made a sharp turn into an adjoining corridor and her foot slipped on the stone floor. She fell against the corner, smashing the young prince's back against the stone.

She came down in such a way that she fell on top of the boy, and she could hear the bone crack as both his ankles twisted and broke under her weight. Mephibosheth howled in pain. His ligaments had torn, and his feet turned blue and swollen. Crying, she got up painfully, and picked up the prince, carrying him from Jonathan's house.

In a convoy of three wagons, the royal family fled Gibeah with their servants and only the bare necessities, escorted by all twenty of the city guards as they rode to Mahanaim. Rizpah held her large belly, feeling her unborn child kick inside of her.

Queen Ahinoam watched fearfully as her people scattered around her beloved city. They were frantic, and streamed out in a crush of bodies, as they abandoned Gibeah. She could not stop looking at them—their expressions, the tears of the children, the cries. The sight would haunt her forever.

Finally, the massive walls disappeared behind the horizon. She had lost her entire family in a single day. She feared for her daughters and their families. *Would they make it safely?*

Where would they go? Would she ever see them again? She held her grandchild to her, and the sight of his broken body was too much for her to bear, and the queen broke down in her sorrow.

⚜

The people of Israel beyond the valley and on the other side of the Jordan River heard that the warriors of Israel had fled and that Saul and his sons had died. There was great mourning, and the men and women deserted their homes and escaped. The Philistines entered the territories of Israel and lived in the cities, ransacking the houses through the night and stealing whatever they could.

The next day when the Philistines returned to the battlefield to strip the slain and collect weapons, they found Saul and his three sons fallen in the dry earth on Mount Gilboa.

With great howling, they cut off Saul's head and removed his armor. Achish ordered that his suit be put in the house of Ashtaroth, and he sent the decaying head with a herald into the land of the Philistines. It was shown all around as a victory-trophy, displaying it in the houses of their idols and flaunting it among the people. As a final savage act of power that same day, the Philistines nailed the king's decapitated and mutilated body, and the three princes' remains to the wall of Beth-shan. The façade was covered with the stinking severed limbs of the conquered soldiers, the blood staining the limestone walls red. The heathen danced and celebrated beneath the gory corpses as the harsh light of a large bonfire washed over them.

⚜

Brave men from Jabesh-Gilead had heard about the disgrace done to Saul's remains, and they gathered their men and traveled through the night. They came to the city at early

417

dawn, and under the cover of darkness, they stole to the walls of Beth-shan. There were no Philistine sentries and the men presumed that they had fallen asleep after too much drink.

One man kept watch in the distant trees waiting anxiously as the other eleven men went to the walls. They had to search the massive bloody walls before they saw the abused royal family. Quietly, the smaller men climbed onto the shoulders of the stronger and reached for the dangling bodies. Their flesh stunk and flies buzzed around the rotting remains. The men gasped for air and jerked harshly at the corpses. Their limbs tore from the iron nails that held them and dropped to the ground with loud thuds. The men were smeared with old blood, but they did not mind. Gingerly, they slid off the shoulders of their comrades and lugged the bodies back to the cover of the trees. With dedication, they hauled them to the city of Jabesh. In honor of the noble men, they would burn the bodies, and they decided that they would bury their bones under a tamarisk tree in Jabesh. They would mourn seven days for the deceased.

CHAPTER THIRTY-SIX

David stood before the ruined gates of Ziklag. The blackened gateway, debris, and wreckage of the houses offered no comfort to the son of Jesse as he entered his city.

There was much to be done before they could call it home again. The roofs had to be rebuilt and the walls plastered and mended. The gardens had been trampled and the trees set alight with heated grease, and the streets had to be cleared of rubble and ashes.

David found a suitable building with adequate privacy and summoned his council. There was much to discuss. The men sat on the floor in the dilapidated shelter in a circle, in cinders and dust, rays of light flowing from the tattered roof mottling the place. David began with a prayer.

"There is one thing that I want done before anything else happens," David said without preliminaries. He was anxious to get things completed. He was not a man for extended patience, and he had been long-suffering since he had been anointed at seventeen.

"I want men sent with half of the spoils of the Amalekites to the elders of Judah, with a message. Perhaps something like: 'Behold, a present for you from the spoils of the enemies of

Jehovah.' Asahel, you are in charge of choosing strong and swift men to do this. I trust you will deal with it quickly."

Asahel nodded.

"Send it to the people in Bethel and to Ramah in the southern part of Judah, and to the inhabitants in the towns of Jattir, Aroer, Siphmoth, Eshtemoa, and Racal; to the clan of Jerahmeel, to the Kenites. Yes, and also to the men and women in the towns of Hormah, Borashan, Athach, and Hebron. And lastly, deliver it to all the places where our men and I have roamed," David added when he saw Asahel memorizing the list.

"The rest of us have the immense task of rebuilding a town. Pelet, you and Joab are in charge of erecting a makeshift barracks. Then recruit a third of the men to ensure the permanent guarding of the gates. We'll need scouts and sentries, as well as patrols. Eliab and my brothers, I want you to take another third to work on the houses. Let's first get the roofs fixed before the winter rains. My nephews and I will oversee the rest, and then we'll assist in the construction. Agreed?"

The council nodded silently, and smiled at their leader.

Three days later while the men were working under the burning sun, a man, whose skin was pierced with iron rings, ran into the city and fell to the ground, shoveling dust over his head as he wailed into the wilderness. His clothes were torn and his skin was coated with dirt, his throat hoarse from screaming.

He had slipped around the Philistine armies to avoided capture and it had taken him days to arrive at Ziklag.

Two guards brought the man before David and he fell to the earth, parched and fatigued. He bowed at his feet. David was bare-chested, gleaming with sweat as he plastered a mud-brick wall.

"Where do you come from?" David asked, immediately concerned. He recognized the man as an Amalekite, and he frowned at him with revulsion.

"I've escaped out of the camp of Israel," he said, and shock stabbed at David's heart. Instinctively he knew what must have happened, and he sat on his haunches, gripping the man by his arm.

"How did the matter go? I pray you, tell me."

"The people have fled from the battle, and many Israelite warriors have fallen," the messenger said and hesitated. David shook him aggressively, his face tight with anguish.

"What else? Tell me!" David demanded.

"Saul and his sons are dead," he stammered and David jumped to his feet, tears flowing into his beard.

"How— how do you know that Saul and his son Jonathan sleep with their fathers?" David asked, downcast. The man hung his head and looked down at the ground. He was afraid at what he was about to do. The young man had found Saul's impaled body on the battlefield and he had stolen Saul's diadem and golden wristband. He believed that the son of Jesse, Saul's enemy, would be inaugurated as the new king of Israel after the death of the king. He had intended to deceive David and gain his favor with his lies. He reasoned that if he gave David the deceased king's crown, he would be rewarded. He would be esteemed in the prince's eyes, perhaps even receive high rank in his kingdom. But now that he bowed before the powerful man, he faltered.

"As I happened to be on Mount Gilboa, I saw Saul leaning on his spear exhausted, and the Philistines chariots and horsemen following hard after him," the young Amalekite spoke simply. "When he looked back, he saw me and called to me. I answered him, 'Here I am.' Then Saul asked me who I was, and I told him that I'm an Amalekite. He asked me to stand over him and kill him because he was still strong, though wounded, and he was gripped by anguish at what the Philistines would do to him if they found him alive."

David was horrified by what he heard, and felt his anger rise. He did not say a word and listened as the uncircumcised Amalekite spoke, his mind working.

"Then I stood over the king and I slew him, because I knew he would not live long after he had fallen."

David gasped, his hands quivering with rage.

"I took the crown from his head and the bracelet from his arm, and have brought them here to my lord."

David arched his back as he screamed and tore at his rich skirt. The men gathered around David also mourned, ripping their clothing. They keened loudly for Jonathan and his king. Suddenly David remembered the messenger again, and glared at the man maliciously.

"Where are you from?"

"I am the son of a stranger, an Amalekite," the man said tremulously.

"Why weren't you afraid to stretch forth your hand against Jehovah's anointed?" David demanded through gritted teeth. The man shrank back at the words. He dropped back on his buttocks from his kneeling, and he shifted away from David through the sand. David's eyes bored into him.

"You, come here," David ordered an armed soldier. The man was fierce, and he glanced at the Amalekite. "Kill him."

The Amalekite screamed as he sprang to his feet, and ran. The guard was quick and fell upon him, stabbing the fleeing man in the back. He stumbled with the spear lodged in his heart, and plunged into the earth, writhing. The people watched him die, and as he fell silent, they looked at David, uncertain what to think.

"Your blood is on your head, because you testified against yourself with your own mouth," David announced, not moving his eyes from the corpse. "When you killed God's anointed, you condemned yourself."

David was silent, and then he turned to his people. He was crying and his eyes were gentle with sorrow.

David chanted a death dirge over Saul and over his son Jonathan.

"The beauty of Israel is slain upon your high places! How are the mighty fallen! Tell it not in Gath, don't let it be known in the streets of Ashkelon, lest the daughters of the Philistines rejoice, lest the daughters of the uncircumcised triumph. Mountains of Gilboa, let not dew or rain be on you, nor fields of offerings. For there the shield of the mighty has been evilly cast away, the shield of Saul not anointed with oil. From the blood of the slain, from the fat of the mighty, the bow of Jonathan didn't turn back, and the sword of Saul didn't return empty. Saul and Jonathan were lovely and pleasant in their lives, and in their death they were not divided. They were swifter than eagles; they were stronger than lions. Daughters of Israel, weep over Saul, who clothed you in scarlet and with delights; who put ornaments of gold on your clothes. How are the mighty fallen in the midst of the battle! Jonathan is slain on your high places. I am distressed for you, my brother Jonathan. Very pleasant you have been to me. Your love to me was wonderful, more than the love of women," David sang emotionally, and he sobbed. "How are the mighty fallen, and the weapons of war perished!"

The people wept and lamented with David. They fasted until the evening for Saul and for his son Jonathan. They fasted for the people of Jehovah and for the house of Israel, because so many had died by the sword.

David ordered that all the sons of Judah be taught "The Song of the Bow."

Abiathar wore the linen ephod. He was silent and his eyes were closed as he came before the Lord. It was a harsh time in Israel. The king was dead and the Philistines occupied many of the cities.

The people watched in tense silence. Would they be able to go back to Israel? They all longed for it, and now it could be safe for them to cross over the borders.

Abiathar opened his eyes, power gleaming in them.

"I have inquired of Jehovah for David and He has answered me," Abiathar said, his voice projecting over the scores of people. "I asked Him if David should go up into any of the cities of Judah. The answer was '*Yes!*'" The people cheered, breaking into dances and singing at the news. They were going home! After a year and four months, they would leave the heathen lands and return to their holy inheritance. They could worship at the tabernacle again and partake in the monthly festivals and offerings. There was great joy among all, and David did not try to quiet them. He celebrated and embraced his brothers.

He had missed the pastures of Judah beyond all measure.

After some time Abiathar spoke again. "Then I asked of Jehovah to what place should David go up, and He has answered me, '*To Hebron.*'" David joyfully took the priest's hand in a soldier's grip.

"Praise be to Jehovah! Make the necessary preparations. We leave at once," David declared loudly to his people.

Early that morning, David and his wives, Ahinoam of Jezreel and Abigail of Carmel, left for Judah. David brought every man and their households with him, and they lived in the cities of Hebron.

EPILOGUE

The priest Abiathar came from the holy tent holding the curved ram's horn. David was tense with exultation.

He stood outside of the city of Hebron and swept his gaze over all the people of Judah. They were the largest and strongest of the twelve tribes, made up of more than half of the number of all Israel.

They were silent and he knew they approved. They had all come to see him crowned. His hands trembled at the prospect.

David watched intently as Abiathar came before him. The priest smiled at him, and nodded. Abiathar understood David's guarded expression. He would have immense power and respect, and with it, terrible responsibilities. The horn was smooth against the priest's fingers as he stepped beside David ben Jesse. His hanging sleeves of scarlet slid over David's skin as he lifted the container above his head.

David closed his eyes.

The priest tilted the brown horn over David's forehead and warm oil dripped onto his face. He felt energy course through his veins, and he clenched his fists. The smell of cinnamon filled his nose from the fragrant anointing oil and he tasted the spiced flavor of the olive oil on his lips. The sensation of the emollient running into his beard and staining his silk robe, which was richly embroidered with gold wire and hemmed with colorful tassels, was strange. He immediately recalled the sensation when the prophet, Samuel, had anointed him king so long ago. He had survived the turbulent years—the fear, the uncertainty, the sorrow. He took in a powerful breath. It had all been worth it.

"Let King David live!" Abiathar said loudly. The afternoon silence shattered as thousands of people shouted the same words, like the thunder of a massive waterfall.

David opened his eyes, authoritative energy pouring off him.

Abner stood beside Ish-bosheth, Saul's son. He was the prince of Israel, and Abner had never thought that he would be crowned king. His father and brothers were dead, and now he would succeed them. It was a bittersweet thing to him.

Dressed regally in silk and gold, Ish-bosheth gazed over the men and women of Israel who had come to witness his inauguration. He waited impatiently for the old priest to come from the holy tent. General Abner had gathered the elders of the tribes of Israel and had demanded that one of Saul's bloodline continue to sit on the throne. The old man had great influence with the tribes; he was royalty and now solely commanded the armies.

Abner was a great man. He had not been wrong in his claims, and after a short deliberation, the elders submitted. Within a week, they had gathered at Mahanaim, and now stared up at Saul's fourth son with mixed feelings. If it hadn't been for the general's demands and threats, they would have seen David crowned king.

Ahijah emerged holding the ceremonial ram's horn.

At age forty, gray hairs streaked through Ish-bosheth's dark beard, and he was haughtily silent as the priest came before him. He was anxious, and breathed with shallow breaths as the oil spilled over him.

"Let King Ish-bosheth over Gilead, and the Ashurites, and over Jezreel, and Ephraim, and Benjamin, and over all Israel—live!"

A man blew loudly on the shofar, and the musicians began playing the flutes. David grinned as he walked to a decorated mule and sat comfortably in the saddle. The Judeans cheered and danced in a whirl of color and movement around him as he rode into his city. David looked out straight ahead. His war council marched beside him dressed formally and splendidly armored.

The people showered him with flowers from the high roofs as he rode underneath the heavy gates in a long slow procession. David waved at them through the cascade of rose and lavender petals wafting gently across the busy streets.

The mule brayed as Eliab pulled at the beast's reins, leading him to the town square. David reached out to the men and women, kissing their hands. As they turned right, a wide stone square opened up before them, and in the center, on a circular cedar wood foundation stood a large stone and ivory throne with David's name inscribed on the base in golden letters. Close in front of the structure was an altar, and fatted oxen and sheep. The donkey stopped and David slid from the animal. People streamed in at the four entrances of the public gathering place and surrounded David as the priests prepared for the ceremonial sacrifice.

In a stately manner David ascended the small steps, his cloak of brilliant violet and white trailing behind him over the cobblestones. The people were quiet in anticipation.

David stood before his throne touching his jeweled belt of pure gold, and bowed to his people. There was complete silence.

David rested his hands on the armrests behind him, and closed his eyes. He hesitated and then sat down in the royal seat. The masses exploded with thunderous cheers, rocking the structure supporting his chair.

Then Abiathar rested a thin golden diadem on his head, and in another wave the crush of Judeans roared and applauded.

"Let King David ben Jesse live!" they shouted. David fingered the jewels on the iron band, and with a deep breath, he opened his eyes.

A king.

CONTINUED IN THE HOLY BIBLE
IN THE BOOKS II SAMUEL AND I KINGS

BIBLIOGRAPHY

Richard A. Gabriel, *The Military History of Ancient Israel* with foreword by Mordechai Gichon (Praeger Publishers, 2003), ISBN: 0-275-97798-6

Jerry M. Landay, *Silent Cities, Sacred Stones* (Jerusalem: Weidenfeld and Nicolson, 1971), ISBN: 0-297-00426-3

Ancient Jerusalem Revealed with foreword by Hillel Geva (The Israel Exploration Society, 1994), ISBN: 965-221-021-8

Ancient Israel: From Abraham to the Roman Destruction of the Temple (The Biblical Archeology Society / Prentice Hall, 1999), ISBN: 1-880317-53-2

Chaim Herzog and Mordechai Gichon, *Battles of the Bible* (London: Weidenfeld and Nicolson, 1978), ISBN: 0-297-77524-3

Yohanan Aharoni, *The Archaeology of the Land of Israel*, translated by Anson F. Rainey (Philadelphia: The Westminster Press, 1982), ISBN: 0-664-21384-7

Juan Bosch, *David: the Biography of a King*, translated by John Marks (London: Chatto & Windus, 1966)

E-Sword was used as a reference for various translations, commentaries, and Hebrew words in the biblical text.

For any comments or questions about the David Series or future fictions from David J. Ferreira's pen, kindly write to the author at kingdavidnovel@gmail.com.